Could this delectable, lovely young creature be the boy Ed?

A young woman dressed in an extremely fetching buttercup-yellow dress stood by the window, her hands clasped at her trim waist. Small and as slender as a willow, she was watching him warily. Without taking his eyes off her, Adam moved toward her, staring in disbelief.

"Good Lord!" The words were uttered on a breath. "I should have known." She had a femininity he could have put to his lips and drunk, and she was so close he could feel her breathing, feel the warmth of her, and smell her natural scent. She was quite enchanting.

Rather nervously Edwina withstood the intensity of his gaze. His dark brows lifted a fraction in inquiry.

"Well, Ed? What do you have to say for this deception?"

* * *

The Earl and the Pickpocket
Harlequin® Historical #201—December 2006

HELEN DICKSON

was born and still lives in south Yorkshire, England, with her husband, on a busy arable farm where she combines writing with keeping a chaotic farmhouse. An incurable romantic, she writes for pleasure, owing much of her inspiration to the beauty of the surrounding countryside. She enjoys reading and music. History has always captivated her, and she likes travel and visiting ancient buildings.

The
EARL
and the
PICKPOCKET

—◦◦◦◦—

HELEN DICKSON

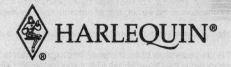

TORONTO • NEW YORK • LONDON
AMSTERDAM • PARIS • SYDNEY • HAMBURG
STOCKHOLM • ATHENS • TOKYO • MILAN • MADRID
PRAGUE • WARSAW • BUDAPEST • AUCKLAND

ISBN-13: 978-0-373-30510-0
ISBN-10:   0-373-30510-9

THE EARL AND THE PICKPOCKET

Copyright © 2005 by Helen Dickson

First North American Publication 2006

Available from Harlequin® Historical and
HELEN DICKSON

DON'T MISS THESE OTHER
NOVELS AVAILABLE NOW:

Chapter One

London, 1770

A murky haze hung over the narrow alleyways and squalid, rickety hovels in the secret world of St Giles—a wretched, brutal, frightening place, cramped, dark and noisy, where violence and death were an inescapable fact of life. The air was foul, and the humid, sweltering heat pressed down on its inhabitants—a churning crush of people, the flotsam of human life. These were thieves, cutthroats and beggars, painted harlots and scavengers, a ragged, unwashed assortment of men, women and children, most of them prematurely aged by poverty and hunger, their only recourse to be found in the gin shops. This tax-free liquor was in plentiful supply, its consumption endemic—a perfect antidote for dulling pain, replacing lost dreams and deepening despair.

Moving among the jostling crowd, Adam carefully scrutinised every face, searching for one that was familiar, unaware of the youth following him closely—a slight, inconspicuous-looking lad in shabby garb and a shapeless hat pulled well down over his ears, who nimbly danced out of his sight whenever he turned about.

Adam was so deeply engrossed in his mission that it was

a moment before he reacted to the body suddenly thrust against him, and the pull at his watch. Clapping his hand to his chest, a vicious curse exploded from him when he found he had been relieved of his timepiece by somebody with the manual dexterity of a practised thief. He whirled in time to see a ragged urchin dart away. Immediately he gave chase, following him through a network of narrow alleyways.

Eventually the lad was delivered up to him by a couple of youths anticipating a reward. Tossing them a shilling apiece, Adam gripped the young thief's arm, ignoring his strangled squawk as he dragged him aside. He grasped the thin arm more tightly as the lad struggled against him, wincing and loosening his hold when he felt a boot rebound against his shin.

Slipping from Adam's grasp, in a blur of panic the youth turned to run, only to find a long booted leg thrust out, obstructing his path. Unable to check his momentum, he stumbled and fell, landing on his stomach in a mud puddle. His posterior pointing skywards, he lay for a moment winded and stunned, successfully managing to hold back tears of shame and humiliation that gathered in his eyes. Covered in mud and slime, he was heaved from his ignoble position by the seat of his breeches, and with a string of outraged curses he quickly danced away and whipped a knife from his belt, wielding it in front of him.

'I'll have your blood,' he snarled, glaring at his abuser as ferociously as a wild animal.

Like lightning Adam drew his sword, placing the point at the lad's throat, locking eyes—the youth momentarily mesmerised by the terrible deadly grace of the stranger's swift manoeuvre.

'I wouldn't try it,' Adam ground out, backing his captive into a corner. 'Do not add murder to your crime. Lower your weapon and give it to me,' he coolly ordered, 'and slowly, if you please. I am far from amused.'

Glowering out of a dirty face at him, breathing fast, his cheeks pink with a combination of rage and fear, reluctantly the youth did as he was told. Adam gave the knife no more than a cursory glance before sliding it down the top of his boot and sheathing his sword. 'A nasty weapon for a boy,' he remarked, his stern gaze raking the lad. 'Very clever, you young guttersnipe. However, you should have studied your craft more and not allowed yourself to be caught.'

Adam's fingers had bit painfully into the lad's arm, who now rubbed the offended member, still scowling up at the giant who loomed above him, looking very small and fragile now he had no weapon with which to defend himself.

'What's the matter?' Adam growled. 'Afraid of the law, are you?'

'You hurt my arm,' the lad snapped, his eyes narrowed accusingly.

'Rob me again and I'll hurt more than your arm, you young whelp,' Adam promised direly. He held out his hand. 'My watch, if you please.'

The youth's clear blue-green eyes glared hotly back at Adam, and he continued to fidget beneath his close inspection. He felt anger towards the stranger for catching him, but most of his anger was directed against himself for getting caught. He was aware of the painful gnawing of his stomach, and the dinner the proceeds of selling such a fine watch would have provided—after Jack had had his cut.

'I repeat. Give me back my watch.' Adam's eyes narrowed when the lad remained mute, and there was a glint in his eyes that warned the youngster against pushing his luck further. Taking him by the front of his jacket with both hands, Adam lifted him so the toes of his ill-fitting boots barely brushed the ground, thrusting his face close to the slim, arrogant nose. 'I dare say a constable will bring you to your senses, lad.'

Adam had the satisfaction of seeing his captive squirm uneasily and his face blanch. To be publicly conveyed through the streets by this tall stranger, and subsequently brought before the magistrate and thrown into prison for thieving—the utter humiliation of this ordeal would be so mortifying that it had the lad delving into the pocket of his baggy breeches and producing the purloined watch.

'Here, take it. I—I am sorry I took it,' he muttered, the apology almost sticking in his throat.

Adam released his hold on the jacket and retrieved his timepiece, noticing how small the lad's hands were—a necessary asset to any thief, he thought wryly. He was certain this young scamp possessed a healthy concern for his miserable hide, and knew fear was the determining factor in his decision to return his watch.

'Being sorry won't undo what you've done.'

Silent and antagonistic, the lad looked up at the stranger, meeting eyes of vivid blue set in a face tanned by the sun. The man was tall, his body hard, lean and muscular, giving the appearance of someone who rode, fenced and hunted. Beneath his tricorn hat dark brown hair was drawn back and fastened at the nape, accentuating his leanly covered cheekbones and firm, angular jaw. His nose was aquiline, and beneath it were generous, but at present, unsmiling lips.

The lad guessed him to be at least twenty-eight. There was an aggressive confidence and strength of purpose in his features, and also something serious, studious, almost. He detected an air of breeding about him, a quality that displayed itself in his crisp manner, neat apparel and austere mien. The man's stern eyes, holding his captive, seemed capable of piercing his soul, laying bare his innermost secrets, causing a chill of fear to sear through him and his eyes to dart about, looking for a means of escape, but the man barred his passage.

Adam was calmly giving the lad the self-same scrutiny, seeing a boy of no more than thirteen or fourteen. Feeling a stirring of compassion—an emotion that was completely alien to him—he gradually allowed his anger to recede and his stern visage softened. The small, slight form was clad in ill-fitting garments, and he was as dirty and undernourished as any other juvenile who inhabited St Giles, but there was an air and manner about him that held his attention.

Adam's look became enquiring as he continued to study the lad—and realized he was educated, recalling how he had blistered him in French in so diverse a manner when he'd hoisted him out of the puddle by his backside.

'Now, what shall I do with you? You're naught but a boy. It'd be more fitting to give you the spanking you deserve than to deliver you up to the magistrate.'

A feral light gleamed in the lucid depths of the lad's eyes. 'You lay one finger on me, and I promise you you'll live to regret it,' he ground out in a low, husky voice.

In the face of this dire threat Adam leaned forward deliberately until his eyes were on a level with the lad's, little more than a foot apart. His eyes were hard and ice cold, yet when he spoke his voice was soft and slow.

'Be careful, boy. Don't you dare me, or I'll administer the punishment you deserve. I abhor the abuse of children—so don't tempt me, otherwise I might change my ways.' The lad stared at him, and when Adam considered he was sufficiently chastened and humbled, he drew himself erect. 'Do you make a living out of stealing other people's property, knowing you could land in gaol—or be hanged for it?'

A brief, reluctant nod gave Adam his answer. 'Better than starving,' he mumbled.

Adam suppressed a smile and directed a stern countenance at the young rapscallion. 'And do your parents know?' he enquired, knowing as he asked the question, being a student in human nature, that his parents would more than likely be the receivers of their son's stolen goods.

Still glaring his defiance, the lad raised cold bright eyes to

Adam's and his chin came up belligerently. 'What's that to you?'

Adam shrugged. Re-attaching his watch to the empty chain and shoving it inside the breast pocket of his waistcoat, he continued to study him thoughtfully. 'Do they know where you are?'

Thrusting his hands deep into his pocket, the lad scuffed the dirt with his oversized boots and averted his angry eyes. 'They're both dead,' he revealed in sullen tones.

'I see,' Adam said with more understanding. Hearing a low growl come from the lad's stomach, he took pity on him. 'I was about to get something to eat. Would you care to join me—or will that pride of yours stand in the way of allowing your victim to put food in your belly? You look as if you haven't had a decent meal in a month or more.'

The lad's eyes betrayed a large measure of distrust and he held back. A thief couldn't afford to hang around his victim. 'I don't take charity. I can take care of myself.'

'I know,' Adam remarked drily. 'You prefer to steal it.'

'I'm particular as to whom I eat with.'

'Suit yourself.' Adam turned abruptly and strode away.

Gnawing on his bottom lip, the lad watched him go, the hollow ache in his middle reminding him how hungry he was. It had been hours since he'd eaten, and the stale bread and mouldy cheese had been less than appetising. Hunger pains overcame his sense of outrage and, unable to let the chance of a meal slip by he scrambled in the stranger's wake.

'Wait. I suppose I could manage a bite,' he said, though it chafed him to do so.

Adam smiled to himself and glanced back. 'Then hurry up. You're lagging, boy,' he reproached, heading for the nearest alehouse.

The youth glowered at the broad back. The man was infuriatingly sublime in his amusement. If he weren't so desperate to eat, he'd cheerfully tell him to go and jump in the Thames.

Avoiding the drunks, they entered a tavern. It was scruffy, noisy and dark, the walls blackened with the heavy smoke of the fire, candles and tobacco smoke. When they were seated in a dark corner and food ordered, Adam looked across the table at his companion. He sat erect, his small chin raised, and Adam could see him putting up a valiant fight for control— a fight he won. Despite his ragged garb he looked incongruously like a proud young prince, his eyes sparkling like twin jewels. Adam's granite features softened and his eyes warmed, as if he understood how humiliated the lad felt.

Pity stirred his heart. The lad was just one of hundreds of London's lost children with thin, dirty faces, their eyes dull and lifeless, children who would never know their parents, since many whose parents could not support them had been deserted, and their only means of survival was to steal or beg.

His thoughts shifted to another young boy, a bastard of the same blood as himself—that he too might be a ragged street urchin, condemned to a life of disease and hunger. Deprived of the prosperity he was accustomed to, had he survived— this? With this in mind he looked again at the lad and felt himself drawn to him. Why, he could not say, but he was in a position to ease his lot in life—if only a temporary ease—and perhaps the lad could be of help to him.

'Since we are to eat together, we might as well get better acquainted. My name's Adam. What's yours?'

The lad met Adam's gaze, serious, intent on his own. He had the uneasy thought that his companion was like a tall, predatory hawk, and that he was a tiny disadvantaged bird, or a mouse about to be pounced on.

'What's that to you?' he questioned suspiciously.

Adam's curiosity increased. He arched a brow and peered at his companion, shrugging casually. 'Just curious. You do have a name, don't you?' he enquired with a trace of sarcasm. When the lad made no further comment Adam glanced at him sideways, prompting, feeling his resistance.

'Ed,' the lad mumbled reluctantly.

'Ed? Ed what?'

'Just Ed,' he retorted sharply, not wishing to become too friendly.

'Right. Just Ed it is then.'

Ed began to fidget and his expression became pained. Removing his hat to scratch his head, he exposed an unevenly cropped thatch of an indeterminate colour.

Adam grinned at the tousled-haired youth. 'It's time you took yourself in hand and gave yourself a bath.'

'I can take care of myself,' Ed bit back irately, pulling his hat back on. 'Besides, baths are for the gentry—not the likes of me.' Uneasy beneath Adam's close scrutiny, he pulled his hat further down. Sometimes daylight had a habit of revealing more than it ought.

Adam continued to watch him, reminding himself that here was no innocent. But he could not help but wonder at the gist of the lad. 'Where do you live, Ed—when you're not relieving people of their possessions, that is?'

Ed's eyes sparked, and his fine-boned face tilted obstinately to betray his mutinous thoughts. Why did he have to pry? 'You ask too many questions,' he snapped.

'It's a habit of mine. Besides, in the light of your theft of my watch, I reckon you owe me a few answers.'

Ed saw Adam's blue eyes were not without humour, but there was censure in the set of his jaw. 'I—I have a room.'

'With friends?'

'No. I'm selective about who I call friends,' he said reflectively, some of his cockiness fading. 'I don't need them. Some people do, but I don't. People are not always what they seem—and not to be trusted. I only need myself. It's best that way—easier, and less complicated.'

'In that case you must be lonely.'

Ed looked at Adam, considering the word. Lonely, he thought. Yes, he was lonely; in fact, he had never imagined he could be so lonely, but, worse than that, he was afraid—afraid of getting caught. He hated robbing people, and he hated St Giles. He desperately wanted to stop and be respectable, and not spend his life feeling scared. When he'd found himself in London's substructure six months ago, he'd had no choice but to face a world he could never understand, and a tyrant who might end his life at a whim.

'I can see that in your line of business,' Adam continued, 'there must be a great many things you wish to protect from intruders.'

Ed frowned. 'Secrets, perhaps, not things. I don't own anything.'

'You own yourself,' Adam responded quietly.

'Do I?' he asked, thinking of Jack, and wondering what this stranger would have to say about that, since Jack regarded him as his most valuable possession. 'I've never really thought about it. Do you?'

'All the time,' Adam replied, studying Ed gravely, having decided that Ed was a young person of no ordinary cleverness. 'You seem to be an intelligent lad so I'm sure you care about yourself, about what you do—but not enough, it would seem, and for all the wrong reasons. Perhaps you don't have enough faith in yourself—or pride. If you did, you wouldn't steal things. Why do you steal, Ed? Don't you have an alternative?'

Ed looked at him steadily, his eyes darkening at some secret memory. 'Oh, yes—I do,' he said quietly. 'But this is far, far better.'

'I see. You might give some thought to what I said.'

Ed nodded, fascinated. Adam's eyes were frank and interesting. 'I have—and I do believe in myself,' he confided. 'I don't like stealing things and I intend to stop—one day. And I will. I want so many things—somewhere special, and safe, that I can call my own. I will change my entire life, when I've figured out a way how to do it.'

Adam believed him. He was troubled by the intensity of his statement. It was born of deep conviction—and perhaps more than a little pain. Ed's eyes were wide and intense, showing in their depths a strong will that as yet knew neither strength nor direction. He was surprised at the feelings of tenderness this youth aroused in him. He sounded so ingenuous about what he wanted that he wanted to reassure him.

'Don't take too long,' he said gently. 'Those who make thieving their profession are destined for an early death on the gallows. Next time you get caught, the person you rob might not be as lenient as me. Have you always been a child of the streets? Have you never lived anywhere else?' When he got no response he lifted a questioning brow. 'France, perhaps?'

Ed stiffened, suddenly wary. 'Why should you think that?'

'When I pulled you out of the puddle, your cursing in that language was most proficient.'

Immediately the shutters came down over Ed's eyes and his expression became guarded. He didn't like talking about himself, especially not with strangers. 'I told you—you ask too many questions,' he replied sharply, averting his eyes.

Adam smiled, nodding slowly. He assumed there was a past that Ed was trying to forget. 'I beg your pardon. I can see I intrude on your privacy too much. Being a private person myself, I respect it in others. You can relax. See, our food has arrived.'

Faced with warm buttered bread, hot, succulent meat pies and tarts packed with apples and pears, a significant battle to conduct himself properly was fought and lost in a matter of seconds as Ed was unable to override the demands of hunger. Eating more leisurely, Adam watched in amusement as the ravenous youth gorged himself. Studying the remarkable face and unable to resist the temptation to draw the lad, he took a small sketchpad and a piece of charcoal from his pocket and began to sketch quickly, effortlessly.

As the food filled and warmed his belly, Ed began to eat

more slowly, savouring the taste fully. When his hunger was satisfied, he took a rag from his pocket and wiped his mouth and sat back, lulled into a harmony he thought he'd lost. He became aware of Adam's preoccupation as he sketched, his fingers long and lean—the fingers of a creative man of some refinement—and how he raised his eyes every now and then to glance at him. How remote he was, he thought, how detached. Stung with curiosity, he leaned across the table.

'Can I see?'

'Of course. Here, what do you think of yourself?' Adam turned the pad round to show him.

Ed gasped, staring incredulously at the image of himself. Adam had captured his likeness expertly. His face was all angles and shades, his eyes sad and thoughtful. 'Is that how you see me?' he asked, without taking his eyes off the sketch.

'I'd have made a better job of it if I'd had longer.'

'You're very good. You really ought to take it up professionally.'

'I'm glad you like it. And I promise to give serious thought to your suggestion,' Adam replied, with a teasing smile in his voice and a knowing glint in his eyes.

'You should,' Ed said with gentle, but unshakeable firmness. 'You could make a fortune. May I keep it?'

'My pleasure.' Adam tore the sketch off the pad and passed it to him, touched to see how carefully Ed handled it and placed it flat beneath his jacket so as not to crease it, as if it were the most precious object.

'Do you feel better with food in your belly?' Adam asked.

Ed nodded, remembering his manners. 'Thank you. I am grateful.'

'You're welcome.'

Ed's earlier anger had receded, leaving nothing to bolster his flagging courage. Adam's eyes were still fixed on him so avidly that he blushed. There was an intensity, a pointedness about his look that for some reason unnerved him. He was curious to know more about the man whose watch he had stolen and who could sketch so artistically. He wondered why he hadn't handed him over to the law, as others he stole from would have done. He cocked his head to one side and took stock of him. He really was a striking-looking man.

'You're a gentleman, I can tell, so what's a gentleman doing in St Giles?' he asked. 'I don't believe you came to take a stroll, or take the air.' Suddenly his dark scowl vanished. He laughed out loud, a mischievous twinkle dancing in his eyes as the obvious reason occurred to him. 'Were you looking for something that might be of interest to your habits?' he remarked boldly. 'If it's a whore you're after, there are plenty to be had, but 'tis the pox you'll get for your sins.'

Adam caught his breath. 'I don't buy my pleasures—I've never had to. I can attract my own women—and I never barter.' He became silent and thoughtful as he seemed to mull something over. 'I'm looking for a boy,' he told Ed bluntly.

After six months as a resident of St Giles, it took no straining of Ed's mental process to conclude his companion might be one of those depraved characters who practised wicked vices.

Aware as to the tenor of Ed's thoughts, which Adam found nauseating in the extreme—that this young lad should believe he could stoop to something so corrupt, so vile—his expression became rigid, his eyes glittering like shards of ice.

'I do not take solace from young boys of the street. The boy I am looking for is a relative of mine. He disappeared two months ago, and I'm anxious to locate him.'

'Why? Did he run away?'

'No. He was taken.'

'And you think he's here—in St Giles?'

'I have reason to believe so. He was last seen in the company of a man and woman. I have a network of people combing the city, but this was where he was last seen. I often come myself, but unfortunately there are places my spies and I can't penetrate, unlike someone who is familiar with the buildings and alleyways—someone like yourself,' he said quietly, watching Ed closely. 'Maybe you could make enquiries—discreetly, mind.'

Ed eyed him warily. 'I've got things to do. I've got my work cut out picking pockets.'

Adam's firm lips twisted with irony. 'I suppose one could call thieving a lucrative career if one is prepared to cast aside all moral principles.'

Ed wanted to shout it was his living, that the mean and filthy streets were his home, and that Jack was the wretch that made him steal and wouldn't let him go, but all he said was, 'It's what I do.'

Adam sat forward and rested his arms on the table, sensing Ed had learned the hard way how to survive among the odious hovels and alleyways of St Giles. 'Come now. Let us make a bargain.'

His voice was husky and attractive, putting Ed instantly on his guard. 'A bargain? I'll do no bargain.'

'Ah, lad—not so hasty. Hear what I have to say. I tell you what,' he said mockingly, his blue eyes snapping with amusement as he reached with his fingers to chuck him under the chin. 'I don't think I need remind you that you have just robbed me of my watch, which is a serious criminal offence—and, as the watch is valued at more than a shilling, a hanging offence, is it not? So, I'll do you a favour. I shall not summon the sheriff's forces if you agree to help me.'

Ed shot him a sullen look. 'That isn't a favour. It's blackmail.'

Adam arched an eyebrow. 'You might stand to profit by it. You will be well rewarded, I promise you. You wish to change your life, you say—to improve your lot. I am offering you the means to do just that. All you have to do is keep your eyes open. The lad is nine years old, slight, with brown eyes and black hair and answers to the name of Toby.'

'You have just described hundreds of boys in St Giles. And two months you say he's been here?' Ed smiled wryly, shaking his head slowly. 'If he's survived the life, he'll be unrecognisable.'

Adam's expression became grim. 'I think not.'

'Certain, are you?'

He nodded. 'Born with his right leg shorter than the left and his foot turned in, he is unable to walk without the aid of a crutch. Toby is a cripple.'

Ed found this regrettable, but his expression did not change. 'So are many others, some deformed from birth, but many of them are mutilated on purpose, usually by those who wish to capitalise on their misfortune by making them beg and displaying them to the curious.'

Taking a purse from his pocket, Adam passed it discreetly across the table. 'Take this for now. Inside you will find five guineas. When I return four days hence there will be more.'

Ed felt the purse. Five guineas was more money than he had seen in a long time. Hope blossomed in his chest, but he'd learned not to trust the future. He looked at Adam with a sceptical eye. 'And all I have to do is look for the boy?'

Adam nodded. 'You don't have to speak to him. Just tell me where he can be found and I will do the rest. You'd be a fool for certain if you didn't accept.'

'How do you know I won't take your money and not come back?'

'Call it intuition. I like your spirit. I trust you, Ed.'

Tears threatened. No one had ever said that to him before. 'Thank you,' he whispered. 'I've given you no reason to trust me. I don't deserve it.'

Adam grinned. 'No, you don't,' he agreed, 'so don't let me down.'

'I'll try not to.'

Sensing Adam's deep concern for the boy, Ed studied the face opposite. His hair was thick and unruly and the colour of walnuts. Dark brows and lashes defined his features in an attractive way, and masculine strength was carved into the tough line of his jaw and chin. His voice was deep and compelling, and the tiny lines at the corners of his eyes testified to his sense of humour. There was a self-assurance about him, which was slightly marred by arrogance, but as Ed looked steadily into his eyes he detected neither cruelty nor dishonesty. He was unquestionably the most handsome male he had ever seen. Deciding he liked Adam, Ed was contrite.

'I'm sorry I robbed you. If the boy Toby is here, I'll do my best to find him.'

'Good.' Adam believed him, and, if Ed didn't come back, he knew it would be through no fault of Ed's. He raised his flagon. 'To success,' he said, tossing down the contents. 'And here, you'd better have this.' He passed Ed the knife he'd taken from him earlier. 'Unless you have a death wish, I advise you to keep it in your belt.'

On leaving the alehouse, after arranging to meet in the same place at noon four days hence, Adam stood and watched his young companion melt into the intricate web of narrow alleyways and yards of St Giles, silent as mist.

Chapter Two

Pushing open the door of a vermin-infested house in a yard off Spittle Alley, Heloise Edwina Marchant stepped inside. The air was thick with stagnant odours hardly fit for a human being to breathe, and little natural light penetrated the grime-covered windows. She groped her way up the narrow, broken staircase to the landing above, closing her ears to the children screaming behind closed doors, and men and women, many of them sodden with gin, arguing loudly and bitterly because of their frustrations.

Weeks before, the sights and sounds that made up her everyday life would have sickened Edwina. Now she didn't even turn away. The squalor of St Giles had lost all its terror for her in its abundance.

She let herself into the small room Jack Pierce had allocated to her when he'd put her to work. She often shared it with other boys who worked for Jack, until they either disappeared or went to live at Ma Pratchet's, a gin-soaked old widow woman of gargantuan proportions by all accounts. Ma Pratchet was employed by Jack to look after the younger children he plucked off the streets, children who had been abandoned. The older, more experience boys trained them to pick pockets.

The wretched plight of these children had seared Edwina's heart when she had first come to St Giles. She had wanted to help them all, to gather them round her and ease their suffering if just a little, but she had soon realised that, in order to survive herself, these kind of emotions would not help her.

The light from the window she had scrubbed clean fell on broken bits of furniture, a few kitchen utensils and a narrow straw pallet shoved against the wall. Pulling off her hat, she laid down on the thin coverlet, resting her head on the pillow. It was hard and smelled of poverty.

Something stirred within her—a yearning for beauty, for luxury and comfort. Closing her eyes, she did something she had not done in a long time and allowed her mind to drift, remembering a time when she had lain between white linen, fresh and sweet smelling, when there had been maids to do her bidding and pander to her every whim. Opening her eyes, she gazed up at the cracked ceiling, the thought of her former life bringing pain more intense than her physical discomfort. The memories filled her with a weary sadness, and thoughts of her father and home seemed like a faraway dream.

Perhaps it was her encounter with Adam that had made her resurrect her past and sharpen the pang of homesickness, but before she could journey too far back along that path reality rushed back at her, a harsh, ugly reality, and, with a hardness of mind born of necessity, she flinched away from memories of the life she had once known. They would not help her now, and feeling sorry for herself would do her no good.

Taking the purse that Adam had given her from her pocket, she clutched it to her breast. Five guineas made it possible for her to leave Jack and make her own way in life—to go to France and look for her mother's people, which was what she had intended doing from the start.

No one knew how badly she wanted to escape her increasingly odious role as a thief, but every day that passed drew her deeper into Jack's debt. She wondered if she dare keep the money and not tell him—but she dare not. Everything she stole she gave to Jack, and when he had sold it on he would give her a small portion of the sale. Silently she considered this grossly unfair, but she would never argue with Jack. Besides, if she were to find the boy Toby, she would need Jack to help her.

He was clever, was Jack—the cleverest person she'd ever met—but her meeting with him when she had arrived in London had been her introduction to the world of crime. When Jack had arrived in the city three years ago, he had been on the run from the law, and St Giles was a perfect place for a man like Jack to develop contacts and start to carve out a reputation for himself.

He had convinced her there was no safer place to hide than the alleyways of London town, and so desperate had she been to escape her past and recoup the money she'd had stolen from her on her journey south from Hertfordshire that she had believed him. At first it had been frightening to be so far away from what she knew. Everything was so different, but she'd willed herself to think of the present and put past and future away if she hoped to survive.

Though eighteen years old, she had masqueraded as a lad since running away from her uncle's house. Being slight, with features that could pass as a boy's, and cutting off her copper tresses, which would have proved a liability she could ill afford, had lent well to her disguise. Until the day came when she had enough money to enable her to go France, this was a time for survival.

Not even Jack knew her secret. It had been Jack who had taught her how to steal, and right lucky it was for him that she'd proved a natural-born pickpocket. She'd learned fast to develop and hone her skills. She was agile, her fingers small and quick, her mind alert. She hated doing it, but she didn't tell Jack.

He became angry when she didn't steal enough, and she

was afraid of his anger. Once, she had sold her spoils to another receiver, praying Jack wouldn't find out, but he did, and his wrath had been terrible. Now she knew better than to try to deceive him, which was why she would have to hand over the five guineas. She felt her cheeks burning—they always did when she was angry, or ashamed—and she was ashamed now, ashamed for putting her trust in Jack in the first place.

Being a master of manipulation, he played on her desperation, and he knew how to use the right combination of charm and menace to ensure her absolute loyalty. They said he was evil, said he was dangerous. They said Jack had killed a man.

He lived alone above a pawnbroker's shop on Fleet Street, but he was never really alone. Others, vulnerable like herself, worked for him, and he carried them around in his head—moving them around like chess pieces as he played his deadly game. He controlled them all. No one could stand against Jack. He had many friends in St Giles, but few were cleverer, bigger, stronger or more terrifyingly ruthless than Jack.

Hearing heavy footfalls on the stairway, she got up and lit her one remaining precious candle—the rats had made a meal of the rest—watching as the meagre yellow flame cast a soft glow around the cheerless room. She started when the door burst open to admit Jack. A man of medium height, thickset and with heavy features, he wore a tall, battered black hat, and the crow's feather stuck into its brim hung limp like the tattered lace at his wrists. His stained dark-green velveteen coat, which strained across his bulky shoulders, had seen better days.

'So here you are, Ed,' he muttered. Pulling out a chair, he sat down, stretching out his legs, his thick calves encased in wrinkled, dirty grey stockings. Placing his hat on the table, he combed his sparse brown hair over his shiny skull, and his deep-set black eyes under bushy brows had a hard glitter when they fastened on her. 'Wondered where you'd got to. It's been a bad day,' he growled in a deep voice. 'Hope you've got more for me than the other lads—a fine watch, perhaps, or a jewelled snuff box…a pretty fan, even, or a lady's purse.'

'No, nothing like that today…but I do have a couple of lace handkerchiefs—and some money.'

Jack's face jerked sideways and his small black eyes fixed her with an investigative stare. It was the quick, sharp movement of an animal watching its prey. 'Money, you say! How much?'

'Five guineas—and there will be more if we help the man who gave them to me to find a boy he's looking for.'

Jack's heavy brow creased in a frown. 'Boy? What boy?'

'His name's Toby.' Edwina gave him a full description of the boy as Adam had given it.

Interest gleamed in Jack's eyes. 'Who is this man? What's his name?'

She shrugged. 'Adam. That's all I know.'

'How much will he give for the boy?'

'He didn't say—only that he would be generous.'

Jack considered this and nodded. 'I'll ask around. Is this man trustworthy?'

'Yes, I'm sure of it. He—he's nice.' Taking her courage in both hands, she said, 'After this I will make my own way, Jack. I told you from the start that when I have enough money I will go to France to look for my mother's people.'

This didn't suit Jack at all. 'So, you're scheming and plotting to run away from me, are you, Ed?' he thundered.

'No. I'm being straight with you. I don't want to do it any more,' she said in a rush, before her courage failed her.

'Not do it?' Jack echoed incredulously, jerking his body in the chair. 'After I went to the trouble of teaching you all you know? Not do it?'

Edwina shook her head, gulping down her fear of him. 'I've thought about it a lot, Jack. I don't mean to sound ungrateful—but I want to stop. I don't want to go on stealing.'

Jack was watching her closely through narrowed eyes. He

had dozens of boys working for him. He was their absolute master and he demanded loyalty. They had to steal when he bade them, or be hanged for refusing after Jack informed them on about some former crime. He would also reap the forty pounds' reward the government offered for anyone providing evidence that would convict a thief.

Ed was good, the best he'd got, but Ed was no fool, and that was the curse of it. Jack knew nothing about him, about who he was or where he had come from. He wasn't interested in that, but Ed was good at picking pockets and Jack was thinking of moving him on to work with the older youths; no matter how many high-falutin ideas he had about going to France, he had no intention of letting the lad run out on him.

'Don't think you can run out on me. It'll do you no good. We're in this together.' Clutching the purse, he folded his arms on the table. 'Sit down. I think you and I should have a little talk. I'm disappointed in you, Ed. I thought you and I understood one another. It seems I was wrong.'

Edwina faced him across the table, seeing his true character much more clearly now since she had got to know him. She feared him, and knew him to be deadly. He spoke softly, but she could see his anger simmered. He sat regarding her with dilated nostrils and heaving breast. She held her hands in her lap so he wouldn't see them tremble. She had turned pale, and she knew that if he roared at her and she broke down and cried he would have the mastery of her.

Taking a deep breath, she looked at him directly. His rugged features were impenetrable, but there was a pitilessness there that repelled her. 'We do understand one another, Jack. I want to end it, that's all.'

'So, you've had enough of picking pockets. Ungrateful wretch, that's what you are—and there was I, thinking you were fond of me.'

'I—I needed you Jack.'

'And now you don't? Is that what you're sayin'?' His eyes

narrowed suspiciously and he leaned across the table, his face close to hers. 'Hope you're not playin' a double game with me, boy, and keepin' some fancy trinkets for yourself. If you are, I'll tell you this: I'm the boss in this game—always have been and always will be. My God, I'd like to see the lad who dared to double-cross me.'

Edwina raised her head resolutely, choosing to protect herself from Jack's closeness as much as to hide her fear. Her pride ached, but the fear of what lay in store for her if she remained stealing for Jack threatened to reduce her to a trembling, shaking coward. 'I haven't, Jack. I've always been straight with you.'

'You've had an easy time since I took you in and set you to work, and you ought to go down on your knees and thank me for it. I've always had a soft spot for you, Ed,' he said, 'you've got spirit and pluck. Because I liked you and you were cleverer than the other lads, because you were quick to learn and kept your mouth shut, I've treated you like a lamb and let you alone to do pretty much as you please, and if you hadn't had that honour you'd have perished before now.'

'And I'm grateful, Jack. But I need more money if I'm to make my own way.'

Jack glared at her, leaning forward. His face was vicious, and his breath stank of sour rum. His deep, grating voice filled the silence that had fallen between them. 'Are you telling me you're not getting a fair deal?'

'Apart from that time when I took my spoils to another fencer—what you give me scarce covers the food I eat. You haven't been over-generous, Jack,' she said accusingly, emphasising the words to defend her actions, as she fought to prevent the shattered fragments of her life from slipping into an abyss.

Fire blazed in Jack's eyes. 'You young whelp. I'll bring you to heel or hand you in,' he threatened savagely. 'Do you think you can stand against me with your damned impudence? I haven't heard the others complaining.'

'No, because they fear you,' she told him truthfully.

'No harm in that. That way they'll do as they're told.'

'I know,' she said, standing up, her voice threaded with sarcasm. 'Charity and sympathy are not in your nature, are they, Jack?'

'What's charity and sympathy to me?' A sneer twitched the corner of his surly mouth. 'They can be the ruination of many a good man.' Scraping his chair back, he stood up and eyed the youngster narrowly, thoughtfully. 'I'll give you more,' he offered suddenly—after all, a tasty morsel had been known to keep a whining dog quiet.

'It's too late.' Edwina was adamant. She had come this far and would not back down now. 'I've made up my mind. I've had enough.'

Jack blustered angrily, making Edwina's cheeks flame considerably as she listened to the curses and insults he flung at her. She wanted desperately to retaliate, to tell him to go to the devil and be done with it, but she knew the folly of doing that. It was far better to let him say what he had to and let him go. Then she could think what to do.

He grasped her shoulder and twisted her round, thrusting his face close. 'Listen to me, boy, and listen well. Don't try to run from me, because if you stray I swear I'll find you and break every bone in your body.' Seizing her wrist, he doubled her arm behind her back. He laughed caustically when she cried out from the pain of it, thrusting her from him so forcefully that she fell against the table and toppled a chair over. 'That's a foretaste of the punishment you can expect if I have to come lookin' for you.'

Jack's parting words seared into Edwina's memory with the bitter gall of betrayal. The fact that she could have been so stupid as to believe she could go on her way when the fancy took her, that Jack would simply let her walk away, showed her weakness of character, in her mind. Her thoughts traced over the events that had led up to her present predicament, seeking to find the exact moment when she had become Jack's property, and she knew it had been right from the very beginning.

She was thrown into a dilemma as to what to do next. Its solution concealed itself in the chaotic frenzy of her thoughts. With nothing to her name but a few coppers, where could she go? There was no one she could turn to, no safe haven she could seek, and if she ran from Jack her fortune would be what she could make herself.

Feeling a bone weariness creeping over her, she sat and placed her forearms on the table, lowering her head upon them and sighing. 'Oh, Father,' she whispered. 'Why did you have to die? Why did you have to leave me to the mercy of Uncle Henry?'

Gordon Marchant had been a good father to her. She recalled how, handsome and proud, he'd smiled down at her from the saddle that last morning when he'd left Oakwood Hall, their fine Hertfordshire home, with his brother Henry, prepared to meet his creditor Silas Clifford, the Earl of Taplow, and beg for more time to pay back what he owed, and how she had stood on tiptoe to meet his parting embrace. The warmth and safety of his tone enclosed her for a moment.

'Promise me you'll have a care,' she'd said.

'Don't worry, Edwina.' His voice was quiet and he released her gently. 'I'll be back, and, if not, you can trust Henry. He'll take care of you.' Those had been his last words to her.

Henry had brought him home across the saddle of his horse, his fine clothes stained dark crimson with his life's blood. Her heart hardened. He had claimed her father had had a run in with a thief on the road to Taplow Court. She had believed him. Henry had smiled and promised to handle everything—and he'd handled it very well…the blackguard.

Together Henry and the Earl of Taplow had drawn up a marriage contract. The Earl had proposed to disregard his losses and marry her without a dowry. Anger welled up in her, anger at Uncle Henry, at the Earl of Taplow. They had done this to her. She would never forgive them, either of them, ever!

In her mind's eyes she saw Silas Clifford. To a seventeen-year-old girl, at fifty he was an old man. He was thin, his skin pale with prominent veins. His hair was white and he gave the impression of deformity without any obvious malformation. In fact, she had found everything about him displeasing. When he had come across her riding her horse along the lane near Oakwood Hall, his attention had been sharply and decisively arrested.

She recalled how he had called on her father soon after, how he had run his eyes over her, examining her face and figure as he would a prize cow. His hissing intake of breath as he did so had reminded her of a snake, and she had been glad when his business with her father had been concluded and he had gone on his way.

But following his visit her father had been uneasy and nervous, and to this day she did not know why. Soon afterwards he had been killed and Henry had become her guardian, and with it came the suspicion that he had killed her father. His odd behaviour, and the way he had of avoiding her eyes and refusing to speak of the tragic incident that had occurred on the road to Taplow Court, fuelled this suspicion, until she became certain of it.

What would her father think of Henry now? It had never occurred to him to doubt the honour of his own brother. Henry had fooled her father. He had taken his trust and trampled it. By running away she had made him pay for his lies.

Tears of fear, sorrow and frustration welled up in her eyes. 'Oh, Father, why did you desert me? I have lost everything.'

It was a cry from the heart, the cry of a lost and lonely child, but the sorrow that shaped it was soon spent. Jack and his kind would not defeat her. The food Adam had bought her still filled her stomach and lent support to her resolve. All she needed was the courage to remove herself as far away from Jack as she possibly could. She had not escaped from her uncle's clutches only to die a lingering death in the filth and squalor of St Giles, wretched and without hope.

She would not be beaten. She was young. She had the strength and the power to survive and grasp for herself a better future. She would make it happen because, if she didn't, no one else would. What was it Adam had said—that a person must have faith and pride in oneself, must believe in oneself? Well, she did believe in herself, and she would start by taking control of her life.

There would be no more Jack. No more Silas Clifford. No more Uncle Henry. Somehow she must find her way back to her own kind, but first she must have money, and Adam would give her that. She would find the boy Toby and take the reward he had promised for herself.

Her spirits strengthened, the following morning she left her squalid room for the last time and took her first steps into an uncertain future. If Jack caught her, there was no telling what he would do. But maybe he wouldn't catch her. It was a risk she was willing to take.

For three days Edwina scoured the vast network of alleyways and yards of St Giles, certain they had been built for the very purpose of concealment. It was like a vast jungle, which harboured criminals with as great a security as accorded to wild beasts in the jungles of Africa and India.

Careful to avoid the places where she knew Jack would be, she entered and searched places she would have steered clear of before—the meanest hovels, from the cellars to the rooms stacked on top. In the streets clouds of flies hovered over horse dung and offal from the slaughterhouses, mingling with the stench of unwashed humanity. Edwina was oblivious of everything outside her own purpose. She questioned fellow thieves and beggars. Everyone had seen crippled boys, and there were some who did fit Toby's description, but they were nameless.

It was almost dark and Edwina, utterly dejected and suffering from exhaustion, found herself in Covent Garden. Sitting on a low wall at the base of some iron railings, she kept herself awake only by a prodigious effort of will. Her whole body ached as if she had been beaten, and she blinked like a night-bird at the many bright lights around her.

She often found her way to the busy piazza. It was famous for its gaming, rowdy taverns, chocolate and coffee houses, and brothels filled with loose women. Its marvellous fruit and vegetable market and theatres giving it flavour and vitality, Covent Garden was pervaded by an atmosphere of uninhibited pleasure, attracting all kinds of folk—in particular actors, painters and writers—both day and night. Tonight was no different to all the others, as people came to savour the high life. Even in the fading light the vibrant colours drew Edwina into the tableau, and she listened to the din of voices as they laughed and boasted, cursed and argued.

Theatre-goers were beginning to arrive for the evening's performances in fine carriages, and she watched enviously as fashionable men and women in glittering and dazzling attire climbed out, the ladies holding froths of lace dipped in perfume to their noses to kill the unpleasant odour of rotting garbage. Creamy bosoms bedecked with jewels rose out of fitted bodices, slender waists accentuated by flowing skirts.

The gentlemen were no less magnificent in their leather pumps with silver buckles, white silk stockings and knee-length pale-coloured breeches, and superbly tailored frock coats over elaborately embroidered waistcoats. Most of the upper classes, both men and women, wore powdered wigs, but those of lesser means could not afford them. Eager to see the night's performances, with much laughter and light-hearted chatter, they alighted from their carriages and disappeared inside.

Edwina was about to stand up and move on when a carriage carrying two ladies and two gentleman stopped and caught and held her attention. Her eyes became riveted on one of the gentlemen. She watched him spring down and hold out his hand to assist one of the ladies with the tender care of a devoted friend—or lover. She was a tall, glittering young woman dressed in cobalt blue silk, her dark hair arranged superbly on her proudly erect head, the silken tresses threaded with sparkling jewels.

The gentleman was a tall, extremely striking man. He was impeccably dressed, his knee-length claret coat and rich dark hair emphasising the pristine whiteness of the cascade of lace at his throat and wrists. He declined the wearing of the customary wig, and Edwina thought how suited his own hair was to him. Suddenly her heart was beating wildly. She stared wide-eyed at the man, unaware that she had stood up. It was Adam. She was sure it was. If only he would turn his head, so she could see his face more clearly.

As if he felt the pull of her eyes he spun his head round and met her gaze head on. An expression Edwina couldn't recognise flickered across his handsome features, and even from a distance of several yards his eyes seemed very bright. Then one corner of his mouth cocked up in a smile, the same mocking smile she remembered. A sweet longing radiated through her, setting her pulse racing.

Not wishing to embarrass him by drawing further attention to herself, she turned. Just as she was about to disappear into the crowd, something clamped her upper arm like an iron band and spun her round. Rage edged Jack's deep voice as he thrust his face close.

'So, you young guttersnipe. Thought you'd run out on Jack, did you? Thought you'd escape me?' His small black eyes blazed. 'I said I'd find you—told you what would happen.'

Overcome with fear, Edwina panicked. A groan of terror

tore from her constricted chest, and she pulled away, cring-
ing from the blow she knew would follow. When it came she
fell to the ground. Coloured sparks exploded in her eyes and
the world began to spin, before blackness enfolded her.

From across the street, horrified, Adam saw what had happened. His eyes flashed with blue fire. 'Go in, will you,' he
said quickly to his companions. 'I'll join you shortly.' They
watched in stunned amazement as he ran across the street.

The crowd that had gathered around the unconscious youth
parted to let him through. 'Stand back,' he ordered. 'Give the
lad some air.' Crouching down beside Edwina, he raised her
up. Her head fell back limply and blood began to trickle from
the cut on the right side of her small face. Adam raised his
head and looked at the thug responsible, a murderous glint in
his blue eyes.

'Damn you! If the lad doesn't recover, you'll regret this,'
he said, and, for all its quiet, his voice was like a suddenly
unsheathed blade.

Jack turned and lumbered away. He disappeared down an
alley, moving with a speed and agility that could not have
been anticipated in a man of his bulk.

Adam gently raised the broken, pitiful burden into his
arms, and to the amazement of the crowd he carried the lad
off across the square. His arrival at the house just off the piazza with an unconscious street urchin in his arms caused a
furore of bawdy comments from both male and scantily clad
female occupants, who sat around talking and laughing and
openly caressing each other.

With the supreme indifference of a true gentleman toward
lesser mortals, Adam ignored the lewd remarks and addressed
a servant, his voice rich and compelling. 'Fetch Mrs Drinkwater at once.'

Right on cue an elegantly attired woman in middle age
moved slowly down the stairs.

'Why, it's you, Adam. I figured it must be. Who else would

make so much bluster? Still, 'tis a pleasure to see you.' She gave the man she had known since childhood an adoring, almost sainted look, before dropping her gaze to the boy and bending over him with concern. 'Bless me! What have we here?'

Adam's voice was urgent. 'I need your help, Dolly. The lad's injured and needs tending.'

'I can see that. Who is he?'

'A friend.'

Looking at the deeply etched lines of concern and strain on Adam's face, Dolly realised the boy must be quite special. 'Tell me what happened?'

'Some thug being too liberal with his fists,' he ground out.

'Oh, the poor mite. Bring him upstairs. We'll find him a bed right away.'

Following Dolly up the stairs and into a bedroom, Adam gently deposited his burden on the bed and loosened the fastenings at Edwina's throat. She groaned and rolled her head from side to side, but didn't open her eyes.

'Who is he?' Dolly asked as she busied herself with the unpleasant task of pulling off Ed's oversized, almost worn-out boots.

'He lives in St Giles. I hired him to help me find Toby.'

Dolly glanced up. 'Still no news of the lad, then?'

'No, unless Ed has something to offer.'

'I do hope so,' Dolly said sympathetically, knowing how important it was to Adam that he find Toby—his cousin Olivia's boy. 'And your cousin Silas?' she asked quietly, keeping her eyes down. 'What has become of him? It's so long since I had news of any sort from Tap-low—not that I seek it or care.'

Looking at Dolly's bent head and recalling the dreadful business that had forced her to leave Taplow Court, where she had been employed as housekeeper, Adam's expression softened. 'Silas is dead, Dolly—a month ago.'

She looked at him and nodded, digesting his words and straightening her back, knowing Adam would feel no remorse over the demise of that particular gentleman—and she even less—although there was a time when there was nothing she would not have done for Silas Clifford. She had been at Taplow Court just one month when he had taken her into his bed, and, though he didn't have an ounce of affection for her—taking her body night after night without the courtesy of a caress, without the slightest endearment and with less feeling than a dog for a bitch—she became a necessity in his life and she had loved him with a passion that had made her ache.

'Thank God,' she said.

'I always admired the way you put what happened behind you and got on with your life, Dolly. It can't have been easy.'

'It was very hard, Adam. But I cured myself of what Silas did to me before a serious depression could occur. Sadly the same cannot be said of your cousin Olivia—poor thing. What happened to the young lady Silas was to marry?'

Adam shrugged. 'She disappeared without a trace.' His firm lips curved in a wry smile. 'Apparently Silas inspired in her nothing but repugnance and she refused to be forced into marriage. Young women of seventeen do not willingly give themselves in marriage to licentious monsters more than twice their age. When her uncle insisted, it appears she ran away and has not been seen since. I never met her, but, whoever she is, I admire her courage.'

'And what of you, Adam? As heir to your cousin's estate you are now the Earl of Taplow. Are felicitations in order— or commiserations?'

His look was sombre. 'I never sought the title, you know that, Dolly. I always hoped Silas would marry and have children. My profession and my position as the Earl of Taplow do not rest easy together. There are many who would not approve.'

'Since when did Adam Rycroft care what others think?' Dolly remarked quickly. 'In that you and I are alike. Approval and disapproval are not words in my vocabulary, Adam.'

Adam grinned. 'You know me too well, Dolly.'

'In that you are right,' she said, laughing lightly. Thinking of Tap-low Court, she had a vision of happy children playing in the deserted gardens, running through the empty rooms, injecting them with life. 'Some might say Taplow Court is a grim and gloomy place, but despite what happened I liked it there. Silas never appreciated it—he never appreciated anything. What that house needs is a family living in it—children, Adam. You should give it some thought.'

'I have, Dolly, but what I do suits me. It is a part of me. The city is my home.'

'Hertfordshire is only a few hours away from London. You could quite easily reside at Taplow Court and still manage your business here. You don't have to sell your house in town.'

'I suppose you're right, but here I come and go as I please, and no man commands me. At Taplow, where I was never at ease, I shall be forced into habits, restricted, which will eventually kill my initiative—my spontaneity—which is an important part of my work.'

'Being the Earl of Taplow will not necessarily change that.'

'I wish I could be so sure. I do not want to become part of a system that stifles—a cog in a wheel that's forever turning and going nowhere.'

Dolly could understand what he was saying. The tragedies of his personal life had made him cynical.

He combed a rebellious lock of hair from his forehead with an impatient hand, and paced the carpet between the window and the bed with long, vigorous strides, his eyes constantly drawn to the still figure laid out on the bed. Dolly could sense the restlessness in him.

'You haven't been back to Taplow?'

'No, not since I left all those years ago. But I will. I have no choice. As yet I have not divulged my elevation to the title to anyone, Dolly, and I would prefer it to remain so until I've been back to Taplow. Had Toby been legitimate, the estate would have passed to him. You, more than anyone, will remember the circumstances of Toby's birth, and the day Silas threw Olivia out of Taplow Court after slaying her lover.'

Dolly nodded. It was something she had tried so hard to forget, but the memory of Joseph Tyke, Silas's incredibly handsome head groom, his blood pouring from a gaping wound in his chest and draining him of life, of Silas standing over him, gloating, bloodied knife in his hand, meant that she never would. That was the day she had come to hate Silas Clifford with a virulence that almost choked her, and made her turn her back on him and his home. She recalled Lady Olivia as being a demure young woman with a sweet nature, and, unfortunately, very poor health.

'I do. It was a truly wicked, cruel act on his part.'

'I know. He should have been apprehended for what he did—hanged, even, but he had the establishment background, wealth, power, influence, and the bland confidence of a noble lord,' Adam said with snarling bitterness. 'When Olivia knew she was dying, destitute and with no one else to turn to, in desperation she returned to Taplow Court and begged her brother to take care of the boy. You can imagine Silas's reaction.'

'Yes, I can. Your cousin was a man used to his own way, a ruthless man, too unprincipled, too wealthy, with too much of everything, who thought the world should pay obeisance to him.'

'He also found disfigurement of any kind abhorrent...' Adam paused. His face was hard with memory, the muscles tight, and his blue eyes were hard too. 'Silas couldn't bear to look at Toby with his twisted leg, so when Olivia died he cast him out—gave him like a bit of old garbage to some passing tinkers.'

His voice was calm, much too calm, carefully modulated, but Dolly knew that beneath the calm Adam seethed with anger, and the striking gentleman in claret velvet and lace became the youth again, the fervent, embittered boy who had been forced to live under Silas's tyrannical dominance at Taplow Court. He took a deep breath and ran a hand across his brow. When he spoke his voice was still calm, but each word might have been chiselled from ice.

'Olivia wrote to me shortly before she died, explaining her situation, but I was out of the country at the time and when I returned it was too late for me to help her. I failed her, Dolly. I saw Silas when he came to London. He told me what he had done—coldly and without an ounce of remorse. If he hadn't died, I think I would have killed him with my bare hands. I have to find Toby—for Olivia's sake. If it's the last thing I do, I *will* find him.'

His voice was so full of conviction that Dolly believed he would.

Adam stood back as she continued to administer to the inert figure with a cool efficiency he'd always admired. Despite her chosen profession, one that caused her to be shunned and looked down on, he respected Dolly and would defend her to the death. Apart from his parents, she was the only person he had ever loved. She had taken him under her protective wing when, at the age of six, following the tragic death of his parents, he had been sent to Taplow Court to be brought up by his cousin Silas.

Dolly was a shrewd businesswoman. When she'd left Taplow Court she'd come to London and opened a dress shop, which had proved a huge success. She was extremely likeable and vivacious, and she soon became a popular figure.

Having made a huge profit, but not content with that, and liking the sound of clinking gold, she'd opened a gambling house in Covent Garden with investments from some of her wealthy gentlemen friends. The downstairs' rooms were sumptuously decorated and the tables run by competent, attractive young women. Upstairs there were a number of private rooms where these same young ladies, and others whose job it was to please the customers, could retire with well-heeled patrons.

Adam suddenly remembered his companions at the theatre, and knew that Barbara, who was Dolly's niece, would be livid because he'd deserted her. 'I don't think the lad's badly hurt, so, if you don't mind, Dolly, I'll leave him in your capable hands. I have to go. I promised I would escort Barbara to the theatre tonight and had to leave her with Steven Hewitt and his wife. As you know, your niece has temper that would shame the devil. My life won't be worth living if I abandon her completely.'

'You have my sympathy. I know just how difficult Barbara can be—even at the best of times. You'd better go.'

Adam glanced with indecision at the recumbent form on the bed. 'I know you'll take good care of the lad. For some reason I feel responsible for him now. Send for the doctor if need be. I'll be back to see how he is in the morning.'

Chapter Three

Edwina opened her eyes. Darkness pressed around her. She winced at the pain in her head. Gingerly she turned it an inch at a time. Curtains were drawn across a window, so it must be night. She was in a bed, the mattress soft—as soft as her own had been. Tobacco smoke and the sweet, cloying scent of women's perfume permeated the air, and from somewhere beyond the room she could hear voices.

Her hands were resting on top of the covers. Sliding them underneath, she was horrified when she felt her naked body. Someone had removed her clothes—not just her breeches and jacket, but everything. She couldn't remember being without her undergarments, except before she had come to London, when she had taken her bath. Fighting down her panic, she wondered what kind of people would take her clothes and—worse—how many had seen her without them?

Anger flared through her and she sat up, clutching the bedcovers to her body. She must escape, but how could she when she didn't know where she was and had nothing to wear? The pain in her head pushed her back against the soft pillows and, closing her eyes, she drifted back to sleep.

The soft singing of a woman came to Edwina. She opened her eyes to find the cosy room flooded with morning sunlight.

The familiar hubbub of the streets drifted from beyond the walls, and above it all a cacophony of sound from the city's many church bells. From somewhere in the house doors opened and closed, and the smell of warm bread and frying bacon wafted into her room.

She tried to remember what had happened—seeing Jack and how he had lashed out at her in anger. A chill ran through her. She recalled being lifted up by someone else, but she couldn't remember who it had been.

Unable to conjure up his face, she forced herself to relax and enjoy the warmth and safety of the bed, at least for the moment, letting the pleasant smells of the house and the woman's song lull her. Edwina wondered who she was. The singing stopped and whoever it was spoke to someone else. Other voices could be heard now, laughing and giggling.

Hauling herself to a sitting position, she leaned back, pulling the covers up to her chin. After a few moments a young woman came into the room, humming softly under her breath. Her auburn hair spilled to her shoulders in a luxuriant mass. She was bearing a tray weighted down by a pot of tea and a platter of eggs and bacon and bread and butter. The delicious aroma tempted Edwina, who'd had nothing to eat since the previous midday.

The young woman stopped when she saw Edwina sitting up in bed, and a smile stretched across her pretty face. 'Good, you're awake!' she said, her voice as clear as her glowing complexion. She placed the tray in front of Edwina on the bed. 'Here, get that down you. Mrs Drinkwater says you're much too thin for comfort and insists we feed you up.' She took a step back. 'I'm Harriet Crabtree, by the way, and I'm pleased to meet you. How do you feel?'

'Better, thank you—at least I shall when my clothes are returned to me.'

Still smiling, the young woman cocked her head. 'I can't

say that I blame you, but when you were brought here, Mrs Drinkwater refused to let you lie between her clean linen in what you were wearing.'

'Mrs Drinkwater?'

'The owner of this establishment.'

'And what kind of establishment is this?'

Harriet had no time to reply, for at that moment a woman bustled in, carrying some clothes over her arm. She smiled when she saw her young guest sitting up in bed. 'Hello, dear. Dolly Drinkwater,' she introduced herself. 'I'm glad to see you awake at last. You took a nasty knock on the head last night and had us all quite worried, I don't mind telling you.' Her voice was rich and warm like the peach dress she wore. Fifty years old, Dolly Drinkwater had a face that was lined, but her figure was still slender, and there was a sparkle in her eyes that age would not dim.

Draping the clothes over the back of a chair, she stood looking down at Edwina. Despite her outward composure, the poor young thing looked extremely tense, frightened, almost. 'You can put them on when you've eaten and had a bath. We had difficulty with the dress size—you being so small, you understand—but Harriet made a quick adjustment to the seams so that it would fit. I've told one of the maids to have some hot water brought up.'

'Thank you—and thank you for the bed. It's the best I've slept in for a long time. You've been very kind.'

'What's your name, love?'

'E—Ed,' she replied hesitantly, her voice hoarse.

The older woman raised an elegant brow. 'Oh, come now. It was no stripling lad I undressed last night—though you'd have everyone believe that, wouldn't you? You might have fooled Adam, but you can't fool me.'

Edwina's composure began to crumble when she recalled seeing Adam outside the theatre. He must have witnessed what happened and rescued her from Jack. 'Adam? Adam brought me here?'

'That he did, and most concerned he was, too. Now, what's your real name?'

'Edwina.'

'And how old are you?'

'Eighteen.'

Dolly's stare was forthright, her tone gentle. 'Why are you masquerading as a boy? Running away from someone, are you?'

'You—might say that,' she answered, convinced Jack would come after her—or worse, that he would put the law on her.

'Well—you'll be safe now. There's no where safer in the whole of London, dearie, than Dolly's Place. No constable will venture inside this house.'

'No?'

'It's a bordello, love,' Harriet quipped saucily, her eyes twinkling. 'Of the prestigious kind, of course. Don't you worry, though,' she said, winking cheekily. 'You needn't sell your favours if you have no mind to. Although, we could teach you all you need to know to be a fitting companion for the gentlemen who visit here—but,' she went on, wrinkling her nose with distaste at Edwina's greasy hair and dirty face, 'we'd have to fatten you up a bit and do something about your appearance first.'

'Stop it, Harriet,' Dolly reproached, a chuckle taking out the sting. 'You'll embarrass our young guest.'

Edwina stared from one to the other in shocked incomprehension. She was in a bordello, a den of depravity, and this kindly lady was a procuress. 'Companion? You mean whore!' she blurted out hotly. 'I will not sell my body.' She had not given up her life as a thief to become a whore. That would be too much to be borne.

As soon as she had said the words Edwina was contrite. It was a harsh remark, and it must have hurt, she could see that. Harriet didn't reply at first, and then a faint smile curved her lips. The lovely, vivacious young woman with lively, laughing hazel eyes was too worldly to be upset by a remark that must have been hurled at her many times.

'Don't judge me or the other girls who work at Dolly's Place too harshly, Edwina. Life isn't always as clear cut as it might seem.'

'You're right. I, more than most, should know that. I can't tell you how grateful I am to you for helping me. I owe you and Mrs Drinkwater a huge debt of gratitude,' she murmured, smiling at Mrs Drinkwater as she went out. 'I'm sorry, Harriet. I meant no offence.'

'None taken, love. What I do helps pay the rent, and a girl needs all the help she can get. I've no romantic illusions about what I do—I've grown used to having insults thrown at me. Reality surrounds me every day, and I face it resolutely—shoulders squared.' She shrugged and smiled prettily. 'What other way is there? Now, eat your breakfast before it gets cold. I'll go and see where that girl's got to with your bath.'

The maid who carried the water and prepared Edwina's bath could not suppress her curiosity at the young person with cropped hair. But nothing was said, and after laying out soap and towels she left the room. Alone at last, immediately Edwina was out of bed and lowering herself into the hot scented water, revelling in the sheer luxury. She scrubbed weeks-old grime from her skin and soaped the gnarled thatch of hair, careful when she washed over the cut on the side of her face, which was extremely tender.

When she was satisfied that she was clean, she relaxed and closed her eyes. Her body now smelled of roses, and not the hateful stench of poverty. Not knowing what would happen next, and that there was every possibility that she would be turned back out onto to street, she was determined to savour the moment to the full.

It was mid-morning when Adam arrived at Dolly's Place. Striding with a natural exuberance into the spacious hall, with elegant, sumptuously carpeted and furnished gaming rooms leading off, he was met by Dolly herself. She ran her establishment and her girls with stern efficiency and the keen eye of an army commander, and no one seeing her now, bright and cheerful as ever, would suspect that she would not have sought her bed until the dawn light was peeping over the horizon.

With a smile curving her lips, she swept an eye of admiring approval over Adam's well-groomed form. He was attired in buff-coloured breeches above trim brown knee boots, a cream silk waistcoat embroidered with silver fleurs-de-lis, and a superbly cut tan frock coat, the lace tumbling from his jabot and spilling over his wrists of the finest quality.

Darkly handsome and imbued with potent masculine allure, he exuded virility and a casual, lazy confidence. There was little wonder women were eager for his affections, falling over themselves in the rush to get close to him. Seeing him here at her humble establishment was like seeing a royal prince consorting with the commoners.

Mid-morning, and with most of the girls still sleeping off a busy night, the establishment was relatively quiet.

'How's Ed? How does he fare this morning, Dolly?' Adam enquired briskly, removing his gloves and placing them with his tricorn on an occasional table at the bottom of the wide, white marble staircase.

'She's much better—and cleaner,' Dolly replied, preceding him up the stairs. She paused and glanced back at him, her eyes sparkling. 'I think you'll be impressed.'

'She?' Adam asked, standing stock still and staring up at her blankly.

'Yes, she,' Dolly repeated, enjoying his confusion. 'Ed— or perhaps I should say Edwina—my dear Adam, is no boy.'

'He isn't? Don't be ridiculous, Dolly. Have you taken leave of your senses?'

'No—' Dolly chuckled richly '—but you must have if you, of all people, can't tell the difference. You have been completely hoodwinked. Now stop gawping and come and see.'

She ushered Adam inside the room before making herself scarce. A young woman dressed in an extremely fetching buttercup-yellow dress stood by the window, her hands clasped at her trim waist. Small and as slender as a willow, she was watching him warily. Without taking his eyes off her, he moved towards her, staring in disbelief. Could this delectable, lovely young creature be the boy Ed? Reaching out, he cupped her chin in his hand, raising her face. He could only stare in wonder at the face that was unmistakably Ed's.

'Good Lord!' The words were uttered on a breath. 'I should have known.' She had a femininity he could have put to his lips and drunk, and she was so close he could feel her breathing, feel the warmth of her, and smell her natural scent.

Never had he seen such shimmering perfection in his life before, as he did now, when he gazed at her vibrant copper-and-gold-coloured hair curling in soft, feathery wisps, framing a finely proportioned visage, flawless, except for the small cut and purple bruise on her temple. Her eyes were as he remembered, a sparkling shade of blue-green—jade, he now noted with an artist's expert eye. She wore an expression that combined vitality and youthful curiosity, without appearing indelicate or wanton. She was quite enchanting.

Rather nervously Edwina withstood the intensity of his gaze, meeting those disturbing deep blue eyes of his levelled on her own. His dark brows lifted a fraction in bland enquiry.

'Do you mind?'

Edwina continued to stare up at him, aware of two things—his darkly handsome face, and the richly textured deep voice. The combination sent a peculiar warmth up her spine.

'Mind?' she repeated stupidly.

'If I look at you.'

'No—oh, no.'

A chuckle started deep in his chest. 'Well, Ed? What do you have to say for this deception?' he asked, dropping his hand and taking a step back.

His eyes were dark, probing, quizzical. His smile was rakishly winsome, and must have fluttered many feminine hearts. 'I say it was no deception. You seem surprised—about my being a girl, I mean.'

'Frankly, my dear, I believe you to be full of surprises.'

'Are you disappointed?'

'A little. It means I can no longer employ you to look for Toby.'

'I don't see why that should make a difference. I can revert back to Ed any time I choose.'

Adam laughed lightly, not taking her reply seriously. Her voice was soft centred, lovely, creamy. The vivid colour of her dress brought a glow to her pale skin. Without realising it she was standing straight, her head high. There was the hint of the kind of sophistication that seemed natural to young ladies of breeding—straight shoulders, the confidence of a level gaze, smooth line of spine, with no slouch.

'I must thank you for coming to my aid last night. I hope it didn't spoil your evening at the theatre,' Edwina remarked, wondering who the dark-haired woman was and how closely linked they were.

'I was glad to be on hand to render assistance,' he said rather formally. 'I'm afraid the ruffian who attacked you got clean away. Now— explain to me what has prompted you to adopt such a mode of attire.'

'I dressed as a boy for my own protection. As a girl in St Giles I would have been ready bait.' She gazed steadily into his clear blue eyes. 'You are a man, so you will know what I mean.'

'Perfectly. However, you seemed well at home in your boy's clothes—but I like these better,' he murmured in such a way that it brought an embarrassed flush to Edwina's cheeks.

Having played the lad so long, she found the conversion to feminine ways difficult. Besides, with the air positively crackling with Adam's virile presence, for the first time in her life she had met a man who made her feel alert and alive, and curiously stimulated.

'I don't know your reasons for the masquerade,' he went on, recalling their conversation in the alehouse when the boy Ed had told him he had secrets he wished to keep, 'nor do I particularly want to know. Suffice it to say that is your business—not mine. What we must decide is what is to be done with you. Just how old are you?'

'Eighteen.'

'I thought you were much younger. And the man who attacked you? Who was he?'

'That was Jack.'

'Your fence—receiver?'

'Yes.'

'And is he aware of your sex?'

'No. No one is. I told you, it was for my own protection that I dressed as a boy.'

'Yes, I can understand that. Why did he attack you?'

'Because I ran away.'

'Are you afraid of him?'

'I'm afraid he will put the law on me—that I will go to prison—and because I ran away from him nothing would please Jack more than to see me rotting in a filthy cell. If he were to discover I am a girl in boy's clothing, it would simply amuse him, and he would use it against me.'

'Then he would do well to remember that receiving is as much a capital felony as the stealing of the goods.'

'He knows that, but he is shamelessly bold and hardened above cautionary fear, working in an organised and far-ranging manner. He controls shoplifters and housebreakers, but I never progressed further than picking pockets. He despises laws and will carry on with his wicked trade, making sure he never hands over stolen goods himself, but craftsmen he employs—paying them handsomely so that they will keep their mouths shut, making them unidentifiable first.

'He always uses someone else to exchange the spoils for money at a time and place arranged by him.' She looked up into Adam's warm blue eyes. 'I have no money, nothing of my own, and when Jack took me in I knew I was on the road to prison, or worse—to the noose at Tyburn.'

'Why did you stay with him?' Adam asked gently. 'Why didn't you run away sooner?'

'I couldn't. I was afraid—and no one runs away from Jack,' she said quietly. Those few words held a world of meaning that Adam fully understood. 'Jack humbled me, confused me and seriously diminished my own sense of worth, and I could not seem to be able to clamber out of the dark hole into which I had fallen. Besides, it was inconceivable for me to return to my former life. I had nowhere to run to. I couldn't see the point in exchanging one hell for another.' She shrugged. 'What's the difference? When I did finally pluck up the courage and left Jack, hoping to find your Toby and receive payment, I staunchly decided to take charge of my own life and to choose its direction. I made up my mind to live decently, to find work of some kind to support myself.'

'Dolly may be able to help you there,' Adam suggested casually.

Offended by what she thought he was implying, Edwina drew herself up proudly and raised her chin to a lofty angle. 'I may not be honest, sir, but I would never stoop so low as to become a whore.'

Observing that her eyes were dark with anger, Adam suppressed a smile and directed a stern countenance at her. 'I was not suggesting that you should. That was certainly not what I meant.'

'Besides, I'm unattractive and skinny, with none of the curves required to be one of Dolly's girls, and not much hair to speak of, either,' she said, running her fingers through the short, wispy tresses.

Perching his tall frame on the edge of a dresser and folding his arms across his chest, Adam arched his eyebrows, squinting at her with his head cocked to one side as he made a study of her. The purity of her face was quite striking. With her large eyes and unbelievably long dark eyelashes resting against her smooth, high cheeks, she looked innocent and incredibly lovely. She glowed with that strange fragile beauty of a young woman newly awakened to her sex, a nymph, clothed in bright yellow finery. Not for the first time, he wished he could immortalise her on canvas, but could he—or any artist—do justice to her flawless beauty? He smiled inwardly at the poetic bent of his thoughts and the challenge she presented.

'Allow me to disagree. You are a remarkably beautiful young woman. You have the kind of unusual looks that put you in a class by yourself. The colour of your hair is divine—such radiance. You have a good neck and an excellent bone structure, and your features, particularly your eyes, are perfect.'

Edwina's lips twitched slightly as she tried to suppress a smile. 'In the past I've often been called sweet and sometimes pretty, but no one has ever complimented me—in such a matter-of-fact way—about my bone structure or my long neck. I don't quite know whether to feel flattered or offended.'

'I meant it as a compliment. I speak as I find. What happened to the five guineas I gave you?'

'I had to give them to Jack.'

'Had to? I gave the money to you, not Jack,' he admonished sharply, coming to his feet.

'I know better than to cheat him.' Edwina was downcast. 'I'm sorry.'

'Don't be. Having witnessed his brutality at first hand, perhaps it was as well. Did you manage to make enquiries about Toby?'

'Yes. As you know, cripples are a common sight, and no one I asked remembered seeing a boy who answered to that name. One woman vaguely recalled seeing a man and woman with a boy, a crippled boy, about a week ago, but they left St Giles and took to the road.'

Interest flickered in Adam's eyes. 'Anything else?'

'Yes. They had a bear with them.'

Adam lowered his eyelids and reflected for a moment. 'A man and woman, you say?'

She nodded. 'Do you think the boy might be Toby?'

'It's possible,' he replied absently as he began to pace restlessly about the room, frowning thoughtfully.

'Who is this boy? What does he mean to you?'

'He is my cousin's child—the son of a young woman who died a while back. Even though I have never laid eyes on Toby, he means a great deal to me.'

'Do you fear for his safety?'

'Naturally, but I don't think he'll come to harm while he can earn money at freak shows.' His frown deepened. 'A crippled boy and a bear,' he murmured, tossing the image around in his head. 'A useful combination. Unless they have transport of some kind I don't believe they will leave London. I can only surmise the man and woman are to display them to the curious at fairs and markets, and if so I'll find them.'

Edwina's eyes lit with interest. 'Are you going to look for them? If so, will you take me with you?' she asked enthusiastically. 'Two pairs of eyes will be better than one.'

Her words caught all Adam's attention. He ceased pacing and looked at her with narrowed eyes. What she was asking was out of the question. But what was he going to do with her? As a lad he'd have no qualms about taking her along—but this young woman was a different matter entirely.

'No.'

Watching his finely moulded lips form his answer, Edwina was surprised and mortified by his refusal, and also a little angry, but she was even more surprised by the unmistakable regret she'd heard in his voice. 'But why not?' she argued.

'For a start, fairs are known to attract violence and vice. Some are also well known centres for the distribution of stolen goods, places where criminals congregate—although I'm sure you will know all about that,' he remarked with meaningful sarcasm. 'Not only do you run the risk of meeting Jack, but you also risk being robbed or crushed to death—as small as you are.'

'Do you mean to frighten me with a description of what it is like to come into contact with thieves and cutthroats, when I have lived among them for six months of my life?'

'Aye, as an insignificant lad. If you were to appear among them now, looking as you do, you wouldn't last five minutes. You are not an easy woman to ignore.'

Edwina was indignant. Her head lifted and her chin squared up to him, the action saying quite clearly that she was contemptuous of being told what to do by anyone. 'I don't need to be protected,' she said boldly. Her anger made her eyes gleam like green stones, and her mouth hardened to unsmiling resentment.

'And I don't expect to have my decision questioned,' Adam rapped out. Despite his anger he admired her courage. She did not cower, but flashed her sparkling eyes in a defiant challenge to his authority.

Edwina clenched her teeth and held back her retort. Adam's stern, stiff-backed hauteur irritated her. All trace of softness had vanished from his face. His dark brows were drawn together, and his blue eyes were cold. The words were an order, one he expected her to obey.

'The majority of the men swilling ale will be drunk out of their minds, and there is always the possibility of you bumping into Jack. The man is dangerous. It's advisable not to put yourself in his path.'

Edwina met his dark scowl with a heated glower, her fingers drumming upon her slim hips. Her expression dared him to attempt control of her. 'Thank you for your concern, but I don't remember giving you the right to tell me what I can and cannot do. Who do you think you are, anyway?'

'Your saviour, it would seem,' Adam replied drily. 'Listen to what I'm saying, will you, and take heed? I'm more advanced in years than you, so I know what I'm talking about. It's a man's world out there, Ed.'

'You're right, but that does not mean that I have to submit to their will. My own strength was my only weapon when I defied Jack Pierce and ran away, and that will is still as strong as it ever was.'

'Nevertheless, the places I intend searching are no place for a respectable young woman.'

'I am not a respectable young woman,' she argued heatedly, firmly, 'who needs cosseting—to be treated like some fragile sugar confection. I can handle myself.'

'As you did last night? If you could handle yourself you wouldn't be here now,' he pointed out. 'I will not take you with me and that is my final word on the subject.'

These words were delivered in a cold, lethal voice, and Edwina grew pale beneath her own anger. 'If I have a mind I shall return to the streets, and there's not a thing you can do about it.' She was adamant and not to be put off by his anger. He was standing not three feet away from her, looming over her, his blue eyes gleaming with deadly purpose, and the uncompromising lines at the sides of his mouth had not been there before. She could see that same cold rage as when she'd stolen his watch, and also a cynicism and ruthless set of his jaw—things she'd obviously been too blinded by her predicament to see before. 'You can't stop me. I'll disguise myself as a boy again,' Edwina persisted.

'And then Jack would be sure to recognise you—and if he's as angry as you say he is, he'll be looking for you. No, Ed. You must abandon your disguise for good.'

'I will do as I please,' she persisted crossly.

'I'm sure you will, you stubborn, wilful little fool,' Adam retorted, combing his fingers through his hair in exasperation. 'I have been in your company twice and each time you've been in some scrape or other. Little did I realise when I rescued you from that animal's clutches that I was committing myself to certain disaster.'

'My, a proper knight in shining armour, aren't you, Adam? I didn't ask you to interfere,' Edwina snapped.

'Why, you—damn you for an ingrate.' He stood in front of her, looking down at her upturned face. It had whitened with her anger, revealing the pale freckles across her nose. The sunlight lancing through the window brightened her hair to a living flame, making an aureole of light around her small, proud head. He looked at her thoughtfully, touched by her vulnerability. He felt himself dwelling with a good deal of pleasure on what it would be like to get to know her better. But as he looked at her, a kind of rage welled up in him against Jack Pierce, and also against the person or persons who had abandoned her to a life of crime, alone on the streets, through no fault of her own.

'I'm sorry. I didn't mean to sound so brutal. But can't you see that I am concerned about your present distress and offer my assistance only with the kindest intent?' he said on a softer note.

The faintest of smiles curved his lips, so slight it was scarcely discernible. Edwina felt a poignant emotion welling up inside her, a tenderness she never believed she could feel for any human being. Immediately the fight went out of her. She moved closer to him.

'If I offended you, then I beg your pardon. I've been on my own and had to look out for myself for too long. It's such a long time since anyone showed any concern about me, about what I do, that it takes some getting used to. I'm sorry I made you angry. Please don't be. I'd rather we were friends than enemies.' She offered him her hand as was proper.

The gesture made Adam smile suddenly, a slow, startlingly lazy smile as he took her hand in his firm grasp. His gaze scanned her face, and when he raised her hand to his lips the pressure of his mouth lingered longer than was customary.

'Friends we are, Ed, or may I call you Edwina?'

'As you please.'

'Then Edwina it is. So, now that is established, what am I supposed to do with you? You've made it plain that you will feel uncomfortable living here. And you can forget any notion you have of donning your boy's clothes and taking to the streets. You've done with that.'

'Then what am I to do? I must earn some money. How else am I to live?'

Adam's eyes narrowed, studying her with unnerving intensity for a moment as he considered her situation carefully. Ever since their first meeting the lad 'Ed' had haunted him. And now he'd been transformed into female form, he couldn't let this young woman with the most remarkable face he'd ever seen simply walk out of his life.

Aware that his fascination was rapidly winning out over his common sense, he said to his own utter astonishment, 'You could come and live with me for the time being.' She looked so surprised and so hesitant for a moment that he wished he had not made the extraordinary, impulsive suggestion, but when he saw a little smile tug at the corners of her lips, he knew she was not as shocked as he at first thought.

'Live with you?' she murmured, seeing his blue eyes darken to indigo. 'Do—do you want me to work for you?'

'In a manner of speaking.'

'I—I'm not very good at woman's work. I—I can't cook.'

'I don't need a cook,' he said, mentally shaking his head at the naïvety of her. 'That position is already taken—and I have servants enough to administer to my personal needs.'

'Then what would you require of me?'

'Oh—this and that.' His smile was lazy and infuriatingly secretive.

Misinterpreting his meaning, Edwina flushed scarlet. 'Kindly explain what you mean by "this and that"?' she asked tentatively in an attempt to clarify matters. 'Do you mean to establish me as your paramour? If so, I must tell you that I will be no man's property. I intend standing on my own feet.'

Adam's eyes took on a humorous glint. He placed a finger over her lips. 'Heaven forbid I would dare suggest anything so bold. You would never be my property, Edwina. What I will ask of you will take very little effort on your part, I can promise you that,' he said softly, 'but I think you will enjoy the work. I'll pay you generously, if that's what's worrying you, but I must warn you that I'm a hard taskmaster. Shortly, I have to go away for a while. Since I shall be absent for quite some time you are welcome to make use of my house. Now, I have to go. I have pressing matters to attend to.'

He took her hand, and when he would have raised it once more to his lips she pulled it away and stepped back with an arch smile.

'You take a liberty. Do you make a habit of kissing the hands of all your employees?'

'It's not usual.'

'Then as my employer you'll not kiss mine.' Edwina raised a brow and regarded him with the same amusement he had earlier directed at her.

Adam was clearly at pains to control his laughter as he playfully chucked her under the chin. 'Cheeky as ever! You are a most uncommon, intractable wench, Edwina.'

'I merely protect my honour,' she countered. 'But isn't what you are proposing to do rather shocking and likely to be frowned upon by polite society?'

'Being an unconventional man, I care nothing for polite society.'

She cocked her head to one side, giving him an enquiring look. 'Forgive me, but I can't help noticing that you're on familiar terms with Mrs Drinkwater. Do you often visit her establishment?'

He grinned. 'It's not my habit to visit bordellos. I've known Dolly since I was a small boy. She used to work for my family as housekeeper. When she left she decided to settle for something less respectable, but far more remunerative.'

'And is there a Mr Drinkwater?'

'Once. He was laid to rest many years ago. Dolly and I always keep in touch. I'll have a word with her on my way out and tell her what we've decided.'

He strode towards the door where he turned and looked back at her. For a moment his gaze held hers with penetrating intensity, and unexpectedly Edwina felt an answering frisson of excitement. The slight smile that curved his lips warned her he was aware of that brief response. His eyes moved over her face as if he were memorising it, and then, with a slight satisfied nod of his handsome head, he left her.

Chapter Four

The thought of going with Adam to his home, working for him, had great appeal. It loomed on the horizon of Edwina's mind like a sweet haven...waiting. Peace and quiet was what she wanted. No more Jack. No more Uncle Henry. No more Earl of Taplow.

No sooner had Adam left than Harriet breezed in. She was certainly different to anyone Edwina had ever known, and it was impossible not to warm to her.

'So, you know the great Adam Rycroft!' Harriet exclaimed, sitting on the edge of the silk-covered bed.

'Yes, but not very well. He—he's asked me to work for him.'

'Oh? Doing what?'

'That's just it. I don't know.'

'He comes here often to see Mrs Drinkwater. She's quite fond of him—known him since he was a lad, apparently. He's very popular with the ladies, and he's a connoisseur of beautiful women.'

'And he makes love to them all, I expect,' Edwina said laughing softly. Spectacularly good looking and imbued with potent masculine allure, she was sure Adam Rycroft was rarely refused.

Harriet smiled knowingly, lying back and propping herself

up on her elbow. 'More than likely. He's no saint where women are concerned. But mostly he paints them—professionally, of course.'

Edwina looked at her with surprised amazement, settling herself down on the bed facing her. 'He's an artist?' Recalling the sketch Adam had made of her, she should have known. She shook her head at the mysterious combination of gentleman and painter. 'Is he good?'

'I'm no judge, but some say he's the best—a genius. His pictures cost the earth. You, I wager, are going to be the subject of a painting. He must want you to sit for him, that'll be what he wants you to do.'

'Sit?'

'Be a model—so he can paint you. Make the most of it, love. Duchesses and the like consider it a privilege to sit for the great man. There are many women who would die to be in your shoes.'

Edwina was impressed. 'You obviously like him.'

'Oh, he's quite endearing, really. He's rich, has oodles of charm when he chooses to employ it, but the man's like a human whirlwind and a positive despot when he's at his easel. Don't let him browbeat and bully you. When he's involved in a painting he loses all track of time. He'll have you sitting there for hours if you let him. I sat for him once—once was enough, believe me. A girl could catch her death sitting for him.'

'Oh?'

'He's a master of the human form, love—the female form—and there's more than one model he's painted in the nude. Mind you, he has to pay extra for a girl to take her clothes off. Titled ladies flock to have him paint them, and they all fall prey to his fatal attraction. By the time he's finished they're head over heels in love with him—and more than one husband regrets his choice of artist to paint his wife.'

'Goodness! Why on earth would he want to paint me?'

'Probably because you're different to all the other models

who grace his couch. Your face is unusual—interesting, he would call it. He probably sees you as a challenge, love. Who knows—' she laughed, tossing her head so her auburn curls bounced '—you might turn out to be his greatest masterpiece yet. He might even make you famous.'

'I sincerely hope not. I don't want to be famous. That kind of notoriety I can do without,' she said, thinking of Uncle Henry. Her uncle was a man of fine tastes. In particular he was an avid admirer of paintings, and had built up an enviable collection over the years. Many of the paintings he hung for their quality rather than decoration, which was the case in many houses. If he were to see one of her, he would know exactly where to come looking for her. Her mind shied away from the thought. 'But what's Adam like, Harriet, really?'

'Well,' she said, lowering her eyes and reflecting for a moment, 'he's certainly a complex character, and he can be utterly ruthless at times. So be warned, Edwina. His fury is unequalled when roused—as I and some of the other girls who have sat for him know to our cost, having been on the receiving end.'

'Is he married?' Edwina asked, thinking of the stunningly beautiful brunette she had seen him with outside the theatre.

'No, love. Adam Rycroft is a self-proclaimed single man, although he's always careful to choose a mistress whose company he enjoys. She has to be unmarried, passionate and experienced, and highly pleasurable in bed, a woman who will not mistake lovemaking and desire with love—who will make no demands and expect no promises.'

'Goodness, you make him sound cold hearted and self-centred.'

'He's certainly volatile. I don't think anyone's got his true measure—except Mrs Drinkwater, perhaps, but she guards her tongue whenever she speaks of him. He's totally committed to his work, a perfectionist, and he won't allow anything or anyone to interfere with that. Have you given any thought as to where you will live?'

'He—he's offered to let me stay in his house.'

The words brought Harriet upright. 'Ooh—now that is a first! And you said yes.'

She nodded. 'I've nowhere else to go, Harriet—only back to the streets and my life as a thief.'

Harriet's eyes opened wide in shocked amazement. 'Thief?'

'Yes. I picked pockets.' Edwina smiled, feeling a slight unease at disclosing her criminal past, but somehow she didn't think Harriet would judge her.

She was right. Harriet sat up with a joyous laugh. 'I insist that you tell me every single detail of this unbelievable story if I have to wring it out of you with my own bare hands. Now, begin at the beginning.'

Edwina started to refuse, but Harriet looked so determined that it was useless. Besides, she suddenly wanted to talk about it, and found herself giving Harriet a brief account of what her life had been like working for Jack for the past six months, talking to this engaging girl as she had never talked to anyone before. At the end of the story Harriet stared at her with a combination of mirth and wonder. 'Does that shock you?'

'No more than you were, when you realised the great Adam Rycroft had brought you to a brothel and I was one of Mrs Drinkwater's whores,' she remarked, gulping down a giggle. 'It's too delicious for words.'

'Do you live here, Harriet?'

'No. Some of the girls do, but I don't. I've got a room over a bakery off Drury Lane. It's not very big, and it's by no means grand, but it's mine. Every night I work one of the gaming tables at Dolly's Place, and afterwards...' she shrugged, unabashed '...well, you know.'

'Yes. Haven't you got a family, Harriet?'

She nodded. 'Across the river in Rotherhithe. Why?'

'And—do they approve of what you do?'

A frown marred Harriet's smooth forehead as she considered the question for a moment before replying. 'I suppose not. It did cross my mind in the beginning that there is something to be ashamed of in my profession—and, in fact, there is, but my mother is poor with four little ones to bring up alone since my father died. He worked in the shipbuilding trade and met with an accident, which killed him. I send my mother what I can. She doesn't question me how I earn it.' She shrugged. 'It doesn't mean she doesn't love me. It doesn't matter,' she said simply.

Edwina shook her head, unconvinced, and then, placing a hand over Harriet's, said, 'It doesn't matter to me, either, Harriet.' There could be nothing wonderful or exciting about Harriet's profession, but her open friendliness spoke volumes about her. There was something about her that inspired trust and put one completely at ease. Harriet Crabtree might be a whore and wicked in the eyes of some, but in this age of cruelty and unconcern she had a caring nature and a kind heart, and these were rare. 'Do you know, I'm glad I've met you.'

'Really? I feel the same way,' Harriet confessed ingenuously. 'I wish you weren't leaving.' With a disheartened sigh she stood up, eyeing the dress Edwina was wearing. 'I'm glad the dress fits. I'll try and find you some more clothes. You'll have to have something to wear until you can buy some of your own.' She smiled, holding out her hand. 'Before the great man comes to fetch you, come and meet the others girls—the ones who have managed to crawl out of bed, that is.'

The afternoon was hot and sultry when Edwina, clad in her donated finery, climbed into Adam Rycroft's shiny black carriage. It was drawn by a matching pair of prancing bays and driven by a scarlet-and-gold-liveried servant. She settled back against the luxurious cream upholstery, wondering if all that was happening to her was a continuing dream. Was she really sitting in a grand carriage with a handsome stranger, travelling across London to goodness knows where? She also wondered how foolhardy she had been to accept Adam's proposal that she stay at his house.

The driver whipped up the horses and the carriage slowly negotiated the congested, twisting alleyways. Covent Garden had long been the most popular haunt of painters, with several resident on the piazza, so Edwina was pleasantly surprised when the carriage rumbled north towards Mayfair, where Adam told her he had a house on the Grosvenor Estate.

No one took any notice of the man standing across the street from Dolly's place. It was Jack Pierce. After his assault on Edwina, but before disappearing into London's back streets, he'd glanced back just in time to see Adam carry the unconscious form inside Dolly's Place. Determined not to let Ed slip away without him seeing, he'd come back to watch the building and learn the identity of the man who'd interfered, surprised to discover his name was Adam Rycroft, the man who'd hired Ed to find the boy Toby. Jack had thought his luck was in when Rycroft appeared earlier in his carriage and entered the building. Convinced they would emerge together, he'd been disappointed when he left with a young woman and drove away.

Seated across from Edwina, Adam stretched his long legs out, crossing them at the ankles. He eyed her in watchful curiosity, dwelling on the perverse quirk of fate that had caused her to be sitting opposite him, and wondering what he had let himself in for by inviting this curious, fascinating young woman into his home. Hers was not a soothing or a restful presence, and he strongly suspected that she did not intend it to be. The impression she conveyed was one of confidence and intense and challenging self-knowledge, defying anyone to catch her out in complacency or self-delusion, but he was not to know that at that moment, under his watchful and penetrating gaze, some of Edwina's confidence was sliding away.

Studying him surreptitiously, she sensed that beneath his relaxed exterior there was a power and forcefulness carefully restrained, and she wondered how different the tyrannical artist Harriet had described to her differed from this gentleman of leisure. It had been so long since she had conversed with people other than beggars and thieves, that now she found herself alone with Adam she suddenly felt gauche and ill at ease.

'So, Edwina,' Adam said at length. 'No doubt Harriet or one of the other girls has enlightened you as to what your work will involve.'

Edwina watched him settle himself more comfortably with that same natural grace that seemed so much a part of him. She gave him a direct, appraising stare. 'Not very much, it would seem. Do you really want to paint me?'

'I do. I must,' he replied quietly, watching her.

'I can't imagine why.'

Adam's brows lifted over sardonic blue eyes. 'I can.'

She flushed softly, deciding it best not to proceed along this path, and to turn the conversation from herself. 'What else do you paint—or do you just paint people?'

'I paint all manner of things—landscapes and whatever else takes my fancy, but painting people is my bread and butter. I find it necessary to cater to the whims and predilections of my commissioners.'

'In which case I would imagine it's unlikely that such paintings will have appeal to anyone other than the client.'

'True. Unfortunately most of my clients are infatuated with "face painting", and fill their houses with family portraits, leaving little scope for the artist to indulge upon. These paintings rarely enter the open market. No one wants to buy paintings of another person's family.'

'I can understand that. And are you good at what you do?'

'I think the people who view my paintings are the ones you ought to ask.'

He was watching her thoughtfully, a strange, unfathomable smile tugging at his lips. He seemed so strong, so self-assured, appearing to hold himself apart from the world, and yet, with his mere presence, dominating the scene around him as he did now. His voice was rich and pleasing to the ear, and Edwina began to wonder if he had any flaw she could touch upon. Watching the satisfied look on his face, she gave up trying to discern what his faults might be. Tipping her head on one side she remarked, 'You look rather pleased with yourself.'

'I should. I have just acquired the most enchanting model. You played the part of a lad so well it's difficult to keep in mind you are, in fact, a very lovely young lady. I look forward to painting you Edwina…?'

His gaze was searching, delving, and Edwina met it directly. 'Just Edwina,' she replied, feeling no compunction to enlighten him beyond that. She was not yet ready to divulge her surname, and she liked and respected him too much to lie by fabricating another. Besides, precepts of conscience forbade it. 'I don't think you need to know more than that if all you are going to do is paint me.'

The bright blue eyes considered the young woman opposite without a hint of expression. When he realised that she had no intention of elaborating further, with slow deliberation he nodded. 'I have many skeletons in my own cupboard, Edwina, that I'm careful not to rattle for fear of which one will tumble out first. Since you are obviously reluctant to share your name with me, I will respect your wish for privacy and not persist.'

'I am obliged,' she said, thinking it a strange thing for him to say and wondering at his own secrets. 'Do you have a family?' she asked, unable to staunch her own curiosity about him.

His expression became guarded. All his life he had kept his emotions locked in an iron heart. He wasn't about to change that. 'My parents died when I was a boy. I have no other relatives.'

'I see. I'm sorry.'

'Don't be. That's how I like it,' he retorted, his tone harsher than he intended as he turned away.

Edwina watched him. She sensed that his ruthlessness, his power over others, the sheer devil-may-care brilliance of his life, were not the reality of him. He seemed to have come from nowhere. He didn't have a father or mother. That struck a perfect chord in Edwina. That was how she came to detect the loneliness in him.

'Why did you offer to let me stay at your house? According to Harriet, you never extend the same hospitality to any of your other models.'

'That's because my other models are not usually homeless. You are. Besides, I consider you an investment. I don't want you disappearing when I'm halfway through painting you. There is, of course, the rather delicate matter of your reputation to consider. It's hardly a respectable situation. I trust there will be no irate relative who will come and snatch you away?'

'Being respectable doesn't concern me any more. It's a little late in the day to begin worrying about my reputation. Whatever reputation I had to speak of was shredded long ago. I took care of that myself,' she said quietly.

The blue eyes lightly swept her, and, catching her own, held them with a smiling warmth. 'Do you never think about your life before you became a thief?'

'Not if I can help it. That way life is bearable. I am no longer the girl I was before I came to London. That girl has ceased to exist. In her place stands another, no longer a prisoner of convention, but most of all a woman who is mistress of her own fate. So, you see, you needn't worry, Adam. No irate relative will come knocking at your door.' After a moment she said, 'Harriet says you're extremely talented.'

'Do you doubt it?'

'No. That sketch you did of me was very good. I still have it,' she said, patting the brocade-and-beaded bag by her side, which one of Mrs Drinkwater's girls had given to her. 'I shall keep it always.'

'Why? It was done in a hurry and is not very good. I'll sketch you another—a better one.'

'I shall still keep that one. It will always remind me of a time when I was as low as I could get and pretty desperate—and prevent me from ever becoming that desperate again.' She fixed him with a level gaze. 'How much will you pay me for being a model?'

Adam became thoughtful. In any of his business ventures he was regarded as a tough negotiator and he would never ruin his own negotiating position by helping his opponents to see the worth of what they held, and the beneficial terms they might extract from him because of it. In Edwina's case, however, he would do just that. 'What are your terms?' he countered. 'I've made no secret of how much I want to paint you. I'm scarcely in a position to argue.'

Edwina hesitated, half-embarrassed. She hadn't expected him to tip the balance of power into her hands. 'I suppose we'll have to negotiate,' she said with imperturbable feminine logic.

'That seems reasonable to me.'

'Money is the solution to all my troubles. Of course, I do understand that, if you are to house and feed me until the painting is completed, you will have to deduct the cost from whatever I earn as your muse. I—I shall want enough to take me to France.'

'Done,' he agreed with alacrity, while wondering what there was for her in France that was so important. 'I will be generous with you, Edwina,' he said gently. 'You hold something of value that I want. I am willing to pay you dearly. When the painting is finished I will furnish you with more than enough money to take you round the world if need be.'

Edwina saw the admiration in his smile and smiled a little in return. 'Thank you—but I have no wish to travel to such lengths. France will do. In return, I will endeavour to be a good model and keep very quiet so as not to distract you from your work.'

Adam grinned. 'Never waver when you've successfully negotiated terms and won. Would you like what we've agreed written down and witnessed, or—in the light of your recent masquerade—shall we shake on it and call it a gentleman's agreement?'

Edwina's smile widened at the teasing light that twinkled in his eyes. She reached out and shook his proffered hand firmly. 'A gentleman's agreement will suffice, I think. I trust you implicitly. Am I likely to meet any of your other models?'

'At present, no. One model at a time is enough for any artist to have to cope with.'

'But what about all those people who commission you to paint them?'

'I've put them on hold for the time being. I have a far more interesting subject to paint,' he murmured, his voice silky soft.

The effect of that warmly intimate look in his eyes, which was vibrantly, alarmingly alive, and the full import of the risk she was taking by being with him, made Edwina quake inside. She did not know this man at all, and yet he was watching her with a look that was much too personal—and possessive. 'I—I have never considered myself interesting,' she stammered. 'I've never had any pretensions to beauty—in fact, I've always considered my looks, like my views, uncon- ventional.'

'I won't argue with that. To me you are unusual, Edwina,

an individual, and luckily for you, you are sufficiently sensible to be neither ostracised nor derided for it, but admired, which is the reaction I hope my painting of you will provoke in those who look at it.' He grinned when he saw his remark pleased her. 'Don't let it go to your head. If you're to sit for me, you'll have to learn to sit still and not fidget like that,' he chided gently, observing how uneasy she seemed to be. With her hands fluttering in her lap, she radiated a nervous energy. 'We'll begin work in the morning. Early.'

She scowled across at him, irritated by his imperious tone. 'I do hope you're not going to turn out to be the temperamental monster everyone accuses you of being?'

He arched a lazy black brow. 'Everyone?'

'Harriet,' she confessed. 'She also told me you have a vile temper.'

'Harriet always did have plenty to say,' he retorted drily. 'You'll have to get used to the way I am. We're going to be spending a lot of time together.' He chuckled. 'Does my being a monster worry you?'

She shrugged, giving a little laugh that Adam found utterly endearing. 'No. I can be temperamental myself on occasion.'

'Intractable and impudent, too, and frequently stubborn, I don't doubt. You'll probably be more troublesome than all my other models put together.'

'Only if you drive me to it.'

'My temper can be awesome—that I freely admit, but Harriet maligns me most dreadfully and does me a terrible injustice. You shouldn't believe all the gossip you hear about me. In fact,' he murmured, a slow, roguish grin dawning across his handsome features, 'I can be quite delightful—malleable, too, in the right hands.'

Edwina's lips curved slightly with wry amusement, trying hard to ignore the gentle caress in his voice and the pull in his eyes. 'From now on I fully intend to keep my hands to myself,' she remarked pointedly, 'and I shall reserve judgement as to the true nature of your character until I have gotten the full measure of you.'

'And I should have known that a defiant young pickpocket with an unpredictable disposition and no regard for convention would insist on prolonging a disagreement instead of politely letting the matter drop,' Adam said smoothly.

'My disposition!' Edwin exclaimed sharply, her delicate brows snapping together. 'There is nothing wrong with my disposition.'

'No? I find it quarrelsome,' he told her, losing the battle to suppress his smile.

'And still you want to paint me. Are you sure you're up to the challenge?' she quipped playfully.

'I shall prevail, you'll see,' he told her firmly. 'However, I foresee many skirmishes ahead.'

He laughed and Edwina felt curiously lightened by it. 'Then I shall strive to have the upper hand every time and out-manoeuvre you at every turn.'

Adam looked at her for a long moment with those magnificent deep blue eyes, knowing that undoubtedly she would pit her will against his, and he already looked forward to the challenge. His firm chiselled lips curved in a slow smile. 'I wouldn't advise it. I always win,' he stated, with the supreme confidence of one who succeeded in all he set out to do, and with the experience gained from years of intimate dalliance with the opposite sex.

Edwina returned his smile calmly. 'We'll see about that,' she told him, at which she decided to let the matter rest. She directed her gaze to the passing scenery, but felt almost smothered by a perusal she knew by instinct never left her. She smiled to herself, knowing that the time she was with him would probably be the most exciting and stimulating time of her life.

They were travelling through a more rural neighbourhood, where the streets were wide and straight, the houses spacious and more gracious, with white columns. The carriage came to a halt before a large three-storey building with a plain brick façade. Suddenly nervous about beginning this new stage in her life, which would happen the moment she entered this grand house—the kind of house that she was familiar with and rekindled memories of a past she had put behind her—she shrank back.

'This—this is where you live?'

'It is my home. Do you like it?'

'It—it's very grand.'

'I'm glad you think so.'

'And—this is where I am to stay?'

Adam's lips twitched with wry amusement. 'It's not outside the realms of possibility—if you should feel inclined to stay. Come in and meet Mrs Harrison.' Still she held back. In silence he contemplated her face. She was pale, with just a faint smattering of pale golden freckles over her nose. Sunlight gilded her hair, which was a mass of short, wispy copper curls. Her large eyes were a darkly anxious shade of green. He sensed she was afraid. 'You look nervous.'

'Forgive me, but I can't help it.'

Adam leisurely raised an eyebrow. 'It is uncommonly warm. You don't feel faint?' he queried with a hint of mockery.

She gave him a withering look. 'I never faint.'

Adam smiled to himself. He should have known better than to ask. 'Good. Don't be nervous. You'll be perfectly safe here with me. Mrs Harrison is my housekeeper. Come. I instructed her to have cold drinks ready on our arrival, and a room has been prepared for you. Tomorrow I'll show you my studio.'

'Studio? What studio?' The absurdity of her stilted words struck her, but her stomach had worked itself into such a knot she was unable to help it.

'Where I work.'

On entering the house they were met by Mrs Harrison, a

neat little woman of a cheerful disposition. She was dressed in black, the only relief being a white lace collar and cap, which completely concealed her hair. Out of her lined, round face peered two faded grey eyes.

'So, this is your guest, sir?'

'Quite right, Mrs Harrison. I trust you have everything prepared?'

'Indeed I have.'

'My name is Edwina,' Edwina offered.

'Oh, but I couldn't possibly address you by your Christian name,' Mrs Harrison countered, clearly shocked at the very idea of it. 'It would be most disrespectful.'

'Please do. Everyone else does.'

'I'd do as she says, Mrs Harrison,' Adam commented with irony. 'I don't doubt for one minute that Edwina has good reason for keeping her surname to herself.'

Mrs Harrison silently conveyed her disapproval to the master but could only resign herself. When she had told him he was behaving in an extraordinary manner—moving a young lady he knew nothing about into his house and hastily packing his apprentices off on holiday—he had grinned quite boyishly and told her there was nothing ordinary about his guest. And as she looked at her she completely agreed.

Her eyes settled on Edwina warmly, wondering what on earth could have happened to her hair. She was so very different from all the other models that came to be painted. What she saw was a young girl no bigger than herself—yes, a girl, she thought, until she looked into her eyes. There she saw pride and intelligence, and a quiet suffering that gave her a maturity beyond her years. From the corner of her eyes Mrs Harrison carefully noted the warmth of the master's smile, the absorbed way he watched this young woman as he introduced her, and the fact that he was standing closer than was necessary.

'You may show Edwina to her room and have some refreshment sent up. Perhaps you would care to freshen up before dinner,' Adam said, addressing Edwina. 'Mrs Harrison will get you anything you need.'

'That I will, sir. The young lady only has to ask.' Taking Edwina's small valise from a footman, she faced Edwina with a cheery smile. 'Please follow me, miss. I'm sure you'll appreciate a bath after spending all that time in the carriage. This hot weather is so very trying, don't you think?'

'So it is,' Edwina agreed. 'And I'd love a bath.' She was unable to believe her good fortune that, after being deprived of this simple pleasure for six months, one she had once taken for granted like the air she breathed, she was to be allowed the luxury of two in one day.

'Unfortunately I have to go out and may not be back to dine with you, Edwina,' Adam said as she was about to turn away. 'In which case I shall expect to see you in my studio in the morning. Seven o'clock sharp. That's not too early for you, is it?' he queried, half-expecting her to argue. Instead she favoured him with a charming smile.

'Considering the unsociable hours I've grown accustomed to of late, seven o'clock will be fine.'

Biting back an admiring smile, Adam watched her follow Mrs Harrison up the white stone staircase before turning and striding back towards the door.

Chapter Five

When Edwina emerged from her room in a lavender dress the following morning, her first impression of the house was one of airy spaciousness and light. Decorated in delicate shades of pale grey and white, it had a subtle patina of elegance and an air of comfort. No floor was with carpeting, and the supply of beautiful, tasteful furniture was full. Like most houses in the area it had numerous services close at hand, notably the mews situated between the streets and lined with stables and coach houses, and occupied by armies of grooms and coachmen. The house was run by Mrs Harrison and a silent body of servants.

After partaking of a hearty breakfast alone in the dining room, a footman directed Edwina to the studio, which was located on the top floor of the house. Moving down a long landing with doors on either side, she pushed open a door at the end and paused. The long room stretched out before her presented a strange sight. Adam stood at the far end, cleaning some brushes.

With his glossy, unruly dark brown hair falling over his forehead he looked different to when she'd seen him before. He wore black pumps on his feet and white silk stockings moulded his muscular calves below black knee breeches. His loose shirt was carelessly tucked into the waistband and the sleeves were rolled up, exposing his muscular forearms, the white fabric stained with blue and orange paint. Upon seeing her he stopped what he was doing and quickly strode towards to her. Greeting her with a mock scowl on his face, he pulled her further inside and closed the door.

'Here you are. I thought I'd have to come and haul you out of bed.'

'No doubt the prospect of doing so and dragging me to your studio if I failed to meet your deadline would give you satisfaction, so I'm pleased to have deprived you of that pleasure,' she responded sweetly. 'If you check your clock, you will observe that I am five minutes ahead of schedule.'

'If you say so,' he said without shifting his gaze from her glowing face. 'Now, welcome to my studio. Look around if you like—familiarise yourself with it before we get down to work. You'll get to know it inside out before we're through.'

She wrinkled her small nose with such distaste that he grinned. 'What's that smell?'

'Turpentine and paint. You don't like it?'

'Not much, but I suppose I'll get used to it.'

'After a couple of days you'll hardly notice it.'

While Adam went back to cleaning his brushes, Edwina wandered about, looking at everything. Windows along one side overlooked a well-kept garden and sunlight streamed in through a skylight. Dirty rags, sketchpads, pots of pigment and jars of brushes and dilutants littered tabletops. It was a large, well-lit room with sloping ceilings, and filled from top to bottom with pictures of every size and description: ladies in sparkling jewels and fabulous gowns, whole families and their pets, landscapes and some of an equestrian theme. She was lost in wonder and astonishment—so many beautiful pictures she could hardly believe her eyes.

One particular painting on an easel caught her eye. She crossed over to it and studied the face of an attractive woman with golden hair and sparkling blue eyes. Her lips were curved in a smile that bespoke both provocation and innocence. The colours and the subject had so much vibrancy that the painting seemed to spring to life before her very eyes. Adam stopped what he was doing and perched a hip on the edge of a table, crossing his arms over his chest and watching her in fascination, his leg swinging lazily to and fro.

'How long will it take you to paint me?' she asked without taking her eyes off the painting.

'Weeks—months. We'll see.'

'As long as that? And will you make me look like this?'

'No. The painting of you will be better.'

'I find that hard to believe. The lady is beautiful? Who is she?'

'Lady Annabel Ripley. Her husband is a distinguished member of his Majesty's government.'

Tentatively Edwina reached out and touched the face, feeling the silky smoothness of the oils. She valued the portrait's taste and for what it revealed about the exquisite sensibility of the subject. 'It must give you great satisfaction to be able to record the beauty of life so well, so vividly.'

'Thank you for the compliment,' he said softly. 'There is satisfaction in the accomplishment, I grant you.'

'I know very little about art, but even to my inexperienced eye it is plain that you are a true master, a genius.'

'No. I've had great success because I am talented, but I see genius in others, not in me. What I do has nothing to do with genius. To paint my subjects takes what talent I possess. That is not greatness.'

Edwina faced him in surprise, seeing a different Adam Rycroft. He was no carefree rake with no ambition or direction. He was absorbed, an artist who cared deeply about colour and light. She was drawn to his intensity, and she wanted to know more. 'How do you define greatness?'

'I can't. I can smell it, touch it and feel it, but what I know is that I do not possess it.'

Glancing at the picture of the young woman once more, Edwina could not agree with him. 'How can you pass judgement on yourself like that—so harshly? Where did you learn to paint like this?' she asked, looking at him. 'Did you go to an academy?'

'Yes. I aspired to be a painter from an early age. Lacking experience and eager to learn from the works of great painters past and present, I attended a school in St Martin's Lane—which was the main London art school until it merged with the Royal Academy two years ago. Both Joshua Reynolds and Gainsborough worked there.'

'And did you set yourself up with your own studio after that?'

'Not right away. Before establishing myself as a portraitist, to enhance my credentials and to give myself a cultural distinction as an arbiter of taste, I undertook the Grand Tour. I visited the great collections in Paris before travelling to Italy—the cradle of classical civilisation.'

'Do most artists do that?'

He nodded. 'On their return they reap the benefits of their time abroad. An artist labours under a disadvantage if he hasn't seen and studied the treasures of Italy and contemplated the great works of classical antiquity. How else can one interpret whether works of art are original, fraudulent, good or bad?'

Edwina frowned, mulling over his words. 'I see what you mean. I hadn't thought of that. Where do you show your work?'

'Exhibitions and auction rooms. I intend exhibiting the painting I shall do of you at the Royal Academy. This house is also an important commercial function. I have a small gallery here that contains a selection of my finished portraits and volumes of prints.'

She moved closer to him, her expression one of genuine interest. 'Can I see it?'

'Of course, but not now. Later you can peruse to your heart's content.'

'Do you paint all your models in here?'

'If you must know, I paint my more aristocratic patrons in another, well-appointed room,' he informed her lightly. 'It is decorated and furnished in the same manner as their own private residences—intended to make them feel more at home and to convey the taste of the artist, you understand. There are many artists in London, Edwina, and it is important that I have a studio to match those of my rivals'.'

Unable to resist teasing him, a puckish smile tugged at the corners of Edwina's lips as she sidled towards him, her head tilted sideways, her gaze capturing his. 'I'm impressed. So—let me get this right. You say you have one room for the respectable, and one for the disreputable. Bearing this in mind, tell me, Adam—in which category do you place me?'

A lazy, devastating smile suddenly swept across his handsome features, a smile that was familiar to several of his models and almost stole Edwina's breath. 'Neither,' he replied, his eyes moving leisurely over her fragile features, pausing at length on her soft mouth. 'You are unlike any of them. Believe me, Edwina, there are more disreputable characters among my more wealthy, aristocratic clients than those of more humble means.'

'Do they ever turn up together—the disreputables and the respectable aristocrats?'

'Not by design, I assure you,' he chuckled richly. 'I do try to maintain distinctions. The room I use for my more distinguished clients is adequately furnished to allow sitters' friends to accompany them.'

'Doesn't that distract you?'

'No. It relieves me of the task of painting and conversing at the same time. As a public figure, my rooms are often used as a rendezvous for my own friends and acquaintances, as well as those who accompany my patrons. However, I am sure you will be relieved when I tell you that I have given strict instructions to Mrs Harrison that she is not to allow anyone up here for the time being. If they wish to see me, they must make an appointment.'

'Goodness!' she gasped with mock horror. 'Do you mean to keep me all to yourself?'

He smiled at her, amused by her choice of words. 'Absolutely. It's highly irregular, I know, but I will not introduce you to anyone until after the painting is finished—by which time the mystery and suspense that surrounds my latest model will have driven everyone to the very limits of frustration and increased its value considerably.'

'And in which case I shall become well established as your paramour,' Edwina retorted coolly. 'I will not take kindly to my name being bandied about.'

Adam gave her a slow smile. 'I wish I could soothe your fears, but unfortunately I can't. Quite often the artist is of far less consequence than the subject of his portraits. Be prepared for notoriety.'

She stared at him. 'I sincerely hope not! Good gracious, Adam, I can see you are quite mercenary. I can also see that I have much to learn.'

'I agree, and I will enjoy teaching you. I also have two young apprentices. I do not neglect them. Believe me, I teach them assiduously, but I considered the time had come for them to take a holiday until further notice.'

Edwina felt a quiver of unease at the intensity that she saw in his eyes. She was beginning to realise just how important this painting was to him. His tall, lean body was at ease. There was a contained energy and fierceness in him that attracted her. She was curious about what was behind the sober respectability of his life as a painter. Did anyone really know him? she wondered. 'Where do you want to paint me?'

'In here. This is where I'm most comfortable.'

'And how would you like me to pose? Sitting down or standing up?'

'Sitting will do for now.'

'For now?'

'I'm not going to paint you today. I shall begin by making some preliminary sketches—which is what I do with all my models.'

With the perfect amount of boldness combined with maidenly demureness, she raised her eyes to his handsome face and smiled. 'Artists have a reputation for intrigues, Adam. Do you ever have dalliances with any of your models?' she enquired boldly.

His brow raised in wonder at her sudden audacity, and then he snapped, 'Mind your own business.' Relinquishing his perch, he strode towards a large wing backed chair, which he dragged into the centre of the room. 'Sit down.'

The menacing look in those startling blue eyes should have squelched Edwina's humour, but she jauntily gave him her cheekiest grin. 'It's no concern to me if you sleep with all your models—as long as you make me an exception.'

Taking her arm in a none-too-gentle grasp, he shoved her into the chair. His lazy smile had hardened into a mask of ironic amusement. Placing his hands on the arms of the chair he leaned forward, pinning her to the upholstery with his gaze, his voice soft yet firm.

'Then you would be wise to heed my warning, you saucy wench, and think twice before you give me any encouragement.' Leaning further forward so that his face was only inches from her own, he gave her a wicked grin. 'Of course, you may choose to ignore my advice, in which case I give you leave to encourage me all you like. I don't mind playing my part, but I can't help wondering if I shall be playing with an amateur. Have you made love often enough to know how it's supposed to be done, Edwina?'

'I would not be so reckless,' she whispered truthfully, never having been kissed before, let alone seduced. The nearness and the fresh manly scent of him filled her head, and the heat of his gaze set her blood on fire. 'I'm not like that.'

'Then don't ever complain that I didn't warn you. Marriage has always been out of the question for me.'

'You prefer affairs.'

'In sophisticated affairs the rule is that no one takes anything seriously.'

'I can understand how that must suit you. Actually, I'm not in the market for a husband any more than you are for a wife. I will not be pushed around by anyone. I want my freedom and independence. That is something a husband is unlikely to give me.'

'Then I can see we both agree on that, at least. But have a care, Edwina. You are eighteen years old—a mere babe compared to most of the women of my acquaintance. I'm also older than you, with a lifetime of experience.' His eyes darkened. 'It would be a dangerous game for you to embark upon. Do you understand what I'm saying?'

She nodded. 'Yes.'

His eyes held hers a moment longer, impressed with the clearness of them and the fringelike thickness of her silken lashes. Her mouth was lovely and expressive—one that needed to be kissed. Before his feelings could get the better of him he straightened up and, reaching out, gently rumpled the shining copper hair atop her head, before moving away and picking up a sketchpad. As if nothing unusual had occurred between them, he coolly began to draw, impatient to sketch the image he wished to portray of Edwina—an image that seemed to pulse with motion in his mind—before it slipped completely away.

Edwina realised that as a well-bred young lady, to question a gentleman about his affairs would never have entered her head six months ago, that it was unacceptable and beyond all bounds, but that was before her encounter with Jack Pierce, and her time spent in the company of other miscreants in St Giles.

Suddenly she felt a devilish, triumphant delight course through her. Still in the spirit to needle, she raised her eyes to Adam's as his long fingers, deft and quick, swept the charcoal over the page in rapid sweeps, and said with a radiant smile, 'It must be a fine life being an artist, almost as fine as being an artist's model.'

As if to confirm her words she settled herself into the comfortable chair and tucked her feet beneath her, watching him, thinking how effortless it was, how easy to simply sit there with the sunlight streaming down on her through the skylight. She sighed, content to relax in its warmth and feast her eyes on the tall man who was intent on capturing her on canvas.

Adam did not respond to her quip, but his thoughts seemed to be in turmoil. As he sketched the angles and hollows of Edwina's face, trying not to be distracted by the myriad of emotions playing in her expressive eyes, he could not believe how she managed to be an alluringly beautiful woman and a bewitchingly innocent girl at one and the same time. Until yesterday he had believed her to be a thirteen-year-old boy, and yet in the course of the last twenty-four hours she had treated him with a jaunty impertinence and impudence that he found utterly exhilarating. What an entrancing creature she was—bold and artlessly sophisticated, with the kind of beauty that made his blood stir hotly.

From the moment he had laid eyes on her in her new guise his senses had felt dazed, captured on the brink of time, and he had been unable to think of little else. Her beauty was entirely different from that of any other woman he had ever known. With an artist's passion his desire was to paint her likeness, to bring out the character in her face, the spirit in her, but that same desire was already tightening his loins.

He didn't understand why she had such a volatile effect on him, but he understood that he wanted her. He wanted her warm and willing in his arms, in his bed—and he told himself that it would be by some holy miracle if he managed to keep his hands off her until the painting was finished.

Two days later Adam began to paint. When Edwina entered the studio bright and early, it was to find him already there, pouring over the sketches he had made of her, a cup of steaming coffee on the table. He looked up as she approached, his manner brusque.

'Good morning.' He lifted a brow. 'You slept well, I take it?'

'Very well,' Edwina said.

'And you have eaten?'

'Yes.'

'Good. It's going to be a long day.' Eager to begin work, he gulped down the scalding coffee.

'Where would you like me to pose?' she asked, looking around.

'The couch—but wait,' he barked, as she was about to move towards the *chaise longue*.

'Why, what's wrong?'

'That dress,' he said, looking at her lavender dress with frowning disapproval. 'It won't do. I have something else for you to wear—something that will contrast with your colouring.'

Striding to a large cupboard in the corner of the studio where he kept an assortment of dresses and costumes for his models to wear, he opened it and removed a gown wrapped in soft delicate paper. Whipping the paper away, he shook out an exquisite creamy white satin gown, the cloth rich and lustrous.

'Here, put this on.'

Edwina gasped at its sheer beauty. 'Oh, it's very beautiful,' she ventured softly. 'I do so hope no harm comes to it while I am wearing it. Will it fit, do you think?' she asked, holding it against her.

'It should. I told Dolly what I wanted and she had it made to your size.'

Edwina stared at him. 'How is it possible for anyone to have a gown made so quickly?'

'I can. You can change behind the screen—and don't take too long about it. I want to get started.'

Edwina hurried to do his bidding and struggled out of her dress, refusing to acknowledge the fact that Adam's relentless, impatient gaze was boring holes at her through the screen. She slipped the gorgeous gown over her head, amazed to find it was a perfect fit. It had tight, elbow-length sleeves and a scooped neckline that was low cut. The waist was fitted, the skirt full, spreading around her in shimmering folds. Unfortunately, she found it impossible to fasten the tiny hooks up the back by herself.

'Well,' Adam snapped impatiently, 'are you ready?'

'I can't fasten the hooks up the back.'

'Never mind. I'll do it.'

Edwina's heart leaped when he stepped round the screen. She gasped, about to object, but galvanised with purpose he ignored any maidenly objections she might raise as he forcefully turned her back to him.

'I know I shock you, and that's understandable,' he said, beginning to fasten the tiny hooks with an agility and speed that told Edwina it was not the first time he had hooked a woman into her dress, 'but you've absolutely nothing to worry about. No one is here to pay any attention to us. There, now come and sit on the *chaise longue*.'

Pushing her down on to one of his favourite props, he made her recline sideways and take up a pose, arranging her arms and legs in the position in which he wanted to paint her. Hardly touching her, with great gentleness he draped her arm over the single armrest and put her face slightly in profile. He was looking at her without desire, with abstract thoughtfulness, as he would an object, and this reassured her.

Not until he was satisfied that everything was as he wanted it did he stand back. He drank in the sight of her form, her face, her hair. She resembled a piece of beautifully worked lace. A myriad of glorious colours glinted in her short-cropped, silken and curly hair, and her flawless ivory skin was tinged with rose. Her body was as slender as a willow, and as dainty and fragile as gossamer. Her cheeks were hollow and her clear jade-coloured eyes large and mournful, but they only made her more beautiful to him. His heart swelled, and going to the large canvas on his easel he began to paint—utterly absorbed.

And so the days took on a pattern. Before beginning his day's work Adam always rode in Hyde Park. Most of the hours were spent in the studio, and afterwards he would leave Edwina alone to do as she pleased, while he socialised with his wide circle of friends and acquaintances. He was often to be found at Old Slaughter Coffee House in St Martin's Lane, where he surrounded himself with artists and literary types, and in this snug centre of conversation and conviviality, he would debate and intrigue into the early hours.

His search for Toby among the web of streets and alley-ways of the metropolis took up a great deal of his time. He often disappeared for hours on end when the light was too poor to paint, but all his efforts proved fruitless, which only added to his growing frustration.

His fascination with Edwina and his growing curiosity about her background increased daily. She had been well educated, which was evident from the books she borrowed from his vast library to read, and she was certainly not as impressed or in awe of her surroundings as he would expect any ordinary young woman to be. But then, hadn't he suspected from the very beginning—even when she had been playing the role of Ed—that here was no ordinary being?

She was undaunted by the army of servants he employed.

She always addressed them with polite correctness, and she adjusted to her situation in his house as if she had been born to it—and what he found most unsettling was that there was something about her manner, her natural grace, and the pride in her bearing, which suggested that this might indeed be so.

Edwina took pleasure in browsing through the books in Adam's impressive library and walking in his beautiful garden, delighting in her newfound freedom and adjusting easily to a world that seemed a million miles away from St Giles. She often thought of the beautiful woman she had seen Adam with at the theatre in Covent Garden, but, despite her curiosity, she sensed she would do well not to enquire further about that particular lady.

She had thought modelling for Adam would be easy, but she had quickly come to realise how wrong she was. To remain in one position for hours at a time was gruelling. Her back ached, her neck ached, and if she so much as flexed a muscle Adam would order her to be still. Occasionally when she did complain he would take pity on her and placate her by saying he was making wonderful progress, but on the whole, when he was totally engrossed, her discomforts were ignored and her attempts to bring them to his attention were met with a bark of reproach or grim silence.

Adam intrigued her. He was a strange mixture—an attractive, mature man, slightly eccentric, exotic, even, and much travelled. He had an adventurous, boyish streak and an impressive enthusiasm that was enormously appealing. He was also the kind of man who absorbed a small amount of the best of every culture he met and processed it within himself in a stimulating blend of intellect and wit. But Edwina sensed there was a dark side to his character that he kept hidden from prying eyes.

Slipping out of the house early one morning to clear her head following a night of unpleasant dreams, unbeknown to Adam she had watched him on his ride through the park. He rode his horse hard, like everyone else for the pleasure of it, but she sensed sometimes not for pleasure. Something else drove that man. He rode in the cold grey dawn light, his horse a prancing black stallion, a difficult, temperamental animal. She had watched him disappear from her sight, leaning forward into the wind, horse and rider one—elegance and power gaining velocity together.

Where his work was concerned he was a stern taskmaster, unreasonable and demanding. His moods were as changeable as the seasons and the weather. Sometimes he could be patience personified, infinitely gentle and considerate, that lent him the exuberance of a boy. At other times he was the Devil's own. From her couch Edwina learned to read the lowering of his brows, the tensing of the muscles in his cheeks, and the hardening of his eyes—all heralding a storm.

He was furious when his work didn't go right, taking out his frustrations on her, and treating her like a difficult, recalcitrant halfwit. She fumed and often argued. Outside the studio Adam Rycroft might be a charming gentleman, but with a brush in his hand, at his easel, Harriet was right—he was an absolute tyrant.

Chapter Six

Three weeks into the painting, one afternoon when Edwina hadn't moved for almost an hour, she dared to do the unspeakable and rub her neck.

'Be still,' Adam commanded offhandedly.

'My neck aches,' she complained.

He ignored her. 'Lift your chin a notch—a *notch*,' he rapped when she elevated it to a lofty level.

Edwina met his dark scowl with a heated glower and did as she was told. After a moment's silence she dared to say, 'A drink would be nice.'

He ignored her as he dabbed at the olive green paint on his palette.

'Mrs Harrison has some lemonade cooling on the slab in the pantry.'

'Quiet, wench.' She scowled. 'And don't scowl. It spoils your face.'

'Harriet was right,' Edwina said, her voice hardly above a whisper.

Adam pricked up his ears. 'Harriet? What about Harriet?'

'She said you were a tyrant.'

'And what is your opinion? I take it you must have one.'

'She was right. You are a temperamental type too. Are all artists?' she inquired airily.

'How the hell would I know?'

'I always thought it was important that artists, especially portrait painters, needed a pleasant and obliging temper with a fair share of wit and a measure of good conversation—which is the sign of a true gentleman, I might add—to prevent patrons walking out of the door.'

Adam briefly cast his eyes upward, as if seeking some divine help for keeping his control. His patience was wearing thin. Courage was an admirable trait in a man. In a woman, he decided, it was a pain. The dark line he was painting suddenly went askew. 'Damn it,' he cursed.

'Did you smudge something, Adam?' Edwina patronisingly plied him.

'Yes,' he snapped irately, throwing the brush on to the table. 'I should remember to be more cautious when you begin twitching and complaining.'

'But it was not my doing,' she purred, placing her small feet on the floor and wriggling her toes to get the circulation flowing. 'You were the careless one.'

'Forgive me,' he said contemptuously, 'for ever thinking you were a gracious and well-mannered young lady.'

Edwina tossed her head and adjusted her dress at the shoulders. 'Thank you for the compliment, but I have never professed to be a lady. Gracious and mannerly, most certainly, but never a lady.'

Raking his hair from his brow with his fingers, Adam glowered across at her, before turning and going to the door with ground-devouring strides, mumbling several unintelligible curses along the way. Throwing it open, he curtly ordered a footman to fetch them some of Mrs Harrison's lemonade. Returning to the easel, he picked up a rag and began to rub the paint from his hands.

Taking advantage of the respite, Edwina had left the couch

and was stretching her aching body. She was in profile and Adam paused, beginning to relax. He always found that watching her was fascinating, and in that gorgeous creamy white gown his eyes ravished the bounty of her charms. Exhibiting youth, grace and suppressed energy, she was exquisite, amazing, natural and unselfconscious. Her hair glowed with a subtle iridescence, as though washed in light, yet imbued with such a rich deepness that it glowed.

Her mannerisms were so blatantly those of a young woman, but the memory of the ragged urchin he'd first encountered was brought to mind. He contemplated the features he'd once accepted as those of a youth, and what he now saw was delicately feminine and finely boned. In the three weeks that she had been living under his roof, with ample nourishment and plenty of rest, she had lost that haunted, hungry, street look. More flesh covered her bones, and her cheeks had filled out.

Adam was enjoying painting her, and yet he realised that he knew no more about her now than he had when she'd robbed him of his watch. As she posed there were times when she had a faraway look in her eyes, as if she could see something he could not—but, no, it was more than that. It was the secret she kept hidden. It was the first thing he had seen about her that day they met, and she still had it. Mystery. It made him want to know what was behind that faraway look. It was like having a tiger by the tail, or having charge of some wild, exotic animal of an endangered species.

When Edwina turned and saw him watching her intently, she flushed self-consciously and gave him a gentle, tired smile.

'I'm sorry, Edwina,' he said, moving towards her, a slow, reluctant smile tugging at his sensual lips. 'Harriet is right. I am a tyrant. I demand and expect too much.'

'No, you don't,' she murmured, relieved to see the tension had left him. 'I'm just tired, that's all.'

'Then you'll be pleased to know that the painting is almost finished.'

Her face brightened. 'Can I see?'

'Not yet. You'll have to be patient a while longer.'

'Are you satisfied with what you've achieved?'

'I shall be, when it's complete.'

'Are you satisfied with all your paintings?'

'Alas, no, but I am rather proud of this one. What will you do when it's finished?'

'Go to France, I suppose, which was what I intended doing six months ago—before I was robbed of my money—and before I encountered Jack.'

'So—you're impatient to leave me, Edwina,' he murmured. Reaching out, he gently touched her cheek.

His voice was low and seductive, reproachful, his look direct and unwavering, and this terrified Edwina as much as the sensual look in those deep blue eyes, eyes that touched her like she had never been touched before. She found herself wanting to move closer to him, feeling herself charged with excitement. Her body was alive, a separate entity of its own, not listening to her brain. It was conscious only of the man in front of her.

'No,' she murmured, in answer to his question. She flushed, her mind reeling from his brief touch. 'It's not like that. Going to France is my only option. My future isn't here. It's in France, with relatives—if I can find them.'

He frowned with sudden concern. 'But you do have relatives in France?'

'I—I don't know for sure. I think so,' she replied awkwardly.

'You think so? Don't you know their names—where they reside?' Adam persisted incredulously.

'I know my mother came from Lyons and that she had relatives there, which is where I'll begin my search.'

'Don't you think it would be sensible to make enquiries

before embarking on such a perilous journey? What if you don't find them?'

'Then I'll settle somewhere.' Her announcement was stated with a great deal of resolve and no hint of uncertainty.

'Aren't you being somewhat foolhardy?' Adam reproached harshly, his ire growing as he thought about it. 'What you propose to do—to travel all that way, a young woman alone and friendless in a strange country when you don't even know if you have family there or not—is sheer madness, Edwina.'

'I won't be completely helpless. I do speak the language,' she pointed out, knowing he was right, but her mind was made up.

'Aye, like a native, as I recall,' Adam retorted drily.

'Going to France may seem foolhardy to you, but to me the alternative is far worse.'

'Then why don't you let me help you? Time and again I have wondered what could have happened in your young life that has made you so wary, so withdrawn. You have a shell around you that makes you seem like a prisoner of your own defences—and if you are not careful that shell will become a cage. What are you afraid of?' he demanded forcefully. 'It isn't only Jack Pierce you're running away from, is it?'

She smiled tremulously. 'No,' but her eyes were focused inward.

On a more tender note, he said, 'I sense someone has hurt you badly and you've become locked in that hurt, determined to protect yourself so no one can hurt you again.' He fell silent. Looking down at her, he could see her taut muscles. When he next spoke it was with an intensity that struck to the heart of Edwina's memories. 'You deserve better, Edwina. Don't lock yourself in tighter. Why are you running away? What has brought you to this?'

'I have my pride and my reasons, which I will not discuss with you.'

Adam sighed heavily, seeing her fine-boned profile tilted

obstinately, and he recognised the cool disdain of those clear green eyes as they held his own. He had known no other like her, and he could not help but wonder at the grit of her. 'You are a difficult, stubborn woman, Edwina. Can't you understand that I feel deeply the burden of your present predicament, that I am concerned about you? I feel you need protection since you've attracted the likes of Jack Pierce.'

'Thank you, Adam, but you needn't feel under any obligation. Do not be in any anxiety on my account. If I can survive St Giles, I can survive most things.'

'I made my assessment regarding your success at doing that the first day we met—but I am beginning to change my opinion,' he said, glaring down at her.

Adam was regretting asking her about her family. She had instinctively withdrawn and he recognised how deep her reticence went. She concealed from habit. Initially he had respected her privacy. That she had family in France was all he knew about her. Clearly she was uncomfortable when he questioned her so he gave up, willing to let her find her confidence with him at her own pace. But he would not give up entirely. He would merely stretch out his forcefulness more slowly.

'Do you worry Jack Pierce might find you?'

'Yes. I'm sure he's looking for me.'

'Then let me offer you my continuing protection. I have to leave town for a while—for about a month, I think. You're welcome to make use of this house until I return.'

'Thank you. You have already done me a great service, in making it possible for me to come here and escape an intolerable situation on the streets of St Giles. For this, I owe you much—much more than I can repay.'

'You don't owe me anything, Edwina. It is I who owe you. So, will you stay until I return?'

At that moment a footman entered, carrying a salver with a jug of lemonade and two glasses. After placing it on a table he went out, leaving Edwina to do the honours. Glad to have something to occupy her hands, she poured the cold liquid into the glasses and handed one to Adam. Sipping her drink, she turned away, thoughtful, knowing that because of the feelings she harboured for Adam, the most sensible thing for her to do would be to leave as soon as the final brush stroke was applied to the painting, but she was aware of the deep sense of loss she would feel when he was no longer a part of her life.

As she had sat and watched him paint her, with all his concentration and energy directed on his work—which was the only way a painter could accomplish anything decent, he had informed her—she had come to know every detail of his handsome face, the way his dark brown hair dipped forward in tousled waves over his forehead, the slant of his arched brows, and the smouldering intensity in his blue eyes. Often when he met her gaze his firm lips would part in a heart-stealing smile that set her blood aflame.

She realised that she was becoming too dependent on him for her own happiness. The aftermath of those terrible months in St Giles had left her feeling cast adrift, and it had been too easy to surrender to what Adam offered. It wouldn't be difficult to fall in love with him—and that would be foolish. His rejection of her would strike at her heart.

She knew nothing about his past, and the questions she harboured she would keep hidden, for she doubted her ability to hide her feelings nestling next to her heart like a sleeping tiger. To disturb them would be to breathe life into them. And yet she could see no reason why, during his absence, she shouldn't remain in his house for the time being.

Placing her empty glass down, she turned and faced him once more. He was leaning against the window, his gaze lingering on the elegant perfection of her glowing face. 'Yes, thank you, I will stay until you return, but I do intend to leave for France before you exhibit the painting of me at the Royal Academy.'

'Why? Don't you want to be the toast of London?' he teased gently. 'To have people clamouring to buy prints of your portrait and every hack in Fleet Street wanting to write about you?'

She looked at him in alarm. 'Good heavens, no! Is that what will really happen?'

'I won't consider the painting a success if it doesn't,' he chuckled. 'You've become something of a curiosity among the gossip-mongers already,' he commented with a wayward smile. 'They speculate on the secrecy that surrounds my latest muse. Eventually we shall allow them the opportunity to see that you're not a bear with three heads.'

'I don't want all that fuss. I don't want to be famous in that way.'

'And you're afraid someone might recognise you and come looking for you. Am I right, Edwina?'

He was watching her closely. 'Yes.' Suddenly she smiled, shattering the gravity of the moment. 'Perhaps I should have insisted you paint me as Ed instead. As a dirty, undernourished juvenile, I would be certain to go unrecognised.' She tipped back her head and laughed, her eyes alight with mischief. 'Although, since the only paintings I have seen littered around your studio are of nubile young ladies—some so scantily attired that little is left to the imagination, I might add—perhaps you have an aversion to painting pictures of dirty young street urchins who pick pockets for a living.'

She faced him, slender and proud, and when she laughed like that Adam caught his breath at the promise she gave of unfettered, vibrant woman. His mouth quirked in a half-smile. Straightening from his lounging position, he put down his empty glass and went back to his easel. 'Impertinent baggage. Get back on your couch. We have a painting to finish.'

The painting of Edwina that Adam hoped would be proclaimed by his fellow artists and the public as a masterpiece—

which in his opinion was his best work yet—was finally completed. When he took Edwina's hand and drew her in front of the finished work, he pulled away the cloth covering it as if undressing a beautiful woman. Edwina stared at the mirror image of herself and said nothing for several moments. It was of a young woman wearing a gown in a sumptuous shade of creamy white. Her short, wispy hair encapsulating a heart-shaped face was vibrantly glowing, like a living flame. She had high cheekbones and eyebrows that swept up like the wings of a startled bird.

Edwina was struck by the stillness and purity of the picture, and the haunting light effects that allowed the viewer's attention to focus on the subject. It was a mystical creation, its light apparently coming directly from the reclining woman herself. There was a purity of line, a serenity emphasised by the simplicity of the central design, and intimacy derived from the soulful glance, and yet the face that looked back was full of startling energy. It radiated intense emotion and lacked any hint of sensuality whatsoever. The painting was exquisite, of that there could be no doubt.

'Tell me what you think,' Adam murmured, his eyes watching her expression rather than the picture.

'I—is that really me?' she said, unable to tear her eyes away, quite moved by what she saw. 'Is that how I look?'

'It's how I see you.'

'But—she looks so sad…and yet at the same time quite lovely.'

'I know. I painted her from life,' Adam said gently, smiling down at her youthful face. 'She does look sad, I grant you. The reason why I could only wonder at. And you are right, she is lovely. That's how I see you. In fact, my dear Edwina, I find you enchanting and quite rare, and you are one of the most beautiful young women it has ever been my privilege to paint.'

Tears came unbidden to Edwina's eyes and she looked up

at him, hearing the truth of his words in the deep, compelling timbre of his voice, and seeing it in the warmth of his gaze. 'And that is the nicest thing anyone has ever said to me. Thank you,' she whispered and, forgetting herself, threw her arms around his neck.

Adam encircled her with his arms. 'You're welcome,' he said softly, his lips against her sweet-scented hair. He was touched by the sincerity and innocence of her gesture, and yet he was unable to believe that, after all these weeks of being tormented by her nearness for hours on end each day and not touching her, she was in his arms at last.

Realising what she had done and embarrassed by her unconscious act, surprise and guilt made Edwina draw back, bewildered when he made no move to relinquish his hold. Instead his arms tightened and drew her so close that her breasts were pressed against his chest. His heavy-lidded gaze dropped to her soft lips, lingering hungrily on her mouth.

'Don't go,' he murmured achingly. 'Stay where you are.'

Their gazes met and held. Adam did not move. Edwina realised with mingled joy and apprehension that he wanted to kiss her, and that he wanted her to return his kiss—the invitation was there in those seductive, compelling blue eyes, an invitation that made her heart begin to pound in erratic, confused beats.

Never having been kissed before, shyly she waited, unprepared for the warmth that flooded through her when his lips descended on hers and his hand cupped the back of her head, his fingers sliding against her nape while his other hand sensually stroked her back, moulding her body to his. Part of her brain ordered her to pull free at once, but some deeper, more compelling voice rebelled at such an unjust reaction to Adam's unexpected ardour.

His kiss was deep and endless, one that shook her to the core of her being and made her want more. His lips courted hers with fierce tenderness, moving over them with accomplished persuasion, tasting their sweetness, coaxing them to part, his tongue making a brief, sensuous exploration of the soft warmth within. Lost in a sea of pure sensation that was like buds that burst into blossom, Edwina moaned softly.

All too soon he withdrew his lips, and she caught her breath, gasping, when he buried them in the soft pulsating curve of her throat, before finding her mouth once more. Sliding her hands up his hard chest, she felt the warmth of his skin beneath the thin white cloth of his shirt, before wrapping her arms around his neck, clinging to him, pressing herself closer, feeling the strength in that hard, lean body. She moaned once more, and the sound somehow penetrated Adam's senses.

Finding himself enmeshed in a kiss that was wildly erotic and in danger of getting out of control, he dragged himself back to reality, his sanity slowly returning. Dropping his hands to her narrow waist, he raised his head and stared down into her adorable young face, unable to believe the hunger and the passion she had evoked in him. In all his life, he realised, he had never been kissed like that.

Standing back in his arms, Edwina tried to catch her breath, dragging her embarrassed gaze to his smouldering eyes.

'Good Lord, you are exquisite,' he murmured huskily. 'But I can see I've shocked you.'

It was true, he had, but Edwina was more shocked at herself and her own reaction than anything he had done. 'This— this is madness,' she murmured nervously. 'I—can't believe we did that.'

Adam was astounded to discover how close he had come to losing control. Edwina affected him deeply, but from the beginning he had vowed that his emotions would not become involved. He had made love to many beautiful women, but he had never wanted any of them as he wanted the young woman he still held in the circle of his arms, which was why he must stop now. He could not make her an instrument of his desire and then cast her off like all the others. She deserved better than that; being a man who had always shied away from committing himself to any one woman, he was not about to start now. Besides, based on what little he knew of her background, it might not be in her best interests to embark on a full-blown affair.

'Actually, I wanted to do that the first time I saw you at Dolly's—not as Ed, but as a lovely young woman. But you're right. This is madness,' he agreed, brushing her face gently with the backs of his fingers. For a moment Edwina thought he was about to continue his seduction, but instead he said flatly, 'It was a mistake.'

She averted her eyes, hot-faced and perplexed, for never had she known a man so perplexing.

'This is not what I intended,' Adam went on. 'I think we let the euphoria of the moment get the better of us, but we should stop lest we go too far. If I took you to my bed, it would spoil something that I value highly—our friendship.' There was an edge to his voice, but his expression revealed nothing of his thoughts and his eyes were carefully guarded. 'That must not happen, Edwina, not when we are very soon to say goodbye—tomorrow, in fact.'

In a daze of suspended yearning and confusion, Edwina's gaze flew to his, her magnificent eyes searching deeply into those dark blue depths. Adam saw the sudden anguish in her face, saw her eyes blurring, misting over with her tears. Her hand touched his face, her fingers spreading over his rigid jaw, and her voice was shattered.

'You're leaving tomorrow?'

'Yes.' He stiffened his arms, gently pushing her away from him.

She heard the absolute finality in his voice, and she was so attuned to him that she knew it was useless to argue, but she did. 'Do you have to go?' she asked, wondering what could be so important that took him away from London. She was prompted to ask, but changed her mind, realising it didn't matter were he went, it wouldn't alter the emptiness his going would leave behind.

Adam's voice was resolute. 'I must. Don't make it harder than it already is.'

Edwina wondered how it could possibly be harder. 'I don't want you to—'

His fingertips covered her lips, silencing her words. 'Don't.'

She swallowed and bent her head, staring at his chest. 'I shall miss you,' she whispered.

Adam tipped her face to his, and in that moment he realised that leaving her was going to be the hardest thing he had ever done in his life, but he had to go for this could not be, and he knew it. The regret he saw in Edwina's eyes was sincere and tore at his heart. Her gaze searched his, but the blue depths were deliberately shuttered. 'I'll soon be back,' he said. 'I will leave you some money and my carriage will be at your disposal. Promise me you won't leave for France until I return?'

'Yes. I promise.'

When Edwina went down to the hall the next morning, Adam's bags were being taken out to the waiting coach. She stood and watched him come down the stairs and cross to the door. He was soberly dressed in black breeches and frock coat, a pristine white jabot at his throat. His hair was pulled back and tied at his nape with a thin black ribbon, a V-shaped wave refusing to be tamed dipping rebelliously over his brow. His face was grave, his mouth held in a tight line, and his eyes were expressionless. She followed him out to the coach, and he paused and looked down at her for a long moment.

'I'm sorry I have to go away, Edwina. I wish I didn't have to, but it is necessary.'

'I'm sorry too,' she said, her voice surprisingly calm. 'Goodbye, Adam.'

'If I am needed, Mrs Harrison knows where I can be contacted. Goodbye, Edwina.' He frowned and his eyes grew pained with indecision as he drank in the beauty of her features, and then he turned and climbed into the coach.

Edwina stood and watched it drive away, feeling as if her heart would surely break, and praying he would soon return.

Chapter Seven

Edwina found the peace and solitude of the house welcome after the long days of posing for Adam, but she missed him dreadfully. A procession of visitors came to the house daily. She always managed to avoid meeting any of them, and it was left to Mrs Harrison to politely inform them that Adam was out of town.

To pass the time she read a lot and took long walks in Hyde Park. She also did something she had never done in her life before and went shopping, finding the simple pleasure of purchasing her own clothes delightfully enjoyable. Dipping into the generous amount of money Adam had paid her for her labours, she purchased several plain and sensible yet pleasing gowns that would be suitable for her journey to France.

After a full morning's successful shopping in the Strand and surrounded by packages, she paid no notice when a closed carriage drew alongside, or to the attention the occupant gave her when she recognised the splendid midnight-blue carriage Edwina was travelling in as belonging to Adam Rycroft. With nostrils distended with dislike, the dark-haired occupant watched the carriage disappear along the Strand, before ordering her driver to head for home.

The warm weather continued, and lulled into a sense of lethargy, one afternoon Edwina ventured to Covent Garden. Unable to resist going to Dolly's Place in the hope of seeing Harriet and to thank Mrs Drinkwater once more for the kindness she had shown when Adam had deposited her on her doorstep, she entered the establishment of ill repute, where she was warmly received by the procuress herself, and surrounded by a host of friendly faces.

The girls at Dolly's Place intrigued her, and despite the unease she felt on entering an establishment of ill repute, curiously she felt no disgust for any of them. Some had endured great hardship in their lives, being the victims of brutal fathers and drunken lovers. She expected bitterness and anger to predominate, but all the girls were surprisingly cheerful and content with their lot. They considered themselves lucky to have risen from the gutter and to have work at Dolly's Place. To Dolly they were an investment and she took good care of them, and should any of the customers show signs of abuse, her henchmen would throw them out and they would know not to come back.

Harriet looked startled on seeing Edwina and subjected her to an assessment stare, scarcely able to believe the transformation, then the hazel eyes sparkled and the lovely mouth curved into a delighted smile. 'Edwina!'

'Surprised to see me?' she said brightly.

'Absolutely. I didn't expect to see you here again—and just look at you. How well you look—how refined. I think you've put on a bit of weight—but that's all to the good. You were much too skinny.'

'That is one of the advantages of being fed every day. But you really know how to make a girl feel good about herself.' Edwina laughed.

'Well, who would believe that filthy street urchin Adam brought in that night would turn out to be a raving beauty?'

'Don't exaggerate,' Edwina chided good-humouredly.

'I don't. You are the epitome of aristocratic poise and elegance,' Harriet enthused, giving her a pixie smile. 'Now,' she said, slipping her arm through her new friend's and enveloping her in the scent of jasmine, 'while I've got half an hour to spare, let's have some tea and a chat.'

'I was hoping you'd say that.'

'I'm simply dying to know how you're getting on with the great Adam Rycroft. Rumour has it that his latest muse is of exceptional beauty and everyone is speculating like crazy about her—even putting on wagers as to who she could be. Adam's certainly kept you well hidden, love. I tell you, Edwina, the curiosity you've aroused is eating everyone away.'

Edwina laughed. 'Then I'm happy to tell you that it won't be long before their curiosity will be appeased.'

Harriet conducted her to a delightful room done up in pale blue and white and carpeted in a darker blue and gold, but before they went inside Edwina paused when a dark-haired young woman who had just come down the stairs and was moving in their direction caught her attention.

She was quite tall, and extremely attractive, in a voluptuous, sultry kind of way. Her nose was tipped disdainfully high; when she drew level with Edwina and found her watching her, she met her gaze. Edwina took a step back as mutual recognition leaped into both their faces. The other woman's eyes became hostile as she regarded Edwina with open dislike, suspicion and resentment, and then without a word she swept past and out into the street to a waiting carriage, leaving a sickly sweet smell of cloying perfume in her wake.

'Harriet, who was that?' Edwina asked, sitting across from her friend at a low table.

Harriet poured tea into two delicate china cups and handed one to her. 'That was Barbara Mortimer—Mrs Drinkwater's niece.' She glanced at Edwina sharply. 'She isn't one of the girls, if that's what you think—wouldn't lower herself, that one. She lives with her mother in Chelsea, but calls now and then to see her aunt.'

'She was with Adam at the theatre that night—the night he brought me here. Are—are they close?' she asked, having quickly formed an unfavourable opinion of Mrs Drinkwater's niece.

'Miss "High and Mighty" would like to think so,' Harriet said, her expression indicating her dislike of Miss Barbara Mortimer. 'She sat for him once and has aspirations where he's concerned, but Adam is careful to keep her at arm's length,' she assured her friend, settling back against the chair cushions and sipping her tea. 'I think he only takes her out so as not to offend Mrs Drinkwater. Now, forget about her and tell me what you've been doing—working hard, I'll wager.'

'If you call reclining on a couch for hours on end every day working hard, then, yes, that is exactly what I've been doing,' Edwina answered, finding it difficult to cast Barbara Mortimer from her mind. After taking a sip of tea she leaned over to smell the roses from the silver bowl on the table.

'Is it finished—the painting?'

Edwina nodded.

'And?' Harriet prompted, watching her with rapt attention. 'Is it a masterpiece?'

'Adam is satisfied with his achievement.'

'And when and where is it to be shown?'

'I don't know when—probably in several weeks' time when Adam returns from wherever it is he's disappeared to—but I do know he hopes to show it at the Royal Academy.'

'Goodness!' Harriet exclaimed excitedly. 'I am impressed. Do you have any idea how famous you'll become?'

'No—but I'm beginning to,' Edwina replied, smiling across at her friend, and feeling a good deal better than she had since Adam's departure. 'And I don't intend waiting around to find out.'

'Why, where will you go?'

'France. I...have relatives there,' she said hesitantly, hoping Harriet wouldn't question her about them as Adam had done. 'As soon as Adam returns I shall leave London.'

'And Adam, too, apparently. Are you close to these relatives in France?'

'No. I've never met them, but I have nothing here so it is best that I go—even more so when the painting is revealed to the public. Of course I am afraid of what lies in store for me. I even wonder if it would not be better to stay here, but I know I will go in the end.'

Harriet's look was direct and quizzical. 'What are you running away from, Edwina? It's not just that bully you worked for in St Giles, is it? There's something else.'

'You're right,' she conceded quietly. 'There's someone far more dangerous to me than Jack.'

Edwina's past piqued Harriet's curiosity; however, not being one to pry into another's private life, she wouldn't dream of asking, so she was surprised when Edwina was forthcoming.

'I ran away from a man who wanted to marry me, Harriet—a powerful man, a ruthless man, a man old enough to be my grandfather, a man I hated. I also ran away from my uncle—for good reason, I assure you. I managed to vanish without a trace, and I don't want him to find me. He is a connoisseur of art, and often visits the exhibitions in London. I have no doubt whatsoever that he will eventually see the painting of me when it is shown at the Royal Academy, which is why I am determined to put as much distance between us as possible.'

'I see,' Harriet said in a voice grown suddenly thoughtful. 'This uncle, is he your guardian?'

'Yes.'

'Then he must be a cruel man if, as you say, he is more dangerous to you than Jack Pierce. But France is a long way for you to run to, Edwina. I only hope your relatives treat you kindly. Ultimately, whatever you decide to do, the decision is yours to make. I only hope it turns out to be the right one.'

'So do I.'

'So,' Harriet said, setting her cup down and smoothing out her skirt, deliberately injecting a lightness into the conversation, 'tell me how you got on with Adam? Did he manage to seduce you with that solid-gold charm of his?' she asked, observing Edwina with careful scrutiny.

Edwina felt her cheeks grow hot. 'I—am attracted to him,' she confessed hesitantly, 'Indeed, who could not be?'

'Who indeed?' Harriet laughed. She had a warm, infectious laugh that showed a gleam of sharp, white teeth between her red lips. 'But are you attracted to the man or the artist? You might just as well say you are attracted to the Tower of London or St Paul's.'

'You think it is the same thing? I have to disagree with you, Harriet. Adam is so imposing. He is—' She paused, hunting for a word that would best describe him, but finding nothing strong enough. On a sigh she simply said, 'There is an air of adventure and eccentricity about him that I find fascinating. He is also a remarkable man, considerate, and he has been extremely kind to me.'

'I'm sure he has!' Harriet exclaimed, her eyes dancing with amusement. 'And I know how attractive he can make himself—when he bothers to take the trouble, that is—and it is that which makes his charm. Of course, he is renowned for his wretched temper—which he makes no effort to control— and he's impatient and stubborn and painfully demanding of his models, and despite all this there isn't a woman of his acquaintance who doesn't long to know what this great artist with his handsome looks is like in bed—nor is there a woman who hasn't at some time or other dreamed of lying naked on his couch and have him paint her.'

Not in the least bit shocked by the tone of Harriet's conversation, as she would once have been, Edwina gave her a knowing smile. 'Even you, as I recall you telling me.'

'Yes, I admit it. I am fond of men—that I cannot deny—

particularly attractive ones who resemble Greek gods. But what of Adam? How does he feel about you?'

'I think he finds me attractive, but—there is nothing in it.'

The sudden break in Edwina's voice brought Harriet's observant eyes upon her. It suggested something very like distress.

'What he loves more than anything is his work,' Edwina went on in answer to Harriet's enquiring look. 'There is not much room for love in such a life—and it is no easy task to love a man like that.'

Harriet's eyes opened wide. 'Love? Gracious! Who said anything about love? I have known love only once, Edwina, and I promise you I have no inclination to fall into that particular trap ever again. It's intense, overwhelming and all consuming. It eats you up inside and plays havoc with your emotions. That's not for me. I'll settle for fondness any day.'

Edwina sensed that the simple word of one syllable had gouged a hole in Harriet's emotional barricade. She looked at her with sympathy, seeing a sadness in her eyes. 'Whoever he was, Harriet, this man you loved, you must have loved him deeply.'

She nodded, swallowing hard to rid herself of the lump in her throat. 'I did, love—but I cured myself of that particular affliction the day he sent me to work on the streets.'

'I'm sorry, Harriet. He must have been a wicked man.'

She shrugged and shook her head slowly. 'No, not really. He was utterly selfish and unprincipled and thought the world owed him a living. Like a lot of men he went about getting it the only way he knew how. I lost track of him when I came to work at Dolly's Place. It's reasonable to assume he's still luring unsuspecting girls into his arms before putting them to use. With his handsome looks he will certainly appeal to them, as I know to my cost. Broke my heart, he did. I'll never forgive him for what he brought me to,' she finished quietly.

Hearing the catch in her voice, Edwina reached out and

clasped her hand sympathetically. Harriet smiled her appreciation. Edwina was far more moved than she cared to admit about what Harriet had told her. It was hard to associate this feisty young woman with the broken-hearted young girl who had come to work at Dolly's Place. They were both silent for a few moments when a maid came in to remove the tray of tea things, and then Edwina rose.

'I'd better go, Harriet. I'm sure you have things to do.'

'It was lovely to see you, Edwina,' Harriet said, her sadness of a moment before having left her. She accompanied her to the door. 'You won't go running off to France without coming to say goodbye, will you?'

Edwina smiled and hugged her tightly. 'I won't. I promise. Goodbye, Harriet.'

The driver helped her into the carriage and shut the door. As it pulled away she waved.

Edwina was in the garden cutting roses and putting them into a basket suspended on her arm when Mrs Harrison came to tell her she had a visitor—a lady by the name of Miss Barbara Mortimer. She looked at the elderly housekeeper with surprise.

'Are you sure it's not Adam she has come to see?'

'She specifically asked to see the lady who she saw walking in the park earlier.'

'I see.' Edwina had taken a walk earlier and hadn't realised she had been observed. She hesitated, the knowledge that Barbara Mortimer had sought her out momentarily scattering her defences. 'Where is she?'

'I've shown her into the downstairs sitting room.'

'Very well. I suppose I'd better see her. Will you ask Nora to prepare some tea?'

Feeling a trifle nervous, Edwina walked back to the house, trying to suppress her growing apprehension. Wondering what Mrs Drinkwater's niece could possibly want to see her about, she placed her basket on the hall table, and, taking a fortifying breath, moved towards the sitting room. Miss Mortimer was perched on the edge of a large upholstered chair, her eyes fastened to the door. She rose immediately when Edwina stepped inside, giving her an exacting perusal.

Edwina felt her heart sink at being confronted by Barbara Mortimer—supremely confident in her beauty, impeccably groomed and faultlessly attired in a gorgeous gold-and-green silk gown. She schooled her features into a tight mask and moved with poise and grace towards her. 'I'm sorry to keep you waiting, Miss Mortimer. Please sit down...' she indicated the chair she had vacated '...and my name is Edwina.' She sat on the sofa with unflinching poise under the penetrating inspection.

Barbara resumed her seat opposite. If she had hoped to see a flicker of unease on the younger woman's face, she was disappointed. Quietly she seethed. How dare this upstart behave like the lady of the house? Adam hadn't sought her out for over a month, and she knew his house was closed to visitors while he painted his latest model—a mystery woman, rumour had it, which had given rise to a good deal of gossip and speculation. Having seen a woman in Adam's carriage along the Strand and assuming this must be the same one causing such a furore, and bumping into her again at her aunt's establishment, she had decided to see for herself what type of woman it was that kept Adam from his friends—and her.

Coming straight to the point, she said, 'There have been so many rumours flying about town regarding Adam's latest muse that I decided to come and see for myself what all the fuss is about. I am not mistaken. You are posing for him?'

Sitting straight and stiff, Edwina tried her best to smile and ignore the husky quality of her visitor's voice. 'I was. The painting is finished.' She raised her brows. 'And—do I meet with your approval, Miss Mortimer?'

Barbara nodded concedingly, smiling tightly. 'To be frank,

you are not what I expected. You're quite different—unusual. In fact, you're really quite beautiful.'

'Thank you.' Edwina was surprised by the unexpected flattery. 'Might I return the compliment?'

Barbara merely nodded coolly. 'Didn't I see you at Dolly's Place yesterday?' She cast her an oblique glance. 'Are you one of her girls?'

Edwina's smile was slightly condescending. 'No, Miss Mortimer, I am not. I was there merely to thank Mrs Drinkwater for a kindness she did me a while ago, and to see a friend.'

Barbara paused. She had been so convinced that the creature who occupied Adam's house was a courtesan. Edwina's answer had somewhat blunted her attack. She was disappointed that this assured young woman was no graceless chit, but unusually beautiful, with a confidence and exuberance that surprised her and was unmistakably intriguing. Who was she? What was her background? Why had Adam mysteriously kept her out of sight? Was he infatuated with her? And, more importantly, was she his mistress?

Until now Barbara had been confident that she had no rival for Adam's affections, but now she had seen this woman for herself she was more frightened than she had been in a long time, and saw her own position assailable. On her way home to Chelsea she would call on her aunt and glean what information she could about Edwina 'whoever she was'. Someone must know something about her.

'Are you and Adam good friends?' Edwina asked with mild interest, determined to remain calm and deliberate. Harriet had told her the nature of the relationship between Barbara Mortimer and Adam, but good manners prevented her from revealing this.

'It's no secret that Adam and I are more than friends,' Barbara assured her with a smug smile, determined to fight for something as vital as Adam Rycroft as anything she could have imagined. 'I know him better than most, which is why I am curious to meet the woman he has ensconced in his house—though not too securely, I hope,' she said meaningfully. 'I imagine you must have become well acquainted with him.'

Edwina was watching her with an arrested expression, but her voice was no more than polite when she said, 'Indeed. After spending most of our days alone together, it is inevitable. He hasn't come to call on you, I take it?'

'No.' Barbara sounded regretful and quietly angry, yet she was wise enough to know that she would be painted in a less than generous light if she gave vent to her true feelings.

Edwina's retort was swift. 'And this is your grievance?'

The air fairly crackled with animosity as the two women eyed each other for a moment, Edwina's steady jade-green eyes meeting Barbara's hostile dark ones. Edwina sensed, almost felt, the anger that was being kept under ruthless control. It came to her in waves of heat. Yet the voice was almost indifferently cool when Barbara said,

'I was merely concerned when I heard Adam was not receiving callers. Of course, I do know how serious he is about his work and can become quite intense. He is best suited with no one to bother him and distract him from his work.'

'Yes, I know. It has been rather peaceful—with just Mrs Harrison and the servants for company.'

The remark, spoken calmly and in all innocence, still made Barbara bristle. Her mouth tightened, and her face hardened. 'In his house a man like Adam needs a wife, not the company of servants, and when he returns to London I will tell him so. I know just the sort of woman he should have—and I believe he will choose the right one.'

Edwina met her vicious glare with an infuriating smile. 'Let us hope—for his sake—that he does. I should hate to see such a talented and charming man laid in an early grave because he took the wrong woman for his wife.'

'Please don't misinterpret my words.'

'I don't,' Edwina countered sharply.

Barbara's eyes darkened to pools of stormy brown. 'Be warned, Edwina. I have wanted Adam for a long time, and I mean to have him.'

'I'm sure you do,' Edwina returned, refusing to allow herself to be goaded by Barbara's glowering threat, 'and if you are as determined as all that, then I am sure you will succeed.'

'Do you have an arrangement with him?'

'Be assured,' Edwina returned with icy dignity, 'that I do not. What we have is purely a business relationship. Nothing more. Adam very kindly offered to let me stay in his house until he returns. When he does, I shall be moving on.'

Somewhat reconciled and relaxing her features, Barbara permitted herself a faint, satisfied smile and rose, pulling on her gloves. 'Good. I'm glad we understand each other. I shouldn't like to see you hurt.'

Edwina stood up. 'How very considerate you are. Your concern is touching.' The door opened to admit Nora bringing in the tea. Edwina smiled at her. 'Thank you, Nora. Put it down there and show Miss Mortimer out. She won't be staying for tea.' She gave her visitor an arch look. 'Goodbye Miss Mortimer.'

Barbara was completely disadvantaged by Edwina's soft-spoken defence, and with venomous anger she followed Nora out into the hall.

Alone and feeling her defences begin to crumble, Edwina sank on to the sofa, turning over in her mind what Barbara Mortimer had said. She hated to think of herself as any woman's rival. Clearly her visitor did not like the attention Adam had given her, and she was eager to tell her so—to warn her off. However, despite Miss Mortimer's obvious infatuation with Adam, Edwina doubted very much that the feeling was reciprocated. Still, she had no wish to become embroiled in something that had nothing to do with her. It was imperative, now more than ever, that she removed herself from the scene as soon as possible. But it would be no easy matter leaving Adam, knowing she might never see him again.

After all those weeks spent as a filthy lad, it was pleasant and flattering to see that warmly intimate look in his eyes when he looked at her. But it was wrong of her to allow her thoughts to stray so often to her handsome saviour. She often thought of his intensely dark-blue gaze, and she chided herself for behaving like a green girl. It was dangerous to her peace of mind to indulge in daydreams. She must not allow herself to be swayed by an attractive face that she entirely forgot what she had set out to do. At the thought of leaving Adam she felt a sharp pang of loss, but it was offset by the thought of finding peace in France.

The street outside Dolly's Place when Barbara emerged from seeing her aunt was unusually quiet for the time of day, which was why the man, a suspicious-looking individual loitering in a dark corner across the way, drew her attention.

She was angry and disappointed because her aunt had clearly been reluctant to appease her curiosity about Edwina, other than to tell her that Adam had found her in the street being attacked, and had brought her to Dolly's Place for her aunt to tend. On her way out Barbara had casually chatted to one of the girls, subtly manoeuvring the conversation to Edwina, and when she was told that she had arrived looking like a street urchin attired in boy's clothes, her curiosity about her rival increased.

She had seen the man loitering across the street once before. He seemed to be watching Dolly's Place and she assumed he might be waiting for one of the girls. However, being a burly, untidy fellow, with a battered black hat and a drooping feather stuck into its brim, she knew her aunt would not consider him suitable company for any of her girls. Curious, she crossed the street towards him, and in no time at all she found out his name was Jack Pierce and that he was looking for a boy named Ed.

As he left Covent Garden Jack's mouth was dry with fury, slowly churning in his stomach. There was more to Ed than he'd realised. How dare the little runt? He—she—had made a fool of him and thought to dispose of him like so much rubbish. Well, she wasn't going to find it that easy. As he made his way to Fleet Street gradually his fury gave way to thoughtful calculation. So, she had been holed up with the artist, had she—Adam Rycroft?

If the woman he had just spoken to was to be believed, he was the same man who had hired Ed to find a lad called Toby, and it was the same man who had intervened when he'd cuffed her one in Covent Garden. He had become adept at picking up useful snippets of information about people of note, and he had heard of Adam Rycroft, the famous artist. The keen edge of his ambition was sharpened. Perhaps it would be to his advantage to find out more, and if the lad hadn't turned up, maybe he could locate him himself.

His smile was ruthless. Who knows? he thought with cold calculation, too shrewd to overlook even the smallest opportunity to capitalise on the setback of losing Ed. Toby might prove a useful bargaining tool in the days and weeks ahead.

Taplow Court. Astride his horse Adam gazed to where the massive, brooding, medieval edifice stood on its hill, the dark walls and dull mullioned windows cold and unwelcoming even from a distance. The house was now his, the house where his mother had grown up until she had married his father and left to live in Devonshire. When his beloved parents had been tragically killed in a fire that had swept their home, this was where he, six years old, had been brought to live.

Adam hated the place with a virulence that sickened him, and he had no wish to live in it. He didn't know if he could bear to live with its memories. He shivered and tried shoving them from his mind. Absenting himself from the house had been the only weapon against the demons that inhabited his brain.

The shock of losing his parents so tragically was a wound from which Adam had never recovered. There had been a special kind of bond between him and his father, which his cousin Silas, twenty years his senior, could never understand. As a lonely, grieving child, he had found no comfort in Taplow's silent rooms, echoing with emptiness and full of shadows, and Silas, who resented his presence at Taplow Court, had made his life wretched. Silas had never had any kind of close relationship with his young cousin. There had been no affection, no understanding.

Even after all these years Adam had not forgotten what Silas was like—the rank smell of debauchery that had hung over him, the hostility with which he had treated him as a boy, the cruelty in which he took such sadistic pleasure. He would never forget the strength of will it had taken to withstand his cousin's violent, often drunken tyrannies, of days locked in a dark room when he resisted, of the bullying and continual punishments for misdemeanours invented by Silas.

He had been bewildered by his cousin's antipathy and the terror he had inspired in him. In the beginning, with every nerve Adam had feared him, and his flesh would shrink from his bones whenever he came near, but with each assault his resolve to stand firm and not let him see his fear had increased. There had been no one to whom he could appeal. The servants, in fear of their master and not wishing to visit punishment on themselves by taking Adam's part, had turned a blind eye and closed their ears.

Olivia, Silas's gentle ten-year-old sister, who lived in absolute awe of her brother, had befriended Adam when she dared, but it was Dolly who had been his saviour. Only Dolly had possessed the courage to stand against Silas. At first this had puzzled Adam, but he eventually discovered her duties went far beyond that of housekeeper at Taplow Court, and that at night she warmed his cousin's bed.

It was only as he grew older and taller than Silas that the abuse had stopped, but the hostility remained Adam had thanked God on his knees when he'd been sent away to school, where he'd been encouraged to indulge his passion for painting. Always shying away from feelings of a personal nature and wanting no intrusion into his privacy, he had learned to cover up his feelings, hiding what was deepest in him, building up an intense reserve until all emotion was buried. But it was still there, like an ache on the perimeters of his mind.

Adam had now been at Taplow Court four weeks, going over the accounts and riding about the estate with his bailiff, meeting his tenant farmers and familiarising himself with the running of the place. He was almost ready to return to London, and Edwina. Lord, how he'd missed her. All those weeks of having her within his sights and then being without her was like losing a part of himself. He had rushed through his business affairs at Taplow Court with a ridiculous eagerness in order to see her again.

His mouth twisted with wry derision. He was behaving like a besotted idiot. But Edwina's open warmth drew a whole new response from him, and he felt a peculiar kind of freedom that was entirely new to him, a process that had begun when a street urchin had picked his pocket in St Giles. He indulged his imagination. A dim vision of a bewitching girl floated before his eyes.

'Edwina,' he whispered in pained regret as he remembered she was to leave him. He focused on her image with every fibre of his being and tried to imagine what she was doing now. Closing his eyes, he slowly traced every line and curve of her face in his mind—the face that had become as familiar to him as his own. He relived their kiss over and over again, clinging to the memory of her incredible sweetness.

He would get his business over with and go back to her, and please God she had kept her promise and waited for him and not grown impatient and gone to France. He tried to analyse his feelings for her, and found nothing would serve. He fought shy of the word love. Compulsion was the one that leapt to mind. When he had finished the painting and left her, he had been like someone emerging from an addiction to a strong drug, a drug he would have to wean himself off, but he had to admit that the addiction would always be there.

He turned his horse and rode in the direction of Oakwood Hall, four miles away, where he was to call on Sir Henry Marchant. He wondered if the man's niece had returned, and, if not, what had become of her. It was ironic really, he thought. Both men had young relatives who had disappeared without trace, despite all their efforts to find them.

Adam had some business to discuss with Henry Marchant about an unpaid loan. Apparently Gordon Marchant, Henry's brother, facing certain ruin and afraid that, under the laws of bankruptcy, all his property would be forfeit and he might spend the rest of his days in a debtors' prison, had turned to Silas. Silas had loaned him thirty thousand pounds, and behaving like the penny-pincher he was in both his personal and his business affairs, had demanded a high rate of return, to be repaid over a duration of eighteen months.

When Gordon Marchant had died in mysterious circumstances—he had been stabbed through the heart and his murderer never apprehended—Silas had offered to disregard his losses if the dead man's daughter, Heloise, who had become the object of his adoration, would become his wife. Being the young woman's guardian, Henry had agreed to the terms stated. Unfortunately for Silas and Henry, Heloise would have none of it, and, when pressure was applied by both men, she had run away.

The duration of the loan was at an end and the money specified in the contract had not been paid, so it was up to Adam to go and see Henry Marchant and discuss the matter. He must show clemency if this business was to be resolved quickly. According to his bailiff, Marchant was not a rich man, but he did possess a fine art collection. The property was forfeit but, unlike Silas, he had no intention of turning a man out of his home.

Adam's mood was grim, his eyes ice cold with anger following his visit to Oakwood Hall and what he had learned regarding Silas. He'd already known his cousin was nothing but a common criminal who, because of his rank and the power he held, had considered himself above the law. Adam's hands, holding the reins, clenched with a barely controllable rage at what Henry Marchant had disclosed to him. If Silas were alive today, Adam would personally drag him to the gallows and place the noose around his worthless neck.

Chapter Eight

When Edwina returned from her walk in the park, a beaming Mrs Harrison was quick to inform her that Adam was back. Happiness soared through her and, knowing where he would be without having to be told, she removed her bonnet, thrust it into Mrs Harrison's outstretched hands and, with wings on her heels, hurried up the stairs to his studio. Gingerly she pushed open the door. Knowing he was unaware of her presence, she waited there and allowed her eyes to drink their fill to the point where she was weakened by an excess of tenderness and pure hopeless longing.

He was standing in front of the easel and, having thrown back the cover, gazing at her picture in thoughtful contemplation. Sensing her presence, he turned his head towards her. They faced one another for one breathless moment, acutely aware of each other, as if some indefinable alchemy was at work. Her cheeks were still warm and flushed from her exertions, her eyes aglow, as she waited for him to speak.

His face was rigid, blank, all his emotions withheld by an iron control as he studied her. She was in blue, her hair gleaming red-bronze in the bright light, and it had been skilfully shaped to frame her beauty, emphasising her wide-spaced eyes and warm mouth, making her look a little older, and more sophisticated. A torrent of feeling washed over Adam as his gaze drank its fill, trying to match her image to the picture. He felt the past four weeks slip away and the stunning young woman in the doorway seemed more like a stranger. He found himself moving towards her, his hand outstretched.

'Come in, Edwina. Don't stand in the doorway.'

Wordlessly she allowed him to take her arm and draw her further inside the room. Closer now, she thought he looked weary. The lines of his face had subtly deepened, making it look leaner, harder. He'd been in the sun somewhere, he was as brown as a nut. But he was just as handsome, and as tall, his hair still unruly. There was something so masculine in the strength of his face that her heartbeat quickened. Realising that she was staring at him, she flushed slightly and dropped her gaze. There were times when Adam Rycroft was too attractive for her peace of mind.

'I've missed you,' he said, his hand touching her chin and tipping her face up to his.

'You have?'

'Yes. Have you changed your mind about going to France?'

She shook her head. Though he appeared calm, she sensed the tension in him, and suspected the cause had something to do with where he had been.

'Then since you are intent on going away, I cannot play out my hand with patience,' he said, measuring his words carefully. 'I have a matter to discuss with you and it must be said. Edwina, the thought of you leaving is intolerable to me. I don't want you to go. I am asking you not to.'

Edwina did not move or speak, she simply stared at him, puzzlement on her face. 'Perhaps you would tell me what on earth has brought this on?'

'Yes, I'll tell you. I can't afford the wear and tear on my nerves, the pure agony inside that comes from the mere thought of you going off alone—a million miles out of reach—away from me,' he said finally.

'What?' she whispered, seeing a need reflected in his eyes that had not been there before.

'I want you to stay—here.'

'Are—are you suggesting that I stay with you?'

'Yes, damn it. I am.'

'Adam, are you propositioning me? Are you saying that you want me to remain as—as your mistress?' she asked hesitantly, flinching from the word as she said it.

'Yes. In every sense of the word. Edwina,' he said solemnly, 'you have come to mean a great deal to me. These past weeks of not being close to your have been sheer hell. Does my suggestion offend you?'

Edwina looked him and shook her head in reply. She hadn't known what to expect, but it certainly wasn't this, and knowing how fiercely he guarded his privacy and his freedom, nor had she expected him to ask her to marry him. So why did she feel disappointed and let down? 'Adam,' she implored, taking a step back, her hand flying to her throat like a captive bird, 'what you ask is impossible. Please don't do this. I have to go. I must.'

'Why must you?' he argued harshly, placing his hands firmly on her shoulders and fixing her with a hard, penetrating gaze. 'You can't spend the rest of your life running away. What earthly reason can you give that can justify you leaving London and going to a country to live amongst strangers?' He saw the growing apprehension widening her eyes and sighed heavily, gentling his tone. 'All right, your mother may have been born and raised in France, but you don't belong there.'

'I truly don't know where I belong any more, but—please stop it. I've told you why I have to go. Let's not go over all that again. I—I think we both know what will happen if I stay.'

There was such intensity in his gaze that Edwina felt her heartbeat quicken. 'And would that be so very wrong? Edwina! Can't I make you see the light of reason? I want you—I freely admit that, and asking you to stay with me is merely a first step on a long and unfamiliar road. That you share my feeling is something I know without having to be told.'

'You seem very sure of that.'

'I am. I've seen it in your eyes, felt it in your kiss. From the very beginning you have roused a protective need in me. It has been a long time since anyone touched that chord. In all my relationships with women I have always cauterised my emotions. You are different. Whenever I think of you my thoughts become chaotic. For four weeks I have been tormented by your absence, and I completed my business in double-quick time in order to return to you.

'You fascinate and intrigue me in a way no other woman has before. You are very special to me and I don't want to lose you. Besides, I am reluctant to lose my muse. I have a desire to paint you some more. I shall be quite desolate if you leave,' he said finally.

His gaze met hers without wavering, promising more than Edwina, in good conscience, could accept. 'Until you tire of me and cast me off like all the rest—when you find another diversion. And then where would I be?' she said quietly.

Dropping his hands from her shoulders, he frowned, anger flaming in his eyes. 'You mean more to me than a diversion. It is no simple thing I feel for you, Edwina, but a burning desire to have you with me every moment. I have difficulty putting my feelings into words, and I won't say words of love and embarrass you with sentiments that are meaningless at this time. You deserve better than that. But what I can tell you is that I am never more content than when I am with you. Can you, in all honesty, tell me that you want to walk away?'

As she stared up at him, drinking in every detail of his handsome face and the smouldering promise in his deep blue eyes, she felt her courage wavering. Her thoughts were put to rout, and she shook her head as if to clear it, her eyes dark with torment. 'I haven't any defences against you—except, perhaps, your honour. It would be so very easy to fall in love with you, Adam. And that would be foolish, would it not?'

Adam studied her in silence, his expression guarded. 'I am ready to defend your honour, and yet I realise that what I want to do offends against both of us. We neither of us conform to what convention demands. Freedom, no encumbrances, clearly appeals to us both. At your own insistence I have respected your privacy, and if it weren't that it suits us both to be free of constraints—which you have gone to great lengths to insist upon—I would ask you to marry me. As things are, I believe we have a great deal to give each other.'

The mere idea that he would marry her if they weren't both their own person, first, last and always, put Edwina's thoughts into such disorder that she was rendered momentarily speechless. He stood tall and motionless, watching her reaction with enigmatic eyes, awaiting her reply. Thinking of marriage brought to mind the visit she had had from Barbara Mortimer. She was not at all eager to bring up the matter of this other woman, but if Adam wanted her to stay with him it was important to her that she knew the true nature of their relationship.

'Have you not given a thought to Miss Mortimer?' Edwina asked. 'She called while you were absent and made it quite plain that she has prior claim on you.'

Adam stiffened. He looked at her a long time, very steadily and stony-eyed. 'Barbara Mortimer has aspirations above and beyond what is acceptable to me. As you know, she is Dolly's niece, and as a kindness I have escorted her to the theatre and to the odd ball on occasion. That is all. I have never encouraged her to believe our relationship will ever be anything other than what it is. We are friends, it ends there. The only woman I am interested in right now is you. So, now that we've disposed of that subject,' he said drily, 'will you give serious thought to what I am asking?'

She nodded. 'Hasn't it occurred to you that we don't know the first thing about each other?'

'It has, but it doesn't matter. We know we want each other. Let that be enough.'

'And what shall I do when the picture of me is hung in the Royal Academy? What shall I do when your muse is recognised and someone I have no wish to set eyes on ever again comes looking for me? I am not speaking of Jack,' she finished, unable to keep the anguish from her voice.

'If that is what's worrying you, I won't exhibit the painting. You are more important to me than that. I'll hang it in this house—or one other.'

Knowing how much the painting meant to him, Edwina was deeply touched by his reply. 'No. I could not let you do that. I know how much it means to you—despite what you say.'

Adam's smile and the way he was regarding her with laughter glinting in his eyes lightened the tension between them. 'When the time comes for it to be shown, I could hide you away in the country—in my other house.'

Her eyes widened with surprise. 'You have two houses?'

He nodded.

'Is it a big house?'

'Colossal.'

'I see,' she said, giving him a plucky smile. 'Well, I don't think I like the idea of being entombed in a big house and relegated to hiding like a hunted animal. I would become a woman of mystery—an object of curiosity in the neighbourhood.'

'Then you will have to face the world and be damned to anyone who means you harm. It's time to put the past behind you, Edwina, and savour the joys of living.'

'Nevertheless, I don't think what you are suggesting is altogether a good idea,' she said, looking at his lips and feeling her blood run warm through her veins at the mere thought of them pressed to hers. 'I'd be an absolute, complete and utter fool to get involved with you.'

'I agree,' he said, bending his head and placing a gentle kiss on her neck.

'And you're a dreadful rogue,' she gasped as his lips burned her flesh.

'I agree with that, too,' he murmured, smelling the sweet rose scent of her skin.

'And what if—?'

He raised his head, his eyes dark and slumberous. 'What if?'

She flushed softly. 'What if I—you know—what if I find myself with child?'

He grinned, his smile wolfish. 'Then you will have to marry me, and be damned to all those fanciful ideas you have in that lovely head of yours about freedom and independence.'

Her heart skipped a beat and she smiled. 'Yes, I suppose I will. Tell me, Adam—when I was posing for you on your couch, did you intend seducing me?'

'I behaved in a right and proper manner towards you at all times—but I wanted you.'

Edwina's gaze was warm on his as she gently touched his cheek with the backs of her fingers. 'I wasn't prepared for any of this.'

Holding her gaze with his, he turned his head slightly and planted a warm kiss in the palm of her hand. 'Then I can see I am going to have to persuade you—to destroy your resistance. I will show you how I assert pressure to get what I want.'

She stood before him, small and slender and utterly lovely, and for an endless interval he could only look at her, and when he could bear it no longer he reached out and pulled her down on to the sofa and took her in his arms, crushing her to him in the wild hope that physical contact might accomplish what words could not. When he lowered his mouth and assaulted her softly parted moist lips with a controlled expertise, and she almost eagerly came full against him, he was confident that with a slow, erotic seduction, he would win.

Edwina moaned, unprepared for the blaze of excitement that leaped through her. Returning his kisses with a desperation that equalled his own, her arms circled his neck and she pressed herself close, little realising the devastating effect her softly rounded young body had on him. The hard rack of his chest was taut and flaming with a fiery heat that warmed her whole body. His mouth became demanding, invading, taking hers with a sensual, leisurely thoroughness that had her trembling with a mixture of dread and wanton longing. His hand cupped one soft, round breast against his chest, feeling the nipple hard and erect beneath her dress, and as his lips brushed her temple and pressed ardently on the tiny pulse beating in her throat before hungrily searching for her mouth once more, he ached to sample this woman more thoroughly.

Slowly he raised his head, his burning eyes restlessly caressing her face. It was flushed with desire, her glorious eyes glazed with it. 'You are so damned beautiful.'

'So are you,' she whispered, feeling her breasts beginning to ache with need from his touch.

He smiled. 'Men are not beautiful,' he tried to tease, but his voice was deep and husky from the effect her aroused young body was having on him.

'You are to me,' she said, gazing at his face, dark with the passion he was fighting to keep under control. She slanted a soft smile at him. 'You are strong and gentle, and I cannot believe you are serious about wanting me.'

His finger touched her chin, tipping her face up to his. 'My darling girl, I am twenty-nine years old, and I know exactly what I want.' Sliding his fingers into the silken mass of her short hair, he cupped her head, his lips clinging to hers in another shattering kiss as desire, primitive and potent, poured through his veins.

To Edwina, what he was doing to her was like being imprisoned in a terrifying sensuality where she had no control over herself. Her mind reeled as his tongue caressed her parted lips, then invaded to search and languidly possess the softness within, until she was reduced to a state of mindless, aching desire.

'Stay with me, Edwina,' he murmured, his lips against hers, his breath warm on her face. 'Say you will.'

Edwina forced her mind to return from where it had fled. Pulling away from him a little, she found herself staring at the V in his shirt revealing his chest covered with curly dark hairs. Hesitantly she raised her gaze and searched his face, looking directly into his eyes. There was an intensified look in them, hard and dark and burning with hope, and she realised that she had never wanted anything the way she wanted his mouth, his hands, his body joined to hers. Nothing mattered to her but this man, and that he wanted her to remain with him. At that moment France and all she had intended seemed a long, long way away.

'I will stay,' she conceded in a whisper, the implication of those three words spreading happiness through her until it was so intense she ached from it.

He kissed her lips lightly. 'Thank you,' he murmured. 'We will make no promises, no commitments. Let us just see where it leads us. Anything is possible.'

Tenderly he drew her into his arms and Edwina laid her head against his chest. What he suggested was more than she had dared hope for. He was talking about a love affair, and she was ashamed that it presented some temptation and she was not shocked by it. She told herself that she should never have let their relationship get this far, that she should have left London before he came back, but she had allowed her emotions to become involved and she could not have left without seeing him again if she'd tried.

Reluctantly her mind turned in an unpleasant direction and she twisted round in his arms, looking up at him. 'There is something I would ask of you, Adam, something that needs to be settled, and I would sooner do that now so that it is out of the way.'

'What is it?' Adam asked gravely, gazing down at her beautiful upturned face mirroring concern.

'Will you promise to remain faithful?' she asked quietly. Adam was by no means singular in his attentions where women were concerned, and the very idea of any infidelity made her feel a little forlorn. 'I've seen how women pursue you. They positively adore you.'

For a moment Adam stared blankly at her, then he tightened his arms and placed a kiss atop her shining head. 'I can't help it if they find me irresistible,' he teased gently, but because he knew how much his fidelity meant to her, and the genuine distress it would cause her if he ever strayed, he made his expression appropriately solemn. 'And if your kisses are an indication of your feelings, it seems you are no exception, my love.'

She smiled. 'It would appear not. When you turn on that famous charm of yours, I know just how irresistible you can be, and you're so certain that no woman with fire in her veins can refuse you. With your reputation as a renowned rake I do realise that you might find the renunciation of a lifetime's habit difficult, but I won't share you, Adam,' she said, injecting a seriousness into her voice. 'I could never accept that. If I stay, there must be no one else. If you are ever unfaithful, it will end. Agreed?'

Gazing into her wonderful eyes, he said in quiet earnest, 'Agreed. No man in his right mind would want anyone else if he had you, my love.'

'Thank you. Then that's settled.' To dispel the seriousness of the moment she laughed lightly and stood up, holding out her hand to his, which he took in his warm clasp. 'Come

along. That delicious aroma wafting up the stairs tells me that
it is time for dinner. After walking in the park for the past two
hours I've worked up quite an appetite.'

His grin was wolfish, his words holding a double meaning that was not lost on her. 'So have I. And after we've eaten
we'll celebrate.'

She smiled back, knowing exactly what kind of celebra-
tion he had in mind. 'Good idea.'

Much later in the cosy intimacy of Adam's room, with pale
rays of moonlight spilling through the windows and bathing
the canopied bed in its silver glow and turning Edwina's skin
pure white, with senses soaring Adam took her in his arms
and laid her down on the soft bed.

'My God, you are so beautiful,' he murmured, the words
like a long drawn-out sigh. For a moment he hesitated, fighting his conscience, but when she turned to him, her pupils
dark and full of passion, her lips hungry for his kisses—
kisses so sweet, so soft—it was more than any man could resist.

Lying beside her and propping himself up on his elbow,
he gazed down at her. She was so heartbreakingly lovely, so
young, so eager, so innocent, the most desirable woman he
had ever seen. He seemed to have longed for her, needed her,
for ever. His hand tenderly caressed the rosy bloom of her
skin, his fingers brushing her breasts, small and round and
soft. She was like some wild young creature of the forest, a
fawn, a creature of sunshine and shadows. He bent his head
and planted kisses where his fingers had been before, smelling the sweet scent of her body, her hair, her breath.

Edwina stretched like a kitten as the soothing fingers and
lips roamed over her throat and shoulders, then strayed down,
stroking her taut uplifted breasts and her gently rounded hips,
cool and soft. It was the most wonderful sensation. With her
eyes closed and her head thrown back, she smiled as this man

who was about to make love to her studied and sighed over her.

Adam, watching her face with intense concentration, saw the smile and his own face relaxed as he marvelled at the unconscious allure of the woman lying beside him. Already she was setting his body on fire, his loins hardening in demanding response to her nearness.

His caresses grew bolder, wandering with deliberate slowness over every detail, savouring what he found, exploring the secrets of her body with the expertise of a knowledgeable lover. His lips, firm and insistent, courted hers, as slowly his hands roamed further still, over her stomach towards her slender thighs, his fingers sliding gently into the silky mat of hair between them. Edwina gave a small moan of pleasure. Her body was drugged by the mesmeric motion of his hands and lips, and she could feel herself floating, buoyed up by the unaccustomed rapture spreading through her body. She was alive with longing, her flesh warm and eager, her breasts taut, her thighs welcoming.

When, at last, he penetrated deep within her and the quicksilver pain faded, there was no holding back, no hesitation, no thought of past or future. Nothing else mattered, only Adam and Edwina, for they were committed to one another as only lovers can be. The first act of their lovemaking was as frenzied and wild as a stormy sky, filled with a desperate need, pulsating waves of pleasure and passion as Ed-wina's body arched to meet her lover's, her eyes as dark and deep as the sea as each sought a common goal, moving surely towards it, both wanting it—the fire and the ecstasy that embraced them both.

The second act, with the pleasure of that first time still warm within them, was more lingering, when delay is divine sweet torment that must end soon or sanity would flee. It was shared pleasure, leisurely and lethargic, exquisite sensations, that unhurried exploration of each other, of taste, of touch, of fingertips and caresses, which is only possible when that first hunger is satisfied, and the joy that comes with fulfilment.

Completely content in the union of their bodies, the euphoria of it still with them, damp with perspiration Edwina curled into Adam, feeling his arms wrapped securely around her. For the first time in her life she felt complete. She was unable to believe what had happened to her. Was it possible to feel so much happiness, to feel such joyous elation shimmering inside? She had done wrong, yet she felt no conscience or shame.

Hearing the heavy, rhythmic beating of his heart beneath her cheek, she was profoundly aware she felt something else, something dangerous and forbidden, something that shouldn't exist. What she felt was a love so profound she was shaken by it. She loved Adam with all her heart, her body and her soul, but she would not dream of telling him so, lest his reply was not the one her heart yearned for.

In the aftermath of their love-making she was unhappily aware that the man who had taken her with such tenderness and need, who had made her cry out with passion and feel as if she were the only woman he had ever made love to, had done it with countless beautiful and experienced females before. Placing her lips against his warm, moist chest, she sighed, hoping all that was in the past, and that his need of her would never cease to exist. For now she was sublimely content to let things remain as they were, content to bask in the present and let the future take care of itself.

Later, with early morning sunlight slanting through the curtains and bathing them in its bright glow, Adam kissed the top of Edwina's head, dazed and enchanted with the realisation that making love to this lovely, spirited and innocent human being had been a wondrous, sensuous experience. In all his years of aimless sexual encounters with some of the most beautiful women London and the rest of Europe had to offer, nothing had approached the shattering ecstasy he'd just encountered with Edwina.

He found himself aroused and absorbed by her in a way that startled him. As they had shared the most intimate of experiences she had reached for him and he had discovered the woman in her. He gazed down at her. Her skin had a translucent quality. Her body was glowing and satisfied—awakened.

'What are you thinking about?' he asked.

She tilted her head and found him studying her. 'Oh, nothing too profound,' she replied, smiling softly. She sat up slowly, her body still singing from his touch. Unconscious of her lack of modesty, kneeling in front of him, feeling the chill of perspiration on her forehead, slowly she pushed the damp tendrils off her face. In the morning light his appeal and the broad expanse of his naked chest seemed more pronounced, reminding her rather forcefully how his powerful body had felt pressed against hers. A leisurely smile lifted the corner of his mouth as his eyes passed over her in bold appreciation. Unable to stave off her awareness of him as a handsome, virile male, with a heavy lock of hair dipping over his brow giving him a boyish look, leaning contentedly towards him, she placed a kiss on his lips before resting back on her heels.

'I was thinking how happy you have made me.' Her breath trembled. 'I've never felt like this before; in fact, I never knew I could feel this—this wonderful wanting.'

Adam rolled towards her and propped himself up with his elbow, his body heavy and languid. His gaze probed with flaming warmth into hers, the heat of it setting Edwina's blood on fire and striking sparks along her flesh. His eyes smouldered with desire as they moved with leisured thoroughness over the rosy peaks of her delicately rounded breasts, and down to the slender curve of her waist. With her back to the light, her face and form were in shadow. 'How do you feel?' he asked at length.

She blushed and giggled softly. 'Strange—and I must confess rather decadent. I'm not used to this sort of thing. This—was my first time,' she confessed awkwardly.

He smiled in the face of her innocence. 'I know. I'm honoured.'

Edwina returned his smile. 'Yes, you are.'

'Happy?' he asked, raising his hand to caress her cheek, letting his fingers glide through her silken short tresses.

She nodded, her eyes sparkling.

'Any regrets?'

'No. None.'

Slowly Adam ran his finger down her arm, admiring the smooth lines of her slender body. 'You are truly lovely, do you know that?' he murmured. 'You remind me of a dancer—or a fawn—elusive, wary, beautiful to gaze upon, quick to flee.' Hoisting himself up, he sat with his back braced against the bed head, one knee drawn up, and an arm dangling across it. His gaze never wavered from hers. Looking into her large, dark eyes, his expression became sombre, his gaze long and searching.

'After all these weeks of being with you, with any other woman I would have known virtually everything there is to know about her—her past, her likes and dislikes. With you it is not like that. You are different—enchanting, fascinating and frustrating. You fit into no category that I can think of. In fact, I don't know anything about you.'

As Edwina experienced a sharp feeling of unease, her gaze became steadily fixed on his. 'Are you asking?'

His eyes glowed in the warm light as he gave her a lazy smile. 'No, but I'm prepared for anything. All I know is that when you came to London you were running away from someone. Tell me, Edwina, are you still?'

Chapter Nine

The question was unexpected. Edwina's eyes grew bright suddenly, and wet. But when she spoke her voice became much harder than before. 'I do have a past I'm trying to forget.'

'You have a right to your privacy, Edwina. I respect that.' Adam's voice was warm with compassion, for she spoke in a tone of unutterable sadness, but there was also a hint of reproach. 'But this is a beginning for us. I would rather not start with the secrets of your past between us, but I will not press you to confide in me. What I will ask is this: did you quarrel with your family, and, if so, is it impossible for it to be mended?'

She was quiet and still, her face ashen, her eyes chilled to chips of glass. 'It was more than a quarrel—much, much more than that.'

He took her hand and placed his lips on her fingers. 'I see, and I can see it upsets you to talk about it, so we will say no more on the subject.'

Edwina kept hold of his hand, looking down at it, at the long lean fingers curled round her own, her expression set in a hardness of remembrance. He could not begin to imagine what she had suffered, nor the act committed by her uncle in the name of caring that had caused it. In her heart she felt the time had come for her to tell Adam the truth. After all he had

done for her, she owed it to him. Besides, how could their relationship possibly flourish and survive if there were secrets
between them? Nothing must be kept hidden. At first she
hesitated, but part of her belonged to him now. For the first
time in months she was content and trusting, and suddenly
she wanted him to know everything.

'No, I will tell you. I want to tell you.'

He frowned gravely. 'You don't have to.'

'I know, but there must be no secrets between us.' She
paused, dragging the sheet over her nakedness, before going
on.

'I will start by telling you about my father. He loved me
dearly and was highly protective of me. Unfortunately he
had a great propensity for running into debt. He was a kind,
clever man, but he had a passion for gambling. With a kind
of fever he would place bets on anything—not only on games
of chance and every political contest and sporting event, but
on all manner of happenings. He was driven by the conviction that the next game would be the turning point when his
luck would change.

'Faced with financial ruin, he borrowed money from a
certain gentleman of some standing, pledging his property
against the loan. When he died the gentleman came to me,
demanding it be paid. I told him the debt was my father's, not
mine. I would not be held responsible.'

'Were you his heir?'

'No. Under the entailment his property had to pass to the
oldest son or the next male member of the family, which, in
this case, was my uncle.'

'Then by rights your father's creditor should have approached your uncle.'

'He did when he became aware of the entailment. My
uncle, who is now my guardian, was more obliging,' she said,
unable to conceal the deep, abiding bitterness she felt. 'I
didn't realise until my father died just how much my uncle

had always coveted his estate. You can imagine his bitterness when the burden of my father's debts fell on him and his creditor claimed the property.'

'Is your uncle a wealthy man?'

She shook her head. 'He's a man of modest means, has never married, and is a genuine lover of art.' She smiled at Adam. 'You'd probably get on well. He does own several fine paintings, some bequeathed to him by my grandfather—and which I'm certain would interest you.'

'What's he like, this uncle of yours?'

'A hard man, and cold. There is no love in him, or if there is he hides it—as if it isn't proper to show affection for anyone. After a meeting between my uncle and my father's creditor, my uncle told me that the gentleman held me in great esteem—had done for some time, in fact. Together they had drawn up a marriage contract. The gentleman proposed to disregard his losses and marry me without a dowry. My uncle saw me as a valuable commodity to be used in the barter of the marriage market, and he could not understand my reaction—which was one of horror, disbelief and revulsion. I did not like my suitor in the slightest, you see, and found his attentions utterly distasteful and unwelcome.'

'Why? What is wrong with him?' Adam asked, pleasuring himself with the sight of her perched in front of him like some woodland nymph, the shapely limbs not quite covered by the sheet, and the soft flush that mantled her cheeks.

'Oh,' Edwina mused thoughtfully, 'he possess the prerequisites of title and wealth, but they are the only prerequisites. There is no polite way to describe him. He is a brutal, disgusting old roué, his debauchery much talked about among Society.'

'How old?'

She shrugged. 'At least fifty.'

'That old? Ancient indeed,' Adam murmured, his lips twitching with a mixture of amusement and compassion.

'And ugly.'

'And you did not feel duty bound to marry this man?'

'Certainly not.' She shuddered when she recalled Silas Clifford's heavily veined face with an uncompromisingly cruel mouth. 'I would never be able to conquer my aversion to him—a man who saw me as compensation for an unpaid debt. His face had a cruel asceticism which showed no tolerance of others. At first, when my uncle told me what he intended, I cried; I begged and pleaded with him not to force me into marriage with this man. I can see my uncle now—how he stood with his arms folded, watching me. He was very calm, impersonal. There was no pity or affection for me. It was like being in a trap. I could feel it closing around me. His insistence awoke a sense of rebellion in me. That was when I stopped crying and pleaded no more. That was when I decided to run away.

'I began making plans. I was cautious—outwardly docile, but inwardly I was determined, defiant. I would not meekly submit to my fate. Disguised as a boy and with enough money in my pocket to get me to France, I left at night so no one would see me go. I did not doubt I would succeed—there was no possibility of failure—but I had not counted on being robbed of all my money before I reached London, destroying any hope I might have had of going to France. I met Jack and he promised to find me work. I trusted him—and—well…you know the rest.'

Adam was watching her steadily. Something was bothering him, something he couldn't put his finger on. Deep in the recesses of his male heart he sensed something was not quite right, and yet he did not recognise what it was he knew, or even that he knew anything. It was just below the surface of his conscious mind and he couldn't quite see what it was. Every time he thought it was going to become clear, he couldn't quite catch it.

Edwina's hands were clasped in front of her, small and

very still, and her eyes were large and guarded. Adam felt
a reluctance in her to continue, and suspected there was
something else she was holding back. 'And was this the
only reason you had for running away?' he asked, urging
her on.

She did not answer immediately. Nervously she licked her
bottom lip and averted her eyes, but then she was looking at
him once again. There was something of compulsion in those
eyes, something strangely deep and fierce. 'No,' she answered
quietly. 'That was the second reason.'

'And the first?'

'I—I believed—and I still do—that my uncle killed my
father.'

Scandalised, in dumbfounded amazement, Adam stared at
her. 'It is a grave matter indeed to accuse a man of murder-
ing his own brother, Edwina.'

'I know.'

'So, what makes you think he did?' He was watching her
intently. 'I presume you have good reason.'

She drew an unsteady breath. 'I heard them quarrelling before they left to meet with Father's creditor. They often quar-
relled, but this time it was much, much worse than usual. I
didn't know what the quarrel was about, but it must have been
of a serious nature to cause my father to raise his voice with
such violence. When my uncle brought my father's body
home, his behaviour was most odd. In fact, he refused to discuss it with me, and when I pressed him he became extremely
angry and irrational, which was quite out of character.'

'Then if he really did kill your father, why did you not confront him? Why did you not take legal action? Who could accuse him with greater force than you?'

'Without proof I could not openly condemn him. And there
never will be. My uncle is a clever man and he will see to that.
Everyone who had known my father was scandalised by his
murder, and it caused a great deal of gossip and conjecture at

the time, but failure to find the culprit has caused memories to become dimmed.

'My uncle had much to gain on my father's death—the house, a beautiful old mansion in the Hertfordshire countryside, which had given me so much joy throughout my life, and then unbearable grief; the estate, such as it was when Father died; and, I came to realise, myself, if I married his noble neighbour, which would make me a countess and mistress of one of the finest houses in the country, and would bring him connections that would be worth more than money. So, you see, my uncle was only concerned about what he could reap from the affair.'

As Adam listened for a moment he was unable to absorb the full shock of what she was saying, but then the entire import of what he was hearing slammed into him. He went white as something dark and without form began shaping itself in his brain. His body rigid, his expression tense, he looked at her for a long moment, his eyes hard and penetrating. When he spoke his voice was low and even, belying the rumbling turmoil in his inner self. 'Tell me, Edwina, how did your father die?'

The change that had come over Adam momentarily escaped Edwina's notice as she continued. 'It was when he was travelling with my uncle to meet the gentleman who had loaned him the money. My uncle claimed they were set upon soon after leaving home, and that they never reached their destination.'

'Were his attackers apprehended?'

'No. In fact, the whole matter was mysteriously hushed up.'

'And what is your uncle's name?'

'Sir Henry Marchant.'

Adam's expression did not alter, apart from a muscle that tensed at the side of his mouth. 'And your name? Your full name.'

'Edwina Marchant—Heloise Edwina Marchant, that is.'

This revelation was so different from what he had assumed, Adam had trouble grasping the facts as they were presented to him. 'And the name of the gentleman you were to marry?' he asked, the name he knew she would utter searing through his mind like a blazing arrow before she had time to speak it.

'Silas Clifford—the Earl of Taplow.'

Adam's face went white, his eyes glacial, and his mouth closed in a hard line. Each unbelievable word Edwina uttered scored into his brain. In this, the most painful moment of his life, he was unable to react as he stared at her in blank disbelief. The irrefutable fact that he could not ignore, or disprove, was that the young woman he had shamelessly seduced was Henry Marchant's missing niece—the same young woman Silas had wanted for his wife.

Disgusted, it was all he could do to contain his loathing for himself. The shock of this ghastly revelation had him reeling, and in restless fury he threw himself off the bed and began pulling on his clothes.

Edwina stared at him with stupefaction, feeling a *frisson* of alarm. 'Adam? What is it? What's wrong?'

Appalled at what he had done and bracing himself for the unpalatable task of answering her, Adam forced himself to remain calm and lucid. 'Get dressed. I will instruct Mrs Harrison to see to it that your clothes are packed immediately.'

'But why? I—I thought -'

A muscle move spasmodically in his throat and his glance seared through her. 'It was a mistake, Edwina. Everything we have done has been a mistake,' he said fiercely. 'I should never have taken advantage of you. I blame myself absolutely. I deserve to be horsewhipped.'

'Why—what do you mean?' Edwina asked with quiet desperation, completely bewildered, and wondering why he was so angry all of a sudden. In the highly charged silence that crackled between them as he dressed, she could feel the man who had made love to her with such tender passion mentally withdrawing from her. Fighting tears, struggling to keep her voice under control, she asked, 'Adam, what's wrong? For the love of God, tell me. Where are you sending me?'

'Home.'

'Home?' Edwina paled. There was a harsh, bitter finality in that one word that thoroughly alarmed her. She stared at him in stunned disbelief. Panic jolted through her entire nervous system and her heart began to race wildly. The atmosphere was charged with something she did not like. It was a tension that had a sharp point of a knife piercing it. One that could hurt, though she was not sure why. Adam's eyes had a terrible blankness in them, and about his mouth was a white line of anger. His voice was like ice when he spoke, hard and cutting.

'You must go back to your uncle,' he told her, thrusting his arms into his shirtsleeves. 'You cannot stay here. For your own sake you must go back and become reconciled.'

Shock drained the blood from Edwina's cheeks as she realised what he was saying. It sent her jolting upright while a blaze of animosity and terror erupted through her entire body, giving way to a sudden, almost uncontrollable burst of wrath. 'You are actually going to send me back after all I have told you—without considering my feelings? You can't. I won't let you. You have no authority to do so,' she cried. It penetrated through her anger and alarm that there was something amiss in all of this, something that didn't make any sense.

'I can, Edwina. I must.'

'Do you mind telling me why?' She waited, her fists clenched and her sharp nails digging into the soft palms of her hands to stop them trembling, and when he offered no explanation, she said tersely, 'Don't concern yourself with my affairs, Adam. It has nothing whatsoever to do with you. I will not be ordered about like a maidservant. I won't go. I absolutely refuse.'

'Then I shall take you back by force,' he said, sitting down and yanking on his boots.

Furiously, her eyes blazing, Edwina jumped from the bed, dragging the sheet still draped around her body with her. 'Force? You would force me?'

'If I have to.'

'I see. What I want to know is how you mean to make me.'

'There are ways and means.'

'Is that so? Are you telling me you will forcibly carry me out to the coach?'

He paused in his dressing and for a moment he looked at her, his face a mask of vicious, grinding fury. 'I will.'

'Oh—how dare you!' she flamed, almost as angry as he was, unable to comprehend the heat of his rage, the abrupt unleashing of his temper. 'After running away from him, Uncle Henry would never want to see me any more than I wish to see him.'

'Who could blame him after the mishaps you've treated him to these past months?' Adam remarked curtly.

'Oh, you beast! When I ran away from him I did so with good reason. You, a virtual stranger, can understand none of this.'

Adam towered over her, and his lean, hard face bore no hint of humour. His mind was locked in furious combat against the idea of returning her to Oakwood Hall, the house she had spoken of with such love just a short time before. Try as he might, he could not imagine a caring uncle actually agreeing to marry his niece off to Silas, a man he, and, he now realised since his visit to Oakwood Hall, Henry Marchant had every reason to despise. There was little wonder Edwina had opposed the marriage.

'What I understand is that your uncle regrets his behaviour towards you and wishes to make amends.'

His words stunned Edwina into momentary silence. The room swam before her eyes, then she said, 'You know my uncle?'

Adam nodded. His face was hard, the muscles tight. He was stiff and unyielding. 'Have no fear that he will press you to wed Silas Clifford. Silas is dead,' he informed her coldly, shrugging into his jacket. He took a step towards her, his eyes hard. 'Now you have made your identity known to me, how shall I address you?'

'Edwina will do.'

'Is that how you are addressed by your uncle?'

'Yes. Heloise was of my mother's choosing—after her own mother. My father had an aversion to it, and after my mother died when I was quite young, no one addressed me by that name.' Adam merely nodded. His utter lack of caring smote her heart. She raised her chin in defiance and self-defence. 'I will not go back.'

His eyes flashed. 'I will not debate this any further with you, Edwina. Get dressed. The discussion is at an end.' His face was obdurate, his voice firm. There was no more to be said on the subject, his attitude implied, and he turned away from her and, with long, determined strides, went towards the door.

In the space of a second all Edwina's memories collided head on with the reality of the present, and with a cry of tempestuous fury she flung herself after him, grasping his arm and forcing him to look at her. 'Do not be mistaken, Adam. The argument is far from settled yet. Would you take me back to live with the man who murdered my father, the man who would have sold me like he would a prize cow to a disgusting old man?'

'Henry Marchant did not murder your father, Edwina. I know that for a fact. Now get dressed while I make arrangements for us to leave.'

Not knowing whether to believe him or not, Edwina's eyes narrowed. Innocent or guilty, it changed nothing where her uncle was concerned. 'Whatever the truth of the matter, I will not go back,' she stormed at him, her eyes flashing green fire. 'I will leave your house this instant and you will never see me again.'

Adam's eyes glittered down at her like shards of ice, from a face that was white with rage. 'You do and I will find you.'

'You would come looking for me?'

'Try me. You will do exactly as I say. Defy me, Edwina, and I will make Silas Clifford seem like a saint,' he gritted viciously. 'You would do well in future to remember it.'

Edwina went cold, her mind registering the physical threat in his voice, refusing to believe it. She realised that her revelation had unleashed in him all the hidden forces of a passionate nature, all the more terrible because the strong, intractable will of the man made him normally able to master them.

Releasing her hold on his arm, she stepped back and watched him go as with heartbreaking clarity, all the scattered pieces of the bizarre puzzle fell into place, presenting her with the complete, ghastly picture, in its entire, profane detail. She realised what a complete and utter fool she had been to disclose her identity to a man who knew her uncle and Silas Clifford personally, and she was shamed to the depths of her soul because she had given herself to him willingly, wantonly. Wildly she wondered how she could have been so naïve and infatuated to imagine that she was in love with him. Now the only emotion in her heart as she gathered her clothes together and began to dress was loathing.

Just a short while ago everything had been so wonderful, so perfect, and seemed so simple. Now she was experiencing a feeling of helplessness, of being swept along by a too-powerful current in the form of Adam Rycroft. Nothing was the same, and all because she had told him who she was.

The Adam Rycroft she knew had changed and in his place she saw a stranger revealed, whose inimical behaviour was totally foreign to her heart. She did not want and would not have a man who wished to dominate her and bend her to his will. It was an affront to her pride to be dragged home by a man she had trusted, a man she had cared deeply for, and her pride ached for some assuaging vengeance.

In disgust and loathing of what he had done, her first re-action was to run away again, but fearing Jack might find her and drag her back down into his ugly world of crime, com-mon sense prevailed and she decided against it. She would bide her time and take her chances at Oakwood Hall with as much dignity as she could muster.

Adam had told her Silas Clifford was dead, and in her fury she thanked God for it, relieved to know that at least one threat had been removed from her life. And how did he know her uncle hadn't killed her father? He seemed so certain. If what he had told her was the truth and her uncle was innocent of what she had accused him of, then she owed him an expla-nation and an apology. Her pride ached, and the fear of fac-ing him again and what the future had in store for her was in danger of reducing her to a shaking coward.

Resolutely she brushed her hair, trying desperately to keep her emotions under control so that she would be able to think clearly. Adam's furious reaction to her identity and his rea-sons for taking her home with such determined haste were most confusing, but no doubt all would be revealed to her eventually. The scale of her misery was greater than she was equipped to deal with, so she took refuge in anger.

Leaving Edwina and going quickly to find Mrs Harrison, Adam was unable to banish his rage. He was furious because Edwina had kept her identity from him, and furious with himself for having taken advantage of her. He should have known better. Scalding rage seared through him at his own blindness. Ever since he'd set eyes on Edwina as the boy Ed, he'd been blind. But no, he corrected himself with furious self-disgust, that wasn't true. He'd recognised instinctively what she was, someone who was brave and proud and inno-cent—and what had he done?

With bitter cynicism he congratulated himself, for after taking her into his home he had lured her into his bed and turned a virtuous young girl into a social pariah, and all because he couldn't keep his lecherous hands off her. When certain individuals realised who she was and spread the gossip, it would be assumed her character must be of the blackest nature, and she would summarily be avoided and shunned by all decent people.

To avoid such a thing happening and, if she was ever to show her face in society again, to rectify the damage, it was imperative that she become reconciled with her uncle immediately and that he set the wheels in motion to wed her, even though he knew she would fight him and more than likely hate him for it.

He didn't like himself for what he was doing, but this was no time for sentiment or guilt.

When she was ready, taking firm hold of her courage and summoning every shred of dignity to her aid, Edwina went downstairs. Adam was waiting for her.

His fury had abated somewhat; his blue eyes became locked on hers with a frowning intensity. Beneath the brim of her bonnet her face was strained and serious, and she moved with an intent directness he found disconcerting. It was as if she had carefully considered all the alternatives to returning to Oakwood Hall and, having made up her mind, was not to be swayed from her purpose. Pride swelled in him at how valiantly she was rallying. He deeply regretted what had happened and that he was the cause of her misery, and he wanted to make her leave-taking as painless as possible.

'I'm truly sorry it's come to this, Edwina. Had I known who you were, I would have returned you to your uncle sooner.'

She faced him squarely, her beautiful green eyes hurling scornful daggers at him. 'Had I known you would react like this, I would never have told you. I am touched by your concern,' she replied, her tone heavy with sarcasm, 'but I cannot understand how you can do this. You are the most heartless, unfeeling man I have ever met and it will be a pleasure to remove myself from your clutches.

'How I survived being with you all these weeks is a testament to my strength, but says nothing whatsoever for my common sense.' Her eyes went through the open doorway to the street beyond, focusing on the coach waiting to take her to Oakwood Hall. It filled her sights like some ominous black threat. 'I would like to travel alone, if you don't mind.'

'Don't be ridiculous,' he said, his voice sounding harsh and angry. 'Do you not understand what could happen to you—a young woman alone on the road with just the coach driver? Any miscreants abroad would see you as a tempting morsel and lose no time in setting about you.'

Coldly rejecting the logic of his warning, Edwina's eyes struck sparks of fiery indignation. 'How conceited you are, Adam, if you think I welcome your protection or your company. I do not wish to be a burden and I won't accept any more of your charity,' she said caustically, feeling more hurt and degraded than she cared to admit. 'I deeply regret my foolishness in becoming entangled with you.'

He arched a brow. 'Foolishness? Yours or mine?'

'Both,' she bit back. 'Since you clearly want to send me out of your sight, there's no need to inconvenience yourself. I am quite capable of returning to Uncle Henry without your protection.'

'I know you are—but unfortunately I cannot trust you to do so. If your past record is anything to go by, you would vanish back into the streets where I found you before the coach turned the first corner. If you will not consider yourself, then consider what your uncle will have to suffer if you don't go back.'

'I do not owe my uncle anything.'

'No? And Oakwood Hall? You told me you loved the old place, and, having seen it for myself, I cannot say that I blame you. Did it not occur to you when you ran away that the Earl of Taplow might expect reimbursement of his money before he considered the matter settled? Did it not worry you?'

Edwina shrugged her slender shoulders. 'Not unduly. You see, Uncle Henry could always sell some of his paintings to settle the debt. They are rather valuable, I believe. But if, as you say, Silas Clifford is dead, then maybe his replacement will be more generous.'

Edwina's reference to the Earl of Taplow made no apparent impression on Adam. He regarded her with a thoughtful, almost tender expression. When he thought of the night past he realised it had been no meaningless dalliance. With a fresh surge of remorse he recalled her incredible sweetness and unselfish passion in his arms. He couldn't lose her now, he was committed to her, and he desperately wanted to make amends for stealing her innocence. He wanted her—he wanted her to be his wife, and he was impatient to have everything completed.

Not for one moment did he think Henry Marchant would refuse his offer to wed Edwina, and he was confident of his own ability to lure her into his arms. What concerned him was the dissension between Edwina and her uncle, and there was a strong possibility that if she learned what he intended too soon, she might rebel against it merely to defy him and her uncle—and his instincts warned him that if Edwina were placed in an opposing position, headstrong and stubborn, she could become an extremely determined adversary indeed.

His identity could prove to be a complication in their forming a proper relationship. Since she'd had such a low opinion of Silas, he considered it wise to keep it secret until she had become reconciled with her uncle, and he himself had won her over. If he were to disclose it now, in her present mood he would sink even further in her estimation. All the

men she had known had wreaked havoc in her young life—
little wonder she valued her independence—but he was confident he would soon disabuse her of that fanciful idea.

'Knowing how stubborn you can be, with your stupid,
progressive ways, will you give me your word that you won't
try to abscond on the journey?' he asked as he took her arm
and propelled her through the door and out into the street. He
waited expectantly for a reply.

The idea of escape was already eating away at Edwina's
thoughts, but the overriding fear that Adam would come after
her and she would have to deal with his wrath quickly ban-
ished such meanderings of her mind. 'I was hoping for a turn
of fate, but I suppose I must accept it. I will not run away
again.'

A troubled frown appeared on her brow as she wondered
why Adam was taking this irrevocable step to banish her
from his life, which was what she assumed he was doing.
Every fibre of her being believed he felt something for her,
so why did he want to hurt her like this? She paused and
looked up at his handsome face, her eyes searching his. On
impulse she said, 'Yesterday you told me that I am very special to you and you don't want to lose me. You have a strange
way of showing it. If you truly care for me as you claimed,
you would not be doing this. Did last night mean nothing to
you? Do I mean nothing to you?'

As she was about to turn away Adam caught her by the
shoulders and forced her to face him. His voice was intense.
'Edwina, there are some things in my life that cannot easily
be set aside, and you are one of them. My desire for you is
hard-driven and I do care for you, deeply. Whatever you may
think, I never lied about that. I know that when something
good comes along, you have to hang on to it.

'If we are to have any future at all together, then you must
return to your uncle. I do know him. I also know things have
not been easy for him since you ran away, and in taking you

back I realise that your fears are not unfounded. But he has been quite distraught with worry, not knowing what's become of you—and in the light of Toby's disappearance I can fully comprehend what he is going through. I have to take you back, I must, and when you are willing to listen to reason I will explain everything. Be assured that I only have your best interests at heart.'

Stubbornly she gave an impatient toss of her head, rejecting his statement. 'At what price to me? I too care about my best interests, and that does not happen to be at Oakwood Hall. Although perhaps it is the lesser of two evils,' she retorted meaningfully. 'I have little left to be proud of. You have taken care of that. You may force me to return home if you must,' she said, her voice low and frozen hard. 'I seem to be at your mercy. However, I know what I want, and that's not to be the mistress of a monster. I will no more be yours in the future than I am now.'

She turned her back on him when Mrs Harrison emerged from the house. Adam's kindly housekeeper was sorry to see her leave—not that she approved of the master taking Miss Edwina to his bed, but she would never dream of voicing her opinion. All the servants were extremely fond of her. Her smile, her irrepressible laughter, her concern for others, touched many a heart. With her in the house it seemed the days were warmer, and the sun shone brighter, and everyone set about their daily chores with a fresh enthusiasm that had been absent before she came. Mrs Harrison had no idea what had gone amiss between her and the master, but the house would be a quieter, sadder place without her.

After bidding Mrs Harrison a fond farewell, in aloof silence Edwina walked to the coach ahead of Adam. He could not resist the view of the swinging skirts and the trim back he was afforded. Shaking his head slowly in admiration, he walked close behind her. For all her fragile beauty, Heloise Edwina Marchant had more strength than many men.

'Make yourself comfortable,' he said in a conciliatory tone as he assisted her up the steps of the coach.

With her chin raised belligerently, Edwina didn't comment. She ignored him as he seated himself across from her and regarded her in bland silence. His jaw was taut, his mouth drawn into a ruthless, forbidding line. His utter lack of concern only added to her outrage. Her temper rolled restlessly, and her mind festered with a growing resentment for every mile that took her further away from London, although the closer she came to her destination and the confrontation with Uncle Henry, the faster her thoughts churned in fretful turmoil. Though she avoided meeting Adam's eyes, she was vividly aware of the clean, fresh scent of his cologne. But where he was concerned she disregarded him altogether, remaining detached and erecting a freezing wall of silence to achieve that end.

Leaning back into the comfort of the upholstery, Adam calmly studied the slim, cool features opposite. He made no attempt to break the wall of icy silence Edwina had built to insulate herself from him. But he could feel her anger.

The coach was travelling along a tree-lined road, and he gazed at her in leisurely contemplation, watching the dappled shade play across her translucent skin. She was lovely and demure in her lace-trimmed cream and green gown—cool and virginal and stunningly arousing. In such close proximity in the confines of the coach he could feel himself responding. He smiled inwardly, never ceasing to be astounded by the way she affected him. His intention to play out his hand with patience would be no easy matter before the tumult of his passions.

The coach jolted and, drawn from her reverie, Edwina glanced at him. At first she found nothing more intimidating than a slightly perplexed and thoughtful frown on his face, but then she flushed hotly as the blue eyes met hers boldly and without wavering. Feeling somewhat becalmed within the seclusion and comfort of the coach, she experienced a sense of dissatisfaction at the knowledge of what he was doing.

Again she focused her gaze on the passing scenery, and only the rumble of the wheels and the thud of the horses' hoofs covered the silence. Just when she thought she could endure the tense atmosphere in the coach no longer, after four hours' travelling she saw the familiar turrets and tall chimneys of Oakwood Hall.

Chapter Ten

When the coach drew up outside the mellow, pink-washed manor house, which was midway between Taplow Court and the village of Taplow, Adam climbed out, holding out his hand to assist Edwina. Casting him a look of dangerous fire, she ignored it and stepped down on to the gravel drive. Trying not to let the emotion of being back home overwhelm her, she stood and gazed at her surroundings, which were more familiar to her than anywhere else.

All the soft lushness of the daisy-strewn lawns, trees and colourful vegetation cushioned it from the outside world. Autumn had turned the leaves on the tall trees to russet and gold, some fluttering down in the gentle breeze that rustled the branches, carpeting the ground. Wisteria and scarlet creeper covered the walls of the house. Everything looked the same, and yet nothing was as it had been. Breathing deeply, she wondered where her uncle was.

She heard him approaching long before the man himself became visible. His tread on the gravel path that surrounded the house had a measured, almost sinister steadiness. Finally he appeared round the corner of the house. Nothing about his reaction escaped Edwina. Upon seeing her standing next to Adam, he came to an abrupt halt, his eyes becoming fixed on her. An expression she couldn't recognise flickered on his austere face, and, even from where she was standing a short distance away, his pale blue eyes seemed very bright and cold. Then he recollected himself and strode briskly towards them.

As always he was elegantly turned out in a black frock coat and sombre grey waistcoat, his neckcloth, tied by an expert hand, held in place by a gold stud. Whereas Edwina's father had been small in stature and stocky in build, her uncle was quite tall with no excess flesh. His piercing eyes flickered over her, cold and uncompromising.

Henry's eyes narrowed with annoyance as he looked at his niece. Despite what Edwina thought of him he wasn't completely lacking in human feeling, and he had been seriously concerned when she had taken it into her head to run away. However, the relief of having her back—unharmed, he hoped—vanished the moment he met her defiant stare. Even now, after all she had done, there was regal grace in her bearing, and a stubborn pride in the set of her small chin. She had disgraced him abominably but she still walked with her head high.

'So, you've come back,' he said in a curt way.

Edwina went rigid at his harsh tone. There was no welcome, no love or affection. She wanted to close her eyes and put her hands over her ears to shut him out completely. Why did it always have to be like this? Why couldn't he show some softness, some feeling for her?

'As you see, Uncle,' she answered, and did not care that she sounded ungracious. Tension tightened her throat suddenly, and a stone settled on her heart. Already she was wishing she had defied Adam and broken free before they had arrived at Oakwood Hall. There was no sign of the concern on her uncle's stony features that Adam had spoken of earlier, although his hair was whiter than it had been, and the lines around his eyes and at the sides of his thin mouth had increased and were deeper than she remembered. She would like to believe the changes had been brought about because of his concern over her disappearance, but she doubted it.

'And do you return of your own free will?' he asked.

'On the contrary. I am here under duress. Were it up to me, I would have stayed in London,' she said, throwing Adam a heated glare. She knew how much her answer would infuriate him, but after his harsh treatment of her, his feelings were the last thing she wanted to consider at that moment.

Henry nodded. 'I see.' His eyes narrowed as he shifted his gaze to Adam, who stood several feet back, his shoulders squared and his jaw set with implacable determination, seeming to emanate the restrained power and unyielding authority Henry had sensed on their previous meeting, when he had called to discuss the outstanding debt.

The meeting had gone better than he'd dared to hope. The new Earl of Taplow had been more generous than his predecessor. Henry had made him a gift of two of the finest paintings in his collection, but their worth was still several thousand pounds' short of the amount of money Gordon had borrowed from Silas Clifford: Adam Rycroft had been duly satisfied and told him the debt was settled, compounding it in writing.

'I hope you will accept my gratitude for bringing back my niece. There's no telling where she would have ended up had it not been for you. She has a great deal of explaining to do.'

Adam moved forward and fixed the older man with his impassive gaze. Where Edwina was concerned, he had all the patience and understanding in the world—with her uncle, however, he had none. In fact, he had small liking for the man, but when he had called at Oakwood Hall, Henry Marchant's anxiety over his niece's disappearance had been genuine and heartfelt. Adam just wished the man would show a little more caring and compassion now that she had come back safe and well, instead of this cold antagonism.

'Be thankful she is returned to you unharmed. I confess to

having known Edwina for several weeks, Sir Henry, but her true identity was not made known to me until today. Shall we go inside? I would appreciate a private word with you before I leave.'

When the three of them entered the house, Henry nodded a curt dismissal to the three hovering female servants, their eyes focused on Edwina in joyous stupefaction that she had returned, dispelling all their fears that something dreadful had happened to her in the wake of her father's tragic death. While they waited for the servants to disappear, the ominous silence in the hallway seemed to crackle with tension. As the door to the domestic quarters closed behind the last of them, unable to contain his anger a moment longer Henry turned to his niece.

'Have you any idea of the trouble you've caused? That any girl should disobey her elders is unheard of, but that she should bring such disgrace to her family by openly defying her guardian and leaving home without a "by your leave" to anyone is monstrous. You set the whole household afire when you ran off like that, exposing yourself to savages and brutes and all manner of corruption. A delicately raised seventeen-year-old girl doesn't know how to take care of herself—how to guard against—'

'I managed,' Edwina retorted, interrupting him coldly.

Unrepentant, there was such venom in her voice, such anguish in her eyes, that Henry was taken aback. Something flickered in their green depths, something dark and secret. He was troubled by the intensity of her statement. Those two words were born of her experiences, and, he sensed, more than a little pain. What had happened to her? She had run from him with a heart brimming with a hate he'd been unable to see—or overcome if he had. The change in her was evident. There was a strength about her that had not been there before—perhaps some would call it hardness.

So often in the past her father had given way to her, this

wilful, headstrong daughter of his, but Henry had vowed he would stand firm. Unfortunately he had no idea how to handle a seventeen-year-old girl, and that once she got some aversion in her head—like marrying Silas Clifford—she'd follow it through, no matter what.

'I would like to go straight to my room—if I can still call it that,' Edwina said, glancing towards the stairs, eager to be alone.

'Of course. You will find everything just as you left it.'

'Thank you.'

Henry halted her as she was about to turn away. 'You have made your point, Edwina, now I will make mine,' he said coldly. 'Before you leave us, do you give me your word you will not abscond again? I have spent a considerable amount of time and money I can ill afford trying to trace you. If you run away again—though it pains me to say it, I shall wash my hands of you.'

'Do you threaten me, Uncle?'

'I am merely stating your position. Well?'

'You have my word.'

'That is an immense relief to me.'

Henry turned on his heel and disappeared through the open doorway into his study, expecting Adam to follow. As Edwina was about to walk away, Adam halted her.

'A moment, if you please, Edwina.'

For the first time since leaving London she spoke to him, fixing him with her cold gaze, her voice heavy with resentment. 'I don't please.'

He frowned. 'You're making this very unpleasant.'

'Really?' She was not to be appeased. 'Then why have you done this to me? Why have you brought me back here? Do you know what you've done? I never want to see you again. Ever. I shall hate you until the day I die.'

Despite her haughty stance and angry words, Adam saw her eyes were glittering with unshed tears. She held herself with pride. It reminded him that she was the daughter of a gentleman, and because of that he could not treat her as a common whore and drag her to his bed to assuage his lust.

Ignoring her threat, he said gently, 'No, you won't, and I'm sorry to hear you say it, because I think you are the most wonderful, beautiful young woman I have ever met.' He sighed, gently tracing his finger down the curve of her cheek. 'Last night when you were in my arms, it wasn't hatred you were feeling then. You wanted what I wanted—you still do. The taste of your lips is still warm on mine, Edwina.'

She stared at him, unable to reply, impeded by the knowledge that he spoke the truth. She was shaken by the wave of longing that flooded through her and fiercely resisted the anguished burning of her flesh. They both knew what her traitorous body was capable of. Confused and miserable, she looked away, her spirit shattered.

'Some day you will forgive me,' Adam went on gently. 'You cannot hate me for ever.'

'Don't be so certain of that,' she remarked fiercely, taking refuge in her anger. She turned from him, but Adam caught her arm and spun her round. His eyes sought and held hers. 'Let go of me,' she hissed, trying to wrench herself away from him. His grip tightened.

'Stop it, Edwina. That's enough,' he ordered firmly yet quietly. He knew just how determined she could be. Underneath her delicate façade there was a layer of iron. 'In time you will thank me. I'll call on you in a day or so—when you are in a better frame of mind. I'll make it up to you, I promise. You are owed explanations. We'll discuss them then.'

Infuriated by his imperious tone, she snatched her arm from his grasp and turned away. 'Go away, Adam. I curse the day I met you.'

As she reached the stairs he said in a low, authoritative voice, 'I meant it, Edwina. 'I'll call on you in a day or so.'

It was on the tip of Edwina's tongue to tell him he would

be wasting his time, that he was the last person she wanted to see, but she was in such an emotional turmoil she couldn't bring herself to speak.

Upon reaching her room she was met by Maggie. Maggie was her nurse, her maid, her friend and confidante, and she had been all these things to her before that. At almost sixty years old she was still slender and elegantly erect, her dark hair beneath the white lace cap threaded with silver. A worried shadow darkened her grey eyes as she waited for Edwina, her hands clasped at her waist.

'I am so happy—happy and relieved that you've come home. I shudder to think what your poor mother would have made of all this.'

'If she were still alive, Maggie, I would never have run away. None of this would have happened.'

'No, maybe not. Thank God you are safe—and that is how it must stay. You poor child,' she said emotionally, enfolding Edwina in a tight embrace before holding her at arm's length. 'How have you been?'

'I could have fared worse, I suppose.' The warmth and love in Maggie's words brought tears to Edwina's eyes. She dearly loved her elderly maid, and she was deeply mortified by the thought of what Maggie must have gone through on her behalf. She had deserved better than the scribbled note telling her not to worry that Edwina had left on her dressing table when she had departed Oakwood Hall. 'It was an experience. I am none the worse for it.'

'Well, I thank God you're home. I've missed you. I've thought and worried about you all the time.'

'I'm sorry, Maggie,' Edwina said guiltily, giving her a warm hug. 'It was thoughtless of me to run off like that. But you, more than anyone, should know why I had to.'

Maggie's face hardened as her mind filled with the memories of the wretched tears Edwina had shed in her misery before she had disappeared. The pressure put on her by her uncle to wed Silas Clifford had affected her visibly. She had shunned all social functions, growing tense and pale. Maggie wished she'd had the courage to face Sir Henry on Edwina's behalf, but it would have served no purpose and she might have found herself out on her ear. And then where would Edwina be without her?

'Aye, I do that—and there's none can blame you. But you have been away so long. I hope you are not going away again.'

'No. There is much for Uncle Henry and I to discuss. I know the Earl of Taplow is dead, Maggie, so I don't feel threatened from that direction any more, thank goodness.' Removing her bonnet, she wandered about the room, happy to see that nothing had changed.

Frowning, Maggie watched her intently. 'You look different, Edwina. I saw the change in you the moment you entered the room.'

'Yes, I have changed.' She sank on to the stool in front of her dressing table and looked at the serious face looking back at her from the mirror. 'A lot has happened to me Maggie— some things not so pleasant. I am my own person now. I will no longer be told what I must and must not do by anyone— especially not by Uncle Henry.'

'Despite his harshness, Edwina, I know your uncle will be relieved to have you home. He's been most anxious about you—about your whereabouts. He's had people scouring the whole county and beyond in an attempt to find you. He's been quite beside himself with worry.'

Edwina's lips curved in a grim smile. 'Has he? You wouldn't think so by his greeting.'

'Nevertheless, where have you been? We were beginning to think you would never come back and that something dreadful might have befallen you.'

Edwina's eyes hardened and she was unable to conceal the anger that still burned inside her against Adam. 'I had no intention of coming back, Maggie. I had every intention of going to France to seek out my mother's people—until a certain gentleman of my acquaintance forced me back here when he discovered who I am.' Edwina told Maggie about her meeting with Adam, about the painting and the Royal Academy and staying at his house, and how he had forced her to return to Oakwood Hall.

'Oh, I see. That's interesting,' Maggie said, watching her questioningly. 'That explains it.'

Edwina met Maggie's eyes in the mirror. 'Explains what?'

'That the gentleman you speak of—who, as I remember, was here at Oakwood Hall calling on Sir Henry just the other day—must be responsible for the change in you. Living in his house and being with him every day—you must have become close—emotionally involved.'

'He—he is different from any man I have ever known, Maggie—but I am aware of the sort of man he is.'

She became silent as she fiercely struggled against her emotions and tried to banish the images of their shared night of passion, but it was difficult. They paraded across her mind, cruelly taunting her, tormenting her with vivid scenes of a mindless, besotted girl who had thought she was in love. She had been a fool, easy prey for his lusts, she thought bitterly. How nauseating it all seemed to her now. Focusing her gaze on the face in the mirror, she watched it harden as she coldly rejected the memory

'Adam Rycroft has a way with women, that's certain,' she went on, unable to conceal her bitterness and the hurt he had caused her from Maggie, 'with his easy arrogant charm, and his assumption that every female who comes near him will succumb to his smile.'

Maggie looked anxiously at her flushed face, sensing the torrent of conflicting emotions battling against each other inside her. 'And did you?'

'Did I what?'

'Why, become a victim of this philanderer?'

'Yes,' she confessed quietly. 'I did. But he should never have made me come back.'

'Haven't you stopped to think that he might have been be-having in your best interests—that he might care about you, very much?'

'Well, if he does, he certainly has a peculiar way of show-ing it,' Edwina retorted heatedly. Getting up, she leaned against the bedpost with her arms folded across her chest. Ever since that awful moment when Adam had firmly told her he was taking her home, she had tried to find excuses for his actions, tried to forgive his betrayal, but to no avail. Although blunted, her hatred remained as strong as the love she wanted so much to deny.

A dark scowl puckered her brow as she declared, 'I now know him for what he is—a bully and a beast. So you see, Maggie, why I never wish to set eyes on that particular gen-tleman again.'

Maggie turned away, smiling inwardly. 'No, I'm afraid I don't. I'm not convinced.'

After a short discussion with Sir Henry, Adam left the house without seeing Edwina. Climbing into the coach, he in-structed the coachman to take him to Taplow Court.

In answer to her uncle's summons that she present herself in the dining room, Edwina went downstairs. The anger that had engulfed her earlier was not in evidence. The young woman who entered the dining room was cool, self-assured and determined.

Her uncle was standing at the window, looking out with his hands clasped behind his back. Deep in thought, he only half-turned when she entered, as though it pained him to look at her. His manner was cool, and Edwina was certain his manner would be characteristically disagreeable.

'Well? I trust you found everything in your room as you left it?'

'Yes—thank you.' Edwina moved closer towards the still figure. 'What did Adam tell you, Uncle?'

'Not much.' What he said was true. Adam Rycroft was of the opinion that it was up to Edwina to give him an account of what she had been up to since leaving home. However, the man had astounded him by informing him he had developed a *tendre* for Edwina, and had calmly made an offer for her hand in marriage, generously declining any dowry—but stressing that she know nothing of this. Henry had considered the possibilities. Naturally Edwina's strong aversion to Adam's predecessor was uppermost in his mind, but having no desire to make an enemy of the new earl, with a satisfied nod he'd given his permission.

Rycroft had then extracted a promise from him not to tell Edwina he had inherited Taplow Court until he'd been given the opportunity to do so himself, pointing out that she had quite enough to contend with at present. Henry had agreed, although he thought the request most peculiar.

Henry turned and looked at her, and Edwina felt the full force of his unwavering, disapproving stare focused on her hair. Seeing her without her bonnet, he opened his eyes wide with horror at her cropped hair, still rather short, though considerably longer than when Adam had found her in St Giles.

'Good Lord! What the devil have you done to your hair?'

Edwina lightly fingered the copper and gold curls. 'I found myself in a situation where it was necessary for me to cut it off.'

'Why, it looks most unfeminine. What you got up to when you left here I cannot begin to imagine, and I can only hope that your behaviour was discreet. The fact that you ran away is known only to those in this house—and Silas Clifford. Everyone else believes you to be away staying with friends in the west country. Please God don't let it be discovered you've been running wild. I have no wish to see your name bandied about in the gutter press.'

'Neither have I, Uncle,' she replied drily.

'Adam Rycroft tells me he came upon you at a friend's house, and that you agreed to pose for a painting, which is now complete. He also informed me that with my permission it is shortly to be exhibited at the Royal Academy.'

Slowly moving over the thick piled carpet, Edwina trailed her fingers over the highly polished table top, her gaze wandering over familiar objects in the room. 'Did he? And have you given your permission, Uncle?'

He nodded. 'I have, though I was reluctant to do so. I was appalled to learn that you have spent your months of absence posing on an artist's couch, and the mere idea that a painting of my niece is about to be subjected to scrutiny galls me.'

Her uncle's biased, almost pious viewpoint caused a look of veiled amusement to cross Edwina's face for a split second. Almost instantly the expression was bland once more. 'I am surprised to hear that, considering the amount of time you spend gazing at them yourself. I am not ashamed of posing for the painting, Uncle. In fact, it's rather splendid.'

'Sarcasm does not become you, Edwina,' he reproached sternly. On a gentler note he said, 'You have clearly spent a great deal of time with Adam Rycroft. What is your opinion of him? Does he impress you?'

Edwina was looking out of the window at the lawns that sloped away from the terrace. She could feel her uncle's eyes watching her closely. As she tried to hide what she truly felt for that particular gentleman, she focused her gaze on a rather splendid cock pheasant strutting across the grass in pursuit of a hen. It put her in mind of Adam, and brought a wry smile to her lips. 'Adam Rycroft is an impressive person, Uncle. However, I find him autocratic, dictatorial, conceited and too good looking for his own good, if you must know. Why do you ask?'

'I am merely interested to know what you think of him. I have not known him long, but my own opinion of him is quite different from yours. He is a man of importance and considerable wealth—respected too, and reputed to be a fine artist, although I am not familiar with his work as yet, and I shall make a point of travelling to the Royal Academy to view his painting of you. He also strikes me as being a man who adheres to reason and fair play.'

'Goodness! You make him sound too good to be true, Uncle—a man without fault, in fact.'

Henry scowled darkly at his niece, ignoring her irony. 'I'm sure he has many faults, Edwina. No one is perfect.' He fell silent, fixing her with a level gaze, 'Now, as for this business of running away, I await your explanation. What became of you after you left here? What had you in mind?'

'I remembered Mother telling me she had relatives in France—in Lyons. My intention was to find them—to make a new life for myself. Unfortunately my money was stolen before I reached London, which meant I either had to return home or seek employment. I chose the latter.'

'Employment?' He regarded her ominously and his jaw tightened. 'What kind of employment? he demanded. 'Respectable, I trust?'

'It—it was shop work—a milliner's,' she said, averting her eyes so he would not see the lie. Nothing would induce her to tell him about her meeting with Jack and her role as a thief. The shame of it ran deep. 'Later I met Adam. When he asked if he could paint me and offered me a monumental sum of money if I would, I agreed. He had no idea of my true identity until earlier today—at which he behaved most oddly, and insisted on bringing me back here.'

'I am delighted that the gentleman was so sensible. Would you have told him who you were had you known the two of us were acquainted?'

'No.'

'That is what I thought. When I became your guardian I thought you had obtained sufficient maturity to know that a young woman must do as her guardian bids, that she should abide by his wishes, but I can see you're as troublesome and headstrong as ever.'

'I don't mean to be. I have always done my duty. Father always told me to do what is fit and right, but marrying Silas Clifford did not serve in my best interests. I know you wanted the marriage very badly, and you went to great lengths to point out how honoured and grateful I should be to receive such an offer, that it was an immense opportunity, and in your opinion I could never be entirely happy if I threw it away.'

'I put your objections down to your youth and inexperience. In my opinion, at the time, you were a fool to refuse him.'

Her eyes flashed angrily. 'Then a fool I would rather be, Uncle, and a happy fool, than married to an odious, unprincipled old man I could not abide. At the time my wishes counted for nothing. Clearly you were hoping I would come to my senses and my attitude would change when I realised you were set upon the union. Your refusal to listen to what I had to say was one of the reasons why I ran away. I could not fight both you and the Earl. I felt no sorrow or regret when I learned of his demise, only profound relief. What was his reaction when he discovered I had run away?'

'He was furious. As soon as he learned of your disappearance he would have set off after you himself. However, he suffered an apoplexy and never recovered.'

'No doubt brought on by his rage at being thwarted by a mere girl,' Edwina retorted without remorse.

'As it turns out, had you wed him the marriage would have been of short duration and you would now be an extremely wealthy young woman and a countess,' Henry pointed out sharply. 'You should have realised that I am your wisest counsellor, Edwina. Clearly you needed my guidance. You should have listened to me. That you could take care of yourself, I was always sure of. What worried me was your defiance.

When you ran away you overruled my authority, an authority vested in me by your father. When he died I made many sacrifices on your behalf, and not once did I hear or see you show your gratitude. I have been grossly and consistently insulted by what I consider to be your irresponsible and dishonourable actions.'

'Father made you my guardian, believing he could not be leaving me in better hands. Sadly he was mistaken. Honour means keeping faith with your family and your house. You showed precious little of that towards me or my father's memory,' Edwina declared bitterly.

'Speaking of your father reminds me that there is something that has to be cleared up between us.'

He paused to collect his thoughts and marshal the facts. Secretly he'd dreaded this moment when he would have to bring the matter that was uppermost in both their minds into the open—the matter that was a like a gaping wound in his side. He approached the table where Edwina stood and cleared his throat sharply. It was apparent to her that he had something on his mind, but a long moment of silence passed between them before he came to the point.

'I—understand that one of the reasons why you ran away was because you thought I killed your father—my brother.'

'Yes,' she answered, seeing no reason to deny it any longer. 'I did.'

'Do you still think that?'

'I don't know any more. I no longer feel entirely right—I don't feel wrong, either. Your behaviour was most peculiar at the time, as I recall. You wouldn't talk to me. You wouldn't tell me what had really happened on the road that day. Despite your claim that you were set upon by thieves on your way to Taplow Court, nothing was taken from you and you were left unharmed. When I questioned you, you became so angry, so secretive.'

'It was to protect you.'

'From what, Uncle? The truth? Tell me. Did you see Silas Clifford that day?'

His eyes hardened with remembrance. 'Yes,' he replied without preamble. 'He rode from Taplow Court to meet us.'

'Oh, my God!' Edwina said in a low, explosive voice as the truth hit her. Shocked to the depths of her being, she stared blankly at him. 'It was Silas who killed him, wasn't it? Was that the reason why you were so secretive?'

'Yes. While he was alive it was a great burden for me to bear, but now I can tell you the truth.'

Chapter Eleven

Edwina stood quite still as the pain of her father's death hit her anew. The idea that her uncle had kept this to himself all this time was as unspeakable as the moment when she had accused him in her mind of killing his brother, her father. 'But why did he kill him? For what reason?'

Henry bowed his head. In the face of her coldness, her anger, he felt something akin to helplessness, which made him feel old in an instant. Several months of fending for herself had brought Edwina's dominant personality to the surface. He was no longer a guardian berating a naughty child, but an adult trying to reason with another adult.

'Silas tried making a bargain with Gordon. You were a part of that bargain even then. Gordon refused to consider his offer of marriage to you in exchange for the repayment of what he owed. He would have none of it.'

'You mean—the Earl had already approached Father about me? He didn't tell me,' she whispered, upset to learn this. 'So—when he refused, Silas Clifford killed him. Is that what happened?'

'Something to that effect. Angry words were exchanged. Silas was livid, demented. Gordon scorned him, mocked him.'

His expression became grim. 'Men of Silas Clifford's position do not stand for that treatment from anyone—especially not from a man who owes him a considerable sum of money. He drew a knife. His thrust was unexpected and swift. It was over in a flash. I couldn't help my brother—though I tried. I did try.'

Edwina listened to him with a feeling of outrage and disbelief. Pain clouded his eyes and his voice was touched with remorse, but in her anger she ignored it. 'The man was a monster,' she whispered. 'It was a truly courageous thing my father did. But you disagreed with his decision. That was what you were arguing about that day, wasn't it—before you left for Taplow Court? You wanted me to wed Silas Clifford even then.'

'Gordon was prepared to risk being locked up in a debtors' prison rather than give you to Silas Clifford in marriage.'

'My poor father. It was a pity you didn't show me the same consideration, Uncle,' she said scornfully. 'Your idea of loyalty is strange, to say the least. Despite what had happened you found a way of increasing your fortunes by selling me off to your brother's murderer, and you didn't care about the outcome.' Her lips turned in contempt. 'What you tried to do was despicable.' She turned away and closed her eyes as she felt the complex web of anger, betrayal and antagonism ride over her.

Her animosity, combined with resentment, brought an angry outburst from Henry. 'Had your father been *considerate,* he would not have gambled away his substantial inheritance and mortgaged the estate,' he pointed out irately. 'As the younger son I inherited little, as you well know, yet I still managed by dint of work and frugality—eschewing the glamorous temptations of Society and excess of any kind—to get by. After all my sacrifices and to my everlasting bitterness, when Gordon died, as his heir, I found fate had contrived to cheat me and I was left to clean up the mess of a reckless, wastrel brother and found myself with a thankless, disobedient niece on my hands.'

'A niece you would go to any lengths to get *off* your hands, apparently,' Edwina bit back, uncaring how deeply her words wounded him, and unaware just how much he regretted his actions.

A silence charged with emotion stretched between them. Edwina had never understood her uncle, but in her heart she comprehended the cause of his bitterness and empathised with it. And to be fair to him, had he been the elder son, he would have been a better manager of the Oakwood estate than her father ever was.

Struggling to keep calm, she said, 'Perhaps you would tell me why, if the Earl of Taplow killed my father, he was not apprehended and made to pay for his crime? He was responsible. It was only right that he was brought to task. He should have been hanged for what he did. Were there any witnesses beside yourself who could testify? A groom, perhaps?'

'There was no one. He was alone.'

'Then why did you not speak out? Why did you not hand him over to the authorities, which is what most men would have done? You were my father's brother, for heaven's sake!' she cried in a shaking voice. 'How could you stand by and let Silas Clifford get away with murder—and then, to add insult to injury, try to force me to wed him as if nothing untoward had happened?'

Her uncle stiffened and then seemed to age. With a ragged sigh he lowered his head. 'I did not act in good faith, I know that.' His voice was heavy as his niece's clear blue-green eyes sought his and held his stare for a moment. He looked away first. 'You must understand that this is difficult for me. You are right to be angry. I realised why you rejected Silas Clifford so vehemently, why you left. But in the beginning—before that tragic incident—when Gordon told me of his offer, I accused him of being a fool to reject it.'

'I know that, but what I cannot understand is why, after he murdered my father, you persisted.' She looked at him pointedly. 'Uncle, were you afraid of him?'

He tensed and for a moment she thought he would deny it. 'Yes, I was afraid,' he answered. The burden, the lingering guilt of keeping the brutal circumstances of his brother's murder for all these long months secret, suddenly made him feel drained and empty. 'Silas Clifford was powerful, a man of influence. No one dared oppose him. His very presence at Taplow Court was a threat. In his own cold, fiendish way he demanded my silence. I was left in no doubt that if I so much as breathed a word about what he had done, I would suffer Gordon's fate.'

'And no doubt in return for your silence he gave you a substantial sum,' Edwina accused scathingly, mercilessly—unjustly, she realised, but taking refuge in anger was the only way she had of dealing with the pain that was tearing at her heart. 'Did he bribe you—pay you off to keep you from spreading what would have become a terrible scandal and the ultimate punishment to himself?'

Henry paled. 'No, he did not.'

Edwina's anger vanished, the sudden spurt of antagonism gone. 'No man is beyond the law,' she said on a gentler note, thinking how old her uncle look suddenly, how the brightness in his eyes had dimmed and his shoulders stooped. 'It was quite wrong of you to shield him.'

'I know. It was a mistake,' he admitted. 'One I regret. But I always knew that because of who he was, without evidence a jury would have found him not guilty, his innocence vindicated.'

'So,' she said quietly and with a deep feeling of regret, 'my father's murderer has gone unpunished.'

Henry regarded her calmly. 'I'm afraid so. Now he's dead there's no point in pursuing it. It would bring a great deal of embarrassment to his successor, and don't forget he saved Gordon the indignity of being sent to prison by loaning him the money in the first place.'

'You're right. It's done with. But the loan remains unpaid.'

'No. It is settled. The new Earl of Taplow, Silas's cousin, came to see me to discuss the matter. We came to an—arrangement.'

'I see. What's he like? Is he anything like his cousin?'

'Nothing like him. He's tall, good looking—a bachelor. I have no doubt you'll meet him very soon. Edwina, if I could undo what I did, I swear I would do it. Do you think some day you will be able to forgive me?'

She studied him. The coldness, the aloofness that antagonised people had vanished, and in its place… For the first time, there was warmth and human emotion. But did he really think he could atone for his complicity in the murder of her father by saying he was sorry? She answered him honestly. 'I don't know. All things considered, it will be difficult—but I will try.'

He nodded, a little reassured by her answer. 'I ask no more than that.'

When Edwina had left to change for dinner, as he stared at the closed door Henry wondered how she would take it when the identity of the new Earl of Taplow was revealed to her, and that, like his predecessor, he fully intended to wed her. If her manner towards Adam Rycroft was an indication of how she felt about him—and he had not missed the furious look she had thrown at him, as if she loathed the very air he breathed—then he suspected she was about to have a battle royal on her hands.

But, he thought, a hard glitter lightening his eyes, he was confident that he could rely on Adam Rycroft to change her mind, and no matter what happened he would not interfere this time. The decision was Edwina's to make regarding their new neighbour.

Edwina slowed her first wild gallop to a walk when she entered the woods and followed a well-beaten track. It was a route she had taken many times before. She loved the seclusion of the trees and the darkness. The air was cold and sharp. Skirting old trees that had fallen, rotting, across her path, she breathed deeply of the full rich scent of decay, laughing when out of the silence she was startled when a pheasant crashed out of the undergrowth, and at the sight of her flew off into the trees.

Plunging into the icy waters of a stream, she guided her horse across as it picked its way over the slippery stones, and she could feel the chill striking up from the wet boulders. On the other side the path was soft with leaf mould, and gradually the trees began to thin out.

On the edge of the wood she reined in her horse in the shadow of a holly tree, its glossy leaves almost black in the dull light, its berries shocking in their abundance. In the distance on its hill stood Taplow Court. It resembled a sleeping giant beneath the dark clouds, heavy with rain, which hung over it. She realised she had ridden further than she'd intended and must turn back. Leaning forward, she stroked the mare's neck.

'You and I fly like the wind,' she whispered, laughing quietly when the horse pricked her ears and whinnied softly at the sound of her voice.

Horses had been a part of Edwina's life ever since she could remember, and Dancer, a strong and meek-eyed submissive dappled-grey mare, had been given to her by her father on her fifteenth birthday. Her habit spattered with mud thrown up by the thundering hooves, her spirits high, she was buoyed up with a sense of freedom. Her face aglow, her heart pounding, she was more at ease than she had been in at any time during the week she had been back at Oakwood Hall. Despite her difficult confrontation with her uncle on her arrival, things had settled down to an uneasy peace between them.

Lulled by the quiet all around her, as so often happened her thoughts turned to Adam. He hadn't called to see her as he had said he would, and, despite her harsh words when they had parted, she was disappointed that he hadn't. A part of her still burned with fury when she thought of him, but another part acknowledged her continuing love for him. A week ago she had hated him for causes she had thought were justified—but that didn't stop her missing him. Giving in to her thoughts, she allowed her mind to dwell on him, which took the sting out of her by slow degrees.

She felt the stabilising force of her anger disappearing and it left her prey to the gentler emotions. She'd missed him more than she would have believed possible. She missed his company, his laughter, his quiet strength, their differences, their loving; her love, that all-consuming, dangerous emotion, still nestled close to her heart. Closing her eyes, she saw again the deep blue eyes with their eternal watchfulness, the handsome, disdainful mouth that could smile with such bewitching charm, the thick dark hair and perfect features. The picture was so vivid that when she opened her eyes they misted with tears.

In the cool leafiness of the trees she sighed and gazed ahead at the house that, had she married Silas, would have been her home. Awesome and ancient it sat atop its hill like some hideous black beast. It was a towering edifice, its many chimneys and roofs pointing upward with a vengeance. In all her life she had never been closer to Taplow Court than she was now, and she'd never had any desire to be. But this time, as she was about to turn away, her curiosity got the better of her, and, gathering up the reins, she urged Dancer forward along the winding road that ran past the bottom of the long, upward sweeping drive.

When she reached the tall, wrought-iron gates she stopped, deciding that she had come far enough and having no wish to go any further. Suddenly it began to rain, sharp and fast, and she guided her horse to the side of the road beneath the trees on the edge of the wood, their branches thick and shielding.

She looked behind her into the quiet world of shifting shadows. It was dark and unnaturally silent, the trees close together, their shadows creeping nearer. Suddenly she became tense, every sense alert. She felt that she was not alone, that she was being watched. Her eyes pierced the darkness of the wood. It seemed deserted. Nothing moved. She jumped when a chittering squirrel scampered up a tree and disappeared. The feeling of being watched became stronger and she felt the hairs on the back of her neck prickling. She could feel danger in the air like a lightning charge, and she harshly reproached herself for riding out alone. She should have known better.

Keeping her movements as natural as possible, she urged Dancer away from the trees. The feeling of an unseen presence was overpowering now. She could feel eyes on her from somewhere in the shifting shadows. She felt the perspiration cold between her shoulder blades as she stared, white-faced, at an ancient oak, its trunk gnarled and broad enough to conceal a regiment of soldiers. Unconsciously she held her breath. Although never of a nervous disposition, she felt her heart begin to race as she watched a tall, lumbering figure swathed in a black cloak step out. Another man appeared behind him and remained where he was as the other moved closer.

When she recognised Jack Pierce her whole being shrank, not with surprise, but an unpleasant sensation more akin to revulsion. She saw the familiar heavy features, set in an expression of perpetual brutal determination, the deep-set, glittering black eyes under bushy brows, the powerful body, and the same misshapen tall black hat with the crow's feather shoved into its brim. How could he be here, so far from London? Had he followed her? And, if so, how had he discovered her secret?

'So, my flyaway bird has come to roost at Taplow. Good afternoon, Ed—or should I call you Edwina? With all my sense and cunning it's not often I'm fooled, but you succeeded. It beats anything I could have believed. What a pretty little lady you've turned out to be,' Jack sneered, giving her a mock bow and smiling that wolfish smile that Edwina had come to hate.

Edwina watched him come closer, positioning himself in her path to prevent her escape. She was discovering that, now she was face to face with him, the vague terrors that had haunted her ever since she had escaped from his clutches had melted away. It was the first time she had been alone with him since that terrible night he had struck her. So many things had changed. Then, she had been a helpless victim in the hands of a brutal and unscrupulous man. Today she had the strength and backing of her uncle and Adam Rycroft. However, she felt intuitively that Jack's sudden appearance boded danger for her, but, despite the small tremor of fear, she managed to stay calm.

'You're a long way from London, Jack.'

'I thought I'd pay my respects—seeing as I was in the neighbourhood.' His voice was mocking, and the eyes that rested on Edwina were as hard as stone.

'You've been watching me?'

'I know where you live, where you go and who with, so, you see, you cannot escape me. I knew if I bided my time you'd show yourself sooner or later. I swore I'd find you and make you sorry you ran from me, but when I found out who you were and realised what it could mean for me, I couldn't believe my good fortune.'

'Please go away and leave me alone. Circumstances drove me to do what I did and now it is over. I am amazed that you should dare to approach me now. I could have you arrested. What is to prevent me?' Jack only laughed, a mirthless, hollow sound, and Edwina felt the cold pricking on her skin.

'Yourself. For one thing, it would do you no good, and, for another, you will have no desire to have me locked up when you hear what I have to say. You and I have some unfinished business. You are compelled to endure my company whether you like it or not.'

Edwina stiffened, fighting off a creeping fear. He seemed so confident, so sure of himself. 'Then say what you have to say and be gone. I no longer work for you. It's over.'

His low laugh was a terrible sound. 'Is that what you think? It's hardly begun.'

Edwina felt the weight of his threat pressing down on her. 'What are you saying?'

Almost leisurely Jack turned his back on her and feasted his eyes on Taplow Court. A prolonged silence ensued, and then he said, 'Grotesque-looking house, don't you think—yet it's stuffed from wall to wall with priceless treasures that could make me a rich man and never want for more.'

Edwina stared at him when he turned back to her. 'Jack!' she gasped incredulously. 'You're not thinking of robbing Taplow Court? I always knew you were involved in house-breaking—but never on this scale. It would be madness.'

'I disagree. With the aid of my accomplice nothing could be simpler. What could be better than having someone assist me on the inside?'

Realising she was the someone he was referring to, she gaped at him incredulously. 'Accomplice? Me? Oh, no, Jack. If you expect me to be a party to your dirty scheme, then you are very much mistaken.'

His smile was evil, his sunken eyes glittering like twin pieces of black coal, piercing and cold. 'I have thought about it. When I discovered you were not the lad you pretended to be, I asked myself, why would a respectable young woman pose as a lad—unless, of course, there was something she wished to hide? Imagine the scandal should it come out where you've been holed up, and what you've been up to for the past months. Picking pockets is hardly a respectable occupation for a gently reared young lady now, is it? A young lady who mixes with the best, who wears feathers in her bonnet and rides a fine horse,' he scoffed.

Edwina drew herself up, her green eyes blazing in her bloodless face. 'You forget that it was a filthy thirteen-year-old lad you forced to steal for you, not a gently reared eighteen-year-old young woman. No one would believe you. Do you think I care what you might do? You can scatter your tales about the entire county for all I care. Do as you please and see where it gets you, but go. I never want to see you again.'

Jack had stopped smiling. His hand reached out and gripped the bridle as Dancer shifted nervously. 'Those are brave words you speak, little lady, but you will never escape me. I can see I'm going to have to teach you obedience all over again. I think your escape from me has gone to your head.'

'I'm not afraid of you, Jack Pierce.'

'You should be,' he countered on a note of hard mockery. Were this the lad Ed brazenly defying him, he would already have dragged him off the horse and given him the pounding he deserved, but, faced with this poised, confident young woman, whose cold hatred seemed to emanate from her person and permeate the very air around him, he restrained himself. 'Knowing your impulsiveness and your passion for disappearing without trace, I've taken additional precautions.'

Edwina eyed him warily, feeling a *frisson* of alarm. 'Precautions? What are you talking about?'

He laughed humourlessly. 'Come now. You are intelligent—which was the thing that always struck me about you. You always were a clever lad, the sharpest in my employ. Surely I don't have to spell it out for you. The precautions I speak of are in the person of another lad—a crippled lad who answers to the name of Toby Clifford.'

Edwina's heart missed a beat and she found herself suddenly at a loss for air. 'Toby?' she gasped.

'The same.'

'You've found him?' Her voice was even despite the sudden pounding of her heart.

He nodded. 'In Wapping—holed up in a stinking hovel with an old man and woman and a bear.'

So, Jack had succeeded where Adam had failed—or had he? Was this just a lie he was spinning to force her into helping him? 'How do I know you're not lying?'

Jack's stare was piercing. 'I have proof. 'Tis a most moving story the lad tells of his dead mother, and how his Uncle Silas gave him to some passing tinkers. Brought me near to tears, it did. How else would I know that unless the lad told he himself?'

Edwina believed him. 'Then you must release him. This has nothing to do with the boy.'

'On the contrary, it has a good deal to do with him. Come, now, even you can't be that naïve. You should know I'm not a man to start a game without several trumps in my hand.'

Knowing how cruel and unscrupulous Jack could be, Edwina feared for Toby. Despite Jack's bland expression, his eyes had the cold steadiness of the fanatic. 'You don't know what you're up against. If you dare harm that boy, Adam Rycroft will kill you. Of that you can be sure. Where is he?'

'In the tender care of friends,' he informed her with a sneer. 'Let's say I'm offering the lad my protection. And just in case you have a mind to inform Rycroft, I have him well protected. No one who values his life ventures into my domain.'

'You'll never get away with it,' Edwina said breathlessly. 'You haven't a hope.'

His eyes narrowed and his nostrils flared. 'You'd better hope we do, lady. Unless you do as I say, the lad is as good as dead and you will know no peace, day or night. I have ways to convince you.' He tipped his head sideways and smiled lazily. 'A face such as yours does not fare well under the knife.'

Edwina paled, shuddering at the callow crudeness of his threat. 'Don't threaten me.'

He shrugged his shoulders. 'I would not like to frighten you. I am more than willing to soothe your fears.'

She slowly arched a brow. 'Aye, Jack Pierce, at a cost,' she hissed with open mockery.

'Remember the lad's life depends on it.'

At a loss to know how to obtain Toby's freedom without becoming involved in his vile scheme, Edwina looked at him in desperation. 'Please don't do this, Jack. Please let him go.'

'You'll get no favours from me,' he snarled, 'until the job's done. Don't you dare fail me.' Jack didn't flinch before the cold fury that flared in her glittering green eyes; the pallor of her face, and the anguish, so clearly written there, had no effect on him. 'If Rycroft wishes to see the lad alive, you will do as I say—but I warn you, if you leak any of this to his lordship and he starts poking his nose into my affairs, the only thing he will find will be a corpse.' He issued his vicious threat with all the desperate ferocity that his cruel nature was capable of.

Edwina felt sick. 'You would kill a boy?'

'Why not? On the other hand, if you behave sensibly and assist me in my new venture of stripping Taplow Court of some of its treasures, then I promise to restore the lad to you unharmed.'

'So you say, but my own nature is less trusting. Do you expect me to believe the word of a—?'

'Thief,' he finished for her. 'It seems you have no choice.' He laughed softly. 'I see you cherish some prejudice against me, lady. I cannot for the life of me suppose what has put it into your head,' he jeered sarcastically. 'When I've made my plans you will assist me in gaining entry into that grand house. My informants tell me there's something going on between you and the Earl. So, if you play your cards right, as the future Countess of Taplow it shouldn't be difficult.'

Edwina sat up straight in the saddle and glared at him with something akin to victory lighting her eyes. 'It cannot be done. I cannot help you. You see, I no longer have the right to enter Taplow Court. The Earl of Taplow, whom I might have wed, is dead.'

'I'm not stupid,' Jack growled angrily. 'Do you think I don't know that? I'm not talking about Silas Clifford.'

'Then who?'

'His successor—the rich and influential and highly talented Adam Rycroft.'

It took a moment for his words to penetrate Edwina's mind, and then she stared at him aghast and speechless, through eyes huge with horror and disbelief, feeling her whole world tilt sideways. 'Adam? The Earl of Taplow? I've never heard anything so preposterous.'

Jack regarded her sourly. 'Come as a surprise, has it?' he growled.

'You're lying.' As she uttered the words she knew it was true. With sudden, heartbreaking clarity, all the pieces of the gruesome picture fell into place. What a fool she had been. Adam had told her he had a house outside London; because he was acquainted with her uncle, she suspected it might be somewhere in the neighbourhood. But not for one moment had she suspected it would be Taplow Court. Never in a hundred years would she have thought that.

Jack shrugged with complete indifference. It mattered not one iota to him what was going on between his young pickpocket and the powerful Earl of Taplow, his main concern was getting the job done. 'Lying, am I? Ask him.' He backed away. 'I'll find you and tell you what to do when I've made my plans, but remember—keep your mouth shut.'

'I hate you,' Edwina said with quiet loathing. 'How I hate you.'

He gave her an ugly, twisted smile before turning away. 'That doesn't disturb me. I'll let you know when I decide to act. I can wait. Sometimes a man profits from biding his time.'

Jack and his accomplice were gone before Edwina could recover enough to reply. She felt an iron band tighten suddenly around her head and there was a taste of ashes in her mouth. As she attempted to check her mounting fury, her fingers, encased in soft black-kid riding gloves, gripped the reins. Adam Rycroft was a devil, a monster. How could she have allowed herself to be so deceived? The truth did not comfort her. It seared like acid, offering nothing to replace the illusion it demolished. She understood it all now. Her whole life was in ruins.

Chapter Twelve

Edwina remained in that wet, dripping world for quite some time as she tried to absorb what Jack had told her and what it was he required of her, placing her in an impossible predicament. She had no intention of helping him in his nefarious scheme, refusing to even contemplate falling in with his plan, but she could not ignore his threats. They had been real. He was a brute and driven by greed, and Toby was as good as dead if she opened her mouth. Anxious for his safety, for his sake she must remain silent, but the thought of that poor crippled boy being held captive in some stinking hovel by Jack tore at her heart. Somehow she must find a way of setting him free, but what could she do? The strain of it all had already begun to weigh heavy on her.

Suddenly her attention was drawn to the sound of horses' hoofs coming from further along the road. Two horsemen appeared and were riding towards her, each shrouded in heavy black cloaks. Afraid that it might be Jack and his companion returning, she drew further back into the shelter of the trees, the raindrops drumming on the leaves. The trunks and the ground all around her glistened with moisture.

It was only when they drew closer that Edwina's gaze became fixed upon the taller of the two men. Her body stiffened. Even with his hat pulled down to shield his face from the now driving rain, Adam Rycroft would be unmistakable anywhere. His companion was also familiar to her; when she recognised William Hewitt, who was the bailiff at Taplow Court, everything Jack had told her was confirmed.

She watched them ride along the road towards her and turn in at the drive leading up to Taplow Court. As if sensing her presence, the two men paused and looked back. In her anger her first instinct was to turn and ride away. It might have been possible if they had not seen her, but both men were looking at her fixedly. Adam said something to his companion, who continued on up the hill. Slowly Adam rode towards her.

Halting in front of her, those deep blue eyes commanded all her attention, and his lean, hard face bore no hint of humour. 'Edwina! We seem destined to meet in the most unusual places, do we not? But what the devil are you doing out in this downpour—and without a groom?' he rebuked harshly, trying to ignore the fact that her eyes were hurling scornful daggers at him.

She gave him an austere smile, pushing the ermine-trimmed hood of her dark blue cloak back on her shoulders. He wouldn't understand the strange need to be alone that had come upon her quite suddenly, as it often did, and unthinking she had obeyed it. 'That is none of your business. However, I have a matter to settle with you.' Her tone was angry, and his brow raised at the seriousness of her manner.

'I thought you might.'

His offhand manner fuelled her anger, and she rushed into her argument headlong. 'How dare you berate me so unfairly for concealing my identity from you, while keeping your own from me—you—you arrogant hypocrite. I know who you are. You are the Earl of Taplow, owner of that noble dwelling there,' she flared with a flick of her hand at the offending edifice, while keeping her eyes locked on his. 'Of all the treacherous, underhand and conniving…' Her voice trembled and broke as she dragged air into her lungs through thick knots of emotion almost choking her. She looked away, blinking back her angry tears.

Reaching out, Adam tipped her chin round, forcing her rebellious eyes to meet his. 'I'm sorry you should think that,' he said with implacable calm. 'I don't mean to be any of those things, and I have most certainly not been conniving in any way. It would appear that you have set your verdict against me without giving me the opportunity to present my case. I admit to being the Earl of Taplow, my cousin's successor, and I will tell you that it is a position I neither sought nor wanted. My inheritance is unwelcome to me. I have never wanted Silas's titles and wealth.'

Jerking her head away, she glared at him. Pushed beyond the bounds of reason by his arrogant calm and the recollection of what she considered to be her own ill use at his hands, she ploughed on with all the ferocity of a hurricane.

'I don't believe you. Of all the men in the whole of London, I had the misfortune to meet you,' she fumed, with all the contempt she could summon. 'I ran away from one Earl of Taplow, only to fall into the hands of his successor—hounded by the first, used and made a trollop of by the second. Ha! It would be hilarious if it weren't so tragic. How it must have amused you playing your little games.'

'I played no games.'

'No? Then what was I—some tender morsel to entertain you on your couch while you painted me—a simple-minded wench to warm your bed after stealing my virtue? Tell me, Adam, did my performance—in your vast experience of women—bear the hallmark of a high-class whore? And, if so, what would a good whore earn in the time I was with you?'

Fury ignited perilously in Adam's eyes and his jaw clenched. 'Stop it, Edwina. Don't try me too far.'

'Try you too far? Dear God in heaven, don't speak to me of being tried. Discovering who you are is like applying fresh fire to a burn, but this time the fire is hotter, the burn deeper.

How could you be so cruel, so heartlessly selfish as to do something so unspeakably despicable? When were you going to tell me? You owe me that. Why did I have to wait to hear it from someone else?'

His eyes in the darkness beneath the trees were narrowed and glittering. 'So, your uncle told you?'

'He never said a word—damn him.' Her unrelenting distress was evident in her tone.

'I asked him not to. I wanted to do that myself.'

Tears blurred Edwina's vision, and she angrily wiped at the twin trails of wetness that coursed down her cheeks. 'I've saved you the trouble. I worked it out for myself just now, when I saw you turn in at the gates with William Hewitt, your cousin's bailiff.' She hated the lie, but in no way could she tell him of her encounter with Jack Pierce. 'When you told me you had a house out of town, why didn't you tell me it was this particular house?' she demanded, enduring the cold blast of his gaze. It dawned on her that he was striving for control of his anger.

'Why should I?' he answered irately. 'There was no reason to. At that point your identity was still unknown to me. Had I known who you were, I would most certainly have told you.'

'And dragged me back to Uncle Henry sooner.'

'Since you ask, yes, I would.' Panther quick, in one effortless motion Adam had dismounted and strode to her horse. Removing his hat and throwing it down, he ground out, 'Get down.'

'Certainly not,' she replied tightly, unwilling to relent, even though he did look as if he had murder in mind. With a toss of her head she gripped the reins, intending to ride off. 'It's raining and I want to go home.'

'I said get down. You and I have to talk.' When she made no move to obey, he snatched the reins from her hands, reached up and dragged her from the saddle, looming over her like some dark, ominous thundercloud.

Taking judicious note of the taut set of his jaw and seeing his expression had become positively savage, Edwina felt the first tendril of fear coil in the pit of her stomach and averted her eyes.

Taking her chin none too gently Adam turned her face to his. 'Look at me, Edwina,' he commanded coldly. 'Look good and hard.' Slowly she did so, meeting his blistering gaze, her chest heaving with indignation at his rough handling. 'I have always believed there is no point arguing with a closed mind, but in this instance I am left with no choice but to try. I am *not* Silas. Silas is dead, and I believe I have more reason than you to be thankful for that fact.' Enunciating what he said, his tone was bitter.

Edwina stared at him for a moment, her eyes on his. The implication of his words was mixed with something else, something immediately veiled. What reason did he have to hate Silas? What had Silas done to him?

'You speak as if I wronged you, and, if so, I apologise,' he went on after a moment's pause. 'But I don't think I need to remind you that we both decided to take our relationship a step further—unless, of course, I exerted more force on you than you understood at the time.'

A lump of nameless emotion constricted Edwina's throat. She swallowed hard. Despite her grievances, the memory of being in his arms was still vibrantly alive in her mind, and at the time what they had done had seemed harmless and irresistibly appealing. She shook her head finally and said, 'No. No, you didn't'

Adam's features relaxed. 'Thank you.'

'Although when you insisted on bringing me back, I hated you.'

'I'm beginning to hate myself,' he said quietly, his anger of a moment ago somewhat diminished. 'There are times when I have acted like a prize idiot. That was one of them. I'm not proud of myself. I should never have reacted so irrationally when I discovered who you were.'

For the past week Adam's mind had been occupied with the explanation he would have to make to Edwina regarding his identity, and how she would react when he asked her to be his wife. She must not think he wanted to marry her out of guilt for taking her virtue, for she was proud and her pride would make her oppose it. She was also stubborn, and if she discovered he had already discussed this with her uncle she would definitely oppose it even more.

The thought did cross his mind that she might want to get her own back for forcing her to return home, and so pretend she didn't want him, but that didn't concern him unduly. She wanted him, that he was sure of—as much as he wanted her.

'Apart from the short time when I knew you as the boy Ed, I saw you as nothing other than what you are—an incredibly beautiful young woman. My desire for you overwhelmed me. I wasn't prepared for you, Edwina. Every day you were within my sights, I saw you as a starving man craves food and drink. You were always so close, and so damned lovely, it became torture for me. I was soundly caught in a trap, my love.

'When I returned from Taplow Court and you told me you still intended going to France, I couldn't for the life of me let you go. I was afraid of losing you.' He cupped her chin, looking intently into her eyes. 'After that wonderful night of our loving, I only wanted you more. I did not want to say this to you yet—but I want to marry you, Edwina.'

Edwina's heart almost stopped beating. 'What?' she whispered.

'I want you to be my wife.'

She opened her mouth, but it was several seconds before any sound came out. 'I—I cannot.'

'Why?'

'Because of who you are. The harm Silas did is still too raw—and your own behaviour towards me of late cannot be ignored.'

'They are not sufficient excuses not to marry me. You are

allowing your pride and foolishness to get in the way of your true feelings, my love, and it is foolishness to spite yourself for the sake of pride,' he mocked while his eyes burned into her. 'So, you judge me by my cousin's crimes?'

'No, but you are of the same family. That is enough. If you feel honour bound to ask me because of what we did, you needn't. Please understand that I cannot marry you, Adam.'

'Because it was consummated before the fact, wedding me might be a necessity.' His reply was quiet and to the point.

The warmth in his tone brought the heat creeping into Edwina's cheeks, and she knew a feeling of panicked defeat that surpassed anything she had ever felt. The fact that she might be carrying his child was a constant worry to her. 'I know. It is hardly a good beginning for a marriage.'

'I didn't force you into my bed, Edwina. You were willing enough, and you gave me the impression of enjoying what we did. However, I won't press the issue. Not now. But I am determined, and I am convinced I shall win you in the end.' Her eyes were lowered, her long curling lashes lying like dark fans, casting shadows on her cheeks. His gaze moved down to her lips, soft and pink, lips that beckoned to be kissed. Adam well remembered the feel of them, and he knew he was going to kiss her. 'Edwina…'

She raised her eyes at the husky note in his voice and found herself gazing into the smouldering depths of his own, his firm, well-chiselled lips poised not far above hers. She gasped softly, knowing what was going to happen if she didn't stop it. 'No,' she whispered. Shaking her head slowly, she took a step back, but, as quick as he was strong, he caught her wrist and held her fast, bringing her full against his hardened frame. His mesmerising blue eyes held hers imprisoned as his lips formed a reply.

'Yes.'

His arms went round her, and Edwina could feel the resistance melting within her. A low moan of protest became stuck in her throat, stifled by the hard possessive kiss when his lips captured hers, parting, gently moving, his tongue possessively exploring each trembling curve. When her lips softened in response, Adam deepened his fiery kiss that warmed her to the core of her being, her resistance crumbling beneath the onslaught of his fervour. She was no longer innocent of the passion he was deliberately and skilfully arousing in her, reminding her of when he had been her lover, ardent and persuasive—wanting.

Clamped within his arms, Edwina could feel the strength and power centred within him. He held her in an unyielding vice, her soft breasts crushed against his chest as he slid one hand downward over her buttock, pressing her to him until she could not ignore the evidence of his burning passion. She was hungry for him, a physical yearning that she could not fight.

He tore his mouth from hers and lavished scorching kisses on her face, her eyes, her neck. 'If we don't stop now, you are going to drive me out of my mind, and I am in danger of throwing you down and repeating what I did to you in London,' he murmured thickly. But apart from a low moan Edwina couldn't answer. His lips had already recaptured hers, hungry and searching, and she was sinking beneath a sea of rapture.

When he finally released her, with her heart pounding chaotically she could only stare at him in wonder, her gaze melting at the raw tenderness she saw in his expression.

'So,' he murmured, 'it's still the same with you.'

Almost in a daze she nodded, unsmiling. 'I'm afraid it looks like it.'

'Then don't fight it. You belong to me, Edwina. From the first you have been mine, and you will be again. But come—it's stopped raining,' he said, stepping away from the temptation of her nearness. 'Before I lose control completely, I'd better take you home.'

'I agree, we should stop now.' A tremor of a smile curved her lips. 'I don't think I could withstand another full-fledged attack of your ardour. But you don't have to ride back with me.'

'Yes, I do. This isn't St Giles. You don't need me to remind you that it isn't done for young ladies to go careering about the countryside unaccompanied. The woods often harbour miscreants. That is why the niece of a baron and the future Countess of Taplow must always have an escort.'

Edwina did not respond to his teasing reference to the title he was so keen to bestow on her. It was an important matter, one she would have to consider seriously in the days ahead.

Having to ride in single file along the narrow path through the wood, above them the trees' thick canopies dripping water, they rode in silence. Perched on her horse, riding side-saddle, her cloak and the green velvet gown she wore beneath spread over her horse's glossy flanks, Edwina had never looked more beautiful to Adam. Watching from the back of his stallion, he viewed her with pride—her head erect, her fine features set, back and shoulders straight, and vibrant wisps of hair curling around the hood of her cloak.

He could sense that she was beginning to yield to him. She had responded to his embrace of her own accord, and had even confessed to being unable to withstand his ardour. Because of the nature of their relationship—and their turbulent ups and down—he had been deprived of the pleasure of courting and winning her in the normal sense, but he sensed victory wasn't too far away, and not for one minute did he doubt that she would marry him. But he wanted her *now,* and was amazed at how much; he realised how helplessly he had become caught in the web of his own desires.

Not until they were in the open once more did Edwina speak. 'Now that you've inherited Taplow Court, will you live there?'

'That is my intention—although I shall still keep the house in London.'

'And you won't find it dreary and tiresome living in the country after living in town for so long, surrounded by so much excitement and activity—the assemblies, the open-air life? All very provincial, don't you think?'

'Oh, I don't know. I enjoy hunting and fishing as much as the next man. It gives one an appetite—although at this moment, when I look at you, my lovely Edwina, I have an appetite of a different kind in mind.' His hooded eyes raked her in a way that brought a wave of colour to her cheeks.

'You are quite incorrigible, Adam Rycroft,' she reproached with gentle laughter, lulled by his tolerant good humour.

'Is that a complaint, my love?' he asked, looking neither chagrined nor apologetic. Instead, he regarded her with an infuriating grin.

'No. Now answer my question properly and tell me what you intend.'

Adam's gaze narrowed on her smiling lips. He was tempted to drag her from her horse and on to his and kiss her again. Instead he sighed and, guiding his horse round a fallen tree, answered her question. 'At first I was reluctant to move into the house—my memories of living there in the past being far from pleasant,' he remarked with a bitter twist to his lips. 'But it's a large house and needs to be lived in. I've been drawing up plans for a studio. It's important that the light is right, and that can only be achieved at the top of the house.'

'You're going to continue painting?'

'Yes—it would be hard not to—but for my own pleasure. I've already cancelled all my commissions and refused to take on more, no matter how remunerative. The builders are to begin work converting part of the lofts into a studio next week—when I shall be away in London.'

'Why are you going away so quickly?' she asked, surprised at the sudden ache that wrenched her heart. She could not deny that she would be reluctant to see him go.

'I must. I still have to find Toby—and, according to one

of the men I've employed to search for him, there has been a sighting of a boy fitting his description in Wapping.'

Edwina paled and looked down at her hands so he wouldn't see the guilt cloud her eyes. She was still reeling from her encounter with Jack, and she knew she should tell Adam that he had found Toby and was holding him captive, but the thought that Jack might carry out his threat and harm the boy silenced her on that particular matter.

'I also have to arrange for a private viewing of my portrait of you at the Academy,' Adam went on, 'primarily for fellow artists and Fleet Street journalists, prior to the public opening. Your uncle is interested in seeing the painting—and, of course, you will have to attend.'

Edwina shot him an indignant look. 'Is that an order, Adam?'

He smiled at her and his eyes were warm. 'Yes, it's an order, but a very humble one.'

She was silent as her indignation fought with temptation. Secretly she would dearly love to go to see the portrait on the opening of its showing.

'I shall benefit from your being there,' Adam went on quietly. 'I'm also looking forward to showing you off. I want everyone to see what a beautiful, enchanting muse I have. A lot of people are going to be curious about the young woman who sat for the portrait, so if you don't wish to be recognised I will arrange for you to see it alone. Otherwise, if you are interested in seeing for yourself the public's reaction and to listen to their comments, you could disguise yourself by wearing a powdered wig and cover your face with a mask,' he teased.

'I—I don't know. You won't tell them who I am, will you?'

'Not if you don't want me to, although I can't see what the problem is now that you're reconciled with your uncle. You have sorted out your differences, I hope?'

'Some of them, although things are still strained between us.'

198 *The Earl and the Pickpocket*

'And you no longer believe he killed your father?'

She shook her head, biting her lip, unprepared for the wave of misery that the mention of her father's name brought. 'No. I realise now that it was quite wrong of me to assume he had when there was no evidence to condemn him, and accuse him the way I did. He told me what happened—that it was Silas who killed him.' She paused and looked across at him. 'You knew that, didn't you, when you forced me to return home?'

'Yes. Your uncle told me when I called on him to discuss your father's loan. Knowing my cousin like I did, his crime came as no surprise to me. Were you close to your father?'

'Yes. I was greatly upset when it happened. I loved him with a gentle love, and that will always have a place in my heart—with my grief.'

Adam was silent as he looked across at her. For a brief moment he had glimpsed the lonely and frightened child inside the still-grieving young woman, and remembered the ragged urchin who had picked his pocket. He could feel her unhappiness wrapped like a tangible cloak around her. He responded with an unlooked-for wave of sympathy. 'I remember how I felt when I lost my own father, so I do understand. Do you want to pursue the matter? I wouldn't blame you if you did.'

She shook her head. 'No. The case is closed, the verdict murder by person or persons unknown. Besides, it would serve no purpose now Silas is dead. He was evil—and God forgive me, but I am glad he is no longer alive. At least I can take comfort in knowing he can't hurt anyone else. Although it doesn't seem fair, does it? Silas strikes a man down in cold blood and gets away with it.'

With much bitterness Adam remembered another man Silas had mercilessly murdered in cold blood—Toby's father—so he could empathise and sympathise with how she felt. Even after all these years the hatred he himself still felt for his cousin was greater than anything he had ever known. It burned through him like fire, like vitriol through his veins.

As if she had read his thoughts, Edwina said, 'You never did tell me about Toby. Adam, did his disappearance have anything to do with Silas?'

Adam's expression tightened, and when he spoke his voice was low and fierce. 'It had everything to do with Silas, damn him. Olivia, his sister, fell in love with his head groom, a man named Joseph Tyke. When she became pregnant and Silas found out, he killed the man in cold blood and cast Olivia out. Dolly witnessed it all. Olivia went to live with Joseph's parents in St Albans. When they died, the rest of the family turned her out. Ill and with nowhere else to go, she threw herself on her brother's mercy. He took her in, but when she died he gave Toby whom he hated for being born and the cripple he was, to some passing tinkers.'

Silent, wide-eyed with horror, Edwina stared at him, shocked to her very soul to learn of this new evil committed by Silas Clifford against his own nephew. Scalding tears rose to her eyes and spilled over her cheeks. 'That is the most terrible story I have ever heard. That poor boy. I cannot believe such wickedness can exist in any human being. Nor can I believe your cousin has conducted the most unspeakable, dreadful crimes and has got away with them. Why did Olivia not approach you instead of Silas?'

'She did write, begging me to help her, but unfortunately I was abroad at the time and did not receive her letter until it was too late. Perhaps now you will understand how important it is to me that I find Toby.'

'Of course I do. Were you there when Silas killed his father?'

'No. If I had, I would have killed Silas myself.' Seeing her tears, Adam reined in his horse. Taking a handkerchief from his pocket, he leaned across and gently dabbed them away. 'Come, no tears. I promise you that I will find Toby if I have to tear every building in London apart with my bare hands, and when I do he will live with me wherever I happen to be.'

'I do hope so.'

'If I could take away the burden of what my cousin did to you from your heart, Edwina, I would do it. Sadly I cannot, but I can promise you that if you agree to become my wife I will never intentionally cause you any unhappiness.'

'Thank you,' she whispered achingly. She had already found in him a sensitivity that made him capable of perceiving her need for tenderness, so his softly spoken words came as no surprise. Reaching across to him, she put her hand in his outstretched palm, feeling strength and reassurance in the firmness of his long lean fingers gripping hers. 'Have I ever told you that you have a considerate and sensitive nature I find most endearing?'

He grinned, subjecting her to an amused scrutiny, amazed at the bizarre turn his courtship of this enchanting creature had taken of late. 'No. I'd sooner hear you use the term irresistible—or tell me that your desire for me is hard driven and that it would be torture for you to live without me, but I suppose sensitive and considerate is as good a place as any to start.'

Observing Edwina's glowing cheeks and sparkling eyes when she returned from her ride, as Henry was about to enter his study he paused to speak to her. 'You should ride more often,' he said. 'It's brought some colour to your cheeks. You've been much too pale since returning home.'

'I enjoyed it, despite the rain,' she said, trying hard to concentrate on her meeting with Adam, rather than her far-from-pleasant encounter with Jack Pierce, and what it was he demanded of her. Removing her cloak she handed it to a young servant girl. 'Thank you, Mary. See that it's put to dry, will you?' When Mary had disappeared to do her bidding, she looked at her uncle directly, pulling off her gloves. 'I met Adam on my ride.'

He glanced at her sharply. 'Oh? Are you still angry with him for bringing you home?'

'No, not any more. I remember the fury I felt at the time. But at the same time I have begun to understand why he made me. He rode back with me just now.' She walked towards her uncle, her gaze fixed steadily on his. 'I know who Adam is, Uncle—that Silas was his cousin.'

'I see. He told you?'

'When I saw him riding towards Taplow Court with William Hewitt, I worked it out for myself. I was a fool not to see it before. It was staring me in the face all the time. From the moment I told him who I was he changed towards me. At the time I could see no reason for his anger, and I confess that I thought it strange that he was acquainted with you, and that he was familiar with the neighbourhood.'

'I would have told you myself, but he asked me not to. It was something he wanted to do himself—when the time was right, you understand. And how do you feel about him now—knowing he is the Earl of Taplow—Silas Clifford's cousin—owner of Taplow Court?'

'The truth of it is, Uncle, I don't know. He—he's asked me to marry him. No doubt you knew that too.'

'I knew he was going to. Will you accept? You should at least give it serious consideration.'

'I cannot ignore it, that's for sure—or Adam.' With a sigh she turned and walked towards the stairs, Adam's proposal filling her thoughts.

Perhaps if she hadn't shared his bed—the decision would not be so difficult to make. It had not been easy to resist him. And the opportunity had been there. How could she walk away when he had beckoned one night and kissed her in the shadows, when he had beguiled her away from what she had always thought was right, and found herself alone with him on a soft bed? With her hand on the banister she paused and looked back.

'He is leaving for London tomorrow. I won't see him again until we go to town for the exhibition of his painting. That gives me two or three weeks to consider his proposal. But how can I marry him, Uncle? How can I possibly marry a man whose cousin murdered my father and live in his house?'

It was just over a week later when Edwina missed her monthly flow. It could mean only one thing: she realised she might have to marry Adam after all.

Chapter Thirteen

The gallery in Pall Mall at the newly founded Royal Academy of Arts was ablaze with light, the occasion attended by only the wealthy and socially prominent, artists, writers and journalists, the ladies—rouged and pomaded—and gentlemen dressed in full splendour. Plumes danced atop powdered wigs, and fashionable satin patches were stuck to cheekbones. There were no outsiders, everyone present having been issued with a gold-embossed invitation.

Liveried footmen moved slowly through the crowd, bearing salvers of glasses brimming with champagne. The paintings on display drew a great deal of interest, and one in particular had attracted a large gathering of admiring people, those at the back trying to press forward to get a better view.

Because of Adam's unusually secretive behaviour of late, and the mysterious identity of the woman who was the subject of his masterpiece, it was an occasion everyone had been looking forward to with much excitement. Who the devil was she? they were asking. The woman was rumoured to be the greatest beauty, though opinions on this were strong and divided, and some would reserve judgement until they saw her for themselves.

When Edwina appeared in the doorway on her uncle's

arm, she paused to take in the sea of laughing, gossiping and whispering faces. Her stomach twisted into knots of nervousness and she was conscious of a state of fear. She was beginning to wish she hadn't left Hertfordshire after all, but after months of fending for herself she had grown restless and stifled at Oakwood Hall, and the undeniable need to see Adam and the city once more had drawn her like metal filings to a magnet.

And, of course, there was the more sinister reason for drawing her to London. Jack Pierce. Since their encounter at Taplow she had neither seen nor heard anything from him. However, it had been apparent to her that Oakwood Hall was being watched by the man who had been with him. He was often in sight when she looked out of the window, and when she rode out with a groom he could be seen openly lounging against a tree somewhere along the route. She displayed little interest in him, but his constant presence gave her a permanent feeling of unease, and she was certain he had followed her to London and was still watching her. She wanted desperately to share her secret, but she knew the folly of that. It was far better to keep it to herself than to jeopardise the young boy's life.

Every day she sent up silent prayers, asking for God's help, while wryly telling herself she had no right to ask for divine intervention when her heart had already become black with sin in the alleyways of St Giles. She had to be ready to face Pierce when he chose to appear—unless she took matters into her own hands and sought him out at his rooms in Fleet Street. When they did meet she must have her wits about her, but she was so tormented by poor Toby's sorry plight that by the time of the exhibition she was in a heightened state of nervous awareness.

Feeling her heart pounding in her chest as she looked around at the animated throng, she glanced at her uncle for reassurance. He was splendidly dressed. His wig was white, his coat burgundy brocade, and his breeches white satin. 'Goodness! I never imagined there would be so many people present,' she remarked with some trepidation.

Henry's perpetually austere face relaxed into a faint smile as his eyes swept and absorbed the full length of the gallery. His cold eyes lighted, as always, when he found himself surrounded by such illustrious company and fine works of art. He recognised many famous and distinguished faces among those present, but the most important of all was Sir Joshua Reynolds. To Henry it was as if the mere presence of this great man had altered the very air itself.

He was unable to believe his good fortune on finding himself in such distinguished company, which, he knew, he owed to Edwina. Gradually his world was beginning to expand beyond Hertfordshire and Oakwood Hall and to take on a whole new meaning. He was eager to view not only the portrait of his niece, but all the other fine paintings on display.

Feeling Edwina's anxious gaze on him, he turned to her, his sympathetic eyes drifting over her pale face. 'Do not vex yourself, Edwina. All will be well,' he told her without a twinge of doubt.

Edwina sincerely hoped it would be as she looked out over the blur of faces, her green eyes searching for one face alone. It wasn't difficult to find him. Being quite the tallest man there, he was a man who dominated his environment, and his mere presence forced people to notice him. He and another gentleman were in deep conversation at the opposite end of the gallery, seemingly oblivious to the noise around them. Of the two, it was Adam who drew the most interested, admiring glances.

Edwina's heart leapt at the sight of him. The very air around him seemed to move forcefully, became snapping with exhilaration and the restless intensity he seemed to discharge. He was splendid in a bronze velvet frock coat, with lace at his throat and wrists. He wore cream-coloured breeches and white stockings, and his waistcoat was gold satin embroidered with silver thread. His hair, tied back at the nape, was glossy in the bright light, and his deep blue eyes glowed with some emotion that seemed to be a mixture of satisfaction, pride in his work, and something else known only to himself—and perhaps to the young woman who looked back at him from the portrait.

'Adam's over there,' she whispered to her uncle.

'So he is, and talking to the great man himself.'

Edwina frowned, glancing at him enquiringly. 'Great man?'

He nodded, an unaccustomed beam animating his features. 'That, Edwina, is none other than Sir Joshua Reynolds himself.'

'Dear me!' Edwina exclaimed. 'So many important people gathered together in one room makes me feel scared.'

Henry gently squeezed her arm. 'Don't be. Everyone present will be dazzled by you.'

He gazed at the composed young woman Edwina had become, outwardly confident and a little eccentric in her love of her own company and her strange abstracted moods. And it was true what he'd said. She was beautiful. However, of late he had observed she had become withdrawn and was clearly troubled by something. Since the strain in their relationship acted as a barrier between them, he knew she would resent him prying into her affairs, so whatever it was that worried her, he hoped it would quickly resolve itself. He was distracted when an acquaintance appeared at his side and he turned to exchange pleasantries.

Clutching her fan in her gloved hands, Edwina nervously edged further into the room, a small, slim figure in saffron silk. She saw Adam lift his head. Their eyes met and she felt the strange shock of recognition shake her as it always did when he looked at her. She had missed him more than she would have thought possible. Excusing himself to his companion, he walked the full length of the room to greet her, approaching with that same natural grace that seemed so much a part of him. Her heart was thumping. His broad shoulders blocked her view of the gallery the closer he came, his blue eyes searching her face, his smile one of welcome and uncertainty.

Taking her hand, he raised it to his lips, and she was startled to find him gazing down at her with a look of profound pride. There were roses in her cheeks and glowing stars in the depths of her smiling eyes, and when his gaze swept the whole of her it changed to that of a starving traveller who had come upon an unexpected banquet.

'Edwina?' he breathed softly. 'I'm glad you decided to attend.'

'I said I would,' she murmured with nervous apprehension. The sound of his warm, masculine voice never failed to bring her senses alive. Close to him at last, she was powerfully aware of everything that was masculine, primitive and demanding, which was always so strong it seemed to be an almost physical force. She was more aware of him than she had ever been, and here, with the whole world looking on, stood the man whose child she was to bear.

'I realise you have been in London for several days and I should have called on you, but I've been tied up here. It's indeed brave of you to appear without a mask.'

'I did intend to—and I see I would not have been alone,' she said, observing other women wearing masks in a variety of colours beneath their powdered wigs. 'But you were right, Adam. I've no reason to hide any more, and I've also decided that in the future I shall no longer let life's tragedies get me down.' With Jack Pierce hovering on the perimeter of her mind, she spoke these words with more conviction than she felt.

'I'm relieved to hear it,' Adam remarked.

Glancing around apprehensively, Edwina was acutely

aware that many eyes had followed her from the moment she entered the room with a kind of bored curiosity, then, when Adam suddenly appeared by her side, surprise and shocked interest flowed over them, snapping them out of their lazy indifference. 'Everyone will find out who I am some time, I suppose, so I thought I'd get it over with.'

Adam sensed a new determination there, strengthened by her experiences. However, sensitive to her every mood, some sixth sense told him that something was wrong, and he was sure it was something other than her nervousness about appearing at the exhibition. Her features were strained, her eyes too large, her smile forced. His smile faded, and he grew serious. 'Now tell me, how are you really?'

Self-consciously she laughed, aware of his penetrating, probing, deep blue gaze as she tried to ignore the sickening ache of guilt around her heart. It seemed heavy and weighted with stone, and it longed for a lightening of its burden. 'I'm fine, Adam. Please don't worry about me.'

By no means convinced, he said quietly, 'I do. What are you hiding from me?'

Edwina's heart flung itself against her ribs with a sickening thud, and the colour drained out of her face. She shook her head in helpless consternation and her eyes flew to his. Adam saw the unspoken anguish that flashed into the green depths, which was soon gone, and his heart twisted. Was it possible that she was with child?

'Hiding?' she asked in trembling, hushed tones, utterly unprepared for the question. 'I'm afraid I do not comprehend you, Adam. I can't think what you mean. I have nothing to hide.' To prove it she instantly put on a mask of normality and fixed a bright smile on her face. Her eyes wide and unblinking, she cast an interested look around, but the fleeting invasion of Jack's face, reminding her that Toby's life was in danger if she uttered one word of what he intended, made her prey to an accusing conscience. She was so consumed with this one thought that it did not occur to her just then that Adam might be thinking along different lines.

Adam was watching her closely through narrowed eyes. 'Do not play with me, Edwina. I don't believe you. I can see perfectly well that something is not right, and silence on the matter will not make it go away. Be assured I will ask you again later,' he said softly. With everyone's eyes turned their way, he decided to let the matter drop for now, but he was determined to get to the bottom of it.

Edwina knew he would, that he would squeeze the truth from her if he could. For a moment she felt her resistance waver, pulling her up short. It was a warning, telling her that she would have to be careful, for Adam had a way of getting beneath her guard that was too worrying for her peace of mind.

His eyes swept over her with warm appreciation, and there was a small quirk of a smile on his lips, and though his gaze took in the whole of her, it lacked the roguish gleam that had oft brought a vivid hue to her cheeks. 'You look absolutely divine, my love. There won't be a hot-blooded male here tonight who'll not want to kiss your lips.'

Now that the awkward moment had passed, the corners of Ed-wina's mouth lifted in a tender smile. Adam's appreciation heartened her. 'And all will be disappointed,' she countered.

'Nevertheless, when some of the doddering ancients among the party set eyes on you, you will send their hearts into palpitations they will never recover from.'

She laughed lightly. 'You tease, Adam. I believe the stress of the exhibition has weakened your mind. There are women here more beautiful than I by far.'

'Not to me.' His voice was husky, and there was such intensity in his gaze that Edwina felt her heartbeat slow. 'Everyone present has seen the portrait and enthused about the subject, but when they see you in the flesh you will astound them all with your beauty. I fear the portrait doesn't do you justice.'

Edwina gave him a wry smile. 'Spare me your honeyed sentiment, Adam. Use it on others if you must, but not on me. The portrait is perfect and you know it.'

A lazy grin drew up the corners of his mouth. ''Tis true. I admit it.'

A hush had fallen over those present who looked at them, anxious to appease their curiosity about the woman who had bewitched Adam Rycroft to such a degree that he had closed his house and studio to his friends until the painting was complete. What they saw had them all agog, for the young woman on his arm was truly a vision to behold, and not in the least what they had expected.

She was small and dainty—a girl, almost a waif, ethereal, and her movements graceful and well-bred. The unusual short cut of her hair had a vibrancy that shone like a beacon in the gallery's bright light, and she wore an expression that combined vitality and youth without appearing indelicate or wanton. At last everyone understood why Adam had kept her a mystery until the portrait was finished. Almost as quickly as the silence fell, so did a chattering medley of voices fill the gallery once more.

'Come. I intend to present you to everyone, but first I want to introduce you to Sir Joshua Reynolds. As you know, he's the most fashionable painter in the country. The respect he commands from his friends stems as much from his literary and social pretensions as from his fame as an artist. As a sovereign judge and arbiter of art, it means a great deal to me that he is here tonight.' He glanced down at Edwina's anxious face, seeing that she was biting her trembling lip. 'Try not to look so overwrought. You look like a fox searching for a bolt-hole,' he chuckled softly.

'Perhaps that's because I feel like a fox searching for a bolt-hole. Unfortunately I can't see one,' she said, trying to keep her voice low. She was intensely aware of the men and women milling around, watching, and, if they were close enough, listening to their conversation.

'It's too late to escape. Besides, it wouldn't be wise to disappoint your public.'

'Nothing I have done in recent months has been wise,' she countered lightly. 'I suppose I'll have to bear it as best I can.'

Adam thought she was going to do very well.

'I never imagined there would be so many people—and why are they all looking at me?'

'Because, my love, you are the star attraction here tonight, the mystery woman everyone has been waiting to see.' He caught her brief, anxious glance and tucked her hand possessively into the crook of his arm, giving her fingers a squeeze of reassurance. 'Stick to my side and you'll be fine. You'll set them all agog,' he whispered, 'and come tomorrow I wager you'll have set a new trend in hairstyles.'

Edwina looked at him, a smile hovering on her lips. The gentleness of his gesture and the soft words meant to put her at her ease plucked at the strings of her heart and set a bittersweet yearning growing within her. 'You remind me of a mother hen shepherding her chick, and the noise of everyone talking at once makes me think of an aviary gone mad,' she murmured as he leisurely led her forward on his arm, completely impervious to the stir he was creating.

Edwina was amazed when the crowd opened a corridor to where Sir Joshua Reynolds stood, close to the portrait of her. So many faces moved past her in a shifting blur of dazzling colours and flashing jewels, but she only had eyes for the man Adam was about to introduce her to.

Sir Joshua Reynolds was the President of the Royal Academy, King George III its patron. The great man was dressed in midnight blue, which threw up the whiteness of his cravat. He had about him an extraordinary air of quiet power. His manner and deportment were amicable and prepossessing, his disposition courtly. Without warning his piercing eyes that spoke of perceptiveness became levelled on Edwina, inspecting her with a barely concealed admiration.

'Edwina,' Adam said, 'may I present Sir Joshua Reynolds. Sir Joshua, Edwina Marchant.'

Edwina sank into a polite curtsy. 'It is indeed an honour to meet you, sir.'

'Likewise, my dear. Likewise,' Sir Joshua said, taking her hand and raising her to her feet. He looked Adam over with a haughty, cocked eyebrow, and a smile turned his lips. 'My compliments, Adam. Miss Marchant is a rare beauty, indeed. How you've managed to keep her out of the public eye for so long absolutely astounds me.' He turned his attention to Edwina. 'I have a great admiration for Adam's work, Miss Marchant, and in my opinion this latest work is his best. I've already indulged my admiration of the portrait, my dear. The whole ambience of the painting is extremely beautiful, and you are even lovelier in the flesh than you are on canvas.'

'Thank you, sir. You are too kind.' Edwina's confidence was slowly returning. Far from being overawed by this famous painter, she was aware of a sensation of a relaxation of tension in finding herself face to face with him.

'It's a remarkable turn-out, don't you agree?' Sir Joshua remarked. 'You have every reason to be delighted in your success, Adam. Your painting has attracted a great deal of attention.'

'Aye, and since my inheritance my attractions will increase a thousandfold.' Adam's tone was not without cynicism.

'Only on the score of your title. You've always had attractions enough,' Sir Joshua pointed out with a low chuckle and a meaningful gleam in his eye, which left Edwina wondering if it was Adam's artistic genius he was referring to, or attractions that were more aesthetically pleasing to the senses. 'An artist, particularly one as talented as Adam, is a vital figure in any civilised society, Miss Marchant, and he will be sadly missed when he retires to his country estate.'

'Taplow Court is only three or four hours away, Sir Joshua, and I have no intention of selling my house here in London.'

'I'm happy to hear it. Now—if you will excuse me, I must have a word with Gainsborough before I leave.'

At the very moment when the great man moved on, a meteor fell. Barbara Mortimer appeared in the doorway with Dolly Drinkwater, shattering everything. Dolly's presence caused quite a stir, for she was a striking woman. A sibilant hiss ran through the gallery as all eyes turned to the well-known, nay, notorious madam, who ran the most popular bordello in Covent Garden.

To those who knew of the strange, close relationship that existed between Dolly Drinkwater and Adam Rycroft, it would come as no surprise that she had been invited to join the gathering. With her hair elegantly coiffed and her slender figure attired in a simple yet fashionable gown of midnight-blue satin, she was not what one would have expected of a procuress of a gaming house and bordello.

Adam's head jerked towards them and he disengaged himself. He strode across the room to receive her, taking both her hands and planting an affectionate kiss on both her cheeks, before turning his attention on Barbara. She looked resplendent in rose pink satin and a high pompadour-styled wig with three fat ringlets brought forward over her shoulder. Adam saw none of this. Aware of her resentment towards Edwina, he was incensed that she'd dared show her face at the exhibition.

'Barbara! I'm surprised to see you here,' he said, trying, with difficulty, to temper his rising ire and his tone.

'Why?' Edwina was standing a short distance away. Barbara's mouth tightened, and an icy coldness hardened her dark eyes as they flicked over her with open distaste. 'You invited me, remember.' Her stance was haughty, her look quietly challenging.

'No, I do not recall inviting you. I invited Dolly,' Adam said impatiently.

'You told Aunt Dolly to bring a companion—so here I am. And I'm simply dying to see the painting that's had everyone on tenterhooks for weeks. Personally I can't for the life of me imagine what all the fuss is about,' she exclaimed peevishly.

Edwina hadn't moved. As Barbara stepped round Adam she looked straight at her, watching her, her own face speculative and predatory. Their stares held for several seconds, and then Barbara looked away with flaunting unconcern and moved off in the direction of the painting.

'I'm so sorry, Adam,' Dolly said when they were alone, gazing up at him fondly, her irrepressible humour and energy a tangible aura around her. 'I had no intention of bringing Barbara along, knowing how things stand between the two of you. But she insisted—and you know how determined she can be when she gets a bee in her bonnet. Had I not brought her with me, she would have come alone.'

Adam squeezed her arm affectionately and smiled. 'Don't worry about it, Dolly. You came, and that's the main thing.'

Her eyes swept the room and she smiled. 'Quite a turn-out, I see. This painting of yours is causing quite a stir.'

He raised an eyebrow. 'And so is my muse, Dolly. Come and say hello to her—and now you're here, I must propose a toast.'

Taking a glass of champagne from the tray of a passing footman, he handed it to Dolly, before taking two more and returning to Edwina. Placing one of the glasses in her hand, he raised his own. The champagne sparkled in the myriad of lights, its pale golden lucidity shot through with countless bubbles, spraying the rim of the glass with a fine mist.

'Ladies and gentlemen,' he said, raising his voice above the buzz of the crowd, his eyes settling on the young woman who was gazing up at him. She was so gracious, so lovely, so flawless. His look was one of unashamed adoration and enormous pride. When everyone fell silent he said, 'A toast to Miss Edwina Marchant, without whom we would not be here to-night.'

Colour spread over Edwina's delicately carved cheek-bones, and her eyes were as brilliant as the champagne as everyone raised their glasses. Adam's eyes were a warm, melting blue as he looked into hers, making her feel that she had accomplished something rare.

At that moment a foppish young gentleman by the name of Lord Brocklehurst, with a florid face and rotund figure attired in garish pink and yellow and whom, it seemed, had drunk his fair share of champagne, swaggered forward, his chest thrust out. Clearly he was quite awed by the portrait.

'And what about the painting, dear sir? I never see a beautiful thing without longing violently to possess it, and since I cannot have the real thing—' he chortled, his rather bulbous eyes raking over Edwina in what both she and Adam considered to be the most insolent manner '—I'd like to make you an offer.'

Adam fixed the man with a cold stare. He had no particular liking for Lord Brocklehurst, who was both a drunk and a fool. He hadn't been invited tonight, but he was the sort who would wheedle his way in to any event by hanging on to someone else's coat tails. 'You'd be wasting your time,' Adam replied, smiling lazily, his voice deceptively mild.

The gentleman looked somewhat startled. 'I would, sir? Come, now, don't tell me someone else has beaten me to it. Why, I would give a thousand guineas to have it hanging above my fireplace.'

'A thousand guineas or not, Lord Brocklehurst—which I very much doubt you can lay claim to since you owe your creditors twenty times that amount—I shall have to disappoint you. The painting is not for sale—not for one thousand or a hundred thousand guineas.'

'Not for sale?' Lord Brocklehurst blustered. 'You mean you are going to keep it?'

The smile did not waver. 'I am indeed. I really have no penchant to sell it.'

'Then it must mean a great deal to you.'

'It does, sir. I admit it. But I appreciate your offer.' Adam gave him a mock bow and turned away.

Angry and disgruntled, Lord Brocklehurst returned to his friends and spoke in a stage whisper that carried some distance beyond his immediate group. 'I am quite mortified. Unquestionably the portrait's a masterpiece—a masterpiece, I say. He'll make that girl the toast of London. The man's a fool not to sell. Prints would sell by the hundreds.'

'And rake in a tidy fortune,' his companion drawled. 'Perhaps the painting means more to him than money—and looking at the young filly, I can see why. She'd prove highly entertaining in a chase. I'd wager Rycroft's in love with that girl.'

When the comment reached Adam's ears he immediately looked at Edwina and smiled. She too had heard the remark and, giving him a sidelong glance, dared to say, 'Well, Adam? What have you to say to that?'

His mouth tilted upward in a roguish grin. 'I do believe I am envied by every man present,' he answered evasively, smoothly. 'And you, my love, are the envy of every woman. Your beauty places every one of them in the shade.'

Edwina would have preferred a different answer to her question, but her smiling face gave no indication that she was disappointed that he chose to prevaricate. 'Flatterer,' she murmured. Her smile faded and she looked at him seriously. 'Did you mean what you said just now, Adam? Are you going to keep the painting?'

'Yes. I shall hang it at Taplow Court in pride of place.' He placed his hand beneath her elbow. 'And now I shall not be content until I have introduced you to all these illustrious people.'

Edwina's was a heady triumph as Adam skilfully guided

her from one group to the next, his whole being filled with a fierce, buoyant pride. It was as if she stood in a blaze of light, with the eyes of the world focused on her. Everyone wanted to be introduced to her—the famous painter, plump and jovial Thomas Gainsborough, whose recent painting, *Blue Boy,* was a great success, and Paul Sanby, both men foundation members of the Academy. Then there was the well-known writer James Boswell, Dr Samuel Johnson of dictionary fame, followed by Sir William Chambers, treasurer and architect, and many more well-known people.

All the gay and handsome young men flirted with her, paying her outrageous compliments—all under the watchful, frequently disapproving eye of the Earl of Taplow. Those who were not well acquainted with the artist stood on the periphery and admired her, while some of the ladies exerted themselves to be complimentary, though several were maliciously finding fault with her hair, her gown and her manners.

Her cheeks flushed and the light of her success shining in her eyes, Edwina was blissfully unaware of their malevolent comments whispered behind unfurled fans. Suddenly, when Adam had turned away to acknowledge an acquaintance, the voice of Barbara Mortimer, cold and brittle as ice, cut into her happy thoughts.

Edwina turned to face her adversary, who was evidently resentful of Adam's lack of attention. Her eyes were bright, too bright Edwina thought, and she swayed slightly—possible signs that she had consumed overmuch of the free-flowing wine.

'So, Miss Marchant, you've successfully managed to monopolise the attentions of everyone present.' Reeking with malice, Barbara tightened her mouth as she cast a contemptuous look over Edwina's pale face and figure. 'I concede that you do look ravishing, which has been remarked upon by several gentlemen who are speculating on your relationship with Adam and would dearly like to get to know you better—on a purely temporary basis, you understand,' she said, making no attempt to hide the cold smirk in her smile.

Edwina stared at her tolerantly. 'What is it you wish to say to me? If all you want to do is to malign me, I have no wish to listen.' She was about to turn away when Barbara's next words froze her to the spot.

'I'm really quite astonished. But I suppose a thief has no trouble outfitting oneself with fine clothes and jewels.' Her gaze fastened on Edwina's exquisite necklace and matching earrings, the diamonds like scintillating teardrops brushing her cheeks. 'Tell me, are those baubles your own, or do they belong to someone else? Are they stolen?'

Edwina went white. She felt as though she were encased in ice. The moment she dreaded had come, and she almost swooned from the anguish of it. Barbara's glittering eyes held hers steadily, accusingly. She could not have orchestrated her attack with greater skill or better timing. 'Not so.' Edwina's grip on her fan tightened and her voice took on a steely edge. 'I assure you that the "baubles" I am wearing are my own, and my mother's before that.'

Barbara's caustic remark had not gone unheard by Adam, who turned. Sensitive to what Edwina was feeling, he moved closer to her and slid his arm about her waist. The possessive gesture, stating the fact that Edwina belonged to him, infuriated Barbara further and increased her resentment. She felt that she could claw Edwina's soft skin till the blood ran and take pleasure from it, but she remained silent as his glacial eyes came to rest on her.

'That's enough, Barbara,' he said in a quiet, controlled voice, his fury tightly in check. 'I think you had better leave before I forget that I am supposed to be a gentleman.'

She gave him a superior smile. 'I intend to. Oh, but before I leave, I have a message for you, Edwina, from your accomplice Jack Pierce—a shady, disreputable character. It would appear that he's been trying to locate you for quite some time.'

Chapter Fourteen

Edwina froze, staring at her as if she'd seen a ghost. 'Jack Pierce?'

Barbara laughed, satisfied that her cruel barb had found its mark. Her eyes were alight with the pleasure of one who has gained the upper hand. 'Yes. The last time Jack saw you, Adam was carrying you into Dolly's Place. The poor man's been hanging about for weeks in the hope of seeing you,' she told her smugly. 'Imagine his astonishment when I told him the lad he was looking for was a girl in boy's clothing—and was even greater when I told him where you could be found.'

Edwina listened with growing horror. Barbara's words receded in her brain and there was such a roaring in her ears that she feared she might faint. She was incensed. Dear God, she could strike her; had the pair of them been alone and not transfixed beneath the interested gaze of so many people, she felt she would have done so. 'So it was you. It was you who told him,' she whispered, her words inaudible to everyone except Adam, who looked down at her with a puzzled frown.

Barbara gave Adam her most charming smile. 'You really should be more careful who you associate with, Adam,' she sneered. 'I would hate to see such a talented man brought down because he placed his trust in a thief.'

Her words were spoken so loudly that men and women around them fell silent and turned their heads attentively to observe the unprecedented altercation. Giving them an apologetic glance, his look indicating that the young woman had partaken of too much champagne, and seizing Barbara's arm, Adam jerked her around, and, placing his palm in the small of her back, shoved her towards the door, which was, thankfully, only yards away. Both Edwina and Dolly followed them out on to the landing, relieved to find it devoid of people.

Looming over Barbara, Adam's expression was murderous, but his voice was ominously soft. 'If you dare use that tone of voice to either Edwina or myself just one more time, I will personally throw you out, regardless of my affection for your aunt.' Sarcastically he added, 'Is that clear to you?'

Barbara threw back her head haughtily. 'I speak as I find,' she pouted and turned away. Taking a few steps, she paused and faced them once more, still furious when her glittering eyes settled on Edwina. 'So, you think yourself established as his mistress, do you?' she hissed. 'Oh, so beautiful, clever Miss Marchant. You were useful to him for a while, as all his muses are, but when the paintings are finished and they are gone he forgets about them completely. He loves and leaves his paramours with frequent ease—isn't that so, Adam? No matter what you are to him, you are still a liar and a thief.'

Edwina saw Adam stiffen at the insult, his expression one of barely controlled rage. She took a deep, shuddering breath, her pride rising to do combat. Her first reaction had been to flee from there, flee from her own disgrace. Her second had been to retaliate in kind, but that would be playing Barbara at her own game, and would be childish and stupid. So she forced herself to smile, knowing that, by remaining calm, she would only infuriate her further.

'I am sure I am not,' she managed to say in a controlled voice. 'It's a pity you are not in full possession of the facts—and your senses,' she retorted drily, when Barbara swayed slightly and had to grasp the back of a chair to stop herself stumbling. 'But what of you? One thing I have learned is that if you purport to be a lady, you set the fashion as to how a lady behaves, and you follow it. That is something you might remember if, in the future, you wish to succeed in winning a gentleman's affections.'

Barbara hid her pain on losing Adam behind her fury. 'At least I don't pretend to be something I'm not.' Her features contorted, she scowled darkly at Edwina, snapping her fan shut as the sharp talons of anger and jealousy clawed at her savagely. 'You are still a thief, a common thief,' she hissed scornfully. 'St Giles was where you picked her up, wasn't it, Adam—in the gutter?' In her desire to see the effect of her cruel words upon her rival, she stepped closer, but she was disappointed. The face Edwina turned to her was one as hard as stone, the look in her eyes one of profound indifference, neither fearful nor sorry.

Having seen them leave, and thinking Edwina looked upset, his curiosity piqued, Henry had followed them. What he saw when he came upon the scene was a dark-haired, brazen young woman so lacking in respect that she stood before them half-drunk, and to his abject horror what he heard was her call Edwina a thief. His whole being rose up in defence of his niece—and also fury, because he suspected there was more than a little truth in her accusation. 'What the devil's going on here?' he thundered. 'Young woman, I heard what you said and you are mistaken.'

Barbara turned and gave him a haughty, resentful stare. 'And you are, sir?'

'Sir Henry Marchant. This young lady you accuse so outrageously of being a thief is my niece. She cannot possibly be the person you speak of. You see, she was living at home until she left, with my full permission, to sit for this gentleman.' He looked at Adam for confirmation. 'Is that not so, sir?'

Looking gigantic in his fury, Adam nodded. 'Indeed it is.'

There was an underlying note to his voice that silenced Barbara, and for the first time she felt a quiver of uncertainty.

'The next time you decide to openly malign someone with such vindictiveness, I advise you to make quite sure of the facts first,' Henry reproached harshly, knowing full well that both the Earl's and Ed-wina's reputations were at stake, as well as his own, and refusing to spare her. 'Consider yourself fortunate I do not file charges of slander against you— but if you persist, then I will.'

'I think you should leave, Barbara. And there will be no scandal,' Adam said, allowing an undertone of menace to enter his voice. His face was very tense, his tall figure dominating them all. 'There would be even less chance, of course, if you keep your mouth shut.'

The expression in Adam's eyes was formidable, and his words were delivered in a cold, lethal voice, but Barbara did not flinch as she tried to clutch at the last remaining particles of her reason, the shredded thoughts that were all she seemed to assemble just then. She cared for nothing now but vengeance, and there was venom in her voice when she hissed, 'It would be worth the scandal to see you brought down.' Her scorching gaze encompassed both Edwina and Adam. 'Both of you,' she spat.

Unable to listen any longer to her niece's appalling outburst, Dolly stepped forward. Giving her the direst of looks, she took her arm. 'Barbara! You wicked girl! How dare you speak to Edwina that way—here of all places, and in front of everyone.'

Barbara shrugged. 'I will make no apologies for what I said, Aunt Dolly.'

Impatient for Barbara to be out of the building and his sight, his hands clenched into fists as he struggle to prevent them from reaching out and strangling her, Adam turned to Dolly. 'For God's sake, take her home, Dolly, before I do something I will not regret. I know I don't need to ask you to be discreet.'

'You should. Discretion is my stock in trade.' Shaking her head with something like despair, Dolly watched her niece make a less-than-dignified retreat.

Barbara's spirits sagged as she left them and tears glistened in her eyes, which she blinked back angrily. No one must know of her misery. She knew that her conduct had been disgraceful and unforgiv-able, but with her courage fortified by too much wine she had been unable to help herself. She hated herself, and she hated everyone else with all the fury of her thwarted first love.

Before Edwina Marchant had appeared on the scene she had been so sure of Adam, compounded by her own vanity and the confidence of her beauty and charm. After this, Adam would hate her—and who could blame him? She should never have confronted Miss Marchant and accused her in such a disgraceful manner. She had underestimated her rival and lost Adam; even worse was the humiliation and the fear that she had made a public spectacle of herself and that everyone would be laughing at her.

'I should have known Barbara would show her claws tonight,' Dolly remarked. 'Possessed of a tempestuous nature, she's been like a simmering pot for weeks. It grieves me to say that my niece is an excessively passionate woman who bears her grudges badly, and she is vindictive enough to try to destroy Edwina for crossing swords with her.' She sighed heavily and her frown was one of concern as she stared after Barbara's retreating figure. 'But I know Barbara, and I also know that later she will regret her outburst—if she doesn't already. I'll go after her. Be so good as to order the carriage, will you, Adam?'

Alone with her uncle, Edwina looked at him a little nervously. 'Thank you, Uncle.' When he swung to face her, his face a cold, ivory mask, she felt her stomach clench warningly.

'How else was I to avoid a scandal and the condemnation of the whole of society?' he thundered. 'Well? Is it true? Were you a thief?'

She nodded and whispered somewhat ashamedly, 'Yes.'

With exasperation his eyes flew heavenward. 'God above! That any niece of mine could reduce herself to a common thief beggars belief. I should have known something like this would happen. I should have remembered your capacity for creating mayhem. So you were lying when you told me you found respectable employment.'

'I had no choice.' She gave him a brief account of what had happened to her when she had run away, of the loss of her money and her meeting with Jack Pierce. 'He promised he would show me how to earn some more money. Unfortunately he introduced me to a world of crime. I was afraid of him. I couldn't deal with him. I wasn't strong enough to fight back. If I didn't do as he told me, he would always resort to threats and violence. That is the only language men like him understand. Before him I was powerless.'

'Why didn't you return home?' Henry demanded.

Tears sprang to her eyes. 'I couldn't. No matter where I went, I knew he would come after me. I couldn't fight him. I was trapped. My dreams had come to nothing. To keep myself sane, I kept a tenuous thread of hope deep inside me— that one day I would have enough money to take me to France, and the courage to leave him. You can have no idea what it was like.'

'Was it so dreadful?'

'Worse than that. Jack Pierce was a savage.' She fell silent and looked into her uncle's face, unaware of the transparency of her expression, and her eyes large and bright with unshed tears. What she had endured at Jack's hands was all there for him to read—fear, hope, frustration. ''Tis a pathetic tale, is it not, Uncle? The tale of a young girl in unusual and tragic circumstances, running away from all she held most dear—

out of pique and more than a little pride, perhaps—and all because of a terrible misunderstanding.'

Henry thought he had never heard such desolation. For an instant longer he remained motionless, staring at the wall in front of him, listening to the chaotic beating of his own heart as it slowly returned to normal. Brushing a hand over his forehead, he found that it was trembling slightly. Looking at Edwina, he saw an expression of desperation on her pale face, and at the pitiful sight his anger relaxed its demon grip at last. Compassion for his niece stirred in his breast, a compassion reinforced by her pain, and the horrors she had known. He could not begin to imagine what she must have suffered. With a deep sigh he placed his hand on her arm and cleared his throat.

'There have been misunderstandings on both sides, Edwina. I had no idea of the hurt I inflicted on you—without meaning to—and there are times when you make me feel ashamed. You are right. It is a pathetic tale, one we will relegate to the past. Should that young woman decide to make trouble, then be assured that I shall stand by you. You will have my absolute support. Now, let there be no further discussion on the subject.'

Blinking back her tears she gave him a tremulous smile. 'Thank you, Uncle. Your support means a great deal to me.'

'Do you feel up to going back inside?'

'I think I should, otherwise I'll never be able to hold up my head in society again.'

'That's the spirit. I've never known you to be a coward.'

'I just hope no one heard Barbara Mortimer accuse me of being a thief? What if they did and they cut me dead?'

'They wouldn't dare,' said Adam, striding towards her, having seen Barbara off the premises himself. Placing his hands on Edwina's shoulders, he looked deep into her eyes. 'Barbara's behaviour was inexcusable. When we return to the party we will make it appear that we regard her outburst as nothing more than a harmless overindulgence of champagne. I trust you're suffering no ill effects from her tirade?' he inquired in a soft tone.

Edwina's chin lifted and she smiled, the corners of her eyes crinkling. 'Inasmuch as I feel partly responsible for the ill feeling she so clearly harbours against me, my pride's a bit dented, I confess, and I shall find it difficult to forgive her for humiliating me so publicly. Still, on the whole I'm none the worse for it. Now, if I am to salvage some of my shattered pride you had best escort me back inside. If anyone did hear Barbara's remark about my wicked past, then I shall be like a martyr entering an amphitheatre full of lions. I shall rely on you to stop them eating me up.'

Adam stared down into the lovely face upturned to his and felt a spurt of admiration for her courage. 'Then wipe that martyred expression off your face, my love, and smile congenially.'

Adam offered her his arm and she placed her trembling hand on it, arranging her features into a reasonably calm mask. On entering the gallery there was an odd hush that made Edwina catch her breath and glance round uncertainly as all eyes seemed to focus on her. Then, relieved beyond words, the explosion of conversation erupted once more, Barbara Mortimer's sudden outburst forgotten.

For the time they were in London, Edwina and her uncle were staying with Mr and Mrs Templeton at their house in Long Acre. Friends of long standing of both Edwina's late father and Henry, they were a quiet, elderly couple whose four offspring had flown the nest years ago.

On the morning following the exhibition, finding herself alone in the house and with the enormity of Jack's threat so terrifyingly visible, Edwina donned her cloak, and without a word to the servants set off for Fleet Street. She would go to Jack's rooms and confront him, and she was fully prepared to sell the jewels she had inherited from her mother to bring about Toby's release if she had to.

Fleet Street was loud with hawkers lustily proclaiming their wares, and busy with all manner of traffic. People strolled in and out of shops, keeping close to the walls to avoid the slops, which were frequently thrown from upper-storey windows, and on their guard from the pickpockets who infested every street and alleyway.

Entering a small, dark and dingy court, Edwina went to the pawnbroker's shop where Jack had his rooms. She entered, starting when a bell over the door jingled loudly. Looking towards a passage where a staircase disappeared upwards, she moved towards it, halting when a voice rang out and the middle-aged pawnbroker with a piercing stare emerged from the back of the shop.

'Hey! Where do you think you're going?'

'I—I'm looking for Mr Pierce—Jack Pierce. I've been told he has rooms in this building.'

'Not any longer, he doesn't. Up and left, he did, without a by your leave.' He squinted down at her. 'Friend of 'is, are you?'

'No—no,' she hastened to tell him. 'I—I have something to sell and I thought he might be interested in buying it. How long has he been gone?'

'Three weeks—give or take a day or two either way.'

Disappointment swamped Edwina. She felt as though every part of her was set in a mould of ice. She had been prepared to find Jack not at home—but to discover he had left his rooms for good was a disaster. 'Do you know where he went, where I might find him?'

The pawnbroker scratched his head. 'No, but if it's something to sell you're after, then Samuel Bland's the name and I'm the man to help you.'

Edwina backed towards the door. 'No—thank you. I'll try and find Mr Pierce.'

The pawnbroker shrugged. 'Suit yerself.' He ambled back into the dirty shop, which was cluttered with all manner of items people had pawned in the hope of one day being able to buy them back.

Edwina shivered as she left the court and stood in the street. She drew her cloak tightly about her. Profoundly disappointed that her journey had proved fruitless, there was nothing for it but to go back to Long Acre. As she hurried in the direction of the Strand, she was unaware of the tall man emerging from a print-seller's across the way.

On seeing the young woman in a dark blue cloak emerge from the small court and push her way through the crowd, Adam halted in mid-stride and looked at her. There was something about her that drew his attention, and he was sure he recognised that dark blue cloak with its fur trim. His brow raised sharply as he realised the young woman's slight stature was just about the right size for—Edwina. This was confirmed when the cowl of her cloak slipped back to reveal a short crop of bright copper-and-gold coloured hair. He stared, unable to believe it was her. But it must be. He watched the small figure pull the cowl back over her hair and dart away.

Mouthing a startled oath he went after her, wondering what the hell she was doing in Fleet Street—alone. His long strides cleared the distance between them, and just when he thought he was gaining on her he was forced to step back when a stout woman emerged from a doorway and threw a bucket of slops into the street. After the short delay, when Adam again looked ahead there was no sign of Edwina.

Cursing savagely, he retraced his steps to the court from which he had seen her emerge, and entered the pawnbroker's shop to question the owner. He was stunned by the information he was given, which gave way to a white hot fury unlike anything he'd ever experienced, turning his mind into a volcano of boiling rage. Why had she come looking for Jack

Pierce? For what reason? Infuriated, he immediately went in search of his carriage, instructing the coachman to head for Long Acre.

When the carriage was about to turn up Chancery Lane, he caught sight of Edwina's small figure once more, ordered the driver to stop and climbed out. Still reeling from her failure to locate Jack, Edwina didn't see him until he was directly in front of her. She halted and stared at him in startled horror, feeling a prickle of unease and foreboding.

'Adam!'

Standing beside the carriage he held the door open. 'Get in,' he said, his voice like ice.

'But I—'

'I said get in,' he bit out between his teeth.

There was such lethal intent in the command that Edwina did as she was bade, realising that, beneath his bland sophistication, Adam Rycroft was blazingly furious. Ordering the coachman to take them to his house in Mayfair, he climbed in behind her. When Edwina opened her mouth to object, the withering look he threw at her stilled her tongue.

Seated across from him, her heart beating painfully in great erratic thumps, unconsciously Edwina pressed herself into the upholstery, waiting for the explosion of fury she expected and feared. His face, turned to the window, was hard, his jaw clenched. She wished he would speak to her, tell her what was wrong, but when he turned his ice-cold gaze on her, his eyes empty, a glacial blue emptiness that told her nothing of what he felt, and said in an absolutely chilling voice, 'Why were you looking for Jack Pierce?' she wished he hadn't said anything at all.

She stared at him mutely, her mind a complete turmoil, and when she didn't reply he snarled, 'Answer me, damn it, before I shake it out of you.'

She swallowed nervously. 'What makes you think I was looking for Jack Pierce?'

'Don't play me for a fool, Edwina. I saw you coming out of the alley where he has rooms—or had.'

'How do you know that?'

His gaze snapped to her face, and he spoke sarcastically. 'I asked the pawnbroker.'

'Oh,' she whispered.

Adam looked at her beautiful, frightened face, but he refused to spare her. 'Edwina, I will ask you again. Why were you looking for Jack Pierce?'

'I—I…' The words fell away and she dropped her eyes, desperately floundering for something to tell him—anything but the truth.

'Don't even think of lying to me,' he hissed. 'And look at me. I must know if you are telling me the whole truth.'

Edwina looked up as he bade her and her green eyes met those of the man across from her. She froze at the murderous look in those deep blue eyes, shrinking from the suggestion of contempt and the hint of distrust in his voice. Never in all her life had she witnessed such controlled, menacing fury. What had happened to the man of last night, who had looked at her with such warmth and affection in those penetrating, soul-searching eyes? She could never have believed he would look at her as he did now, with so much anger and contempt.

'I—I can't tell you.'

'Can't, or won't?' he asked with deadly calm.

'I can't.'

'You can and you will,' he stated implacably. 'Tell me this, Edwina. Have you seen Jack Pierce since that night I rescued you from his clutches?'

She nodded and whispered through dry lips, 'Yes.'

'Where the devil did he spring from? Where and when did you see him?'

Unable to endure his hard, accusing gaze, Edwina focused her eyes on a point outside the window, wondering a little wildly when his questioning was going to end. 'It—it was at

Taplow—when I was out riding. He was waiting for me in the woods. It was on the same day I met you.'

'Before or after?'

'Before.'

Adam was incredulous. 'So, you had just been speaking to Jack Pierce and you didn't think it important enough to tell me?'

She looked at him directly, her stomach in knots. 'It was important, which was why I couldn't.'

'And how did he know where to find you?'

'At first I was puzzled by that, but it's obvious to me now. When Barbara told him I was staying with you, he must have watched the house and followed us to Taplow.'

Adam looked at her hard. He'd wondered what she had meant when she had been confronted by Barbara at the exhibition, and she had quietly uttered 'so it was you'. Now he knew—like he knew it was Jack Pierce who had been the cause of the anxiety he had seen in her eyes at the exhibition, and not the conclusion he had arrived at, that she was carrying his child. His jaw hardened as he coldly rejected the memory. 'My compliments,' he mocked, 'on your duplicity.'

'Please don't say that,' she implored.

'What does he want from you?' Adam demanded. 'Does he want you to steal for him again?'

She nodded.

'What else?'

'There is nothing else.'

'Yes, there is.' Her stubborn determination to remain silent finally snapped his fragile self-control. Leaning towards her, he gripped her arms and thrust his face close to hers, wanting to shake it out of her. 'The rest, Edwina. I want to know the rest,' he demanded in a silky voice that nevertheless rang with authority. 'I shall give you no peace until you tell me. Why did you go looking for Pierce today?' His lips twisted cruelly, his eyes full of mockery. 'Could it be that you liked stealing after all—liked the excitement, so you want to try it again?' His words were like hammer blows.

'How dare you say that to me?' Her cry was like a shot ripping across the distance between them, and she reared up like an enraged, courageous young angel of retribution. With her green eyes hurling daggers at him, her chest rising and falling with anger, Adam thought she was the most magnificent creature he had ever beheld, and he was sorely tempted to drag her into his arms and kiss her soundly, but his admiration for her courage was instantly demolished in his determination to get at the truth.

'You can't believe I liked thieving for Jack,' she flared, feeling his grip tighten on her arms. 'I hated it. You know I did. You'll be accusing me next of being a professional fortune hunter who sets out to entrap, to ensnare, and that I wormed my way into your life and your house determined not to miss a chance. But I'm not like that. You know I'm not.' Her words did not lack force—she felt crushed beneath the weight that he might think so ill of her.

'Then what? Did he hurt you? Did he threaten you? Has he threatened to tell everyone that you were nothing but a common thief if you don't do as he tells you?'

The questions were fired at her like shot from a gun, but she hesitated only a moment. 'Yes. He will see to it that everyone knows it.'

'And you believed him? The man hasn't a leg to stand on,' Adam said with a bitter laugh, relinquishing his hold on her arms and raking the hair from his brow with impatient fingers. 'He must know that. He's trying to frighten you. When you worked for him he was under the impression that you were a lad. Who is there to testify that you were anything else? There is nothing he can do to prove it.'

'Jack is clever. He will find something,' Edwina retorted, rubbing her arms.

'Be assured, Dolly and her girls will keep your secret—

and Barbara knows better than to open her mouth again. So you see, Edwina, he no longer has the power to manipulate you—to terrorise you. Now,' he said, his attention fastened on her deathly pale face, relentlessly determined to get to the bottom of this nonsensical affair, 'pray continue. I know there's more.'

Edwina swallowed hard, most of her determination having gone out of her decision to keep the truth from him. 'He—he knows how closely acquainted I am to you. He also knows of your inheritance, and he wants me to assist him in stripping Taplow Court of some of its valuables.'

Adam stared at her in stupefaction, all trace of anger having vanished from his expression. His face was very tense. 'Does he, by God?' he uttered at length. 'He thinks he can do that? This is fantastic! Insane! Tell me more.'

Without mentioning Toby, few words were needed to tell Adam what Jack required of her and what he intended. As Edwina spoke she was able to follow the swift succession of emotions reflected on his face—surprise, anger, indignation and contempt. For the time it took in telling he watched her in silence, then he shook his head slowly.

'The scoundrel must be caught. We'll see what the law has to say.'

'You can't go to the law, Adam,' Edwina said quietly. 'You mustn't tell anyone.' She took the last plunge into the truth. 'Jack has found Toby. He—he said that if I told anyone, he would kill him.'

In all the time she had known Adam, Edwina had never seen him immobilised by any emotion or event. Now, however, he stared at her as if unable to absorb what she had just told him. 'What did you say?' he said finally, his expression completely blank.

'I said that Jack has found Toby,' she repeated, just as the carriage drew level with the steps of his house.

Chapter Fifteen

Adam's blistering gaze sliced over her before he yanked open the carriage door and climbed down, almost dragging her after him. He marched her into the house and across the hall, striding past an astonished Mrs Harrison and almost colliding with a footman before entering the drawing room. Closing the door none too gently, he strode across the room to a bureau against the wall and poured himself a large brandy. Raising the glass to his lips, he drained the fiery amber liquid and put it down. Deep in thought he paced the carpet, eventually stopping in front of Edwina.

She looked up at him and froze at the inexplicable fury in his eyes when they finally settled on hers. She felt cold inside, and numb, as she stood without moving in the heavy silence, waiting for him to speak.

'That bastard has had Toby in his clutches for more than three weeks, and you didn't tell me? You didn't believe in me enough to tell me?'

With a physical effort, Edwina willed her body to stand erect. 'I wanted to tell you,' she said. 'But you must understand now why I couldn't.'

'No, I do not. Didn't you consider for one minute the tortures he is capable of inflicting on the boy the longer he remains in his clutches?'

'Of course I did,' she cried. 'I, more that anyone, know what Jack is capable of. Do you think me so unfeeling? I am almost pulled apart every time I think of him.'

'And you agreed to comply,' Adam said roughly. 'Knowing him as you do, you agreed, blindly! It did not occur to you that he could have been lying about Toby, that it was simply a ruse to get you to fall in with his plans.'

Two bright spots of indignation appeared on Edwina's cheeks. 'I did not agree to help him, but I knew I would have to make it look as though I would co-operate to protect Toby's life. If you must know, I went to look for Jack today to beg him to release Toby. I would have given him everything I possess to have him freed.'

'How very touching,' Adam retorted with biting sarcasm, walking away from her. 'Was Pierce telling the truth? Are you sure he has Toby?'

'I believe him. Neither of us can afford not to believe him. If Jack even suspects I have told you, it could put Toby's life in great peril. Who knows what that man will do? If it's a matter of acquiring a fortune, he will not ease his determination until he has it.'

'And just when does Pierce plan to burgle Taplow Court?'

'I don't know, exactly,' she admitted. 'When I become a regular visitor to the house—or when I am your wife, I suppose.'

The muscles of Adam's face clenched so tightly a nerve in his cheek began to throb. 'My wife?' he repeated cynically, moving closer while his gaze locked on hers. 'Are you telling me you are willing to accept my proposal after all?'

'Yes—if you still want me.' He continued to stare at her, rigid as steel. Her mouth went dry and her heart began to beat in terrifying dread as she sensed Adam had withdrawn from her, that he might no longer want to marry her. It was as if the closeness they had shared had never existed.

'In that case,' he drawled, 'for Toby's sake I shall obtain a special licence. We will be married within days. I sincerely hope you will raise no objection to that?'

Swallowing her rising panic, Edwina shook her head. 'No, of course not,' she answered, determined at all costs to conduct herself with calm maturity, and to make it infinitely clear to him that she was sorry she had kept her encounter with Jack Pierce from him. 'I realise I should have told you. I can see my failure to do so has angered you.'

'How very observant of you,' he mocked coldly.

Ignoring his sarcasm, Edwina persevered in what she considered to be a reasonable tone. 'Your accusations of complicity and treachery I do not deserve and deeply resent, Adam. I did what I thought was right and for the good of Toby. Jack threatened to kill him to ensure my silence and my co-operation. And ever since I saw him that day he has been having me watched. What could I do? Based on those things, I didn't tell you. If you can't see that, then I'm sorry.'

Adam looked at her sharply. 'Having you watched? How do you know that?'

'He left his accomplice behind at Oakwood. I saw him almost every day. He made no attempt to conceal himself, and I am certain he has followed me to London. What will you do?'

'I've no intention of sitting back and waiting for him to contact you, if that's what you think. I intend to be one step ahead. First I shall find Toby. Then I am going to do everything I can to ruin Jack Pierce.' His voice was low and filled with hatred, his hands clenched into fists by his sides. 'However long it takes, whatever I have to do, I'll make him pay for this. I'll see him rot in hell.'

Edwina shrank from the violence glittering in his eyes, eyes as cold as blue steel.

'In a day or two I'll tell you more,' he went on, 'but now I want you to return to Long Acre.'

The tone, lightly contemptuous, made Edwina's hackles rise. A surge of anger shot through her. 'In your present mood I can see that is the sensible thing to do. Perhaps when you are able to see things more clearly it will occur to you that I love you so much I was prepared to lay down my life for you and Toby. Goodbye, Adam.' Without more ado she turned and walked away from him, her head held high and her back ramrod straight, but her parting words were said in a tone of doleful resignation and with such humility that found a chink in Adam's armour.

He felt the full weight of her confession, of her beauty, and if any bit of anger and irritation remained about her failure to inform him about Jack Pierce, it immediately vanished at the sight of her retreating figure. Quietly he said, 'Edwina.' She paused without turning. His tone was softer now. 'I do understand. I also understand that you went to find Pierce for Toby's sake, and in return I rewarded you with callousness and mistrust. I apologise. Please forgive me.' When she failed to turn and look at him, he said, 'Come here.'

Edwina turned and faced him. The distance between them stretched like a mile. Slowly she retraced her steps and stood before the handsome, grave man who was watching her intently. She met his gaze, which was warmer now. 'Forget Toby for the moment, Adam—if you can. This is about you and me. I asked you if you wanted me. You still haven't answered. If I am to be your wife, it's important to me. I have to know.'

Taking her face between his hands, he looked deep into her glorious eyes. His expression held no laughter when he searched the hidden depths with his own, and when he spoke his voice was husky.

'Want you? How can you ask me that? Little fool. My attraction to you is both powerful and undeniable. I have wanted you from the moment I knew you were no longer a thirteen-year-old lad, one minute filled with childlike innocence, and the next with the wisdom of someone twice your age. You are still full of strange, shifting shadows, and I ask myself if I shall ever truly know who you are.'

'Know that I am only a woman who loves you. That is the truth.'

Adam's strong, lean hands left her face and folded round her, drawing her close to his hard chest, and suddenly his lips were on her eyes, her cheeks, seeking her mouth. Trembling with a joy that was almost impossible to contain, Edwina abandoned herself to his embrace, pressing herself close to him and closing her eyes, which were full of tears. Their kiss was full of longing, tasting of salt and bittersweet, and when at last they drew apart, Adam took Edwina's chin between his fingers and tilted her head until the light shone in the green depths of her eyes.

'There is one thing more I have to ask you, my love. Have you told me everything? Are there any more secrets lurking in that pretty head of yours that I should know about?'

She stared at him, a soft pink flush mantling her cheeks, knowing perfectly well what it was he wanted to know. With a raised brow he waited silently, expectantly, for her answer. She swallowed, tears of joy and relief constricting her breathing. 'Why—I—yes,' she said softly, shyly. 'Since you ask, there is just one very small secret you should know about. It—it concerns a baby. Our baby.'

His heart ecstatic in its joy, with a groan Adam pulled her against his chest with stunning force, crushing her against him. 'My beautiful, darling girl, thank you,' he whispered hoarsely, burying his face in her fragrant hair. His exultation was boundless as she moulded her body to the rigid contours of his. After a moment he held her at arm's length and gazed down into her melting green eyes, seeing they were wet with tears, but a smile was trembling on her rosy lips.

'You are certain?'

Her mouth curved in a sublime smile while her eyes grew

dark. 'It's early days, I know, but I'm as certain as I can be at this time. I can see the prospect of being a father pleases you.'

'Pleases me?' He laughed loud with jubilant delight. 'That is an understatement. I am overjoyed. I've no experience in dealing with babies, but it fills me with happiness—and gratitude, my love. I had never imagined that when you gave yourself to me it would be so wonderful, and now you are to present me with what I've always wanted—a child, which is a rare gift indeed—makes it complete.'

He strode across the room and went to fill two glasses with wine, coming back and handing one to Edwina. 'Let us drink the health of our child, Edwina,' he said, raising his glass, 'and tell me how I can give you back a little of the happiness you have brought me.'

'I have happiness enough, Adam,' she replied, her eyes shining rapturously, 'and when we have found your Toby, it will be complete.'

It wasn't until later, when Edwina was alone at the house in Long Acre, that the full realisation of what she was about to do set in: she would be married to Adam within days. Just the thought of being his wife warmed her heart and set her pulses racing, but she was disappointed that he hadn't told her that he loved her, which would make their union perfect.

Taplow Court was to be her home after all. A coldness crept over her when she thought of this, and she wondered what it would be like living there with Adam—as his countess—instead of Silas. Before she had so much as set foot inside the place she could already feel its oppression, its emptiness and her lack of belonging. Built to impress—and intimidate—centuries before, Silas had inhabited it fully. There he had reigned like a black spider in the centre of his web, and she would always think of Taplow Court as being his house.

Her thoughts turned to Adam, and she wondered what it had

been like for him, living there with his much older cousin. She felt his bitterness whenever he spoke of Silas and Taplow Court, reflecting some inner battle as yet unresolved, which told her that whatever had befallen him there had left scars—scars that were of a personal nature—and had nothing to do with what Silas had done to Toby's father and to Toby himself.

This was confirmed by Dolly when she called on her to apologise for Barbara's behaviour at the exhibition. Edwina studied her visitor, not critically, nor with the kind of fascination with which many upper-class ladies would gaze at animals in a zoo, just as though women of Dolly's profession were another species. Rather it was with an assessing frankness, and even an admiration one woman directs at another, when she sincerely believes that woman to be worthy of it.

Attired in a modestly styled dark-green velvet dress and bonnet and a little paint, she resembled a respectable middle-aged lady about town, rather than the madam of a bordello in Covent Garden.

'I fear that young lady is not the meek, obedient daughter my sister might have wished for,' Dolly said as she swept into the sitting room, a subtle cloud of expensive perfume following in her wake. She seated herself beside Edwina on the sofa, glad that the two of them were alone, for there were things she wanted to say to this lovely young woman that were for her ears alone.

'Unfortunately your niece treats me with contempt whenever we meet,' Edwina remarked ruefully.

'Barbara treats everyone so. She is, as you see, a great beauty. She is also extremely spirited and opinionated and suffers from her own passionate nature. As for her contempt of you, your closeness to Adam is the reason for that. Adam is an authoritative man who demands loyalty and commands respect from his friends. Barbara has done herself no favours with her outburst—and no one is more aware of that than she is. She deeply regrets telling Jack Pierce where you could be found, and at this very moment she is at home in Chelsea, wallowing in humiliation and self-pity.

'You and I and Adam know the truth behind her accusation—and Barbara too in small measure—despite your uncle's gallant ride to the rescue, but sadly she would never be able to understand the hold Jack Pierce had over you, and how you were driven to do what you did out of fear. I am so glad your uncle rose quickly to your defence.'

'So am I.' Her lips curved in a slow smile when she thought of Uncle Henry. 'My uncle has said and done many things since I returned home that have pleasantly surprised me. How is Barbara feeling today?'

'Miserable, extremely foolish and very ashamed.' Dolly's lips curved in a smile. 'I doubt she will venture far from Chelsea for some time. I always knew her hunger for praise and admiration—for Adam—would be her downfall one day. She had set her heart upon a future with him—a small dream, perhaps, but one beyond her grasp now.'

'I can see that. She came to see me when Adam went to Taplow. Did you know?'

'Yes, she told me. Edwina, I am extremely fond of my niece, but she was not made for Adam—however much she may try to persuade herself otherwise. Whereas you, my dear, will be perfect for him.'

'I will?'

'Adam has told me he has asked you to be his wife.'

'That is true—and I have accepted,' Edwina replied with a soft smile.

'I'm glad. You will be good for him. You will also make a beautiful countess,' she said appraisingly. 'Do you love him, Edwina?'

'Yes, and I told him so.'

'You have excellent judgement.'

'Perhaps I shouldn't have. I think I may have embarrassed him with sentiments he cannot return. But I do love him, Dolly. I have come to care for him deeply. But rather than lose him I am prepared to accept what we have.'

Dolly noticed the tell-tale flush on her cheeks, and the softness in her eyes that bespoke the true depth of her feelings for Adam. 'No matter what you have heard regarding his exploits with women, Edwina, Adam's reputation has been grossly exaggerated. Because of the past, he has always vowed never to let his emotions become engaged, and he only ever gives so much of himself. But he is more than fond of you. Anyone can see he adores you. I have never seen him look at a woman the way he looks at you. Oh, yes, he loves you. I was beginning to despair he would ever find it.'

Troubled, Edwina looked at her. 'You say he loves me. How can you know that? He is attracted to me and feels a deep affection for me, I know, but he has never spoken of love.'

'I have known Adam since he was six years old. I know his moods—often better than he knows them himself. Barbara was right about one thing. Women have always been attracted to him. He warms them, but he can burn them too. He loves and leaves his paramours with frequent ease. You see, he has never wanted any of them. What he has with you is more meaningful.

'Oh, yes, he loves you, but as yet it's more than he cares to admit. He may not even know it, and when he does he will be surprised. He does not give of himself lightly or easily, but I truly believe he will be your most devoted slave. Beneath his often overbearing and imperious manner, Adam is a sensitive man and capable of great gentleness. He is a fine man.'

'And you would know that.' Edwina smiled.

'Yes, I do. When you become his wife and he takes you to live at Taplow Court, be patient. The house and the memories that dwell there will be hard for him to come to terms with.'

'Adam always speaks of Taplow Court and his cousin with such bitterness. What happened there to harden his heart so, Dolly? Was it dreadful for him?' she asked quietly.

'It wasn't pleasant, Silas being what he was.'

'He was a terrible man.'

A shadow came over Dolly's face. 'Yes, yes, he was. You know I was the housekeeper at Taplow Court for several years, don't you?'

Edwina nodded, watching her closely.

'I was also Silas's mistress.'

Edwina stared at her in astonishment. 'You were in love with him?'

'To my shame, yes, I was—deeply—but gradually my love turned to hate. Silas never loved anyone or anything in his life. Only when he had brought his prey to its knees, humbled and in fear-maddened pain, could he find the only form of love that could content him. He was close to the devil where making people wretched was concerned. He was an evil man, Edwina, and he did some terrible things.'

Edwina reached over and placed her hand over Dolly's. 'If you are referring to the time when he killed Toby's father, Dolly, and how he gave Toby to some tinkers because he couldn't stand the sight of him, I know about that. Adam told me.'

'I'm glad he has. That—that was a terrible time,' she whispered. 'That was when I truly hated Silas. He liked hurting people. He got immense pleasure out of seeing them suffer. At six years old Adam didn't stand a chance.'

'Was that how old he was when he went to live at Taplow Court?'

Dolly nodded in reply. 'It was difficult for him when his parents died. Silas gave him a hard time.' She gave Edwina a brief account of Adam's miserable childhood and the cruelties inflicted on him by Silas on a daily basis. 'He became withdrawn, learned to hide his feelings. He still does. School was the best thing that happened to him. Being able to indulge his passion for painting, and encouraged to do so by his tutors, stripped away some of his reserve, but not all of it.

'As he got older and taller, I recall once when he returned to Tap-low and strode into the house with that particular long-legged stride, that lounging grace…' she smiled '…you must have noticed that arrogant way of walking he has—well, it put Silas's back up and he began to leave him alone. But Silas left him a bitter legacy. He taught him not to believe in the inherent goodness of anyone. He became restrained, cynical, and guarded, and beneath the sophisticated veneer he shows to the world, he is still the same.

'His life was damaged by experiences you and I cannot imagine. I was the only one who saw, the only one he would open up to. I was the only one who knew something of the person beneath.' She looked at Edwina and patted her hand, smiling. 'And now you. Perhaps you can strip away the remaining layers.'

'I will try.'

'I know you will, and I am sure you will succeed. I am sure that as his wife you will release him from the bondage of that awful time. Think yourself fortunate you didn't marry Silas.'

'I do. Every day. Has Adam told you that Silas killed my father.'

Now it was Dolly's turn to look surprised. 'No. What are you saying?' she enquired, aghast.

'It's a long story.' Edwina began haltingly with her father's decline into bankruptcy and his appeal to Silas for a loan, and as her story progressed beneath the sharp eyes that never faltered in their gaze, the sickening horror of it all came back to her. When she had finished she dropped her eyes and waited for Dolly to speak. The silence was so prolonged she wondered if the older woman could have failed to comprehend what she had told her. Finally the voice that spoke to her was low and shook with outrage.

'Mercy me! So, Silas had killed again.'

'Yes. Adam told me you were there when he killed Toby's father.'

She nodded. 'I saw him thrust the knife into his heart. Joseph Tyke, his name was—a fine man. He and Olivia had planned to wed, but, of course, Joseph being of low birth and nothing but a stable hand in Silas's eyes, Silas wouldn't hear of it. When Olivia left Taplow Court to go and live with Joseph's parents in St Albans—distraught and broken-hearted, poor girl—I left too. Sadly I lost track of her after that.'

A deep sorrow entered Dolly's eyes and there was a hint of tears as her gaze became focused on a point beyond Edwina's shoulder. 'Perhaps if I hadn't she wouldn't have thrown herself on Silas's mercy when she was dying—perhaps she wouldn't have died and Silas wouldn't have given Toby to some passing tinkers,' she said quietly. Shaking her head, she looked down at her hands, swallowing down her tears, tears she hadn't shed since she had left Taplow Court all those years ago. 'Perhaps you will understand why, even now, I continue to hate Silas. I despise him still, even though he is in his grave and can do no more harm.'

Edwina had gone white. 'Dear Lord. I ask myself what manner of man, or monster, was Silas Clifford, to whom I was almost bound? What depths of evil and sadistic cruelty lay behind the face he showed to the world?' She peered into Dolly's face and swallowed hard. 'But—didn't you tell anyone of what he had done? Surely he should have been apprehended for killing a man in cold blood.'

Dolly smiled thinly. 'I was only the housekeeper. Silas was a powerful man—so powerful that he could use his influence to protect himself from the law. No one would have believed me, and poor Olivia was too weak and too afraid of him to stand against him. But why didn't you, when he killed your father?'

'I only found out recently, when I returned home and my

uncle told me the full facts. Silas was dead, the case closed, the verdict murder by person or persons unknown. I saw little point in having the case re-opened.'

'I can understand that. When I think of the pain Adam would suffer as a consequence, I would have done the same. It's best confined to the past and that everyone concentrates on the future.' Dolly got up to go, pulling on her gloves.

Edwina rose and placed her hand on the older woman's arm. 'Thank you for coming here and telling me all this, Dolly. It has answered a lot of questions.'

'Yes, I thought it might.'

'Won't you stay and meet Uncle Henry? Sir Joshua Reynolds has very kindly invited him to drop in at his studio to view his latest work in progress. Mr and Mrs Templeton have accompanied him. They've been gone some time, so I don't think it will be long before they return. I don't believe you were properly introduced to Uncle Henry at the exhibition last night.'

'I'd better not. I have to get back. The girls tend to get up to all manner of mischief when I'm not there. Besides, Edwina,' she said, bending a satiric glance on the young woman, 'last night your uncle didn't know I am one of the most notorious women in Covent Garden. By now I am sure he will, and, being a respectable gentleman, he would not thank you for an introduction and would make haste to remove himself from my vicinity at once.'

As she turned to go, with Edwina saying she would call and see Harriet some time during the next few days, Dolly smiled inwardly, for there were many respectable gentleman who patronised Dolly's Place, nice men like Edwina's Uncle Henry, men with families, whose wives believed bordellos were only visited by common, vulgar men. It would never occur to them that their husbands could possibly seek out such low women, and actually pay them for their services.

As Edwina showed her visitor out, she made no attempt

to contradict her, for what Dolly had said was true. But she was not as green as Dolly evidently thought her to be. During her time in St Giles she had seen many high-born, respectable gents—the rich, the fêted, the distinguished, men of all classes and occupations, in their expensive coats and rich waistcoats—seek out harlots to indulge their indelicate practices. Men of Uncle Henry's ilk were no exception.

Adam and Edwina were married a week later. Neither of them wanted to surround the ceremony with pomp, yet the preparations were frantic. There was nothing constrained in the joy with which her uncle and Mr and Mrs Templeton had received the news of their impending marriage. Mr and Mrs Templeton were highly delighted to have Edwina married from their house and, for their part, were looking forward to the modest celebrations.

Edwina saw Adam only twice during this time. She was disappointed at not seeing him and tried not to think about it too much as she was carried along on a whirl of preparations. In brief notes transmitted by one of his footmen, he kept her informed about arrangements as he embarked on an undercover operation to try to locate Jack Pierce. But Jack was like a fox that had gone to earth.

When the day of the wedding finally arrived, in a pearl-encrusted wedding gown of cream satin, her riotous curls brushed to a gleaming mass, Edwina went to meet her husband to be at the church of St Clement Danes in the Strand. His tall frame resplendent in claret velvet, Adam looked down at his glorious, beautiful bride with gentle pride. 'You are beautiful,' he murmured, for her ears alone. Her happiness showed in the sheen of her skin and the glow of her hair, and in the clear depths of her green eyes. Taking her hand in his strong, reassuring grasp, he led her to the altar.

Bathed in sunlight pouring in through the windows, they

knelt on two prayer stools. The priest took his stand in front of them and recited the prayers and customary phrases, the bridal couple responding. When they were pronounced husband and wife, Adam claimed the right to kiss his bride.

Afterwards, in the elegance of Mr and Mrs Templeton's gilt and white salon, standing beside Adam and receiving their guests, smiling uncertainly at everyone as she sipped her champagne, the whole affair had a distinct aura of unreality for Edwina. Sensing her nervousness, Adam went to unprecedented efforts to put her at her ease, for which she was grateful.

After the wedding breakfast, finding a moment to have a word with her alone, Adam took her hand and drew her to one side. He looked down into those twin green orbs, and something in their depths and in her shallow breathing made him frown in puzzlement, until he finally realised Edwina was afraid.

'What is it?' he asked gently, feeling her tremble when he ran his finger up her arm. 'What are you afraid of?'

Edwina gazed at the tall, daunting man who would do all manner of things to her later, and gave him a quivering smile. 'Not afraid. It's ridiculous, I know, but I'm nervous, that's all. It stems from what I know will come later,' she confessed quietly, and yet she trembled from excitement, impatience and fear before this virile husband of hers. 'I cannot for the life of me understand why I should feel this way about something I've done before, for which I am carrying your child.' She kept her voice low so that no one would overhear, for her condition was a matter they had agreed to keep to themselves for the time being.

With a tender smile Adam touched her pale cheek with his finger, before bending his head and gently placing his lips on the same spot, his senses coming alive to the elusive perfume scent of her. He thought of the night to come when she would be his once more, and his blood stirred hotly. 'Don't worry,' he murmured. 'We'll leave soon.'

'I confess I can't wait to escape all these people.'

Raising her hand to his lips, he placed a kiss on the gold band he had slipped on to her small finger in the church, locking his possessive, intense gaze onto hers. 'You can't escape me, my adorable, obedient wife. You belong to me now, and I won't let you.'

'I don't want to escape from you, Adam. Ever.'

'You make a beautiful Countess.'

'I confess I don't feel very much like one.' Detecting a roguish glint in his eyes, one she was beginning to recognise, one that must surely be what had charmed half the females in London, she cocked her head to one side. 'Now what are you thinking?'

A slow smile covered his lips. 'I'm trying to envisage you bedecked in rubies and diamonds as befits your station—and nothing else.'

'Adam Rycroft!' she reproached with a gurgle of laughter. 'Have you no shame?'

'None whatsoever,' he boasted wickedly. 'I've never made love to a countess before. It appeals to me.'

Impatient to have her to himself, an hour later Adam assisted her into his shiny black coach with the Earl of Taplow's coat of arms emblazoned on its door, and travelled the short distance to his house in Mayfair.

Chapter Sixteen

In the pale, watery light of dawn, emerging from heavy slumber, Edwina stretched in the huge bed. Nestling close to the man beside her, feeling his warm, firm flesh next to hers, she felt a deep contentment and languorous peace, having spent the most erotic night of her life as prey of this creature of the darkness—*her husband*—who had taken her with tender violence and had had his will with her after rousing her to heights of unbelievable, unbearable, passion, which erupted inside her, exploding with a force that tore a cry from her throat.

Awake, Adam tenderly kissed her shining head and placed his arm about her, his fingers stroking the smooth velvet flesh and following the curve of waist and hip. Half-opening her eyes, Edwina tilted her head and smiled up at him—the happy smile of a sated wife in love with her husband. He was staring up at the tester.

'You look disgustingly wide awake, my love,' she murmured sleepily, wriggling against him until she was in a position to place a soft kiss on the mat of dark curls covering his broad chest, 'and deep in thought.' She sighed and raised her head, searching his face, while an uneasy, inexplicable feeling of change hit her. His profile was harsh, and, his passion dimmed, his eyes were cool now, his mouth tight, and when he lifted his free hand and rubbed the muscles up the side of his neck as if he was tense, she felt a chill inside her.

'Adam, what are you thinking about? What is it?'

He didn't answer at once. He took a deep breath in a valiant effort to control himself. When he spoke his voice was calm, but each word might have been chiselled from ice. 'Jack Pierce.'

Edwina sighed. The sweet drift of happiness she had felt on waking shattered away. 'Must you think of him now?'

Angry, impotent frustration ran rampant through every fibre of Adam's being at his failure to locate Jack Pierce. 'Until he's found, until I have found Toby, I can think of little else. That blackguard seems to have disappeared into thin air. He could be anywhere in London.'

'I'm certain he's in St Giles.'

'Maybe you're right. Maybe we're jumping to conclusions. We cannot be sure of anything. I suppose it's too much to be hoped he will abandon his idea to burgle Taplow Court, and release Toby.'

'Jack is determined, Adam. He is merely biding his time. My belief is that he will show his hand when we return to Taplow.'

'Then we will let it be known that we are to go there three days hence.' He cursed savagely and thumped the bed in frustration. 'A whole week of looking, of making discreet enquiries, alternating with threats, promises and bribes, prevailing upon scoundrels like himself to undertake my commission to drag him from his lair—and nothing at the end of it. The immense number of alleyways, courts and bye-places of St Giles is like hell on earth, a place of abandonment for lost souls, and might have been intended for the purpose of concealment.'

The prudence of Adam's line of enquiries was obvious, but Edwina was apprehensive about it, and it was not the first time she had raised an objection. Lying on her stomach, she pulled herself up on her elbows and regarded him closely. His black brows were gathered in a harsh frown, but she lost none of her purposefulness. 'I am afraid that if Jack finds out you're looking for him, the game will be up—and that would be worse for Toby than for you.'

'I know that. I am sure of one thing: that Pierce is still having us watched. Whether it's the same man who followed you to London I have no way of knowing, but there is someone watching the house on a daily basis. At first I was tempted to confront the scoundrel, but I realise that if I were to do so it would alert Pierce and he may harm Toby. To lull suspicion I try to behave as though nothing is amiss. But I must get hold of Pierce somehow. Where is he hiding, and where does he store his stolen goods? He must have a warehouse, a building, somewhere, and employ craftsmen to make the jewellery and snuff boxes and suchlike unidentifiable before selling them on.'

'He does, but I don't know where. I was never made privy to the inside workings of his gang. Jack's band of thieves may not be as large as some that inhabits St Giles, but he is well organised—a criminal genius—and enjoys near-immunity from arrest. To find him will take someone who is as familiar with those rookeries of crime as he is himself.'

'That I know. One thing I have learned is that Jack Pierce is much feared and respected in the criminal underworld. How can I know who to trust—who is capable of tracking him down in his lair, without raising his suspicions?'

'Ed could do it.'

The words, spoken low and sure, hit Adam like a rock. At first he stared at her with amazed disbelief, his face rigid, then he reared up and rolled Edwina on to her back, looming over her like some gigantic black cloud. He recognised that stubborn thrust of her lovely chin. Her eyes were challenging and there was a hint of determination in their depths, and her expression had turned mutinous. When Edwina looked like that he knew to be wary.

'Ed will not,' he bit out. 'Don't you even think about it.' Pinning her to the bed, there was a dreadful blankness in his eyes. His voice was so cold, so full of terrifying menace, that Edwina's heart pounded, and she was gripped by a worried fear that she might have gone too far. 'Whatever is going on in that head of yours, Edwina, forget it. Don't even think of reverting back to Ed. He's in the past. Forgotten. Do you understand me?'

'Of course I do, but I was serious, Adam.'

'I know. That's what concerns me. It is not only ridiculous, but beset with perils.'

He was eyeing her with the menacing air that told Edwina her plan would not be tolerated. 'I am prepared to do anything to help you find Toby,' she persisted bravely. 'At least think about it.'

'I won't waste time thinking about it. The answer is no.' He was adamant.

Edwina's pert nose lifted in a manner of prim confidence. 'I know the bye-places and alleyways of St Giles. I know the houses where those who work for Jack lodge. If anyone can find him in St Giles, I believe I can.'

'I have every faith in your ability,' Adam ground out sarcastically, 'but I will not change my mind. I do not care to think of what that—that reprobate would do to you if he were to recognise you. Don't you dare disobey me. You know how dangerous St Giles is. You are now my wife and soon-to-be mother of my child. If you defy me, I'll lock you in your room until it's born.'

'You wouldn't.'

'Try my patience too far, Edwina, and you will learn what I can and cannot do,' he warned softly. 'Swear to me that you will do nothing to place yourself at risk.'

To her consternation Edwina felt her cheeks grow hot. Eager to dispel the fury she had aroused in him, in an unconsciously childlike gesture, she draped her arm around his neck and pulled his head down to hers. 'No, Adam, I won't swear. You must trust me.'

'Trust you?' he retorted, his lips hovering only inches above hers, feeling the heat of her, the softness of her flesh, of her touch as she trailed her fingers provocatively over his chest.

He could find no satisfaction in her reply, and was not about to let it die a beggar's death, but her soothing caress awoke his lust in places he tried to ignore. He tried to hold on to his anger, but this betrayal by his own body aroused an impatient vexation. He had thought that all the burning fires of the night past would have cooled by now, and would be slow to rekindle, but he was becoming increasingly aware of the folly of that conclusion.

'My love, you have a penchant for foolishness and trouble that outweighs all considerations of common sense. It concerns me deeply.'

Her lovely mouth curved in a soft, haunting sweet smile. 'It needn't.' She pressed closer to him and rested her palm on his cheek. His eyes were no longer cold and angry. They were warm now, full of affection, and his mouth curved in a languorous, sensual smile. 'Don't be cross, Adam—especially not today—the first day of our lives together. Perhaps you'll be in better humour when you've bathed and eaten,' she whispered, feeling his body begin to relax.

Adam was weakening. 'Sounds delightful,' he murmured, unable to tear his eyes from her. 'And afterwards?'

'I'm sure we'll find something to do,' she replied huskily, meaningfully, raising her head slightly to meet his lips, and planting a kiss on them. It was brief and light and meant to tease. She made a move to get out of bed, uncovering her shapely legs and supple young body. With a groan Adam reached out and pulled her back.

'Not yet.' His voice was hoarse with need, his eyes sultry. 'A few minutes more.'

Edwina recognised the look and laughed softly. 'I suppose I could spare a few.'

Pulling her beneath him once more, Adam's mouth covered hers, devouring, fondling her breasts, his lips leaving hers and following a trail to where a pulse was beating erratically in her neck. His warm breath touched her cheek, and he nibbled at her ear, sending delicious sensations through her. Beneath his tender assault she moaned softly and threw back her head, pressing herself even closer.

'I love you, Adam,' she whispered, in a barely breathed whisper. 'I love you so much.'

'Convince me.' Finding her lips once more, his heavy eyelids drooping over his eyes, Adam kissed her long and deep as she arched beneath him. The movement robbed him of his thinking, her soft moan acting on him like an aphrodisiac. As he claimed her with his hands and then his body, he could not believe the passion of his lovely young wife, nor the need, the violence of his body's craving for her. She was completely female, womanly and beautiful, sensual and wanton without being conscious of it.

The following day when Adam left for the Academy to meet up with friends, Edwina cautiously left the house by a back exit, slipping away into the dusk like a shadow, foiling Jack's accomplice watching the front of the house.

Garbed as a lad, having purloined breeches and boots and an old jacket from one of the stable lads when he'd been busy with the horses—whom she would recompense when she returned—she'd had no qualms at cutting her hair a little shorter and rubbing soot and grease into it to dull its lustre, before liberally applying it to her face and clothes. Much as she hated it, her disguise was necessary and something she would have to contend with.

Keeping to the shadows, she went in the direction of St Giles, bravely and sure-footedly. By the time she reached this vicious, amoral world she had hoped she would never have to set foot in again, it was almost dark, with just a pale light in the sky from the setting sun to percolate the twilight. The cloud of smoke and soot that hung over St Giles covered buildings and inhabitants with grime, thickening the atmosphere to such a degree as to be a hazard to visibility and to health. Edwina realised, with a sense of relief, that she was drawing near to places that were familiar to her, but the chaotic uncontrollability, the corruption and dissolution, the stench, reached out and clung to her.

The streets were just as she remembered—wild and rushing headlong. Men and women, drunk out of their minds, lay wallowing in the gutters or propped themselves up against the walls. Lords and ladies and street vendors rubbed shoulders with beggars and ragged urchins and tawdry whores, who brazenly pulled open their dresses to display their wares. An overflowing rag cart had overturned, spilling its contents into the street and causing a stoppage. A din and clamour ensued. Someone cried 'stop thief', and everyone looked to their pockets. A pistol was fired, but the rogue had fled.

Shuddering with revulsion and fear, Edwina moved on, penetrating deeper into St Giles to look for some of Jack's workers. Beggars appeared out of the dark recesses, most barefoot and in tattered clothes. After half an hour or so she paused and looked across the street. A youth was leaning idly against a tavern wall in an attitude of close observation. Edwina returned his look and smiled inwardly on recognising Jonathan Ward, one of Jack's more experienced workers. Aged about fifteen, Jonathan was a person of few words, small for his age and as dirty as the rest. His overlarge coat hung on his narrow shoulders and flapped about his skinny legs. With extra pockets stitched into the lining, it was an ideal garment for secreting away stolen goods.

Pushing her hands down into her pockets, Edwina sidled cautiously forward.

'Hullo, Ed,' Jonathan said. 'Surprised to see you back 'ere.

Put Jack in a black frenzy when you ran off, it did. Where've you been?'

Edwina shrugged and leaned on the wall beside him. 'Here and there. Across the river mostly—Southwark.'

'Rich pickings, were there?'

She shook her head. 'Not much. Thought I'd come back and try my luck with Jack again. Is he about?'

'Somewhere,' Jonathan replied, continuing to watch the passers-by with more interest than he was displaying. 'Don't reckon much to your chances when he gets his hands on you.' He sliced a finger across his neck to indicate what Jack would do.

Edwina grinned bravely in the face of it. 'I'll risk it.'

'Where're you lodging?'

'Haven't got any—no money, either.'

'Suppose you could sleep at Ma Pratchet's place—if you've come back to work for Jack. Come on,' he said, shoving himself away from the wall. 'I'll take you since there's not much doin' round here tonight.'

With nothing to lose and much to gain, Edwina followed him. She was remembering all she'd heard about Ma Pratchet.

Jonathan took her to Crow Alley and entered a small yard. She looked round at the knot of cramped houses and the filth piled up in corners and shuddered. This was where some of Jack's thieves were housed—not in the attics where they might see the light of day, but in the deepest place in the house, the basement and damp cellars, with no ventilation or light, the boys packed inside keeping company with pigs, chickens and vermin, the air impregnated with filthy odour.

Edwina followed Jonathan down a narrow flight of stone steps and into what could only be described as the underworld of lost souls. Jack's boys filled the place, crouched together on the floor on straw mattresses, with hardly a spare inch between. Her heart wrenched at the pathetic sight as she looked at the motionless young bodies, some of them crouched in the foetal position as they slept, some surveying her with large empty eyes and with the air of people much older.

To the men and women of St Giles there was of necessity a moral insensibility towards children, a lack of finer feelings that allowed them to be unmoved by the wretchedness of these small creatures who, because of their weakness and poverty, were forced to do work as thieves for brutal, ruthless men like Jack Pierce. Edwina herself had had to harden herself, to become tough and insensitive to the suffering of those weaker than herself in order to survive it. Nevertheless, her heart wrenched with pity and helplessness at the sight of them.

Candles flickered listlessly, stuck into any receptacle that would hold them, great globs of wax fixing them to the surfaces on which they stood. A large deal table piled up with dirty plates and bottles of distilled spirit stood before a dull fire, teetering crookedly, one leg being shorter than the rest. A sooty iron pot suspended from a hook had something bubbling in it, spitting into the fire as Mrs Pratchet stirred the unsavoury contents. The stench of unwashed bodies, stale food and excrement was so appalling it filled Edwina's nose and head. She could taste and feel it. She clamped her lips tight, finding it difficult to contain her nausea. Already Adam and the comforts of her Mayfair home had receded a million miles.

Ma Pratchet was everything she had imagined—and worse. She was a huge, dour-faced old crone with lank grey hair, almost bent beneath the weight of her enormous bosoms. Seeing Jonathan, she left her cauldron and shuffled towards them. Not recognising Edwina, she held a candle above her head to get a better look. She had a bestial face. Dirt rested in the creases and folds of her skin and in the deep rings around her grey eyes. She scrutinised Edwina's every detail.

'Well, what have we here?'

'Another one for yer, Ma,' Jonathan said. 'His name's Ed.

Worked for Jack afore so he knows what he's about. He's no lodgings, so I brought him here.'

It was a common enough occurrence for Jonathan to bring new lads in from the street, so Ma Pratchet wasn't surprised. She poked Edwina sharply in the ribs. 'Not a bag of bones like some. Someone's been feeding yer,' she grumbled reproachfully. Placing the candle on the table, she stuck her hands on her massive hips and looked Edwina up and down as she would a prize cow. 'So—yer another o' Jack's boys. Well, suppose ye'd best sleep over there.' Grudgingly indicating a spare mattress in a corner of the room, she thrust her face close to Edwina's. 'But I'll warn yer. I keep a quiet house—no trouble, see?'

'I won't be,' Edwina replied roughly, stepping back from the stench of Ma Pratchet's foul gin-laden breath and her penetrating eyes, beneath which she was beginning to feel extraordinarily self-conscious. She glanced around fearfully, fully expecting Jack to materialise out of the gloom at any second, but if he was running true to form, he'd be at some alehouse at this time and wouldn't show himself until daylight.

'I'll be going.' Jonathan began to move away. 'Want to come?'

Edwina shook her head. 'I'll stay and get some sleep.' Looking around at the sleeping bodies, she wondered if any of them had seen Jack with Toby; if so, they might be able to throw some light on where the boy was being held.

'Suit yerself,' Jonathan said. He sauntered to the door, whistling jauntily as he swaggered out.

Edwina lay on her foul-smelling straw mattress on the trodden earth and pretended to sleep, watching Ma Pratchet as she sat before the fire and took a bottle of gin from the hearth. Hoping it wouldn't be too long before the old crone fell into a stupor, Edwina looked around her, trying not to think about Adam. When he returned and discovered she'd disappeared, his initial reaction would be one of deep concern, but then he would remember the conversation they'd had during the early hours of their first morning as man and wife, and he would put two and two together and come up with the right conclusion. She could well surmise how he would react.

What tomorrow held for her she could neither fathom nor raise a care for just then. It seemed an eternity away. It wasn't long before she began to itch and started to scratch vigorously, realising with a shudder of revulsion that she was being invaded by her old enemies—fleas. After what seemed like an eternity she saw Ma Pratchet's head loll back against the back of her chair and she began to snore loudly. Edwina looked to see if any of the boys were awake so she could question them, but they all had their eyes closed.

She sighed and stirred herself; then, seeing something that resembled a small crutch leaning against the wall beside a boy who was lying apart from the rest, her eyes froze on the object. Immediately she sat bolt upright and looked at its owner—a small, skinny boy with a thatch of greasy black hair.

Her heart began to hammer in her chest. Slowly, so as not to draw any undue attention to herself, she crept between the sleeping bodies. When she was close to the crippled boy she collapsed on to her knees beside him. Leaning over, she looked at his face closely. He was sleeping, the long dark eyelashes heavy against his pale cheeks.

Was it possible that this boy was Toby? No, it couldn't be. It could not be that easy. There were hundreds of crippled boys in London, and Jack often put them to work to distract the victims' attention from his more experienced thieves before they robbed them. Besides, Jack would never be so lax as to leave a boy he was holding for ransom with Ma Pratchet. Would he?

She touched his arm. 'Toby?' she whispered. When he didn't respond she gave him a gentle shake. 'Toby?' she repeated. He squirmed and his eyes flickered open—brown, just as Adam had told her.

'What do you want?' he mumbled, sounding very young. He rubbed his eyes with the backs of his hands.

Edwina was barely able to contain herself as she asked, 'Is your name Toby? Toby Clifford?'

He rolled on to his back and met her eyes. 'Yes. Who are you?'

Edwina's mind stumbled with relief. 'A friend. I've come to take you away from here.'

'I'm not supposed to go anywhere. Jack will be angry.'

'Don't you want to leave here, Toby?'

He nodded, rubbing his eyes.

'Then come quickly, while Ma Pratchet's asleep. Trust me, Toby. I am here to help you.'

The hour was late when Adam returned home. Unfastening his cravat as he went, he climbed the stairs to the chamber he shared with Edwina. He was tired, angry and frustrated because his business at the Academy had kept him away from his wife longer than he had intended, so, entering his dressing room, he sent his weary valet off to bed. His frustration began to dissipate when he thought of Edwina waiting for him in the adjoining room, and he smiled at the thought of waking her with a kiss. With that tender thought came several more of a similar nature. Unbuttoning his shirt, he opened the connecting door. The maid hadn't quite drawn the curtains over the window and moonlight spilled across the floor on to the bed.

He froze. The bed was empty and had not been slept in.

Where was Edwina? Lighting the candle on her dressing table, he looked around the room as if he expected to see her hiding in the shadows, but the room was empty. He was about to walk away when something bright beside her hairbrush caught his eye. It was copper and gold—a curl—Edwina's hair. He stared down at it in horror, and then slowly picked it up, letting the feathery wisps fall between his fingers. Glancing down at the rubbish bin beside the dressing table, he saw more curls. The conversation he'd had with his wife the previous morning came crashing back into his mind, where something dark and sinister was already beginning to form. There was only one reason he could think of that would have made Edwina cut her hair.

Striding back into his dressing room, he pulled the bell chord to summon his valet back. He was scowling darkly when he appeared several minutes later. 'Have you seen my wife?' he asked abruptly.

Quaking beneath his master's wrath, the poor man shook his head. 'No, sir. Not since this afternoon.'

Adam's scowl took on the creases of his growing concern. 'Summon her maid at once.'

Refastening his cravat, he paced the floor of his dressing room, his brain working restlessly, crossing bridges before he reached them. His mind registered disbelief that she would defy him, it shouted denials, even while something within him began to crumble. More minutes later, attired in her night robe and sleepy eyed, Edwina's young maid, Amelia, appeared.

'No, sir,' she answered in reply to his question, rapped out impatiently. 'My mistress sent me to bed early—said she could manage by herself tonight, which I thought slightly odd at the time.'

Adam confirmed this action was unprecedented. Immediately he ordered his valet to rouse the whole household and for them to assemble in the hall. Reining in his temper with a supreme effort as he waited for his orders to be carried out, when his servants appeared he asked them icily if they had seen his wife. When no one could throw any light on where she could be, after ordering the groom to have his carriage made ready at once, he dismissed them.

By God, Edwina had actually gone to St Giles. Adam could hardly contain his fury. He could not believe she would defy him, her husband, so brazenly. But then, with her defiance of anything that smacked of conformity, with grim cynicism he immediately changed his mind. That wench was capable of anything. She had a mind of her own and there was no telling what she would do next.

Raking his fingers through his dark hair, his emotions veering from disbelief to fury, Adam knew a wrath that was beyond anything he had ever felt in his life. Thrusting his arms into his jacket and cursing savagely, he left the house with ground-devouring strides, taking grim pleasure in thinking up methods he would use to punish his wife for her treachery and deceit and rebellion.

Meanwhile, deep inside St Giles, Edwina and Toby were negotiating the complicated web of alleyways with difficulty. Toby hadn't said a word when they had left Ma Pratchet's. Even though he knew nothing about Edwina, he seemed to trust her and followed her resignedly and without question. Very little light shone to show them their way. The night was filled with the noise of vice, the air cold, their breath leaving their mouths in clouds of condensed air. Edwina kept her eyes fixed straight ahead, too afraid to look in the dark recesses where menace lurked—old lechers and skulking thieves. When Toby faltered behind her she glanced back.

Toby stared at his protector apologetically. The tip of his crutch had become lodged between two cobbles. 'I'm sorry. I can't move quickly with my crutch.'

'Don't worry. I'll help you.'

Edwina helped him pull the crutch free. Noting how he shivered in his shirtsleeves, she removed her jacket and helped him to slip it on. He smiled gratefully and then they were off again, pausing every now and then to let him rest. They progressed slowly and clumsily, Edwina attuned to all the dangers of discovery. She didn't look back. Jack might not have gone to the alehouse tonight, and decided to visit to Ma Pratchet after all. Might they not be hunted at this very moment? She felt the beginnings of panic, but forced the emotion to subside.

Edwina was sure Ma Pratchet, in her inebriated state, wouldn't notice that Toby was gone until morning, and if Jack followed his usual pattern neither would he. Even so, she hurried faster. When Jack found out Toby had disappeared he would give chase, especially when Ma Pratchet told him a boy called Ed had also gone—and Jack would remember Ed.

Sooner or later he would come after them. She had witnessed the fierce turmoil of his spirit, experienced the deep well of his cruelty, and she cringed from the absolute determination that drove him beyond the bounds of normal men. Fear drove her faster. Jack would never let them escape. Somewhere, some time, he would retaliate, implacable and not to be denied.

There would be some explaining to do to Adam when she reached the house, and he would be furious, but she would leave the soothing to Toby, whose presence would be far more effective than anything that she had to say.

Dawn was breaking when they broke free of the squalor of St Giles and carried on towards the elegance of Mayfair. Already the birds were singing and the air was sweeter.

Chapter Seventeen

Close to the house Toby stopped and gazed up at it. Taking a step back and leaning against the wall for support, he shook his head. 'I can't go in there.'

This was the first time since Edwina had found him that he showed fear. He seemed to shrink inside himself. 'Toby, what is it?'

His eyes were wide and filled with terror when he looked at her. 'Does Uncle Silas live here?'

Edwina understood what was going through his mind and was quick to allay his fears. 'No. Your Uncle Silas is dead. This is Adam's house. Your mother and Adam were cousins. Being next in line, Adam inherited the title and the estate from your uncle.'

He looked at her sharply. 'Taplow Court?'

'Yes. You'll like him, Toby, I promise you. He's been trying to find you for a long time.'

Hope flickered in the dark eyes. 'Has he?' When his strange companion nodded, he cocked his head to one side and eyed her curiously. He was certain his rescuer was a youth, not much taller than himself, and yet he spoke like a female. 'Then who are you?'

Edwina smiled, her teeth gleaming white in her grimy face. 'My name's Edwina. Adam is my husband.'

With wide-eyed astonishment Toby looked her up and down. 'You're a woman?' he gasped.

She laughed lightly. 'I know I don't look very much like one dressed like this, but I assure you I am.'

'Then why are you dressed like that?'

'It's a long story, Toby, and I will tell you. But it will have to keep until later. Come—let me show you your new home.'

When they entered two footmen stared at them, the surprise on their faces yielding to obvious bewilderment. Mrs Harrison emerged from the kitchen and paused on seeing them.

'Just a minute,' her voice rang out as they were about to enter the hall.

They stood stock-still and waited for her to reach them, fully prepared to be chastised like two naughty children. She looked from one to the other and then returned her astonished gaze to the taller of the two. Seeing the mistress behind the guise of the unwashed urchin she appeared to be repulsed by what she saw and stepped back, wrinkling her nose in disgust when the stench of St Giles reached her sensitive nostrils.

'Gracious me! It's the mistress! My goodness!'

Edwina gave her a dirty-faced grin. 'I'm sorry to startle you, Mrs Harrison, but my disguise was necessary.'

'Well—if you say so. I'm glad you're back safely.'

Taking Toby's hand Edwina drew him forward. 'This is Toby, Mrs Harrison. Toby Clifford—the boy my husband has been looking for.'

Mrs Harrison's expression softened when she looked at the lad balancing on his crutch, his crippled leg bent beside the other. Tears pricked the backs of her eyes. 'Indeed it is, and it gladdens my heart to see him at long last. There have been times when the master's been out of his mind with worrying about what could have befallen you. I swear there isn't a street or alleyway in London that he hasn't scoured in his search.'

'I—is Adam still in bed?' Edwina asked tentatively.

'In bed? Lordy me—no. When he found out you'd gone he left to look for you. Quite beside himself he was, too, I can tell you—with his temper raised to boiling point.' The last few words were added not so much as an afterthought, but to warn this young woman of what to expect when her husband eventually returned home. Miss Edwina was the only woman who could provoke such unprecedented emotional reactions in the master.

Edwina's heart beat with a combination of fear and dread at the thought of confronting Adam. Drop by precious drop she could feel her confidence draining away. 'Oh, well, perhaps his temper will have cooled by the time he returns. Will you have a room made ready for Toby, and I'm sure he must be ravenous.' She smiled at the boy, who was gazing about him with awe. 'I'm sure a tub and some hot water won't go amiss—for either of us. Mrs Harrison will take care you, Toby. I'll see you in a little while.'

Not wanting Adam to see her dressed like this, she hurried up the stairs. While Amelia filled the bath and laid out the soap and towels, Edwina removed her filthy clothes and dropped them into a heap. Free of restraint, she climbed into the bath and sank into the steaming hot scented water, a long sigh of pleasure escaping her lips. Closing her eyes, she leaned her head back against the rim, the heat and water lapping over her, transforming her weariness into a languid insensibility.

She was just about the reach for the soap to wash her hair when the door was flung wide and her husband strode in. The thunderous look on his face spurred her to seek the protection of the water, and she sank beneath the suds so that only her head and neck were exposed.

Adam's eyes immediately focused on the big brass tub in

front of the fire, Edwina's bedraggled mop of filthy hair just
visible over the top. The speed with which he crossed the carpet to his wife's bath was eloquent of his consuming rage. He
glared down at her. The dirty, dishevelled scamp bore no resemblance to his lovely young wife.

Aware of her maid standing like a petrified statue by the
bed, he glowered at her. 'Leave us,' he said flatly.

His tone was cutting. Amelia's distress showed in her face
and widened eyes and brought a protest bubbling to Edwina's
lips. 'Adam—I need Amelia to help me—'

'Leave us,' Adam repeated on a softer note, indicating the
door with a nod and a look, which Amelia completely
understood.

Warned by something in her husband's eyes, Edwina
looked at her maid. 'It's all right, Amelia. Do as my husband
says. You can return in a few minutes.'

Taking a step closer to the tub, Adam kicked against the
discarded clothes. When he realised what they were, he saw
red. 'Wait,' he bellowed as Amelia was about to scamper out
like a terrified rabbit. He pointed to the heap. 'Take those with
you and burn them. The less there is to remind me of that
filthy vagabond, the better I shall feel.'

Amelia rushed to do his bidding, piling the clothes and
boots in her arms and fleeing as if her feet were on fire.

Alone with his wife, Adam gave her the full force of his
attention. His emotions veered crazily from colossal relief to
fury as he beheld her. The urge to murder her resurrected itself, followed immediately by the opposing urge to drag her
out of the water and wrap his arms about her.

'So, you decided to come back.' His voice snarled like that
of an animal goaded beyond endurance, and he showed no
sign of appeasement. 'I might have known you would dem-
onstrate your rebellion by reverting to Ed to defy and provoke
me.'

Edwina flinched before the cold, ruthless fury. Her husband's shoulders were squared, his jaw set with implacable determination, and emanating restrained power and unyielding authority. He loomed over her like a hawk about to take its prey, and she was aware that there was some dreadful destructive power in him which, if released would hurt her.

At any other time the menacing look in those dark blue eyes would have been enough to make her want to disappear under the suds, but she was so pleased with the result of her trek into St Giles that, after a brief moment, she collected enough of her wits to murmur in a voice that was a pure shade of innocence, 'Oh, dear. You do appear to be vexed up. Does my husband chafe at something?'

Adam's narrowed eyes glittering down at her were like shards of ice. 'Chafe? You young whelp! I could cheerfully strangle you,' he warned, her lack of contrition making his longing for vengeance more apparent. 'You've made your point, now I will make mine. If you ever defy me again, I will cheerfully—'

'What?' Edwina interrupted him, in such a mood to extend his frustration to the limit. 'Strangle me?'

'Exactly.'

She sighed ruefully. 'And after I have survived the extremes of St Giles without scars, too.'

'Don't push me,' Adam seethed. 'For the entire night I have walked every alleyway and searched every squalid yard in St Giles.'

'I'm sorry, Adam,' Edwina crooned, as if in sympathy, taking the soap and beginning to lather her arms. 'Is there still no sign of Jack?'

'My search has been for my wife,' he bit back, in no mood to spare her. In a state of frenetic restlessness and frustration he began pacing the carpet, circling the tub like a fox trying to mesmerise a hen out of a tree. 'I've had my pockets filched. I've been involved in a public dispute with a drunk who accused me of eyeing his "lady" too boldly, and I've been propositioned by every harlot in St Giles.'

The image this presented to Edwina was almost comical. Her lips twitched as she tried to suppress a smile, and a glow of mischief brightened her eyes. 'Which is why you stink like a midden, my lord, and look as if you've slept in one,' she dared to quip on a teasing note, noting that he was attired in the exact same clothes he'd been wearing for the Royal Academy the previous day, and would no doubt follow her own on to the fire. 'My bath will be free shortly—if you would like to share my water.'

Adam glared at her. His patience was wearing thin. 'When I bathe I prefer my own water—clean water,' he stressed.

She shrugged. 'Suit yourself.'

Adam's lean cheeks flexed tensely. 'Edwina! Do you have any notion how exasperating you are?' The rising fire of the volcano suddenly flared in his eyes and he flung up a hand irritably. 'Odd's blood! Have you no comprehension of the dangers you put yourself in? What the hell did you think you were doing?'

'If you will stop yelling at me, I'll tell you,' she replied calmly.

'I am not yelling.'

'Yes, you are. I take it you haven't spoken to Mrs Harrison—or anyone else, come to that.'

'Only one of the footmen who told me you were back. Mrs Harrison was elsewhere.'

Edwina smiled serenely as she brazenly raised one shapely leg above the suds and began to soap it. 'Bathing Toby, I should think.' If she had wanted to stun her husband, she'd succeeded admirably.

'Toby?' A peculiar expression passed over his face. The fury vanished and he looked perplexed. 'You—you've found Toby?' he uttered in a strained voice. 'You tracked him down?'

'Mmm. In the end it wasn't difficult. I'll tell you about it. But why don't you go and see him first?'

For a full minute he stared at her, and then, without another word, with one swift movement he turned on his heel and went out.

Laughing lightly, Edwina watched him go, and after submerging her head beneath the water began to lather her hair.

When Jack Pierce left Ma Pratchet's, having been told that Toby had disappeared during the night with a lad called Ed, his ears were filled with a roaring, like a huge wind unleashed. He was oblivious to everything—images were blurred, voices faded. His hands were clenched into fists so tightly they ached, and there was hate in his glaring eyes. The scope of the monstrous thing that had happened began to register, and with it came a rage that threatened to run out of control.

His thoughts were a riot. He wanted to lash out. He contemplated having them killed, but on reflection he decided that was entirely too quick. He wanted something more lasting. After a long time his scorching fury became a simmering anger and his thoughts became more rational. He would defer retaliation until they were at Taplow Court, and then 'Ed' and Adam Rycroft would find out the extent of his vengeance. It struck him that nothing could be more suitable than destroying them bit by bit. Pleasurably he began entertaining various means.

His mouth curved up at the corners and he gave a short, brittle laugh, walking on with a new spring in his stride. He swore he would teach them a lesson for trying to get one over him. No one did that to Jack Pierce and got away with it. He would make them pay. He would make them burn.

Scrubbed and fed, Toby was in bed when Adam entered the room, which was where Mrs Harrison insisted he remain until he was well rested and she had sorted him out some clothes to wear. The door still open, Adam stared at what he momentarily thought was a hallucination, a trick of the light falling on to the huge bed in which the small boy lay, and then he realised the vision was real. Edwina really had found Toby and brought him home. He was so overwhelmed with gratitude and relief that he was almost unmanned.

Trying to buy time, he closed the door and walked slowly towards the bed. In the many months of searching for him, he'd wondered how he would react when at last they came face to face, and now the time had come he was speechless. Seeing the pale face against the pillows, a chasm of feeling began to grow within him. He was relieved that Toby took the initiative and broke the silence.

'Hello. Are you Adam?' he asked, his voice boyish and clear.

A lump appeared in Adam's throat, which he swallowed down. 'Yes, and you are Toby.' Despite his raven-black hair, which he got from his father and which rose high on his forehead, he took after his mother, whose brown eyes and translucent skin he had inherited. 'Of course it's a few years since I last saw your mother, but you are very like her.'

Not wishing to intimidate the boy, he removed his jacket and sat on the bed so their faces were on a level. 'I've been searching for you for a long time, Toby—ever since your mother died. Things must have been very difficult for you.'

'Yes, they were.' His gaze was steady and direct. 'Did you know Uncle Silas?'

'I did, although he was much older than I was. When my parents died I went to live at Taplow Court.'

'Did you know my father?'

'Yes—Joseph Tyke. He was the head groom at Taplow Court. I remember him well.'

'Did you like him?'

'Very much. He would often accompany me on my rides.'

'Uncle Silas killed him,' Toby suddenly exclaimed. 'Did you know?'

Adam winced. 'How do you know that?'

'My grandparents told me. They never stopped reminding Mama. It used to upset her and she would cry a lot, but she was too afraid of them to speak out. They were strict and abided by the teachings of their Christian faith and never lied, so it must be true. They died within weeks of each other, leaving Mama to fend for herself.'

'I know.' Adam glimpsed in his eyes the pain of a boy deeply wounded by his mother's sad plight.

'She had nowhere to go and wasn't well, so she went to live with Uncle Silas.' His eyes clouded and became focused on something across the room. 'He hated me, and always referred to me as "Tyke's bastard",' he said quietly, less emphatic. His gaze shifted to Adam. 'Why didn't she come to you instead?'

'When I left Taplow Court, sadly your mother and I lost touch. When your grandparents died, she did write to me. Unfortunately I was in France just then, and by the time I received her letter she had died.' Recalling how shocked and hurt he had been at the time, Adam lowered his head. It was still difficult for him to imagine a world in which that gentle, caring woman had no place. 'When I learned Silas had given you away I tried to find you. I have been looking for you ever since. Tell me—what happened? How did those people treat you?'

Toby paused before answering. How did they treat him? How did a brutal man treat a disobedient dog? His dark eyes blazed from his pale face. He began to speak rapidly. 'Mr and Mrs Quincey made me work. I had to look after them and the bear—which was the one good thing about being with them. We were friends. He liked me. If I didn't work hard enough, the Quinceys would beat me. There was never enough to eat—for them, yes, but not for me. People never give their money to fat boys. We travelled around a lot, fairs and markets, and that sort of thing—always where there were crowds of people.'

'In London?'

He shook his head. 'Not at first. We went to Kent and Sussex. They came to London for the winter months.'

'That explains why I couldn't find you. Did you ever try to leave them?'

'When I grew tired of the beatings I did try to run away once, but I couldn't move very fast and they found me. They were living in a house in Wapping at the time. They took away my crutch and put me in the cellar and fed me on bread and water. That was the worst time. I had to fight off the rats. I had nightmares every night and used to wake up trembling. I was only let out when they wanted me to beg.'

Fighting the pain within him, Adam tightened his fist in the folds of the quilt and his face became set in hard lines. The thought of this tender, intelligent young boy being starved of food and locked in a cellar for weeks on end made his throat constrict. A vision of how it must have been flashed through his mind—the sounds, the smell, the rats, deprived of his freedom and his dignity. Frustrated by his own inability to relieve Toby's sufferings, he was in a new kind of rage, one whose edge was blunted by compassion for the boy.

'You've had a bad time, I can see that, and I am glad to see the experience hasn't destroyed you. What happened to you is in the past. You must not allow it to fester, Toby, otherwise it will eat you away.'

Toby frowned, puzzled by Adam's words, and wondered what had prompted him to say them with such intense feeling. 'I won't. You speak as if you know how it feels.'

'I do, in a way. You see, there was a time, many years ago, when I was a boy, that I suffered as you have. I was angry and thought I hated the world, and that everyone hated me. But the intervening years have taught me a tolerance, if not an overall wisdom, which that boy would have scorned.' He smiled and ruffled Toby's hair to dispel the solemnity of the moment. 'Now, tell me how you came to meet Jack Pierce.'

'He bought me from the Quinceys and took me to St Giles. A horrid old woman watched me all the time. Jack threatened me with violence if I so much as stepped outside. And then Edwina came.' Suddenly he smiled, the smile robbing him of his gravity, and the display of white teeth increased his resemblance to his mother. 'Imagine that! I thought she was a boy— one of Jack's boys.'

Adam grimaced, but he was unable to suppress a fleeting smile. 'I can well understand why you thought that. My wife took it upon herself to venture into St Giles last night. There are times when Edwina is possibly the most infuriating female in the world—but she has her moments.'

Toby looked straight into Adam's eyes. 'I'm glad Jack Pierce didn't find her. I hate him,' he said vehemently, 'and I never want to go back there.'

'Never fear. You won't have to. You are here now, and in my care.' Adam reached out and squeezed Toby's arm to reassure him. There was something aloof about him. For one so young, his expression was austere. Adam imagined it would become more so as he got older. It was not the face of a boy—it was too serious, too mature, too sad. Silas had much to answer for. 'Edwina and I want you here with us, Toby. Never doubt it. We are the closest family you have. You belong with us. Do you want to stay here?'

Toby felt a growing warmth inside him. Adam's words gave him a strange but pleasant feeling. Almost shyly, he said, 'Yes. I would like that very much.'

'Good, then that's settled. We are to stay in London for a few more days and then we will leave for Taplow Court.' When he saw Toby tense, he frowned. 'Do you have any objections to that?'

'Not really. I hated Uncle Silas and wouldn't go if he still lived there, but now he's dead I don't suppose it matters. Why did he kill my father?'

'I can't answer that, Toby. I wasn't there.' How terrible was the intensity of Toby's hatred, and Adam was someone who could well understand where that hatred came from. 'I comprehend your bitterness. I know why you scorn your uncle. I did myself, for my own reasons.'

'Then you won't tell me that I am too young for such mature emotions?'

'No. Has anyone?'

'Mama.'

Wishing to smooth away his frown, Adam said, 'I trust your bitterness will find a softening as you grow older.'

Toby smiled. 'Maybe I will, if one day I find a woman to match your Edwina.'

Adam's eyes gleamed. 'Ah, Edwina is a rare treasure.' Toby covered his mouth to hide a yawn he couldn't hold back. Adam smiled. 'I can see a hot bath and Mrs Harrison's food are beginning to have their effect. I'll leave you to sleep.' Standing up, he picked up his jacket. He paused and looked down at the boy—so mature for one so young. 'Eventually you will find someone. I want so much for you to be happy.'

Happy? Toby snuggled down beneath the sweet smelling covers. He thought he could remember being happy. His thoughts inevitably went to his dear mama.

When Adam returned to Edwina she was attired in her robe and seated before the mirror at her dressing table. Calmly assessing his mood, she watched his strong, vigorous figure approach through the mirror. His white lawn shirt was open at the throat, the full sleeves rolled up over his forearms. His dark brown hair was mussed, and there were faint shadows under his eyes. He looked weary, she thought, which wasn't surprising after what she had just put him through, and his night spent scouring the streets of St Giles.

When he stood behind her he bent and looked at her in the mirror, his heart melting as he confronted that misty gaze. Her hair was still damp and clung to her face in feathery wisps, giving her a fragile, elfin look. Without a word he placed his lips in the soft curve of her neck, kissing it lightly, then the blue eyes raised slowly until they met hers once more.

'I swear that if you ever put me through a night like that again I will—'

'I know—strangle me,' she whispered, feeling tears clog the back of her throat and burn her eyes.

'I shall be sorely tempted. You might have told me.'

'I wanted to surprise you.'

'I don't like surprises.'

'I shall endeavour to remember that when next I am tempted to embark upon some escapade or other.'

Adam's eyes met hers in a wide, admiring smile, a smile that tugged at his firm lips. 'For your sake I hope you do, my love. However, despite my ranting and chastising, I am nevertheless impressed with the sheer daring of your escapade. I'll be for ever grateful—I think I speak for Toby, too.' Again Adam nuzzled her neck, caught up in emotions he could no longer conceal behind stubborn pride. 'Did I ever tell you that I love you?'

Edwina's heart soared and she thought she might expire of joy. 'No. You've said many things to me in our time together—some disparaging, some nice—but never that.'

'Then it is long overdue.' Taking her hand, he raised her up from the stool and placed her in front of him, looking deep into her eyes with tender solemnity. 'I love you, Edwina. I have never said that to a living soul—apart from Dolly, and in a different context. But I do. You make me happier than I have ever been before. I love you deeply—even though you are the most unpredictable young woman I have ever met.'

'Better that than being predictable. That would be so dull. Don't you agree?'

'How can I possibly answer that? I haven't had a predicable minute since I met you. You are the most wilful, stubborn wench I have ever known.'

'I will always be that—just like you will always be volatile, mercurial and moody. But as an artist I suppose you are
entitled to be, and I suppose we will always have disagree-
ments.'

'I hope so, my love,' he murmured achingly. 'It will make
making up all the sweeter.' Unable to restrain himself a moment longer, he pulled her tightly against him. Heavy eyelids
drooped over his eyes. His lips were parted, ready to savour
hers, which he took in a long, compelling kiss. She kissed him
back, curling her arms around his neck and holding him
fiercely to her, delirious in the knowledge that he loved her
and that he had told her so at last.

Despite everything he had gone through and the wall he
had built around himself, she had managed to breach that barricade. Already the layers of bitterness and reserve that Dolly
had spoken of were being stripped away, and she was beginning to discover the softness underneath, to find the boy he
must have been, and to find the man he had become, tender
with love.

His embrace was crushing, his mouth moving against hers
with hungry urgency, his hands shifting possessively over her
spine and hips. Dragging his mouth from hers, he gazed
down at her, his eyes dark with passion. 'I want you very
badly, Edwina.'

She smiled, the tell-tale flush on her cheeks telling him that
she felt the same. However, she pulled away a little and wrinkled her nose. 'I know you do, Adam—and even though I love
you dearly and think you are the most wonderful man I know,
until you have washed away the stench of St Giles, that kiss
will have to suffice for now.'

'In that case I won't try to corrupt you with intimate dis-
tractions until later.'

'Oh? How late?' she asked, smiling up at him.

'Tonight.' His eyes were aglow with anticipation. 'Is that
late enough?'

Tilting her head to one side, she pretended to think about it. 'It could be earlier,' she told him after a moment.

'You can count on it,' he told her. 'I shall have my valet prepare me a bath this minute. His hand came up and he drew a caressing finger gently down her cheek, before touching her cropped hair. 'Did you have to cut your hair?'

'I wanted to look convincing.'

'How did you manage to find Toby so quickly?'

'I told you it was easy.' Edwina gave him a brief account of her meeting with Jonathan Ward, of going to Ma Pratchet's and finding Toby. 'When the old woman fell into a drunken stupor we left. I was amazed that we managed to get out of St Giles so quickly and unmolested—but I hope I never have to set foot in the place again. How is Toby?'

'He's been through a tremendous ordeal for one so young. To suddenly find himself thrust into a brutal world and unable to rely on his mother to shield him from the pain of it, he's come through remarkably well. He's had a hard lesson and has come out of it better than most. But then again, perhaps the pain will never be expunged. Yet I took it as a hopeful sign that he was able to speak of it.'

'And I expect you could empathise with him.'

Adam glanced at her sharply, his expression at once stiff and aloof. He lifted a brow.

'Dolly came to see me after the exhibition,' Edwina explained quickly. 'She told me just how difficult it was for you growing up at Taplow Court—with Silas.' She felt his slight withdrawal.

'Did she?' His voice was terse.

Edwina took his hand and on tiptoe she placed a featherlight kiss on his lips. 'I think after the awful experiences both you and Toby have suffered, a new beginning is in order—don't you? Silas is dead. He can't hurt anyone again. You and Toby and our child are the only ones who matter now.'

He took her hand and gently kissed her palm, then lowered it. Resting his hands on her shoulders, he looked deep into her eyes. 'And you, Edwina,' he amended in an aching and husky voice. 'Nothing matters to me but you.'

Tears shimmered in her eyes. 'And me,' she repeated. 'I'll make you happy, Adam, I swear I will. Remember, it is the future that counts.'

'I couldn't agree more. I couldn't survive without you.'

'Don't you dare try. Now—off you go to your dressing room and bathe, before I take you out into the yard and dunk you in the horse trough. Imagine the amusement that would create among the servants.'

Adam made a face and turned away. At the door he looked back, chuckling softly. 'Permit me to say, my love, that you are beginning to sound like a proper wife.'

She smiled a little at that, her eyes aglow. 'I am a proper wife, Adam. Never doubt it.'

Chapter Eighteen

Great were Edwina's misgivings when she saw Taplow Court up close. A black and grey, gloomy-looking house, it was built around three sides of a single court. The mullioned windows with small panes of glass, black and unreflective, frowned down on her like a many-eyed beast, as if contemplating what torments it could inflict on those who dared to enter. On either side of the shallow steps leading up to the heavy iron-studded door, two grotesque stone lions stood guard. Around the large portal carved in stone, imps and snakes frolicked and slithered with all manner of beasts with horns and pointed tails, creating a bizarre and hideous tapestry—an unwelcoming sight for any visitor to the house.

The moment Edwina set foot in the vast, medieval hall she did not like it, and she knew she could never be happy there. The atmosphere was oppressive. The great house was silent; it smelled old and musty—the damp, cold smell of emptiness. It was also dark and full of shadows. She had been right. This was Silas Clifford's house, and even though he was dead his spirit still lurked inside its rooms and corridors, hugging the walls like some dispossessed ghost. It was as if he had left his venomous evil behind to poison the very air itself.

Adam was watching her reaction closely, and if he sensed her unease he did not show it. Her instinct told her that Toby felt the same. His young face was expressionless as he gazed about the lofty hall, and she was sure she saw him shudder.

The days took on a pattern as Edwina and the newly appointed servants tried to give the house a lived-in feel. The china and glass were washed and furniture polished until it gleamed, giving the rooms that extra glow. Adam had much to do on the estate, and when that didn't claim him the alterations he was having done for his studio up in the rafters did.

Edwina was unable to banish the unease she felt about the house. Everything—the dark wood, the ornate staircase and pillars and posts, the decor and the heavy furniture—was characteristic of its former owner. The silence became something tangible, oppressive and heavy with threat. Like a slight *frisson* of movement on the air, it followed her round the house as if it were listening, almost holding its breath. Often the skin on the back of her neck prickled. Did a shadow stir in a dark corner?

Closing her eyes for a moment, she would take a deep breath, trying to steady herself, silently reproaching herself for such foolish imaginings—things that weren't there. She thrust down the dour thoughts and got on with her work, but they surfaced every time she entered a darkened room or corridor and a shadow moved.

Adam became concerned about her. Her face was thin and she looked tired and tense. Coming upon her in a large sitting room at the back of the house, he paused in the doorway. The low winter sun was slanting in at the windows, throwing patches of warm light on the floor.

The room overlooked the gardens—the only aspect of Taplow Court Edwina liked. To the right of the gardens were the stables, coach houses and administrative buildings, a walled-in orchard and rose garden. Standing by the window and gazing at the park beyond the gardens, Edwina watched as Toby rode a frisky chestnut-coloured horse, a gift from Adam, through the park. With all his energies centred on his mount, the youth rode well and it gave him tremendous enjoyment, for it was the one thing he could do unimpeded by his crippled leg.

Adam came up behind his wife and placed his hands on her shoulders. He could feel the tension inside her as he firmly massaged the back of her neck with his fingers.

Edwina sighed, feeling the residual tension from her forehead and the back of her neck receding with every stroke. When his arms came round her she leaned into him, finding his presence comforting and reassuring.

Adam followed her gaze and smiled on seeing Toby skim his mount effortlessly over a particularly difficult obstacle, and he could well imagine the huge grin that would be spread across his young face on his success. 'He rides well and appears to like the horse.'

'He adores it. It's just what he needs to take his mind off things, and unleash some of that pent-up energy inside him. I just hope he's careful. It worries me when he rides so fast. He seems quite fearless when he's astride that horse.'

'He's a good, competent rider. Obviously he gets that from his father, who was a superb horseman.' Adam's arms tightened around her. 'He also appears to be extremely fond of you, my love.'

'We do get on, I'm happy to say. He's a lovely boy and seems to be recovering well from his ordeal.'

Adam chuckled. 'You may be right, but it will be some time before he recovers from seeing you as Ed. In fact, I would say you bedazzle him. If he weren't so young, I dare say I'd be jealous.'

She smiled. 'It's all part of growing up, I suppose.'

Adam bent his head and placed a gentle kiss on her cheek. 'You look tired, Edwina. I hope you're not overdoing it.'

'No, of course not. I—I like to keep busy.'

He noticed the slight catch in her voice and frowned. 'Why? Because it stops you thinking about the house? I'm not blind, Edwina, nor am I insensitive. Something is wrong, and it's more than just tiredness and the baby. You hate this house, don't you?'

Unable to lie, she nodded. 'I do try not to let it get to me.'

'But it does.'

'Yes,' she admitted quietly. 'There's an atmosphere. I can feel it. It's heavy and tangible—almost like a brooding resentment, a chill, which has nothing to do with the physical cold of the house. And what about you? What do you feel about this place?'

'Cold, mostly.' And uneasy, he was going to say, and that in spite of himself he found himself listening and glancing towards the darker corners, but not wishing to unnerve her further he said nothing more.

'It—it's Silas I feel,' Edwina went on. 'It's silly, I know, but I feel that he's in every room, watching—and that even at night when—when we—'

'Edwina, stop it,' Adam said sharply, turning her round in his arms to face him. 'Are you talking about a ghost? Silas's ghost?' He raised an eyebrow, watching her intently, studying her face.

She smiled wanly and gave a nervous laugh. 'I don't believe in ghosts—or spirits or demons, come to that. They don't exist—not in real life. It's complete nonsense.'

'Thank God for that. It's only the smell of cold and damp, Edwina.' His voice was gentle. 'Surely there's nothing else here to frighten you—not with hundreds of candles lighting the place, and an army of servants to keep you company. It's not so frightening.'

'I'm not frightened—just a little uneasy, that's all.' She was slightly scornful, then she sighed and placed her cheek against his chest as he held her. 'I'm sorry, Adam. Take no notice of me. I'm being silly. Perhaps my pregnancy is to blame—perhaps it makes my mind more fertile. Women do grow fanciful at such times.'

'That may be so, but I think you've allowed the past to play on your mind. I know it hasn't been easy, coming here. I do understand.'

'It hasn't been easy for you and Toby, either.'

'I know. But too much of all our worlds has been spent in pain and strife. This is a time to forget the past and seek out the better moments of whatever the future has to offer. Ere long there will be a child—and, God willing, more, and laughter will ring within these walls. But you do look tired, my love. You've been doing too much. You should relax and rest more.'

'Yes, I will try,' she said. But she didn't want to relax, because when she did, that was when the stillness and the silence—the kind of silence that inhabits a tomb—became more profound and threatening. That was when the slumbering silence stirred and the shadows would detach themselves and move closer to her.

When he felt her shudder Adam held her closer. 'What you need is a distraction—visitors—and how about a ball? Or perhaps you would prefer to return to London for a while?'

Edwina felt her spirits rise. She glanced up to find him looking down at her with an expression of such tenderness and concern that she felt a lump rise in her throat. 'Yes. Yes, I would like that.' Her gaze travelled beyond him and through the window. The bright winter sun had vanished behind a cloud, and the garden looked suddenly very bleak and cold.

Night had fallen when Adam was crossing the courtyard and he thought he saw a movement at one of the ground-floor windows in the east wing. Because it was the only part of the house still uninhabited, he was puzzled as to why anyone would want to go there. Deciding to investigate, he let himself in through the creaking door. He paused, certain it was footsteps he could hear echoing from above.

At the bottom of a narrow flight of stairs he stopped, his hand resting on the newel post. He looked up into total darkness. It was intensely cold. A fire hadn't been lit in this part of the house since Silas had died, and the winter chill had penetrated deep into the walls. Straining his eyes, he was certain something moved. He had the feeling that there was someone up there, up in the shadows, waiting, watching. He frowned and began to climb slowly, hearing the protesting creak of wood. A gust of wind struck the house, and he almost felt it shudder with the strength of it.

At the top of the stairs he stepped on to the narrow landing, his concentration focused on the doors opening off it. Cautiously he peered ahead. The moon trickled in through the windows, shedding a little light. He wasn't sure now what he'd heard, but he could feel rather than see there was someone there. He wished he had a weapon to hand. Stealthily he went from room to room, but there was no one there. He paused and listened to the hollow moaning in the chimneys. The wind buffeted the house from all directions, knocking the creeper against the window, sounding like someone demanding entry.

On the landing once more, he went towards the stairs. He was halfway there when he thought he heard a movement behind him. Spinning round he looked back, straining his eyes in the gloom. Still nothing. For a moment he was tempted to retrace his steps, but, deciding his mind was playing tricks, that it was probably the wind creating disturbances in the house, impatiently he walked purposefully back down the stairs, oblivious to the shadowy figure standing motionless beside a tall cupboard, watching him.

The fire started later that night in the east wing. Adam woke with a strange feeling of dread. He sat up, smelling smoke. Immediately he was out of bed and at the window. Clouds of sparks and bits of burning matter were blowing past, borne on the wind. Flames could be seen coming from the wing, wisps of smoke curling through the rafters. Going back to the bed, he shook Edwina awake.

'What is it?' she mumbled, not at all pleased to be woken up so roughly.

'Get up and get dressed, Edwina,' Adam said urgently, struggling into his clothes. 'There's a fire, and it looks bad. It's started in the east wing, and it will spread unless the wind calms down. Wake Toby and the servants and go outside. I'll see what can be done.'

In the courtyard, household servants and estate workers were already running about in wild confusion, slamming into each other as they went, shouting at one another, some forming a human chain with buckets full of water, while others disappeared inside the burning building and hauled out anything that could be salvaged. Seeing William Hewitt, his bailiff, carrying a bucket, he strode towards him.

'How in God's name did this happen, Will?' he asked, having to shout above the roaring of the fire and the wind.

'Don't know, but it took hold fast in the wind. One of the men told me he saw someone in there—didn't recognise him, though, and he must be trapped inside because no one's seen him come out.'

Adam stared at the burning house, thinking of earlier when he had searched the east wing himself. Perhaps there had been someone in there after all.

When Edwina emerged from the house, closely followed by Toby hurrying as fast as he was able on his crutch, she scoured the courtyard for Adam. Seeing him with Will, dousing himself with water so his clothes would not be so flammable, she picked up her skirts and rushed across to him frantically.

'Adam! What are you doing?'

His voice was urgent. 'There's someone trapped inside. I've got to try and get him out.'

'But you can't go in there. You'll be killed.' Tears started to her eyes. 'Please, Adam. Please don't,' she cried, unable to think of anything other than the mortal danger he was placing himself in.

'Don't worry. I don't intend anything happening to me. I'll be back, I promise.'

Edwina watched wide-eyed as he raced towards the burning building and plunged into the clouds of smoke billowing out of the doorway.

The heat inside was fierce, the fire quickly consuming the wooden floors and beams. Adam stopped in the doorway to one of the rooms. Inside he glimpsed a hulking form. He wiped his stinging eyes and focused on the figure, taking note of a bulging sack on the floor beside him. He could hardly believe his eyes when he saw that the man was none other than Jack Pierce. He was holding a heavy silver candlestick, and Adam realised he'd been in the process of robbing the house.

'Pierce? What the hell do you think you're doing here?' he yelled as smoke hid the other man for a moment.

Startled, Jack Pierce looked towards the door, just able to make out Adam. With a growl he darted forward, still clutching the candlestick.

When he was close, Adam saw his visage was red with scorching rage, and that his eyes held an irrational light. He moved aside as the lumbering, demented man lashed out with a roar, catching him on the side of the face with the candlestick. Adam stumbled and almost fell. Pierce dashed away. His head throbbing, his vision blurred, Adam went after him as he blundered towards the worst of the fire.

The orange flames were spreading quickly, and black smoke was curling along the white plasterwork ceiling. Pierce staggered suddenly, just as a beam burned in half and fell,

striking him on the head and trapping him underneath. He
screamed as his sparse hair caught fire and his arms flailed
the air wildly, his legs sprawled in a grotesque fashion. Adam
rushed to try to save him, but flames leapt between them and
drove him back. Unable to stand the intense heat and in danger of being roasted alive, coughing and gasping for breath,
he ran to the door. Having inhaled so much smoke, Adam felt
his lungs were about to burst.

Great tongues of fire were licking out of the shattered windows, and he could hear woodwork cracking and beams
crashing down behind him. Outside he glanced back, seeing
that part of the east wing was already starting to collapse, and
that the wind-driven fire was raging out of control and was
beginning to taking hold of the central block. There was nothing anyone could do to stop it, he could see that. The house
was just dry tinder to the flames. Soon the whole building
would be gone.

The night sky was full of blazing wood and glowing ash,
and he had to dodge the airborne burning debris falling all
around him. After fortifying himself from a bucket of water,
he placed his hands on a low wall and bowed his head as he
fought to bring his breathing under control.

Standing with her arm round Toby's shoulders from a safe
distance, Edwina had watched the doorway through which her
husband had disappeared with paralysed anguish. When she
saw him emerge alone she immediately ran towards him, her
eyes streaming with the effects of the smoke.

'You are alive! Oh, thank God! I thought I'd lost you.' She
looked ready to weep, yet there was overwhelming relief and
joy in her voice.

Adam stood upright and folded her fiercely in his arms,
burying his face in her hair, too overcome with emotion to
speak.

'Did you see anyone in there?' Edwina asked after a full
minute had elapsed.

He straightened and looked down into her upturned face. 'I did.'

'Who—who was it? Did you recognise him?' she asked hesitantly, her eyes, full of wonder and admiration, tempered by a cold knot of fear that was forming in her stomach. 'Is he dead?' The look in Adam's eyes told her this was so. 'Did—did he start the fire?'

'I believe so. And we need look no further than Jack Pierce.'

Edwina was stunned.

'Yes, it was Jack Pierce. He wanted to harm us. He'd already stripped the house of some of its valuables.'

'So, he tried to carry out his threat after all.'

'It looks like it. It is my belief that he set fire to the house with the intention of grilling us alive while we slept. Why he didn't make a run for it while he had the chance, God knows.'

Will appeared to confirm what he said. He was accompanied by one of the grooms, who was dragging another man along by a piece of rope that fastened his wrists together. With his head bent, the prisoner presented a wretched creature.

'This man was apprehended running away from the house when the fire started. He was trying to make a dash for it. It appears he came with a man by the name of Jack Pierce to burgle the place. They left their horse and cart along a track in the woods at the back of the house. He was keeping watch and was to help Pierce carry the haul away. When he was about to go in, Pierce torched the house prematurely and his accomplice here got cold feet and ran away. Pierce didn't follow—couldn't bear to leave his haul behind apparently—and this man wasn't going to risk being burned to death to help him get it out.'

'So, Pierce might have carried out his plan had it not been for his own greed, his impatience, and the wind that took immediate hold of the fire. Well, one thing's for sure. He won't be coming out.' Adam shifted his gaze to Jack's accomplice. 'Take this man away, Will. See he's locked up until the constables get here in the morning.'

Noting the intense strain on Edwina's face, Adam slipped his arm about her waist and drew her close to his side. 'It's all right, Edwina,' he reassured her. 'Pierce won't trouble us again, thank God.'

'It takes some getting used to. I can't believe there will be no more fear—for ever afraid of that moment when I would meet him again. I should have known he would retaliate when he discovered Toby had gone, and that Ed had taken him.'

With mixed emotions they stood in silence and watched the inferno. The roof seemed to heave upwards before imploding, as if it were some living creature caught up in howling agony. Unhampered now, the flames shot higher and roared in greedy delight.

'There's no saving it.' The comment came from beside them, and Adam turned to find Henry Marchant at his side. 'I came when I saw the flames. Thank God you're safe—all of you. Is there anything I can do?'

'You can take Edwina and Toby back to Oakwood Hall. I'll be along later. There's nothing to be done here.' Adam's gaze passed on to find that Will had joined them. 'Tell everyone to stop, Will. It's useless. Let it burn itself out.'

With the first light of dawn Edwina met her husband outside Oakwood Hall. Dismounting wearily, he handed the reins to a waiting groom, who led his horse away. Edwina walked into his arms and looked up at him. Parts of his hair had been singed and fell wildly about his grim, blood-streaked face. His waistcoat and breeches were ruined, the sleeves of his once-white shirt were rolled up, exposing his corded forearms, his clothing and his skin smelled of smoke, but to his wife he had never looked more handsome.

Her arms tightened around him, never wanting to let go. Joy

and happiness welled inside her, filling her because this wonderful, vital man belonged to her. His own arms tightened about her waist, and Edwina responded by kissing his sooty cheek.

'You shouldn't worry about me,' he said.

She closed her eyes and placed her head on his chest. 'How can I help it?'

Adam continued to hold her, liking the feel of her so close.

'I thank God you are safe,' she said, tilting her head back and gazing at him.

Adam looked at the young woman in his arms, and in the midst of one of the most achingly poignant moments of his life, he felt a strange lightening of his spirit. Out of all this, there came a new sense of resolve. As he crushed her to him, his laugh rang softly in her ear, and Edwina could feel it rumbling in his chest. 'Indeed, my love. Safe and free.'

Looking up at him, Edwina raised her eyebrows in feigned shock, though the passion in her eyes was compelling and tender. 'Why, one would almost think you are glad the house has burned down.'

'I'm not sorry. It was ugly. It was Silas's house, not ours.'

'What are we going to do now?'

'Live, and be happy. I realise that I am the custodian of a great and beautiful estate, which is mine to safeguard and one day bequeath to my sons and their sons that follow. I also realise that it is a heavy responsibility, but with you by my side I will carry it with honour and pride. We will begin by building another house—not in the same place, but away on the hill to the west. It will be ours, my love. Yours and mine. Our children's house, and Toby's. As long as I have the woman I love, and my work that matters, I don't need anything else.'

Taplow Court was different in every aspect to the old house, the first difference being its position. To reach it involved a steady climb through oak and beech woods. When the house finally came into view one did not fully appreciate its situation—all that was visible was a welcoming house at the end of an approach lined with newly planted limes. It wasn't until one went round to the other side that one realised this mellow redbrick mansion was on top of the world, with lawns reaching its walls and a wide undulating view sinking off into the distance.

Adam's portrait of Edwina had, at the time, caused a sensation. The public had been drawn to the Royal Academy in their hundreds to see it, and not even the fact that it was not for sale, that the artist intended to place it in pride of place in his own home, detracted from the interest.

However, seeing nothing wrong in indulging the public and profiting from the painting himself in some way, Adam had sold the publication rights to an enterprising print-shop owner, who had done very nicely out of it. News sheets had heaped praise on the artist's talent and proclaimed the Countess of Taplow—no longer a woman of mystery—as the most beautiful woman to hit London in a long time, and Society was disappointed when the Earl of Taplow whisked his wife off to his country estate before anyone had the chance to get to know her.

Outside the summerhouse, half-hidden by high banks of shiny green laurels and rhododendrons, with her legs tucked beneath her skirts, Edwina was sitting on the grass with Adam's long lean body stretched out beside her, among the remains of a picnic. The midsummer air was warm and still, the sun a red glow in the hazy blue sky.

They were enjoying the pleasure of watching their two-year-old son Thomas, on stumbling legs, chase a yapping young puppy round a tree. All of a sudden he came to an abrupt halt and fell on his bottom. The puppy dropped down beside him in a heap of tangled legs, its ears flopping pathetically, its tail wagging hopefully, and, in the way of all young dogs, it began to lick Thomas's face ecstatically, wriggling its plump little body into his.

With a squeal of delight Thomas wiped his face on his sleeve and shoved the puppy on to its back. He looked at his parents with his deep blue eyes, and then he chortled and grinned, and Edwina's heart ached and swelled with love and pride. She was constantly amazed that this beautiful child was hers and Adam's. And he was beautiful, with the same breathtaking smile and masculine charm as his father.

The sound of galloping hoofbeats made itself heard, and Toby appeared astride his horse. When they waved he galloped towards them, horse and rider soaring like lightning over a tall hedge. He was on them like a thunderbolt, holding them spellbound by the wild beauty of his gallop, and they were in imminent danger of being ridden down if Toby could not master his horse in time. But there was no question of his mastery of the princely animal that had become his devoted friend.

Those early days when he had been released from a beggar's miserable existence had been a difficult time for Toby. Loving and supportive, Adam and Edwina had nursed and encouraged him through that time, and being of a resilient nature, he had recovered quickly from his hardships, and the memories of those terrible months following his mother's death, until Edwina had found him at Ma Pratchet's, had receded into the distance.

Sadly, having consulted some of the best physicians in London who had examined his crippled leg, they had been told there was nothing that could be done to improve it. There was a proud courage in the way Toby accepted this and refused to be fussed over and cosseted and treated like a sickly cripple. He had a brave spirit and despised anyone's pity. In these, the most exciting days of his life, he refused to be downhearted, and was determined not to let his disability spoil his enjoyment of life and dampen his hunger for adventure.

Upon seeing the youth he adored, Thomas got to his feet

and began to jump up and down with delighted squeals, his arms raised. Toby dismounted and, leaving his crutch strapped to his horse, fell to his knees and proceeded to tickle Thomas into helpless laughter, before sitting on the grass and dragging him into his lap and playfully ruffling the giggling child's hair.

In one quick, smooth motion, Adam sat up and leaned his back against a tree, drawing one knee up and draping his arm across it. He sighed, feeling utterly languid and content. He studied his wife for a moment in impassive silence. A tide of love rolled over him. Her face was serene as she watched their son and Toby romp about.

'It's been a lovely afternoon, Edwina. We must do this more often.'

Edwina tore her gaze from the children and looked at him, shuffling to his side. 'Yes, we must.'

'I can't thank you enough for giving me Thomas.' His hand, as it did so often, crept to her swelling abdomen where another child was growing. 'And now we are to be blessed once more.' He leaned close and brushed her lips with his own. 'I love you, Edwina, and you make a beautiful Countess.'

Edwina was aware of nothing but the vigour of him, his strength, the power he emanated, the smoothness of his shaven face, and the faint scent of sandalwood on his cheek that was so close to her own. Since the night the old house had burned down followed by the birth of their son, they had been inseparable. They had planned and watched the building of their new home together, and Edwina had never believed she could be so happy and content. How far she had come from that disillusioned young girl who had run away from her uncle, and found nothing but wretchedness.

'I recall a time when you told me you would have my blood and that I deserved a thrashing—and you also called me a dirty young guttersnipe—a far cry from being a countess, is it not?' she teased, her warm green eyes sparkling with suppressed laughter.

'That was because I couldn't see what a treasure you were beneath all that grime.'

'And now?'

'I've since come to realise that the smartest thing I ever did was to encounter Ed that day I ventured into the alleyways of St Giles. But I was glad when you put aside your boy's breeches and became a woman.'

'So was I,' she murmured, leaning against him.

'So, why do you weep?' he questioned anxiously, seeing the tears glistening on her cheeks.

Edwina lifted her thickly lashed eyelids, and the dazzling brilliance of her eyes was soft and full of love for her husband. 'Happiness makes me weep. Happiness, and also the final destruction of the past, and the conviction that we will both succeed in escaping our yesterdays.'

Adam's arms encircled her, and the strength of those arms was love.

* * * * *

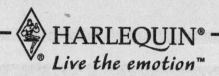

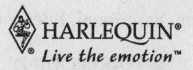

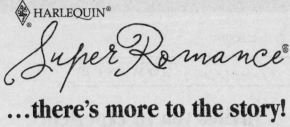
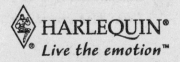

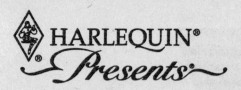

HARLEQUIN®
Presents

The world's bestselling romance series...
The series that brings you your favorite authors,
month after month:

Helen Bianchin...Emma Darcy
Lynne Graham...Penny Jordan
Miranda Lee...Sandra Marton
Anne Mather...Carole Mortimer
Susan Napier...Michelle Reid

and many more uniquely talented authors!

Wealthy, powerful, gorgeous men...
Women who have feelings just like your own...
The stories you love, set in exotic, glamorous locations...

HARLEQUIN®
Presents

Seduction and Passion Guaranteed!

HPDIR104

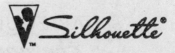

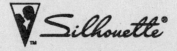